Inscription

Inscription

Fiona Ballard

Troubador Publishing Ltd
Unit E2 Airfield Business Park,
Harrison Road, Market Harborough,
Leicestershire. LE16 7UL
Tel: 0116 2792299
Email: books@troubador.co.uk
Web: www.troubador.co.uk

ISBN 978 1805142 553

British Library Cataloguing in Publication Data.
A catalogue record for this book is available from the British Library.

Printed and bound in Great Britain by 4edge Limited
Typeset in 10.5pt Adobe Garamond Pro by Troubador Publishing Ltd, Leicester, UK

For all the yesterdays that led me to today.

One

Beatrice – 1999

The nearest oncology department, at the Dorset Infirmary, lay over thirty miles away from Ocean Cottage. The appointment letter had arrived two weeks before. She'd hidden it, deciding not to worry Ralph. It would probably be nothing to worry about anyway. Fabienne, her eldest, had offered to drive her. Caught up in their own thoughts, Beatrice chose to concentrate on the beauty of the surrounding countryside in order to take her mind off the impending appointment. Fabienne had been considering her next house move. They remained silent for the entire journey, which was unusual. The drive took them past Corfe Castle, where the family had spent many happy hours. After negotiating the unhelpful one-way system through the market town they parked up outside the sign for the mortuary. Fabienne got them there early, with fifteen minutes to spare.

As Beatrice glanced up at the hospital signage she asked herself why placing the mortuary alongside an oncology department was good estate planning. As they walked the long empty corridor down to the oncology department, the mother and daughter role shifted from one to the other as Fabienne took her hand. For a brief moment she regretted not telling Ralph where she was going. She'd told him only half a lie when he'd asked. The waiting area smelt of plastic and recent disinfectant as she helped herself to a small cup of water in a cone-shaped cup. At ten o'clock, a receptionist called out her name.

"Ms Gardiner? This way please." Smiling, making incessant small talk. The two women stood up and followed behind. The nurse, in the crisp burgundy uniform with white piping, stood alongside Mr Markham, who held out his hand, offering a firm handshake. Laid out in a fan shape on his desk: the recent kidney scan results.

"I'm guessing it's not good news?" Her voice is soft.

"Well, it's not as bad as we'd originally thought. Your scan shows that you do have an eight-millimetre tumour on your right kidney. It is treatable with a minor op and with the correct drugs we can remove it. If it turns out to be benign, that'll be all the treatment you will need. If it turns out to be cancerous you'll need to return for further treatment. But let's wait for the biopsy results, shall we, and not jump too far ahead? They should tell us a bit more." She warmed to his calming manner, found it reassuring. A short-sleeved shirt showed off a recent tan on his forearms. He must like the outdoor life, she thought, trying to distract any naughtier thoughts seeping into her mind. The word "cancer" had never featured in her vocabulary, not a word that many people spoke about. Beatrice knew nobody else who had it. He went on to say, "I'm aware it must be a shock to discover you have a tumour, but kidney ones are quite common."

"How long will I have to wait for the operation?" she asked, clutching her handbag. "The waiting time should be roughly four weeks and we should be able to fit you into the schedule, unless of course you want to take a cancellation?" She nodded "yes" to a cancellation; they all agreed it sounded a good idea. Words failed to describe the joyous feeling as she emerged that everything was going to be ok, and she would make a full recovery. Why trouble Ralph with all this stuff? He'd never been good at emotional stuff. The news came as a relief, because as usual Beatrice had feared the worst.

She didn't want to think negative thoughts and had already made up her mind that the tumour would be benign. She managed to hold back a few tears of relief as they made their way out to the car park. Fabienne offered to collect the car and pick up her mother from the bench outside oncology. Beatrice sat waiting patiently for Fabienne on the hospital bench as instructed.

It seemed the perfect moment to pounce. Samuel had been watching the scenario play out, and chosen his moment exactly to coincide with Beatrice being alone. He heard her voice for the first time and instantly warmed to the soft intonation. He sat down alongside and commented unprompted on the warmth of the sunshine.

"I love the sun at this time of year."

"Sorry, do I know you?" Beatrice hesitated, glancing sideways.

"No, we've not met. My name is Samuel."

Beatrice's face swung across, shocked, before turning ashen, instantly feeling faint. Her vision tunnelled into fine black pinpricks. The cars ahead started to spin, as she clung to the arm of the bench. For a brief moment she closed her eyes. This was surely one of her bad dreams. Could this person be the baby she was forced to give up at birth? How had he traced her to this bench?

"Sorry, I didn't mean to frighten you," continued the bearded man, running his hands through his thick, dark hair.

"I'll be ok, just give me a second. My daughter will be back in a moment. She's gone to get the car."

"Your daughter, ah?" He stroked his bearded chin.

She had a fleeting moment to ask the loaded question.

"So, where are you living these days? Are you local?" He didn't answer straight away.

"Nowhere; actually I don't have a home." Lying came easily. Beatrice immediately took pity on him, as her heart started to melt.

"You must have a home." After a long silence, Samuel deliberated whether to tell more lies or simply wind up the conversation and flee. He didn't fancy meeting any step siblings at that point. Jesus, his plan had all gone horribly wrong.

"This was such a bad idea. Perhaps I could ring you to arrange a better location for another time?" He stood up to leave, buttoning up his coat.

"Yes, yes that's much better." As his voice trailed off, he watched her scribble her home number on an envelope. Samuel hadn't meant to snatch it, but walked quickly away without looking back, towards the bus stop and the perimeter fence. Tucked inside the envelope was the appointment letter with her home address at the top on the right. That was all he needed. Bingo.

From a distance Beatrice thought he looked like a vagrant. Like the ones that seek shelter in shop doorways at night. His old navy greatcoat looked torn, the collar fraying at the edges. The shoes looked worse, worn down on the soles. His gait had been akin to Jack's. But nothing a good bath and a hair wash wouldn't sort out, ran through her mind. Fabienne pulled into the lay-by and wound down the car window.

"You ok, Mum? You look awfully pale. Who was that man?" Beatrice didn't answer and got in the car. Her brain immediately went into meltdown.

How the hell did Samuel know she would be at the hospital at that time? She hoped he hadn't been stalking her. Was Ralph in on the secret even though she hadn't told him where she was going? Random threads cut across her mind, without any foundation or endings. After a slow drive home, Fabienne suggested she cook them lunch as Ralph was out with their neighbour, Freddie. Food always interested Beatrice in whatever form. Pork chops and a couple of wrinkled apples for a sauce would suffice. They stopped off at the village shop to buy some cream.

With stomachs replete, mother and daughter headed down to the beach. Beatrice swam in the sea, and Fabienne lay on a towel reading her book. By late afternoon her mood had brightened and conversations turned to a lighter tone. When Ralph returned, they retired to bed, sticking to their familiar bedtime routine. Whilst she undressed and brushed her teeth she wondered whether she should share the hospital incident with him yet or keep it to herself. Perhaps he knew about it already. She decided to review her decision in the morning when her mind would be thinking more clearly and less befuddled by wine and strong emotions.

Three months later the family had gathered around her hospital bed. Had she had a premonition about her own mortality? Perhaps it had been the real reason for the sudden change of heart? Curled up in a foetal position, she uttered three faint words: "Fabienne, the ring." The family looked up at one another, bemused. Her thick lashes fluttered. Her mouth fell open as though she wanted to say something; but her mind thought better of it. On the other side of the bed stood Ralph Barclay, holding her cool, limp hand, gently smoothing the flattened blue veins under his thumb.

"Rest now," he told her. Together the assembled group thought they had worked out the meaning of her mumblings.

The room, although chilly, felt calm; soft music played in the background on the sound system. The morphine started enhancing her hallucinations again, as she fell deeply into the weirdest of dreams. Her brain questioned if this was real?

With her feet secured firmly in the stirrups she held the reins high, using her calves to urge the horse forward. It responded into a brisk canter. The pale sandy beach spread across the bay for three miles. The vast expanse fired up the chestnut filly to whinny with excitement, kicking out her hind legs. The rider clung tightly to the martingale as the horse sped up. Released from captivity and ready to charge. As they turned into the wind her black mane rippled as their speed increased. The rider going too fast, chasing someone or being chased herself? In the distance stood a solitary figure… in a black cassock and matching Romano cap. Wasn't that Father O'Flynn holding a baby wrapped in a yellow shawl? Shouting into the wind, her voice mute. She pulled up and dismounted, ready to take her baby, but when her feet touched the ground the dark figure holding the baby had vanished. Scanning the horizon, her hand to her forehead, the darkened form resembling the priest had faded.

She awoke to find her bed sheets and nightdress drenched in perspiration. Someone with cool hands had changed her into a dry nightie. How long had she been asleep? The inside of her mouth felt as dry as an old sponge. With her heart still racing, she pressed the button that powered the syringe driver pump, topping up her morphine. The horse ride dream had taken its toll on her strength and she fell back on the pillows, deep into the black hole of more hallucinations. She had always had a deep-rooted fear that she would end up dying alone. Where was he? Who asked a voice? This time she felt a different hand, familiar, larger, more callused. The morphine muddling her crazy thoughts and somewhere in her confusion she'd lost Ralph.

Beatrice had chosen this particular hospice room for its light, to facilitate a peaceful end. An archetypal hospice room with bland decor, tired magnolia walls, an eighties throwback. The windows had metal frames and leaded glass windows. The garden doors swung open onto a terrace. In one of her more lucid moments she relished the cool breeze that drifted through and requested the nurses leave it ajar.

Ralph rechecked his watch: three minutes past three. His beloved Beatrice had just taken her last breath; he allowed himself a muffled sob into his hankie, piercing the silence. The two daughters hugged their father, standing side by side like small children holding hands. Their brother, Douglas, stood on the fringes of the family group, attempting to keep his emotions in check, furiously chewing the inside of his cheek. The door opened as the portly nurse came bustling in, followed by a doctor who asked them to wait outside.

Douglas fled and sought sanctuary in a small corner of the hospice garden. Lighting up, even though the forbidden signs were directly in his eyeline. They were no deterrent. At the rear of the main building he found a low brick wall opposite a large stone feature. So, paused a moment, taking the first drag, he cast his eye over the dozen or more large grey stone boulders in front of him. Trying to puzzle out what they were meant to be. Flattish in shape, laid out in such a pattern to form a walled structure. A steady trickle of water cascaded from the middle stone, streaming neatly into a small fountain. The water feature cleverly drew the eye to the centrepiece as the clear liquid spilled out towards the rectangular pool below. Douglas had read about landscape gardening in a magazine. This particular garden seemed different, though. Vibrant colours splashed around the edges from the carefully positioned plants and shrubs alongside ferns and fuchsias. Obviously it had been built with a calming influence in mind, by an experienced landscape gardener. He drew so hard on his cigarette it sizzled; exhaling the smoke into rings, as he attempted to gather his thoughts. The first of which, "well, how unexpected." He wished he'd taken the hint from his father and visited his mother sooner. Over the last few months he had become more estranged from his family. He held back his tears, scowling in a manly sort of way. Unsure, as emotions didn't fit his toughened persona. Recently he had left his elder sister's calls unanswered, isolating himself further. Today was not the time for recriminations. His phone number had changed so regularly that it made communication difficult. A feeble excuse. Regrets tumbled loosely among his thoughts, too many to consider in one go. Who would he have shared those personal thoughts with anyway? Certainly not Molly, the latest girlfriend.

He'd also felt hurt when Fabienne had referred to him as flaky. What had she meant by that? He knew he'd been given everything as a youngster, but pushed it all away. The memory of Beatrice defending him in an argument with his sister, came to mind. Always looking for danger, and risk mixed with a little heroism. Not too much to ask? He'd failed to notice his second cigarette had come to an abrupt end. Either he lit up another or returned inside to deal with reality. Shivering, he thought it easier to stay outside, where nobody could push him into playing a dutiful part. He had nobody directing him in thoughts or actions. Knowing that Molly was back at the cottage on her own, that would do as an excuse, to escape the oppressive, sterile atmosphere inside.

"Ah, there you are, Douglas. We've decided to make our way home," Ralph announced. Douglas heard it as "The royal *we*; I'm still your dad and can tell you what to do, *we*". Ralph couldn't tell if his son was upset or not.

"Sorry, are you ready to leave, or do you want to go back in the room alone for a few moments?" Ralph, feeling charitable, looked at him expectantly.

"No thanks, I'm done with this hellish place." He was content to remember his mother as she had been in the days before, relaxed and happy, surrounded by her family. Why hang around? There seemed little point, as the focus of their attention had departed. The small party of four silently made their way back to Molly, waiting at the cottage. The atmosphere at home felt strange, as Beatrice was ostensibly still there. Everything as she had left it a few hours before. Coats hanging in the hallway, boots by the back door, a coffee cup with lip balm around the rim on the table. No clearing up had been done, despite Fabienne's firm instructions to Molly, who had been luxuriating in a lavender bubble bath and reading magazines.

Molly opened the door, the dragon tattoo clearly visible on her chest, loosely covered by a cheesecloth shirt. She rushed to hug Douglas close to her in the hallway. He'd badly needed some fresh sea air and another fag. So he took her hand and pulled her out into the garden, where he explained that he wanted to hit the road earlier than they'd planned.

A man of few words, Ralph watched them through the kitchen window and felt struck by Douglas's tenderness towards the girl that none of them really knew. He had never witnessed his son with a proper grown-up girlfriend and thought they seemed in tune with one another. Over the weekend he'd felt a renewed closeness between Douglas and himself but may have misread the signals.

Eloise, the youngest sibling, was born with baby blue eyes that sparkled when she laughed. She kept her hair short and its original blonde colour still held firm. Her beatific smile caught people by surprise. People remarked that her facial expressions were also akin to her father's and sometimes her laugh too, the manner of it rather than the tone. Blessed with a gentle sprinkling of pale freckles across the bridge of her nose that highlighted themselves during the summer. Her trim waistline had thickened slightly after years spent cooking and sampling food in the French kitchens. The long working hours meant she didn't get outside to exercise as much as she would like. Her daily routine was now firmly governed by the restaurant bookings for dinners, rather than a regular exercise routine.

Her childhood memories consisted of playing on the beach at Ocean Cottage, running around the garden and playing in the tree house with her friends. Followed by eating tea on paper plates up in the tree house, with strawberry jam sandwiches, chocolate mini-rolls, and apples sliced straight from the orchard. The children made posters deterring the adults from entry and wrote: NO ENTRY OR DEFF with a wonky skull and crossbones at the bottom. They used yards and yards of Sellotape to attach it to the ladder at the bottom.

The darker memories came when she thought of her brother. Being shoved over on the gravel by Douglas, who quickly became jealous of his new baby sister staggering around outside learning to squat down and balance. The pain to her kneecaps as she went down, and the scream for help. Douglas caused her to tumble over when he thought his mother might be looking the other way. His baby sister ended up covered in bruises and bashes. He liked to snatch her toys away, causing her to sob until Fabienne or Beatrice would notice and chastise him offering her back her pet toy. Douglas enjoyed snatching her toys away causing her to sob until Beatrice would take pity on her and offer her treasured toy back. When Beatrice raised it as a concern with the health visitor she classed it as normal sibling rivalry behaviour.

As soon as Douglas could verbalise his feelings he told his baby sister firmly. "Go home, baby, no like you," as he opened the front door, the toddling baby now exposed to freedom. By chance Beatrice came through the hallway to the living room and noticed the open door. Stepping outside, she found Eloise in the flowerbed picking the heads off the daffodils. Despite the locked gates to the beach it had made Beatrice's heart miss a beat. How did the toddler open the front door? The clue: the small chair that Douglas used to allow his sister some fresh air.

Of the three siblings Eloise proved to be the most sentimental. Often reserving her opinion for fear of being shouted down or drowned out by the more forceful personalities around her. As a teenager she became withdrawn, moody in the usual sort of way. She left home without going to university and took herself off to France to work and study. Perhaps it had been a subconscious decision to live abroad and distance herself from family dramas and conflict. Even-tempered and not known to overdramatise events or situations, unlike her sister.

Romuel, the love of her life, would take her away from her kitchen duties and encourage out onto the water in France. Her father had taught her to sail, so she had grown up without a fear of the open sea. They would take trips out to the undiscovered islands off the west coast. She loved nothing more than to dive off the boat and sink as deep as her lungs would allow, resurfacing in the shape of a mermaid. The water brought the pair calm, after the stresses of working at the restaurant.

They'd met as teenagers whilst working in the kitchens of a large family run hotel, Eloise working as a sous-chef and Romuel as a waiter serving evening covers. They formed an instant connection and found they had much in common. He had been her first real love since arriving in France. Her ambition: to settle and take French citizenship, then train to be a chef at La Cuisine, Corsaire Ecole. He helped her achieve that dream. They went on to marry, and had their first child, Amélie. A bouncing, blonde, blue-eyed baby who cooed and gurgled at everyone she met. Born prematurely, the tot weighed only two kilos and spent the first month of her life in an incubator. Owing to her early arrival the baby's weight was slight. Her petit nose came later with a tiny piercing on the right-hand side of her nostril, near her freckles. Her eyes akin to her grandfather's, with extended dark lashes that curled naturally she had inherited a happy-go-lucky personality. Amélie became their pride and joy.

A year later Eloise miscarried a second baby at thirteen weeks after falling down a step outside the restaurant, landing awkwardly on her side. The doctors advised her not to have any more babies.

La Baule had become a chic upmarket seaside resort in the Seventies. A quaint mix of old and Breton seaside cultures. The restaurants dotted along the twelve-kilometre beach, alongside a swish yachting marina, were testament to the wealth and status of its locals. The French family lifestyle meant they spent their winters skiing. Apart from inheriting her mother's phobia for insects and spiders, Amelie sailed through her teenage years with ambitious plans to go travelling. Recently she had hooked up with Guy, who had passed the parental acid test with flying colours. But those plans were interrupted by an unplanned pregnancy followed by another in quick succession.

If Eloise had one regret about settling in France, it was that she didn't get over to England, to spend time with her parents. Time off from the kitchen proved difficult to secure, and the added complication of distance. Looking back she felt her emotional burdens had always been linked to past family conflicts. For Eloise during those years back home, she'd tried her hardest to avoid any serious conflict or melee. Choosing to tuck herself away in her bedroom, reading or listening to her radio, or strumming her guitar as music became her solace.

Obituary – September 1999

The obituary filled the back page of the *Swanage Echo*. The newspaper column showed an old black-and-white grainy picture of Beatrice in her youth. Ralph had picked his favourite photo of her leaning against a wall holding a bicycle and throwing her head back with laughter. Her hair tied up in a gingham headscarf, wearing blue denim dungarees, it seemed to sum her up beautifully as it captured her perfect smile.

It is with great sadness that Ralph Barclay and family of Ocean Cottage, Swanage, wish to announce the death of Beatrice Hamilton, beloved partner and mother to their three children. Born in Consett, County Durham, in 1949, Beatrice was one of four siblings, Arthur, Albert, and Rosina. She had led a colourful life at home and abroad in France, and always put others before herself. The burial service will take place at St Cuthbert's Church on Friday, September 18th, at 12 noon. The family asks for no flowers. All donations to Barnardo's Children's Homes.

The Funeral

Following Beatrice's death, the promised phone calls from Douglas enquiring after his father's wellbeing all but dried up. Until the time came to read the will, when his interest kicked in again. Fabienne had tried to make contact, eventually leaving a strongly worded answer machine message commanding him to get in touch immediately.

Three weeks later, the family gathered to honour Beatrice with a small private funeral. The church, a modern design with vibrant stained glass windows, had been built in the centre of the village. Most Catholic churches were built within larger cities.

The order of service read:
– The Lord Is My Shepherd
– A Eulogy by Father Munro
– A poem by Henry Wadsworth Longfellow read by Ralph Barclay
– Exit tune. A Celtic hymn, Mountain Thyme

Ralph awoke early on the morning of the funeral, feeling unsettled. He had always disliked public speaking and had somehow agreed with Father Munro to read Beatrice's favourite poem at the service. He'd always disliked funerals in fact the whole process from start to finish. There were sobs from the front row and the sound of weeping coming from the back of the church. Nobody identified the culprit. The local priest, Father Munro, delivered his short eulogy, to sum up: "a life lived that had ended too abruptly". Eloise stared solemnly at the coffin, her eyes focussing intently. Listening to the words from the priest, unable to reconcile the painful fact that she would never see her mother again.

Out of curiosity Samuel had wanted to see for himself what the other immediate members of the family looked like. He remained unchallenged as he hid behind his sunglasses. Nobody had noticed the solitary figure at the back of the church, wearing a long navy coat and peaked cloth cap. All bar one person anyway. The family had failed to notice that behind the trendy sunglasses sat someone who looked like one of the family. The beard and stature were obvious family traits; Fabienne, after a quick glance, didn't recognise him. She thought it impolite to swing her head around and stare and didn't want to appear rude. It played on her mind during the service and afterwards became the focus of her attention. She refrained from asking her father, not wishing to upset him further. Looking around again, she noticed the stranger's seat empty. His exit must have preceded the coffin procession. Why be in such a hurry to leave? she thought. She'd paused by the empty pew, as if looking for a clue, when something caught her eye. A silver lapel badge lay on the floor, sparkling in the sunlight. Stooping, she picked it up, saying nothing to the others.

On the way out, after thanking the priest, she paused to use the restroom. Washing her hands, she remembered the lapel brooch in her pocket. Racking her brains to work out the connection between the brooch and her mother. She turned it over in her palm and examined it more carefully. The brooch, in the shape of a horse, had a rider standing up in stirrups, waving a riding crop in the air. It must have belonged to someone from the horsey world. The family only had one link to the horsing world and that had been through her Uncle Albert. What was the connection, though? Tucking it back inside her coat pocket, she convinced herself it had something to do with the missing gentleman from the pew.

Apart from immediate family, the other faces around the graveside were a few locals from the village. With the burial over, the family spurned tradition and chose to return to the cottage for a small, private wake. Some of the ladies from the village kindly laid the kitchen table with plates of sandwiches, sausage rolls and a rather dry-looking Victoria sponge. At these functions the amount of food normally exceeded the number of attendees. A dozen people at most, including the immediate family, returned to the cottage. Father Munro apologised; he had another burial service to officiate. Leaving quickly after piling his plate high with sandwiches first, though. Freddie offered his condolences before vanishing next door. Ralph scraped the untouched food into the kitchen bin, leaving the cake on the table. He would have a slice later with a cuppa. At four o'clock he remembered he'd forgotten to take his medication. The doctor had upped his dosage for high blood pressure, except the pills had made him nauseous. His new excuse for not taking them: he found the blister packs too difficult to burst with his arthritic fingers.

In the kitchen, Eloise and Fabienne were washing up the last few glasses and cups. Looking into the sink, Eloise noticed a ring on Fabienne's finger through the bubbles. It had belonged to Beatrice and she'd listed it as part of the list of bequests. Why had Fabienne helped herself to their mother's jewellery box before they had buried Beatrice or concluded the reading of the will? The normally passive Eloise decided to have it out with her sister and uttered the first thing that came into her head.

"Is that a new ring, Fabi? I've not seen that one before. It looks similar to one that Mum had."

"It's not new, Ellie." Fabienne tried to spin it round between her fingers under the bubbles, hoping to hide the iridescent stone and avoid any further scrutiny. The bubbles had cleansed the ring and added a glistening sheen to the stone.

"Mum left an emerald ring with a claw setting to me, you know? Dad bought it for her to celebrate my birth. Let's have a look."

"Did he? Oh, I don't remember that," Fabienne answered, pretending she had no knowledge of her mother's bequests, her cheeks colouring with an embarrassed blush. "I'm sure Mum had more than one emerald ring. I admit it does look similar."

Eloise balled her hands into tight fists as she tried to control her temper. How bloody dare her sister just help herself to Beatrice's bequests? Their mother had told both daughters that they had been prepared in a particular way. So what else had Fabienne helped herself to before the clear-out? It wasn't often that Eloise displayed such emotion. Maybe brought about by the intensity of the occasion, she flung down the tea towel and stormed outside to rant at her father. Everyone seemed overwrought; Ralph understood that as these occasions always brought out the worst character traits in families. It seemed Fabienne had already earmarked items soon to be hers. Ralph made a feeble attempt to placate his youngest daughter, with a promise to sort out the bequests before she left. The only one privy to the finer details of the list in the box. Hearing the kettle whistle, he headed inside to offer tea for any remaining visitors. Poking his head round the lounge door, he saw Douglas and Molly preparing to leave. The two sisters had dispersed in opposite directions, leaving an ugly tension hanging in the air. He went upstairs to find the damn list. He dearly wanted to prove to Eloise that everything was under his control. He carried the jewellery box into the lounge and waited for the girls to regroup, confident the list would tell him what he needed to know. Scanning down the list of names, he noted that Eloise had been correct and the emerald ring had indeed been listed by her name. He decided to end any further speculation and show both girls the list. But when he returned to the kitchen he found himself alone. Fabienne had retreated to the beach and Eloise was upstairs packing to leave.

Douglas and Molly had vanished too. Though they'd shouted out "goodbye" to everyone, nobody had responded. Ralph tried not to be hurt. For Douglas, this was not the first time he'd walked away. Eloise came to say her goodbyes. He wanted to give her the ring but it had vanished from the box. Her poor face, still tear-stained, made his heart melt. The tissue in her hand was shredded into small, damp slivers; within days her family were unsettled, grieving for the loss of their mother, at odds with one another. She hated it; her gut reaction to flee had not been a dissimilar feeling to the one Douglas had felt. Ralph showed her the now-crumpled list in his hand.

"Look, you were correct, and I promise I'll sort this out, but I can't find Fabienne." Eloise looked at him pitifully, studying his face and saw how much he'd aged just in the last few days. His features were drawn, and his beard flecked with white rather than brown. The eyes were less twinkly than she remembered. She'd noticed the knuckles starting to gnarl on his right hand where his fingers had succumbed to arthritis. He looked ten years older. Would he sort it out, as in the past she knew he had always favoured Fabienne?

"It's ok, Dad, I'll pursue it another time, I'm not feeling in the greatest of moods today either, so best I get on my way; it's a long journey back. Fabienne always did get her own way when we were younger; I should be used to it by now."

"Ok, love, as you wish," agreed Ralph, nodding and patting her arm. Her sister had been headstrong from a young age, often cutting others down in her wake.

Fabienne arrived back from the beach and sought out her father. Ralph had taken refuge on the sofa in the lounge, staring vacantly out of the window, as she plonked herself down alongside him.

"Sorry, I had no idea Eloise would react that way. Yes, I know I should not have helped myself, but wearing her jewellery made me feel, oh, I don't know, closer to Mum. Especially today at her funeral, I wanted to hand it over to her before she left."

As her eyes focussed on her hands in her lap she gasped. The ring had gone, and was no longer on her finger.

"What? Oh, God, no, what the bloody hell?" And she leapt to her feet. She had been down on the beach twiddling it round on her finger in agitation; it must have slipped off! She would have to go back and look for it. Thank goodness the others had left. She did not feel in the mood for another argument, and knew she should say something quickly but words failed her.

"I'll be back in a moment; wait right there. I've... I've left something behind down on the beach," she stammered and dashed off. Ralph followed her out to the hall to find she'd vanished by the time he'd shuffled to the door. What on earth? Watching from the kitchen, he saw her rushing off to the steps down to the beach. After a few minutes she returned, hot and flustered but looking relieved, the ring firmly back on her finger. She'd found it at the bottom of the steps, lying on the sand. The sparkle of the stones had caught her eye.

When she returned she had only one question left for her father to answer before leaving herself, the ring back on her finger.

"Dad, I found this lapel pin on the floor of a church pew earlier today. Do you recognise it?" She plucked it out of her pocket and placed it in his hand.

"That's unusual. The only connection we have to a horse is through your Uncle Albert. He owned a horse called Harrison's something. It'll come to me in a moment. Now, what was it? Count? Mount? Yes, that's it. I remember now: Harrison's Mount."

"Well, I'd like to trace the owner. They were at the funeral earlier today, and left before I had a chance to say hello."

Ralph frowned. He hadn't noticed anyone strange at the service. Mind you, he was deep in his own melancholy. Fabienne thought it was not the right moment to mention to him it might be connected to the incident at the hospital. She'd wondered if it was the same person who'd approached Beatrice.

The true definition of the word "inscription" varies, from engraving to lettering, an epitaph, a carving, or a simple dedication. The art of inscribing an object dates back centuries to the French posy rings that became popular in England and France. Originally rings symbolised eternity or "declarations of love". Beatrice and Jack had chosen a simple wedding band and she'd thought long and hard about an inscription. What valid reason would you have to inscribe a ring not once but twice over? Perhaps like Beatrice and Jack because you wanted the story to be told in years to come, and not have it hidden away like a guilty secret.

The infighting among the siblings had reached a point where nobody could agree on the exact interpretation of the damn will. The inscription of the ring had led to further arguments and wrangling over paperwork with the solicitors. It had left the family wondering if the words on the ring were perhaps in some form of code. More importantly, what was the significance of the two dates? How could they be interpreted? They speculated like any other youngsters among themselves. Ralph kept his opinions to himself. Secretly, Douglas thought the ring should be sold and the proceeds divided equally. Eloise expressed to the others that she was not fussed about the inscribed ring. She had no desire to possess it. She thought it had brought bad luck upon the family. Fabienne, sharper in her thinking, believed the ring held a backdrop to her mother's past that she was keen to explore further.

Despite notifying Samuel about his mother's passing, Ralph had had no response. At the graveside, there had been no sign of him. He wondered if he even cared a jot that his mother had passed away. Being generous, he thought perhaps the occasion was just too painful. Samuel, one step ahead, had cut out and read the obituary in the local paper. Pinned to his wall like a trophy. No one had approached him at the funeral so the notice remained. He speculated as to what he would have told them if they had spoken with him.

"Hi, I'm Samuel, Beatrice's firstborn and your stepbrother." With his hands in his pockets, avoiding eye contact. No! He'd chosen to take the coward's way out and left the funeral before anyone spotted him lurking in the back pew. Swirling, sickening thoughts were still rushing through his head. Ralph had met him previously with Beatrice in Swanage but he remained unknown to Fabienne and the others. Samuel knew everything; he'd done his research, and was more clued up than any of the step siblings had realised. Happy to double-cross anyone who stood in his way.

At Lucknow and Hardcastle, the family solicitors, he discovered there were two parts of his mother's will that included him. The first part a personal connection linking him to the mysterious ring with two inscriptions. He didn't want it and felt aggrieved to have been left what he considered such a paltry object. The second part of the will concerned an amendment in the form of a codicil that Beatrice had signed not long before her death. Nobody else in the family knew that the change to the will would affect Ralph's future. As Samuel began his plotting, his stepsiblings returned to their respective lives in an attempt to pick up a little normalcy.

PRINT Name.

This last Will & Testament is made by me BEATRICE HAMILTON.

Signed Beatrice Hamilton of

Address: Ocean Cottage, Chapel Lane, Ulwell, Dorset.

I hereby revoke all previous Wills & Codicils.

Executors' I appoint as Executors & Trustees of my Will
Names & Addresses;

1. Rosina Nkosi of Apt 136, Bldg 4, Norberto Ty St, Manila, Philippines.
2. Ralph Barclay of Ocean Cottage, Chapel Lane, Ulwell, Swanage, Dorset...

Specific Gifts & legacies I give;

Samuel Gardiner, a wedding band inscribed.

Fabienne Hamilton a Topaz ring

Eloise Hamilton an Emerald ring

Douglas Hamilton a male onyx signet ring.

Ralph Barclay, The SailDreamer Yacht

X 1 Amended Codicil; To Samuel Gardiner I give the deeds and title to Ocean Cottage, Chapel Lane, Ulwell, Swanage, Dorset.

In the last few weeks Samuel had been spinning too many plates. Described by those who knew him as a lazy, ambitious schemer whose plans never came to fruition. Currently out of work with big money worries. Standing in the bookies, and considering placing another bet, likely to sink him further into debt. He could barely afford it, and needed one more chance. Deluded, his luck had finally run out. His curiosity to find out where and how they lived had become an obsession. What kind of homes did they live in? Were they living in flats, bungalows or houses? How would he infiltrate their lives to see for himself what he had been missing? For Samuel, the mixture of grief, anger and sadness were buried far deeper than he'd cared to admit. How would he manage it? Was he bold enough to act on his own impulses and what would he discover about himself on the journey?

In one of his darker fantasies he'd gone ahead and purchased the properties of his step siblings just to wreak his revenge at what he perceived as something life owed him. In Samuel's fantasies he believed assets were the golden ticket to happiness. The initial plan had been to visit all three step siblings, but he made an abrupt U-turn on that idea. Starting his visits in a particular order. Top of his list: Mr Douglas Hamilton.

The long trek north to Douglas's home on Mull would be worth every effort by the time he had persuaded Douglas to join his latest crazy loan shark scheme. He'd managed to glean the location and address from Ralph, and knew he would have to work doubly hard to win Douglas round. Such was his scheming imagination. There may not be enough time to visit France and his youngest stepsister; that idea would have to wait. Looking at their saddened faces at the funeral, he had already decided that Eloise would be the easier, softer target. He started to consider how much worth there would be attached to her restaurant in France, and whether it was owned in joint names. Considering Fabienne to be the smartest of the three, he decided he would call into London on his return journey from Mull. His unhealthy interest and fascination in her luxury apartment had already begun.

Samuel, as they would soon discover, was a fantasist, who continually lied about his life and achievements. Maintaining a relationship always fell down at this level, as he was unable to be honest about his feelings. The last girlfriend had loaned him money and when the promised repayments failed to happen they'd parted company. The loan had been for the latest model of his favourite car. When the payments dried up the car company retrieved the car. Now he'd moved on to other unsuspecting individuals. Determined to have the assets belonging to each member of his stepfamily, he would need to go to extreme lengths to acquire them. It wasn't just the money he wanted this time; in his twisted mind he became determined to wreak havoc within the family. And now, with Beatrice no longer alive, nobody would stop him. He wanted his share of the family spoils and so much more. It would make up for all the years of anguish and hardship he believed he had suffered.

In some of his darker days he had lain in bed at night and imagined how things could have been. Looking through a rose-tinted lens, he imagined the picture-perfect scenarios. He imagined the family scenes, convivial Sunday lunches perhaps surrounded by everyone seated around a table. Laughter, joking and chatting together; despite his anger, a small tear escaped, and trickled down his cheek landing in his beard. How he'd dreamt of that scene over the years. The smallest of details but with such significant meaning. Already he liked to think he would have a few similar personality traits with Douglas and with that thought uppermost in his mind he planned his visit to Mull with precision.

Fabienne had her suspicions about what was happening at Ocean Cottage. In terms of her father's grieving, she felt powerless to monitor things from her riverside apartment in London. Concerned about her father being left on his own after the formalities of the funeral were over. When the siblings had retreated he had no one close by to monitor things. In the past he had always been a quiet, laid-back individual, with a sharp sense of humour. On the last call home she sensed something amiss, but had not fathomed out what was causing his withdrawal. Perhaps it was a case of unadulterated grief and loneliness.

The next time she visited her GP surgery, Fabienne picked up a leaflet, "The Six Stages of Grief". Once the initial shock surrounding the death had passed, a period of denial and anger would ensue. The next stage sometimes took longer when depression or melancholy set in and smothered the survivor. She could identify with that statement. They can often feel guilty for being alive, for not being the one who has died. In the final stage, acceptance comes much later, she read. Ralph found himself only at stage one on the day of the funeral. Barely able to function. Fabienne was positive that it was only part of his demise; there had to be something else bothering him.

One idea she'd had, was to ask Freddie, the neighbour to check in with her father. He had become a firm friend to her parents. Perhaps he could take him out to the pub for a pint or a sail like the old days. In the past they'd shared fun days out, just the three of them, on the family boat, *SailDreamer*. Freddie's wife had left him for a doctor, ten years younger. This had caused an awkward split among the locals, unsure which side, if any, they should take. Most of the men leant towards the Freddie camp, though Beatrice had leant the other way.

When Fabienne tried to call Freddie, she'd left a message on his answering machine after no one picked up the phone. Had there been some falling out between the two men? Ralph reassured her that the two men were keeping in touch. Frustrated at being thwarted to find the answers, she approached Eloise for further moral support.

"I've tried everything," came her first comment, in a rather overdramatic tone.

"What do you expect me to do from here?" Her sister's voice trailed off after working a ten-day stretch without a break. "I'm nearly four hundred miles away and he doesn't answer my calls either." Fabienne bristled; she didn't want to hear it.

"I always have to pick up the pieces, Eloise. Just for once I'm asking for your help, for God's sake!"

"Where's Douglas in all this?" came the frustrated response. Eloise listened and sighed, staring vacantly through the window. Her attention caught by the sea mist swirling around the bay. She knew at that moment that living abroad had its advantages. She wanted to help, she assured her sister; in reality she felt a little detached from things happening back home. Living in France had its advantages. She would not be at her sister's beck and call at such a distance. She made a mental note to try her father's number again later.

Through the window Eloise's attention had been drawn to a figure limping along the path. A sudden mishap outside required her immediate attention. So she quickly hung up just as Amélie limped through the door. She'd been in a cycling accident on her way back from town. A car had got too close, making her wobble, sending the bike careering off into the grass verge. She had braked hard and flown over the handlebars, landing in a heap. She burst into tears before staggering to her feet. The blood from her mouth looked like a minor gash to her lip. The front tyre had buckled on the chrome rim. With no way of calling for help, she'd had to limp home. Her right thumb had started to swell up under the nail bed, turning a livid purple. On seeing her daughter, Eloise had thrown down the phone and rushed to her aid. "*Quel dommage, ma petite!*" As Amélie burst into tears, Fabienne's request for her to contact their father promptly slipped her mind. It was several days later that she finally got round to contacting her father.

"Hi, Dad, it's me, Ellie. How are you?"

"Hello, love, not too bad. It's so quiet now without your mother's presence filling the cottage. I'm missing her laughter and her cooking. How are the others, Romuel and Amélie?"

"All well, thanks, what about you, Dad, what's been happening over there?"

He could hear the concern in her voice so tried to keep their conversation light-hearted, upbeat.

"Listen, perhaps you'd like to come over for a visit in the summer, Dad? We can take some time off."

"I'm not sure, Ellie, it's a long way to travel on my own." He'd never baulked at the idea before, when her mother had been alive. To Eloise it sounded like the stuffing had been knocked out of him, his spirit deflated. She would try to remember to ring more often as by the end of the chat his mood seemed buoyed by her call, making her feel doubly guilty.

Two

When Ralph looked in the bathroom mirror, he saw a strange unfamiliar face returning his stare. Jeez, he barely recognised the old man with the steely blue gaze. The thicker stubble on his chin, now speckled white, remained unshaven. For several days he had chosen not to wash. This new domestic regime extended to his clothes; he wore the same trousers and threadbare jumper on a continuous loop. The faded blue flannel on the side of the bath remained unused, a sure sign he had stopped having his daily shower. The crinkled soap dried out in an oval dish. His clothes, once his pride and joy, now hung on hangers in the wardrobe, unworn. The rest lay in the dirty linen basket waiting for someone to load them into the washing machine. That had always been Beatrice's job.

The division of labour had been made abundantly clear soon after he'd moved in. He recalled Beatrice screaming at him in despair to leave the "damn" laundry to her in future, as she clutched her best pink cashmere sweater, now a sludgy grey colour and two sizes smaller. Of course, she was no longer there to supervise him, so why bother? Laundry was not important anymore; he never went out.

Fabienne was still determined not to allow their clear-out dates to drift further towards winter. Autumn had clung on by the time Fabienne managed to secure a weekend with her father. Her mother had passed away in late spring and she was hoping to sort out her mother's personal possessions with her father's approval.

Armed with boxes, bin liners and charity sacks, she'd packed her Marigold gloves, the ones with a faux fur trim, in anticipation they would be required.

Ralph's mood lifted after confirmation of her visit and felt secretly pleased to have secured a date. At last something to put in the empty social diary. He entered Fabienne's visit amongst the endless blank social pages. It sat there among the numerous medical appointments.

Looking around, he admitted the cottage looked a bit of a state. Piles of stuff lay everywhere, as he'd been putting off the grisly deed of clearing and sorting things out. He admitted Fabienne's assistance and direction would be timely. Instead of sifting through Beatrice's things, he'd taken a different option, less painful. He'd chosen to sail his boat or go for a swim in the bay. Anything to avoid the inevitable. The rest of the family had been too preoccupied to notice his gradual decline into domestic mayhem and depression, or so he thought.

When Ralph eventually heard from Douglas, the call was full of light-hearted banter. Unsure of his son's motive for the call, he referred him straight to the solicitors for any legal queries. Douglas didn't enquire after his father's wellbeing, so Ralph didn't tell him. Things between them were still feeling strained post funeral. The call had ended with Douglas promising to repay any outstanding debts. Ralph decided he wouldn't hold his breath. Where would his son access that sort of money? He wanted to believe him but past experience told him things were promised but rarely delivered with Douglas. Ralph still had no idea how his son was making a living? They never got to discuss it after the funeral. He remembered thinking, at the time, that he'd chosen the coward's way out. He admitted to himself after ending the call he was impressed by the offer of a repayment of funds.

A few years back he had struggled to align Douglas with the rest of his family after the way he had behaved. Ralph had already suffered his brother Max's wrath and the demands to recompense him for his losses. He'd ended up footing the bill for a replacement car and the missing money from Max's bank account. But had never shared the finer details with Beatrice before her death. At the time he had not wanted to put any undue pressure on their relationship.

Fabienne tooted as she drew up in the driveway outside, sporting a new black driving hat, her hair curled up inside to avoid it blowing in her face. The big cottage clear-out weekend had officially begun. Goodness. She tried to hold back her shock: the man on the front doorstep looked gaunt and shabby in appearance, and did not resemble her father. What the hell had happened to her father? He'd rushed to dress himself less than an hour before her arrival, after scurrying around the kitchen in a vain effort to tidy up the mess. The waft coming from the bin, caught in the back of his throat; he hadn't bothered to empty it. Unbeknown to the outside world, on most days he preferred to lounge around the cottage in his pyjamas, often getting dressed after noon. Some days when it got to four o'clock, he thought: why bother to get dressed at all? His threadbare slippers needed replacing, Fabienne observed before stepping over the piles of newspapers, cans, and bottles on the threshold.

When she went to hug him he stepped back; maybe he'd caught a whiff of his own body odour. Fabienne took a sharp intake of breath, as she leant in to kiss him on a stubbled cheek.

"Hello, Dad, how are you doing?" already knowing the answer at first glance by the state of his appearance. "Take this for me?" Bossing him before she had set foot in the house, she handed over a small box of cleaning materials. Ralph stood there looking sheepish, under a mop of white, uncombed hair. He needed to make an effort, he told himself.

"Hello, darling, you're looking gorgeous as ever. Your hair looks different. The colour, perhaps, or have you changed the way you style your fringe?"

"No, it's the same shade as always, Dad, chestnut brown, Mum used to colour hers the same shade when she was much younger, remember?" Why did she suddenly feel like a schoolgirl again, tossing her tresses over her right shoulder? True, she resembled her mother when it came to her hair and facial features, carrying the famous Hamilton cheekbones with deep-set brown eyes. Ralph stared at her intently; she resembled Beatrice when young. Always devoted to his firstborn, his mind took him back to holding her in his arms within a minute of her birth, swaddled in his arms with a mop of dark hair before the midwife whisked her away. In those early precious moments a deep bonding occurred between them. Jolted out of his daydream, he heard a voice in the distance, and one of his fondest memories interrupted by more pressing matters.

Fabienne was now standing in the kitchen, and impatient to get on with the job of clearing her mother's stuff. Whilst waiting for an answer she glanced over at the sideboard and noticed a small picture frame tucked behind a teapot. Who was that? The baby's face, not one she recognised, had dark curly hair with olive skin, cradled in the arms of a nurse. A definite query for later, she thought.

"Right, Dad, let's make a start in the bedroom."

"Yes, wherever you think is best," came the shaky reply. His heart had not been invested in the clearing-up project. He tried his best not to look at the objects as they landed in the various boxes. The piles on the floor were set out in a fashion only to confuse him further, and he kept getting it wrong. Placing the charity stuff in the "to be sorted" pile. Fabienne went along behind him, rearranging things. So the whole thing took twice as long. He began to feel useless. All this stuff, just material objects that meant nothing without the beloved person to whom they once belonged. Fabienne decided that the story behind the baby photo would have to wait or they would never get the job finished. For the next couple of hours they sorted in silence, neither wishing to start a conversation, deep in their own thoughts.

Finally alone, Ralph breathed a sigh of relief. His peace was short-lived, though, as he heard Fabienne calling him again in that abrupt, sharp tone.

"Daaad," she called out again, "you're not answering me. Where are the trays kept?" She was rummaging through the kitchen cupboards.

"Where they have always been, stored alongside the tall cupboard." After a heavy fish pie supper, they agreed they should retire to their beds and start afresh the following day.

Next morning things failed to improve. Fabienne attempted to hide her dismay, when Ralph arrived in the hallway, ready to set out for breakfast. Standing in front of her dressed in a threadbare navy V-neck jumper, with a gaping hole in the armpit, stood her father. With possibly a bit of last week's fried egg dribbled down the front.

"Dad, I hope you don't mind me saying, that jumper is a bit grubby. Look, there's even a hole; it probably needs throwing out."

"There's nothing wrong with it, it's my favourite; it's my oldest and most treasured jumper, I'll have you know. And your mother bought it for me!" came the offended response, examining the wool and stretching it out in front of him.

"Please go and change it; you can't be seen out in town dressed like a tramp. I'll wait outside in the car." Her words stung. Bossing him about just as her mother would have done. Arguing proved futile, so he retreated inside, shoulders drooping. A few minutes later, he reappeared with the jumper replaced. Now a deep shade of plum, with no hidden debris or holes, his hair brushed neatly.

They drove through the Dorset countryside, admiring the changes to the autumn trees, cascading colours of orange and russet. Although the sun no longer emitted the heat of the summer's warmth, it still cast its golden glow in the skies stretching far out across the water.

His mind was still in a reflective mood when he remembered the conversation between Beatrice and himself, on holiday in Scotland, the year before she died.

It must have been August time, as there were midges galore feasting on any piece of exposed bare skin. Beatrice had asked him a question: would he rather fly like an eagle or swim like a dolphin? He chose the eagle, circling high above the fir trees, with eyes focussed purely on spoils below. Typically, Beatrice had chosen differently, a dolphin, to do with her love of swimming. Dolphins had always been her childhood passion and she took her carefully constructed drawings from picture books.

Ralph's memories had faded out again by the time the car pulled up in the car park, returning him abruptly to reality. The sun felt warm on his face, and the sky was full to bursting with white clouds resembling cotton candy floss, puffed up, voluminous. Life had been perfect, just the two of them.

Fabienne had chosen the Spinnaker Cafe for breakfast. It had always been a firm favourite of her mother's. She had fond memories of the place, with stunning views out towards the little harbour. Small sailing boats, moored alongside, were dancing on the water. It made a perfect setting for an uncomfortable breakfast conversation between father and daughter.

The cafe, operational for over forty years, had served the best breakfasts in the area. The queue formed early at eight o'clock on a Saturday morning, in the height of summer. They were barely through the door at nine, when Julian, the owner, approached them to offer his condolences. Not a great start; Ralph immediately felt his anxiety levels go up a notch.

The decor on the walls saw a mishmash of fishing nets, ropes and small lobster pots. The pictures of sailing yachts all looking tatty and dusty. But the food and drinks were always good quality, and served with care and a cheery greeting.

Fabienne managed to demolish a full English, accompanied by two slices of granary toast, in a mere twenty minutes. During that time her father had only managed to pick at his pork sausage, and left the slice of streaky bacon and some congealed egg, before setting his cutlery down neatly at the side of his plate. Wiping his mouth, his appetite clearly diminished as Fabienne helped herself to her father's plate. In days gone by he would have finished his breakfast, and any other leftovers belonging to the family.

Catching the eye of the waitress with the pierced eyebrow and heavy gothic eyeliner, Fabienne ordered two more coffees. She waited for the right moment to raise the first of the awkward questions. Her previous enquiries had previously met with a rather stony silence, so she started gently. Ralph had always been clever at avoiding emotional questions.

"Ask me another?" he quipped with a half smirk, avoiding eye contact. This time Fabienne grabbed his chair as he went to stand up to leave, causing him to lose his balance and topple forward towards the table.

"Don't... don't ask me now," he faltered, looking directly into her eyes with his own fixed on her face, grabbing her upper arm.

"Dad, please wait, just sit down. I haven't finished and everyone's looking at us,"

"I know. Don't you think I'm not aware of that? I want to leave now and go home." Speaking through clenched teeth. Should she get straight to the point? What harm would it do?

"You cannot hide away in your cottage forever, Dad; you need to get out and face the world. You're depressed, you're grieving. I get it. You also need to tell me about the baby in the photo back at home. Where did it come from?" Fabienne felt herself getting flushed. She had just opened her mouth when her father released his grip, turned on his heel and dashed off towards the toilets at the back of the cafe, taking her by surprise. Surely he wouldn't leave through the rear fire exit door? She knew some subjects were going to be off limits. Fabienne, pushy by nature, would not let him totally off the hook now she'd almost had him cornered.

After what seemed like an age, he returned to the table looking sheepish. Wiping damp hands on the back of his trousers. Fabienne remained seated, looking down at the table. Where to start? she thought. Furiously folding the bright pink serviettes into a neat pile, rearranging the splattered place mats into a semblance of order. A minor thing that her mother used to do when faced with a tricky conversation.

"Come on, Dad, sit down," she persisted, patting the chair. "Tell me the full story behind the ring and the photo." Using a more assertive manner this time, refusing to let it go. "You need to start at the beginning and tell me the truth. Don't try and fob me off, do you hear me? I'm not going to sell my story to the newspapers; my name is not Douglas." Laughing at her own joke, and the throwaway sarcastic reference to her brother. The deadpan expression on the opposite chair remained fixed. Ralph didn't find it amusing and thought Fabienne cruel, referring to Douglas in that manner. He frowned, unable to find the right words before speaking.

Without thinking she reached out and placed her hand on top of his; unaccustomed to the warmth of a human touch, his skin tensed. She found it cool and still slightly damp. Ralph considered his words carefully. He wanted out of this nightmare so the sooner he answered her questions the sooner he would be released.

"Ah yes, the ring," and he explained the significance of the two dates inscribed inside the ring. All relevant in terms of Beatrice's will, and the division of her estate. The first date had celebrated the arrival of Samuel, born to Jack and Beatrice. Jack being her mother's first husband. The second date celebrated a forced marriage, three months after the birth. It didn't take a genius to work out that the birth arrived before the marriage. So their mother had been "with" child when her own parents sent her abroad to avoid a scandal. When she returned to give birth, her father had already signed the baby over for adoption. Underage at the time, her parents deemed her too young herself to sign any papers. So everything had been done without her consent.

So the siblings had an older stepbrother. Is that the baby in the photo? That's him?

"Yes." Her father's face remained stern, studying his hands.

"What does that mean in terms of the will?" asked Fabienne with a quizzical look. After a moment, a slow dawning panned across her face as the full meaning began to sink in; it all started to unravel in her mind.

"Well, isn't it obvious? It means that you have a stepbrother, Samuel, not much older than yourself, actually. He is keen to meet you all, as he is part of your mother's family."

"Why the name Gardiner?"

"After his father, Jack Gardiner, and mother's married name, like I just told you. She reverted to Hamilton when she left him and got divorced."

"Oh I see." She didn't see at all as her eyes filled; she tried not to blink as that would instigate a release. Too late, they burst forth down her cheeks. Pausing the conversation momentarily as she grabbed a serviette.

"Have you met him yet, Dad?" she whispered, dabbing at her face. Ralph thought about lying, knowing Fabienne would never believe him; she knew him too well, or did she?

"No, I have not met him," he fibbed, without flinching. "He did trace your mother recently, though." That bit was true. Had she noticed?

"How?"

"Through the Adoption Lost and Found Agency, and recently he came to meet her."

Fabienne shook her head in disbelief, shocked, hurt that Beatrice had met with the man but chosen not to tell her. Her intention had been to tell all her children. What rattled Fabienne more was the fact that as the eldest child – well, until five minutes ago she always thought she had been – she would be left to pick up the pieces.

The notion of her tight-knit family unit had just been crushed into a thousand pieces. These people had names and feelings. Worst still, would this man want to become part of her inner family? Ralph's opinion had been different from the outset. Why should Samuel be welcomed into their tight-knit family? He wanted to reject the idea from the beginning, allowing Beatrice to influence him. Finding himself easily swayed.

The next question on Fabienne's lips felt unexpected: why had Beatrice been forced to give up her baby? Now Ralph did his best to explain without any hint of bias. He'd hoped by the end of their conversation he had given his daughter an acceptable account of events that had brought them to this point. Ralph had lied to his daughter and he hated himself for doing so. If there were further secrets he had not been party to them. Fabienne knew she would not be able to keep it from her siblings until Christmas, as that would be weeks away. No, she would speak with them both to update them on her plan.

The conversation left Fabienne dismayed. Unable to stem the flow of tears, she grabbed herself another serviette and hurried outside. Her perplexed father left at the table to settle the bill.

They drove back to the cottage, quietly nursing their thoughts, neither wishing to intrude, the car radio belting out a Cliff Richard song, "Living Doll". The Audi weaved its way back, a wild and breezy journey with the roof down. Fabienne angrily threw it around the country lanes, causing her father's stomach to lurch. He found himself holding his breath whilst his white, unbrushed hair stood up in the G-force. He took his eyes off the road briefly and concentrated on the hedges. Looking down at his hands clutching the sides of the leather seat, his knuckles had turned white. The feeling in his forefingers gone, as numbness had crept in.

"Please slow down, darling. One death in the family recently has been more than enough to deal with," Ralph shouted above the noise of the wind. Fabienne shouted back at him; he could hardly hear her above the noise of the wind.

"Sorry, Dad, I suppose I was unprepared for the depth of

Mum's secret, and if I'm honest I'm feeling a little overwhelmed. It took me by surprise, that's all." First we hear about the implications of the baby given away, followed by her failed marriage to Jack. What other secrets had she been hiding away? Her heart must have been ripped out, and so young too.

"Will you tell the others or shall I?"

"No, I intend to tell them both together; perhaps I'll invite them for Christmas. Can you keep it to yourself until then?" He already knew the answer before he completed his sentence. He needed to track down Douglas first, which might take him a while. Fabienne had thought, why spoil their Christmas? What's worse than finding out that type of news on Christmas Eve? No, she would overrule her father and tell them herself, once back in town.

Anyway, nobody knew the whereabouts of her brother. Or did they? The phone calls home to enquire after their father had been non-existent. Douglas blamed a poor signal, dodging reality as he'd opted to cut himself off. Fabienne too had tried to make contact, and left him an urgent message that seemed to convince him.

Before she died Beatrice had pleaded with Ralph not to tell the children for fear it would drive the family apart, and sworn him to secrecy. At the time she felt unable to threaten him with divorce as leverage as they remained unmarried. There had never been talk of a marriage commitment, and Beatrice felt more than happy to comply with his wishes when it became a modern cohabiting relationship. She'd written home explaining her new living arrangements. Her mother, Flo, responded, saying how saddened they were by her actions. Beatrice replied, saying she hoped their differences could be put to one side and invited them to visit and meet Ralph later in the spring when the weather warmed up.

The will explicitly stated that each child should inherit

equally from Beatrice. Fabienne had assumed the cottage would be hers. What about Ralph? Beatrice had not been so kind to the man who had saved her, and written her will to reflect her guilt and love for Samuel over those she felt for Ralph.

Something had been puzzling her about her father. He had more to tell, but had been withholding information. No sooner had the car drawn to a halt than he leapt out, trying to recover his equilibrium. The familiar sea air and his favourite view. Both seemed to appease the aftereffects of his paltry fry-up, combined with some travel nausea from the turbulent driving. He plonked himself on his familiar wooden bench. It offered comfort and solace as he tried to centre his thoughts, already regretting his decision back at the cafe.

To divulge Beatrice's secret to Fabienne had been a reckless move, caught in the moment and under pressure. Had he told her everything? Why hadn't he kept it to himself? He dragged his hand through his hair, fretting he had just made a huge error.

Ralph dusted off the ancient Sunbeam slow cooker that had lain buried in the kitchen cupboards; it must have gone unused for ten years or more. This meant his train of thought had focussed on making a paella in Fabienne's honour. "Oh my goodness," she thought as she caught sight of the shopping list on the table. Ralph took himself off to the local FineFare supermarket to seek out fish, chicken, frozen mussels, peas, peppers, chorizo sausage. Would his local supermarket have such a foreign type of sausage on their shelves, or mussels? The ingredients went into the slow cooker during the afternoon and rice added at the last minute. Fabienne watched from a distance, knowing it was a melting pot for a classic case of food poisoning. She believed if she washed it all down with a copious amount of white wine it might be bearable.

Come seven o'clock she had no way out. Her father had cooked plenty of food, more than enough. The chilli sauce she found at the back of the larder was out of date and came with a warning and a red glow. Probably the safest bet would be to slather the plate with sauce to kill off any lurking bacteria. With dinner served, the tinge of yellow came only from the rice, she hoped. The mussels tasted of old rubber bands, and during the cooking process had turned a dirty grey colour. She discreetly left them to one side. When they'd finished eating, Fabienne silently scraped the remaining forkfuls into the bin. The leftovers were not to be offered to Freddie, as per her instructions.

The remainder of the big clear-out weekend flashed past. Several overfilled boxes appeared by the back door for disposal. Fabienne felt relieved that they had broken the back of it before Sunday afternoon drew to a close. All the sentimental objects had been carefully put to one side for discussion with Eloise at a later date. As she prepared to leave for the drive back to London, her feelings of guilt returned about leaving her father behind. She'd already asked him, "Did he know of someone in the village who might come in and do a spot of cleaning?" Perhaps they could place an advert in the shop? She received no firm acknowledgement to any of her questions, her father following his usual evasive tactic and selective hearing when cornered. Ralph refused to have strangers bossing him about, and chastising him about his lack of domesticity. He didn't want anyone knowing or interfering with his new habit of not getting dressed till noon either.

Fabienne hugged him goodbye, trying not to inhale.

"Promise me you'll get the shower repaired before Christmas." Ralph pulled a face and gave a brief nod, avoiding eye contact. Enough, he thought; she needed to be on her way.

Fabienne pulled her hair into a tight ponytail and wound it round neatly into a makeshift bun. She hugged him again, a little tighter this time. With her driving cap in place, she exited the driveway at speed, scuffing up gravel dust in her wake. Ralph smiled to himself: his daughter would never change, always dashing from one thing to another. Though he admitted that he would not have managed the clear-out without her help. Beatrice's voice in his head told him he should have been more appreciative of her efforts. If she'd been there Beatrice would have chastised him for not being more grateful and remaining a filthy grumpus all weekend.

In the weeks following Beatrice's passing, Ralph retreated into his shell and stopped communicating with the rest of the family. Steeped in his own state of melancholy, he found it difficult to climb out of the trough of grief. Many phone calls had gone unanswered, with the answer machine banished to the garage in an effort to avoid well-meaning inquisitors.

Once Fabienne had left he felt drained of energy and emotion, so retreated to his favoured place. His beloved sofa, where he mulled over the events of the last few days. Heeding Fabienne's advice, he began to make a list of things to do and people to contact. First he would contact Eloise, followed by Samuel, and lastly Douglas. The list stayed on the table, untouched, for the next few days while he procrastinated.

Ralph felt sure Fabienne would beat him to it, and probably be on the phone speaking to one of her siblings the minute she got back to London. He would stick to his promise and get a plumber to look at the shower that had sprung a leak. And he'd agreed that he would call in on Freddie and suggest they take the boat out. Way down at the bottom of his domestic list was the laundry, cleaning the kitchen and valeting the car. In his eyes none of it was urgent.

Samuel successfully traced his stepsiblings, bypassing any

minor obstacles. Now there were five beneficiaries and not four. The rings to be allocated as formal bequests. Beatrice for all her planning had had her own solution: she would leave the inscribed wedding ring to Samuel, believing it would hold the most sentimental value for him. But he had had other ideas. As the family secret had been unleashed after thirty years, he'd decided on his own course of action. He wanted more from the family that he felt had neglected him for so many years. He sought recompense for what he saw as major errors of judgement, and vowed he would make them all pay. Screwing them for every penny if things went his way.

Three

Crows Gather – 1998

It was not that Beatrice had forgotten about Samuel, or her promise to him after his birth. She reminded herself every year of the vow that she'd made back in Elswick, that one day she would look for him. She'd often wondered who his parents were, and where they lived. Did they show him love and affection, and give him the upbringing that he so richly deserved? She had heard horror stories about children who were maltreated and suffered cruelly at the hands of abusive parents. Nobody informed Beatrice that Samuel's placement was in a strict orphanage. One that ruled him by punishments instead of affection. Would she have looked for him any sooner if she had known the background? She'd confided in Ralph prior to her death about the wedding ring, and its sentimental meaning with the connection to Samuel. Ralph always remained unsure how to proceed with the information he had been privy to. In his mind, he could only foresee someone getting hurt.

After a fitful sleep, Beatrice had woken on Saturday morning with a pain over her right eye. She recognised it as the one she suffered at regular intervals. A migraine type of pain that would eventually respond to medication. Whilst she was out on a walk to clear her head, Ralph dialled Samuel's number again. This number is no longer in use. Leaving him confused and frustrated. What had Ralph been up to? He'd hung up the phone looking rather guilty when Beatrice entered the kitchen. He was about to try a different distraction tactic with the offer of a meal out.

"Let's have lunch at the Cobb on Sunday. It's always been your favourite."

"I'm not sure I want to. Can't I decide later?" Beatrice suspected a subplot.

"Well, it's just that the tables get booked up quickly on the weekends."

"Yes, that is true, ok."

Ralph had insisted the drive over to The Cobb pub would cheer her up and take her mind off her recent problems. He'd wanted to placate her, like the tea and toast in bed on a Sunday morning. A ritual they found hard to stop. A strong mug of arabica coffee for himself and a cup of Earl Grey for Beatrice.

Out in the garage stood Ralph's pride and joy. A mustard-coloured Austin Maxi, a first of four British cars in terms of a hatchback. A real jalopy as the suspension bounced on coiled springs. The car needed a run-out; the engine had sounded sluggish. That Sunday, they'd chosen the scenic route through the villages full of beech trees, turning from green to coppery red. They both agreed the surrounding vista looked stunning and how lucky they were to live in such a beautiful part of the world. As they pulled into the pub car park Beatrice flinched at all the Sunday lunch folk already seated at the tables. Her palms felt a little damp. She hoped it would be less crowded inside. Crowds always made her feel weird. It had happened more frequently the older she got, resulting in something akin to a panic attack and a deep anxiety she seemed unable to relinquish. Whenever faced with a situation out of her control, the feelings flooded back. They were associated with the birth of Samuel. So when she saw the crowds outside the pub she instantly felt overcome and wanted to turn around and leave.

Someone had lazily scrawled the Cobb Arms lunchtime menu on a chalkboard outside to lure in the passing trade. All their favourites were on special offer, so it did not take the pair long to make a choice. A roast dinner of beef, pork or chicken with all the trimmings, including Yorkshires. Desserts were limited to three choices: treacle sponge, apple pie, or the latest American sensation, vanilla cheesecake. Ralph chose the beef and Beatrice the chicken. Feeling more upbeat than earlier, they shared a bottle of South African red, despite Beatrice explaining she didn't feel like a heavy red wine, as it was an unwelcome companion to her headaches. Ralph ordered it anyway, despite the protestations, and she left half a glass. He'd planned the lunch with something to confess when the moment seemed appropriate.

First, he had contacted Douglas without mentioning it and he'd also been in touch with Samuel. So, he had committed a double betrayal of sorts. He'd suggested to Samuel that he contact Beatrice himself to arrange his own meeting.

Ralph cleverly steered the conversation as Beatrice neatly avoided his questions and clammed up. He wanted to talk about Samuel and meeting up, but she didn't and paused the conversation. So Ralph took a different tack, knowing what might hook her interest, and suggested they book a holiday. A subject he'd been thinking a lot about recently.

"I thought, while we were here, we might plan our next holiday. We've not had a proper break since last year. Let's go somewhere different, somewhere warm. How about Corfu or Crete, perhaps in June, before it gets too hot?" Beatrice perked up and suddenly became fully engaged.

"What about it, love?"

"I suppose, if you pack your watercolours, I could write some more of my memoirs."

For a split second he felt he had the upper hand. By the time they returned home, in order to avoid any further procrastinations, his mind was made up. Beatrice felt her heart wanted to say, "Yes, let's do it." But her head kept putting forward arguments about why they should stay closer to home. The long list of excuses was getting on his nerves. Tomorrow he would book a damn holiday. They drove home from lunch in silence, each with their own thoughts.

Beatrice suggested a lie-down once they got home. A euphemism of sorts, and her own way of making up to him for being so crabby over the meal. He accepted the invitation willingly. Their sex life had dwindled to almost nothing recently. She had blamed the family dramas and her poor health. He always welcomed any offers to lie down. Beatrice had always taken the lead in the bedroom, and that's how he liked it, a fantastical dominatrix. Leaving him feeling more relaxed in a post-coital daze. Afterwards, they drifted off to sleep. A telephone ringing abruptly shattered their Sunday evening. Ralph came to first and leant over to pick up.

"Hello?" He didn't bother to recite their number.

"Hi, Dad, it's only me. Just so you know, I got Mum's message and I'll be down at the weekend." It was Fabienne and she was in a bright and cheerful mood.

"What message?" questioned a confused Ralph, scratching his head.

"She left a message for me at work to come down as soon as possible."

Ralph scratched his head. Beatrice hadn't mentioned it. What was the rush?

"I'll do my best to get hold of Douglas too."

"Have you spoken with Eloise yet?"

"No, not yet. Listen, I'll get hold of Douglas, don't you worry about that; leave it with me can you, and I'll make contact him?"

"Oh, ok, Dad, it's just that—" She didn't have time to finish her sentence as Ralph snapped her head off.

"Just bloody leave it alone, Fabienne, I'll sort it all out. Be here on Friday as your mother requested, please."

He hung up the call and wandered off to the garden to gather his thoughts. He failed to understand why his life had suddenly become so complicated. It all stemmed from Beatrice's past. He made no reference to Samuel and had not mentioned it to Beatrice either. But he had been in touch with him to arrange a meeting, to introduce the siblings. To his surprise, Samuel had taken charge of the conversation. Ralph remained unaware of how fast the man was moving to get to know the rest of the family. By the time Ralph caught up with him, he had met with the solicitors and travelled up to Mull to seek Douglas. Nobody had heard from him since. They did not know that Samuel had also been down to Swanage, poking about in estate agent windows, and making his own visual inspection of the cottage. For what gain, though? A better understanding of the valuation figure? Not something that was part of any revised plan, either.

The following day, perhaps out of guilt, Ralph gave Beatrice a gift. A canvas painting in muted greys and pink, depicting a sunset merging on the horizon over a wide bay. The colours blended seductively by the artist as the sky met the pale light above coloured sands. She instantly recognised it as one of her favourite local views over the bay. The clever blend of colours suited the living room decor. She would find a place for it to hang alongside the other canvases. To one side of the fireplace there were already three framed canvases; birthday gifts from

Amélie. Completed when she was about ten years old, painted with such artistic flair. First, a butterfly with wings of emerald green and cobalt blue painted in such fine detail you could clearly see the antennae. The second, a solitary magpie with jet-blue-black feathers and a bright white breast, sitting upright on a branch. A third one, a beech tree painted in the autumn months, showing the leaf colour changes from vivid green to a fiery coppery red.

$$\sim\!\!\sim\!\!\circ$$

No one had heard from Douglas to confirm his plans. Initially, he'd cited distance and the cost of fuel might be a problem when he last spoke to Ralph. Now, without telling them, he'd reconsidered. So what had made him change his mind? Perhaps Ralph's second phone call? In the past, the easiest way to deal with his family was to keep them at arm's length. They rarely knew his plans or whereabouts. His sisters thought differently and found his behaviour irksome.

So the crows had gathered. Eloise, the first to arrive, from France, and Fabienne from London, leaving Douglas unaccounted for. With his recent history, they all privately speculated whether he would appear at all.

Whilst out swimming, Eloise had reflected on her own childhood events, brought to mind by the current visit home. Firstly, she felt her mother had always been overprotective of her, perhaps as she'd been born last. She recalled as a child playing for endless hours on the beach. Flashes of pink armbands running in and out of the sea, squealing with excitement. Her brother, who had the meanest streak, took great delight in smashing her sandcastles. She never heard the angry, whispered tones behind the kitchen door, followed by a slam of the front door as her father would

49

head out to the beach to calm down. She never heard her mother crying at night or the heated discussions between her parents. Too young to understand. Her childhood had been mostly idyllic. One or two of her memories were yet to be unearthed.

Before Fabienne could set off for her weekend, she needed to do a quick tidy up at the flat. She'd arrived home from work the previous week to find a "For Sale" board outside. The estate agent had rung to say they had booked someone in for a viewing while she would be away. They had made the booking under the name of Mr Townsend. She never liked to be in attendance when viewings took place. It only caused her dismay when people picked faults with her choices of decor, or commented that the cushions were not plumped, or not set at the correct angle. Some suggested improvements for the interiors. Either the colours didn't suit or the bathroom tiles were the wrong shade of blue. The final straw came when a viewer sneered at her choice of magazines on the coffee table. After that, she steered clear. In the local newspaper, she'd already noted the adjoining apartment had sold for 50k.

Standing outside the apartment in the drizzle was the smart-looking buyer with the peaked cloth cap. They had kept him waiting under his umbrella as the estate agent arrived late and apologetic, caught up in the traffic. Stepping inside, he wiped his feet deliberately, as though not wishing to leave a single footprint. Looking around the apartment, he kept his opinion to himself, despite the gentle interrogation by the agent. The estate agent explained to Mr Townsend that his client would be more than happy to accept an offer at the right price. Samuel played the game and admired the flat with its fantastical river views. Mr Townsend, Samuel's alias, busied himself in the bedroom and turned over a photo frame of a young lady holding a small baby, thinking it might have been him and not realising it was Beatrice and Douglas as a small baby. In the bathroom, he'd already noted the expensive gold-plated taps and the large half-bottle of Chanel No 5. He removed the stopper and inhaled, quickly replacing it, thinking its owner had rather expensive tastes, perhaps above her status. He admired the views of the river and made all the right noises to the estate agent. Had Samuel met his match in Fabienne? He knew he would not buy the place but wanted to see where and how she lived, perhaps a glimpse of a life that he might have had. His plan, to lead them along further, just to be cussed.

~~~

As Fabienne made her way out of the city, she tried to put it all to the back of her mind. She needed to concentrate on her family for the next forty-eight hours. If she accepted any offer on her apartment, her latest plan would be to move into Ocean Cottage, a place she'd dreamt of living since her teenage years. Anyway, she was getting ahead of herself, moving too fast. Besides, her parents were very much alive, so she didn't know why that thought had entered her head.

From Tower Bridge it had taken her three hours due to the heavy Friday afternoon traffic. Running through her mind: speculation as to why the siblings were being summoned at such short notice. The consultant had reassured her the kidney issue would dissipate once her mother had her tumour removed.

Whilst driving, her mind drifted to Douglas. She pondered whether he had found himself a partner, regardless of gender. She'd always found him to be a single-minded individual with no desire to share any personal thoughts. She'd lent him money, with not a penny returned to date.

When he last put in a request for funds, Fabienne lied, saying she was no longer in a position to bail him out, making her feel doubly guilty. After much persistence, he pleaded poverty and, as a last resort, homelessness. The last word had made her soften a little, and she had to check herself not to yield again. Douglas needed money to pay off his bad debts, all the money he'd frittered away, in her opinion. Forgetting about Douglas, she continued to speculate about the reason for the weekend ahead. No, it had nothing to do with him. More likely to be her mother and her will. Beatrice had sworn her to secrecy and asked her not to disclose any recent medical information to her siblings.

Rain hammered noisily on the windscreen, making driving visibility difficult. The wiper blades struggled to keep the torrent of water off the screen. A temporal headache got worse. She pulled over to rummage in her handbag for an aspirin. Once she'd bypassed the tallest spired city of Salisbury, the rain clouds swept themselves away and a milky sunshine appeared. Another hour of driving and she would find out the mystery of the parental summons. She was looking forward to seeing her sister. It had been a long time.

Looking back, she had grown up questioning what the elusive missing piece had been in her mother's life. To date, she had failed to find out. Her mother's face had almost given it away on a couple of occasions. Fabienne felt determined to seek out the dark family secret amongst other things. Maybe Ralph would reveal something to her being the eldest, and not to the other two.

Before she turned off the engine, a figure stepped out of the porch to greet her as she squinted into the late afternoon sun. Father and daughter embraced. Fabienne sensed he wanted to say something, out of earshot, but held back. Wringing his hands together, he looked awkward.

"Where is everybody?" asked Fabienne, plonking herself down in the kitchen.

"Your sister was keen to get a swim in before supper," Beatrice advised, appearing from nowhere.

"Hi, Mum." Fabienne put out her arms and her mother clung to her in a strange childlike manner. She sensed something might be majorly wrong. The appointment with the consultant had been so positive, so what had changed?

"No Romuel?" queried Fabienne. The question went unanswered by both parents. If Romuel had not been included, things wouldn't have been that bad. In her opinion, both parents were behaving oddly and seemed rather distracted.

"Cup of tea?" offered Beatrice. Fabienne politely declined, suggesting something stronger might be in order.

Looking at her watch, Beatrice confirmed, "But it's only five thirty, dear." Fabienne caught a fleeting look between her parents, which summed it up. Despite her advancing age, they would always serve tea first and no alcohol before six o'clock. It had slipped her mind that the sun was not yet over the yardarm.

Eloise returned from her swim and found everyone in the living room, having changed and roughly towel-dried her hair. Her older sister's face lit up. Warm hugs and exclamations on svelte figures, new hairstyles, and jean envy happened whenever they met up. It felt as though no time had elapsed since their last meeting. They put aside the cross words from the recent phone call. Though Fabienne couldn't help but have a dig.

"You promised to ring me back, Ellie."

"Yes, so I did, but something distracted me. Now what was it? Oh yes, Amélie had a serious bike accident and broke her wrist."

"Has Mother told you her important news yet?" queried Fabienne, quickly changing the subject.

"Yes, I can't get my head around it, can you?"

The sisters nodded in agreement, saying that at least they could remove the blasted thing and she could get on with her life. Beatrice, looking resigned and knew she should say more, but didn't want to dampen the jovial atmosphere between the sisters.

As the family gathered in the living room, with one person still absent, Beatrice tried to steer the awkward conversation with her two girls. Fabienne moved across the room to seat herself on the sofa alongside her mother. Putting her arm around her skeletal frame, she felt her fragility and the difference since her last visit. It had forced Beatrice to tell Ralph about their hospital visit.

"So it's not terminal, is it, Mum?" asked Eloise, keen to get started.

"No, they don't believe so. Mr Markham agreed. Once it's removed, things should be fine and settle down again." Trying to make light of it.

"Jesus, Mum, you had us all worried," interjected Eloise, stifling a sob into the arm of her jumper. Ralph wondered how he would manage these strong-minded females once Beatrice had departed. What was he thinking? Nobody need mention dying, so why the sudden turn of conversation to morbidity? "For goodness' sake," he told himself, "get a bloody grip, man." Nobody was going to die this weekend. He needed to just relax and enjoy the precious time with the family. He poured himself a double gin and tonic and went to join the girls, deep in conversation in the living room. Eloise asked if they could take out the boat the following day, just the two of them. Ralph went off to find the tide timetable and check the weather forecast.

~⁓~

Up in Scotland, the day had not started so well. Douglas had grudgingly responded to his father's request to head south to see his mother and sisters. The heightened tension in the car added to his mood. Molly was behind the wheel, weaving in and out of the traffic. They were running late for the morning ferry. She'd grown up on a small island with narrow roads unused to large volumes of traffic. Douglas kept up a running dialogue on what she should and shouldn't do in terms of her driving decisions. It was pissing her right off. She chewed her cheek and tried hard to keep a lid on her fearsome temper. In her head, she wanted to yell at him,

"Shut the hell up and let me drive." But thought better of it.

Still grubby after her night out, which had ended less than twelve hours ago. She could still smell unwashed sex on her clothes. The previous evening she had been out with her old school friends, over on the Isle of Harris, arriving back late on a friend's boat. Getting out of bed at dawn had been a struggle, she admitted. Hence, they were late setting off, and this had irritated Douglas. Not a great start to such a long journey. Her breath still reeked of stale smoke and alcohol, so he wound the window down. With no choice, he needed her to drive him south. He'd too many penalty points on his licence. Only another month to go before they were all spent. The timing could not have been worse. She owed him a couple of favours, so he didn't feel bad for too long.

"Christ! Watch out, Molls, you nearly hit that car. What are you doing for God's sake?" Molly snapped.

"Douglas, who is driving this bloody car? Remember, it's me, so shut up and stop with the hassling or, I'm warning you, I'm gettin oot."

"I have a better idea. Why don't you, go on then?"

Douglas looked at the side of the road and wondered where

she would end up if she did get out. Molly was not dressed for walking among the gorse bushes running alongside the road for the next five miles. She was a feisty hot-head, and being cooped up with her in a moving car was tricky. They were still on Mull, and had not yet reached the mainland. At the ferry, she parked up so close to one of the other cars the passenger door would not open.

"Molls, I'd like to get out for some fresh air. You'll have to move it over an inch, hen."

"Och, nay, the cars are all wedged in now. Can ya not climb over the back seat and outta da boot?"

Douglas gave her a death stare but felt obliged to comply, and wriggled his way over the rear seat and out through the boot. The manoeuvre brought him out in sweat.

Once over the border and into England, Molly's driving slowed to a reasonable speed. More than anything, she needed a stiff drink and some nosh, something greasy. It would help cure the pounding head of her mammoth hangover.

At Ocean Cottage, the family had gathered at the table about to eat, having given up hope of Douglas joining them. The sound of screeching tyres suddenly disrupted the chatter and displaced gravel. A car door slammed, followed by a second. Shadows were moving about outside in the fading light, heaving luggage out of the boot. A strange female face with flame-red hair and large cheap white sunglasses got out of the driver's seat and peered at them through the living room window. Who had tracked him down? The women peered back through the glass.

"It's Douglas!" they shouted in unison.

"No, surely not. It can't be. Look, who is that with him? It looks like he has some chick in tow," announced Fabienne. Her face fell. Such bad timing to introduce a new girlfriend to the family, and so typically selfish of her brother. Perhaps they had some news of their own, she speculated to her sister in a whisper.

"So, who tracked Douglas down?" No response came from those assembled. Ralph had gone to open the front door. He'd found his son's whereabouts through a mutual friend, and kept them from the rest of the family. There had been no mention of bringing a girlfriend when they'd spoken earlier in the week.

"The chick", as Fabienne had put it, stood awkwardly in the hall, smoothing out her white, crumpled miniskirt. Hiding in Douglas's shadow, as though she were trying to ease herself out of the limelight.

"You've made it son; have you seen you-know-who yet?" Ralph spoke in a hushed voice, as he stepped forward to embrace his son.

"Who? Oh, no, not yet," Douglas lied. Why the hell had he just lied to his father? Quickly changing the subject, he continued, "Listen, Dad, I hope you don't mind Molly coming down too. With the long distance we could share the driving." His second lie in less than five minutes. He'd promised himself no more lies on the journey down. The promise must have slipped his mind for reasons he chose not to share with the assembled group. Fabienne and Eloise cast a knowing look at them. To the sisters, it looked as though the prodigal son had returned, everything forgiven and forgotten. He was back. Nothing had changed.

Molly "the chick", left standing in the hallway, was admiring herself in the long mirror. Rearranging her hair into a ponytail and posing, hand on hips. Fabienne caught a glimpse, her hackles on the rise. Why had her stupid brother brought a new girlfriend with him for such an important family weekend? Perhaps Molly had some news of her own. Ralph took pity on the poor lass and led her through, asking how her journey had been, and what her preferred tipple might be.

"Och, mine's a neat voddy on the rocks." He detected a Scottish accent filtering through the missing eye tooth? It meant she spoke with a hint of a lisp. The dialect, difficult to translate at first.

The sisters continued their own private conversation in hushed tones. The rest of the family reunited again. How lovely! thought Beatrice, watching them closely.

"Yes, I can't get my head around it, can you?"

"At least the blasted thing can be easily removed, and she can get on with her life." The sisters nodded in agreement.

"Gave me a right scare, though. Did it you?"

"Yeah, I thought for a minute she was going to say it was terminal," Fabienne piped up.

"Let's hope we can all relax and enjoy the weekend," whispered Eloise, squeezing her sister's hand.

Their mother took Douglas to one side and relayed the news about the kidney operation, sparing him the details. He'd always been squeamish with medical matters. The sight of blood always made him gag and his knees go weak. He didn't like to tell his mother that he knew everything already, just from a brief telephone conversation with his dad.

Beatrice was now keen to discuss the real reason they had been called home. Awkward questions followed. It was true, Beatrice had updated her will and had had her cancer checked out. What had she planned to happen to the box of rings? These were important issues to the female assembled group. At that moment, none of them had an inkling it would be the last time they would all be in the same room. Each sibling had a differing take on the events that unfolded over the next few hours.

Douglas led the sisters out of earshot, one at a time, to make it clear. They needn't ask questions of his new girlfriend. Did they both understand? Ooh, thought Fabienne, that sounded like a warning. Never one to fear her brother's wrath. She wondered why he was so tetchy about Molly being interrogated. What were the couple hiding?

Ralph dug out a bottle from the back of the cupboard. Vodka never went off as he recalled. The girls felt uneasy about the following part of the evening. It had led them to believe their parents wished to discuss private family matters. Wasn't that the essence of the phone call? Fabienne and Eloise felt uneasy about discussing their mother's wishes in front of a stranger. They voiced a concern that they should not share their conversations with Molly. At this point Beatrice chose not to drop the bombshell about Samuel and kept her secret to herself a little longer.

Boldly ignoring her brother's advice, Fabienne suggested Molly might like to sit in the other room with a magazine and her voddy. Douglas suggested she take a long soak in the bath. He needed to keep her as sweet as because she'd be driving him back to Mull. The family needn't know about the recent points on his licence for drink driving. Despite all his broken promises to himself that he would kick his drinking habit, it hadn't lasted.

The short skirt, the bleached blonde hair and long white boots had given Molly a particular look. Nobody had dared ask her what she did for a living; they were politely saving that for the dinner table. But Douglas had already censored questions that referenced his latest girlfriend. He'd briefly mentioned Molly worked in a shop and that was all they needed to know.

The food that evening was a speciality of Beatrice's, home-cooked lasagne and salad. Followed by raspberry trifle. Molly, wide-eyed with vodka, sat nibbling on the salad alongside her pasta, and tried her best to keep up with the pace of the family chatter. The dinner went off without incident; the conversation remained light-hearted. Once they'd cleared up and returned to the lounge, the discussions descended further into childhood memories and school incidents. Beatrice retired to bed early, citing a bad head and too much excitement. Ralph, last to lock up downstairs, caught a brief conversation between Douglas and Molly as they climbed the stairs to their room.

"Why didn't you tell them I was coming? I feel so out of place?" whispered Molly.

"They don't know about my driving ban, that's why," hissed back Douglas.

"That older sister of yours is a right stroppy bitch. She does nay get me, treats me like I'm some idiot. I wanna go home. Can't we go back tomorrow instead, Dougie?" He softened.

"Molls, it's taken a whole day to get here. We have only been here a few hours and you want to go back? I knew it was a bad idea to bring you?" He hissed his words directly into her ear.

"Well, I should have stayed back on Mull, and not listened to you." And she slammed the bedroom door.

Ralph moved into the shadows and waited until they'd shut the bedroom door before he ventured up the stairs. So Douglas had a driving ban? What else had he not told his father? Ralph thought the days of his lies were behind them. It didn't make sense, as Douglas seemed more settled this time.

Saturday flashed past with a family picnic on the beach and more sea swimming. Mid-afternoon saw Eloise and Ralph take the boat out for a short sail. With a gentle offshore breeze blowing, the sails responded kindly. The pair had not sailed together for some time, and the quiet conversations had been enough to carry them contentedly for a couple of brief hours before the light faded.

Ralph deliberately left out the recent information concerning Samuel, who had been in touch to say he had a new job offer, so would not be journeying to meet the family as promised. His natural curiosity would normally have taken over, but he needed the money from his temporary job to fund his trip to Scotland. Samuel also failed to mention to Ralph about his planned trip to London and the viewing of the riverbank apartment.

By Sunday morning, the atmosphere at the cottage had

changed from upbeat to a rather sombre aura. At breakfast, nobody spoke, and Beatrice was absent. She'd felt unwell during the night, woken feeling nauseous, and running a fever. Not wishing to worry her, Ralph thought she looked worse, and offered to take her straight to the hospital. Beatrice wanted to avoid any fuss and see out the weekend with her family.

She knew deep down that this may be the last time they would be together. Tucked out of the way upstairs, she allowed the siblings time to enjoy each other's company. Despite all her best intentions, by mid-afternoon she could no longer bear the pain. Writhing in agony, leaving Ralph no choice, he dialled 999. The emergency services suggested the ambulance take her straight to the hospice. Fabienne accompanied Beatrice in the ambulance and Ralph followed behind with Eloise and Douglas. They left behind a sulky Molly with a sink full of breakfast dishes and the important job of manning the phone. News of an ambulance at Ocean Cottage would be through the village within the hour, and callers to the house would ensue, some with pertinent questions. Was Molly the right person to fend them off?

At the hospice, they had admitted Beatrice to a side room and made comfortable. With the pain under control, the doctors explained that the tumour had changed course. The family was called into an interview room to have a discussion with the doctor.

Each sibling had voiced a differing reason to stay by their mother's bedside. Douglas was keen to be on his way as soon as possible and return to Molly. Fabienne wished to stay and support her father. And Eloise found the whole situation too much to handle and dissolved into a sobbing mess. The doctor advised the family to remain, as they did not expect Beatrice to live beyond Tuesday and they all might like to readjust their travel plans. Nobody had expected or prepared themselves for what followed.

Four

Consett – 1940

September – Florence and Harry Hamilton came from a semi-rural town, fourteen miles outside Newcastle. Consett, originally known as Conside, had its name changed after the development of the local steelworks. The town sat high on the edge of the Pennine Hills, alongside the River Derwent. Roughly nine hundred metres above sea level.

Harry and Florence (Flo) were from an upright, well-respected family. A traditional stay-at-home mother, she had given birth to a mixed brood of four, two boys and two girls. The two eldest, Arthur and Albert, were twins born at home. The babies had arrived swiftly within fifteen minutes of each other. Only one baby survived. He had lain lifeless on the towel with the cord wrapped several times around his neck. Flo rechecked with the midwife that they could do nothing more to revive the poor little mite. She accepted the medical advice that the cord had been the primary cause of death; later confirmed on the death certificate.

Pillars of their local community and good practising

Catholics, the family attended Mass every week. Father O'Flynn, their priest, led the small burial ceremony at their local church. Flo attended, cradling two-week old Albert in her arms. Her husband never spoke of the deceased baby or mentioned his name from that day forward. Harry was profoundly impacted by the death of his son, even though he had a fit and healthy baby in Albert.

Flo thought sometimes he behaved as if Arthur had never been born. She knew Harry rarely displayed emotion, so she found it hard to tell if he was grieving. To create a small memorial to her baby, Flo planted a cherry tree in their garden to commemorate little Arthur. Harry tended to the tree and often sat under its branches whilst in flower. A year later, she fell pregnant again, this time with Rosina, followed by Beatrice in 1949. The children were close in age. When they were first married, Flo had envisaged a much larger family.

Years later, when the three Hamilton siblings had left school, Albert had been eagerly awaiting his papers to join the Household Cavalry. He had always been keen on horses and had mastered some fine equine skills while working as a stable lad on a local farm. The Household Cavalry was made up of two senior regiments, the Blues and Royals and the Life Guards. It had captured young Albert's imagination, and he became enthused by the idea. More than that, he loved the idea of escaping his hometown. He wanted to be a hero alongside his beloved horse. It seemed the perfect solution. He could continue his love of horses, and benefit from some strong army discipline, according to his father. Aware he had lost a twin brother, he always felt he had so much to prove to Harry. He wanted him to be proud of his achievements. Harry wanted his only son to have a military life that he had never experienced.

The third sibling, Rosina, had a different type of career calling. She believed God had given her a special direction.

She would soon join a holy order, courtesy of Father O'Flynn (whose motives were always self-interest and monetary values!). Founded in the early fifties and known as 'The Sisters of Mercy', based in Manila, in the Philippines, according to the leaflet the priest had given her. They specialised in the development of the poor, the sick and the uneducated.

Rosina had been on tenterhooks as any day she should hear. The papers were just a formality. Father O'Flynn had encouraged her parents to sign them, as by the time her ship arrived in the Far East she would be seventeen and able to make her own decisions. In the preceding months, whilst awaiting her joining instructions, she worked at a small drapers' shop in Consett, selling fabric and dresses. Famous for its prime location in the middle of the high street, it stood proudly between Carey's the Ironmongers, and Barnards the Florists. Beatrice, unlike other young women, didn't care for what she described as 'unimportant' things like fashion. Rosina and her sister were like the other youngsters in the neighbourhood who left their education at fifteen.

Beatrice filled her time as a volunteer in a local children's home. She assisted the staff with the younger ones. On some weekends, she bathed and fed the smaller babies. At other times, she took the older ones outside for long walks. Sometimes she would read to them or play games on the sprawling lawns under the trees. The children who were orphans were all awaiting fostering or adoption.

In the 1950s, there were many reasons for the children to be placed in institutions. Some parents had lost their partners during the war and could not cope alone. Some families were destitute and living below the poverty threshold. People prepared most girls of Beatrice's age to go into 'service,' and the boys often worked as labourers on local farms.

Come September that year, Albert and Rosina, both with too much time on their hands, implied it might be time for Beatrice to have her first courtship. They were concerned about their younger sister, soon to be at home with no siblings to socialise with. After much persuasion and brotherly cajoling from Albert, the pair set up an introduction for Beatrice to meet his close friend, Jack Gardiner. A local lad from across the river, he and Albert had been firm friends since primary school days. Beatrice had never considered a romance before and, trusting her siblings' opinions; she seemed suddenly keen to find out more. She asked what this best friend looked like, not realising her father had been listening in the front room (his protective antennae on full alert).

"Now, don't you go getting into any trouble, young Beatrice," shouted Harry. "In my experience, young men like Jack Gardiner only have one thing on their minds and it's not what you think! Anyway, Beattie, I've heard this Jack has a reputation with the ladies. Isn't that true, Albert?" Harry had a firm opinion on the matter, as always.

"Don't you worry, Father. I'm sure everything about Jack is legitimate. After all, he is Bertie's friend," she hollered back, winking at her brother.

"That's what concerns me," replied Harry.

The siblings left the kitchen and continued their conversation in private out in the garden, and well out of earshot. Harry frequently forgot that his youngsters were almost adults, making their own plans for the future. He had always kept such a tight rein on the small group of three.

Sitting out in the garden, Albert gave his sister a brief description of Jack to allay some of her fears.

"So what do you want to know?" He chuckled. "I can tell you that Jack has black hair styled in a short back and sides, liberally slicked back with plenty of Brylcreem, and he dresses like a Teddy boy with all the gear and large shoes that's all the rage right now." Beatrice thought he sounded rather exciting, so they set a mutually agreed date. She had seen the Teddy boys hanging around in town by the American cafe. From a distance, she wanted to be part of their gang, if allowed. She would need to change the style of her clothes to fit in.

On the evening of the blind date, Beatrice went up to her bedroom to get changed. It had not been decorated in years, and still bore the old telltale signs of a bedroom well used. The scuffs and scribbles hidden out of sight behind the chest of drawers. She found several dresses laid across her bed. Rosina had kindly borrowed them from the shop, with her manager's permission. They were on the sale-or-return rail. A simple selection, as she knew her sister had the most basic of wardrobes, full of dowdy-looking dresses that would never attract the notice of any boy. Rosina, not wishing to be left out, fussed around the room. She liked nothing more than telling her younger sister what she should wear, and how to fashion her hair with some of their mother's tortoiseshell combs. Whenever Flo went out, they would practise with her lipstick and powder puff, ending up in fits of laughter at the outcome. That evening was different. Tension sat firmly in the air. Beatrice attempted to back-comb her hair into a style she had seen in the magazines, but made such a mess of it she gave up. She tried to plaster it down at the sides but it would not stay put without kirby grips.

"Rosina, stop your bossing," exclaimed Beatrice.

"I can sort myself out. I'm fifteen now, you know." Looking in the mirror, she held the first one up against her body. Scrunching up her face, she held up the second one, a bright pink number with a plunging neckline. It wasn't her style either, a bright, cheerful fabric without a collar and a shorter hem. She threw it down on the bed, tutting under her breath. Her sister's experience would not help. Poor Rosina had never had a sweetheart either, probably because she'd been saving herself for the Almighty. Beatrice knew her acerbic thoughts were not what her sister deserved. The tension began to seep out of her. Rosina had experience of ladies of all types coming into the shop looking for dresses for courting or fancy parties and summer balls. This would be the first time for Beatrice. True to form, she selected one of her own drab-looking dresses and ignored the brightly coloured ones on the bed. Instead, she chose a frumpy, shapeless, brown linen number with a fussy off-white collar and beige shoes with buckles at the side. Rosina bit her lip and kept her silence. History told her to get out of the bedroom at that moment, as Beatrice was about to explode and lose her temper. Albert, one step braver, poked his head round the bedroom door, and commented that he thought his sister's look would be far more suitable for a schoolteacher than a date. He too disappeared out of the front door at speed, as a shoe came flying in his direction.

Beatrice slumped on the bed, dejected by all the fuss and mayhem around her. Suddenly she had a panic about what she was going to do. What was the point? Why have all this hoo-ha? Everything was ready. With Harry and Flo out for the evening, at least there would be no scrutiny about where she was going with such brightly coloured lips. Beatrice admired herself in the mirror one last time, before she went down to sit by the window in the front room and wait. She sat on the sofa, fidgeting with her hands, checking her watch for the third time, and folding and unfolding her hands. She already felt a fluttering in her stomach. Perhaps they were hunger pangs. She had been far too nervous to eat earlier. Ordinarily, she had a voracious appetite and cleared everything on her plate. As a family, they had no waste at the dinner table after the shortages and rationing years. They encouraged the youngsters to eat everything put in front of them. Albert always ate enough for two, clearing any leftovers. Earlier that day, Flo had not been paying attention to her daughter's plight and failed to notice a plate still piled high with sandwiches, and a piece of leftover fruit cake. The parents shouted goodbye as they left for weekly bingo. They wouldn't be back for hours.

When she heard the double rap on the front door, her heart skipped a beat. What would she find to say to him? Back in school, they spread a story that if you kissed a boy with your mouth open, a black seed would transfer from the boy to the girl, and that's how babies were created. Yikes! What would happen if he kissed her? Would she fall pregnant? Beatrice had already asked her brother if it was true, while he laughed his head off, failing to give her an answer.

What happens if he wants more than just a walk and fish and chips? She had never been out on a date, yet alone thought about sex. They had never discussed the subject at home. Albert might have been sniggering about sex with his friends at school, but at home they never discussed it out loud.

Beatrice, naturally shy, found small talk not her forte. She had always chosen to hide herself in the background behind others, preferring group outings with her siblings or friends. This would be her first official outing alone as a grown woman.

At eighteen, Jack's master plan was not so mature either. They would walk down Lombard Street to pick up fish and chips and call in at his house to say a brief hello to his parents. He had no intention of being seen in the pub with Beatrice on their first date, and he already knew she was underage and his mates would ridicule him about his choice of women. Jack idly wondered if Beatrice would let him touch her at all. Loose was not a word you would naturally attribute to Beatrice. A good Catholic girl could not be loose, as they needed to remain intact, until marriage. Speaking of underage, Jack had not considered that Beatrice, at only fifteen, would make him culpable if anything happened.

Secretly, he already knew that his parents would be out at the bingo that evening, and the house would become a convenient stopping-off point on their way home. If everything went to plan, they would end up with the place to themselves, but first his intention was to get her tipsy with a couple of his mother's Babycham drinks. Taking a tremendous risk, he would use his own house, as his father would offer his opinion brutally if they got caught out.

Jack had been daydreaming about what Beatrice held under her heavy linen dresses. The thought of running his hand along the top of her slender thigh and feeling her flesh through her thick stockings excited him. The top half of her body, he had already noted, ran flat. He would normally have chosen a more buxom girl. Chortling to himself, he slipped his hand deep in his trouser pocket, checking for something that might come in handy later.

Earlier in the day he'd gone to his local barber's for a trim and treated himself to a new tin of Brylcreem. The barber, winking at him, had gone to the back of the shop for an extra something that he might need later that evening.

When he arrived at the Hamiltons', the house sat in semi-darkness. Just as he knocked loudly, the door opened, and he was unprepared for what stood in front of him.

"You look nice." They were the first words that popped into his head, trying to be kind, but honestly, what was the girl wearing?

"So do you," replied Beatrice quickly, but she held back with further compliments after she inhaled the overpowering smell of aftershave mixed with whisky on his breath. She recognised it immediately, Williams Aqua Velva, a particular favourite of Albert's. She liked his outfit and chuckled at the size of his shoes, which looked overly large for his feet. The latest trend, he told her. As she left her house that evening, she had no inkling that her life would be about to change in such a dramatic way.

What the hell does she look like? thought Jack. He was doing his close friend Albert a favour and anyway, what about their bet? The pair stood side by side, feeling awkward, and he noted he was almost the same height as Beatrice. She thought his long arms seemed out of proportion to the rest of his body. At the height of fashion, the burgundy Teddy boy suit, along with his black shoes, neatly finished the look. With a cocky demeanour to match, he lived up to his reputation as a bit of a flirt with the ladies. A real-life 'Jack the Lad', some called him. He'd always proved popular with the opposite sex, and had evidently mastered the patter.

Jack wondered to himself why the girl standing in front of him had worn the ugliest of frocks for their date. It could have easily belonged to his grandmother. Her red lips appeared exaggerated against the smooth pale complexion and a smattering of freckles on the bridge of her nose. Jack tried hard not to stare. Setting off that evening, Beatrice naively thought they were just going for a walk to pick up some fish and chips. The plan had already gone awry when, on the way over to collect her, Jack had taken a quick diversion to the pub and downed a couple of whisky shorts for dutch courage.

The couple made it as far as the fish and chip shop without further mishap. Beatrice looked at the sticky plastic menu pasted on the wall and chose cod and chips. Jack plumped for a fishcake with chips, vinegar and lots of salt. Neither chose mushy peas, which were a particular specialty of the chip shop. They sat side by side on a bench stuffing their hungry faces, making difficult small talk in between the mouthfuls of hot steaming chips. Beatrice struggled to finish hers and asked Jack to help her out. Eventually, he stood up and wiped his hands, taking the lead and stuffing the used newspaper wrappings into the bin. The pair walked off across the bridge towards the cheaper side of town.

The two-bed terraced house where Jack lived with his parents stood in stark contrast to the Hamiltons' home. Small, dark and cramped, the parlour had, until recently, doubled as his grandfather's bedroom. The family were from generations of steelworkers. There had been an accident at the local factory, which resulted in many men being overcome by carbon monoxide poisoning. Jack's grandad had had a lucky escape and left for home early on the day it happened. Townspeople gathered on the street corners as Grandad Gardiner returned home. His lungs never quite recovered from the years of exposure to the gases down below the surface. So, when he died recently, just the three of them remained at the house.

Because of his father's behaviour, Jack spent much of his time out of the house. He wanted out of the family home but first needed to find a job to support himself. He knew the armed forces would not suit him like his best mate Albert, and anyway he objected to all forms of harsh discipline. The idea had crossed his mind briefly, if only to allow him to escape his regular punishments. He liked to think he would run his own business one day; he heard himself bragging to Beatrice as they walked up the path to his front door.

"Come in," whispered Jack. Casting a quick glance down the dark hallway, pretending his parents were in the front room.

"It's so quiet," she commented. "Where are your parents?"

"Oh damn, I forgot, they must be out at bingo." He shrugged without flinching. Lying always came so easily. "Never mind, you can say hello another time." Hoping she didn't see his face in the half light.

"I think my parents are out at the bingo tonight too," Beatrice commented innocently. Jack's face remained unmoved as he took in her last sentence. He did not want the two sets of parents to meet face to face.

As they hung up their hats and coats in the hall, Beatrice noticed a long leather belt with an overly large buckle hanging on one of the coat hooks. Jack's father thought a stint in the steel works would discipline his son. Jack had far bolder ideas for his life. Some of those ideas had recently displeased his father. The man behaved like a bully. He preferred to use his chubby fists and his leather belt.

When his father disliked something Jack had done or spoken, his response would be swift. The ferret-like eyes would penetrate through him as he took another lashing, and he lost control of himself. It would often be a minor misdemeanour, such as not filling the coal bucket before his father returned home from work. Beatrice tried hard to dismiss the thought of why a belt would hang in the hallway. Most people kept them in a wardrobe, didn't they? Well, her father and brother did. She felt compelled to ask.

"Why is there a belt hanging in the hall?"

"I don't know what it's doing there," came Jack's answer. Beatrice took her seat on the sofa, placing her hands neatly in her lap. Jack plonked himself alongside and quickly made his move. He lunged at her, unsure how to respond at first. She wrinkled her nose at his smoky whisky breath and caught the faintest whiff left over from their fish supper. This kissing lark was all new to her. The salt lingered in his mouth. She tried to close her lips, but his thick tongue probed them apart, making her gag as it flicked in and out. She tried not to think about the black seed story from her school playground days.

Jack appeared taken aback by Beatrice's reaction. What happened? Things were not going to plan. He paused his fumbling and tried another tack. He moved over to the cabinet, helping himself to his mother's favourite tipple. The bottles of Babycham stood neatly in a row alongside the eggnog with a dark green bottle of Stones Ginger Wine. All the bottles were previous

Christmas leftovers. Plonking the last tired-looking cherry into the glass, he watched as it sank slowly to the bottom. And motes of dust rose to the surface, disguised amongst the bubbles.

"Sorry, we seem to have run out of cocktail sticks." That sounded posher than reality. Taking a risk in helping himself to the Babycham, confident his mother wouldn't say anything. Though he would need to remember to dispose of any evidence before they returned.

Beatrice started to relax, mainly thanks to the effect of the drink. Her head felt fuzzy and her arms a little heavy. Should he work on his technique? The great Jack Gardiner wouldn't be losing his touch? The doubts crept into his head all the same. Should he try again?

"Another one, Beatrice?"

"Why nooot?" This time her voice slurred a little and the rest of the evening followed the course of his great master plan. Jack whooped with delight and rubbed his hands to warm them up.

With one swift movement, he slid it in, and quickly satiated himself before withdrawing clumsily. When he rolled away and stood up, he noticed a small, damp, pink stain on the sofa. He sped off to the kitchen to find a cloth and carefully placed a cushion over the offending spot. Beatrice experienced a sudden and intense pain. She rushed off to find the bathroom and sat on the cold wooden toilet, clutching her stomach, shivering. Horrified, she noticed blood on her knickers and grabbed some toilet paper and rolled it into a pad. The toilet paper made a loud crinkly sound as she walked. The family didn't have any soft tissue paper.

Jack had got what he wanted that evening, though not in the best or most comfortable circumstances. A purely selfish, lustful act, and he felt a modicum of guilt when he stopped to think about what they had done. It had not been all Jack's fault, as Beatrice had enjoyed the thrill of it all, well, up to the last moment, at least. The big flaw in his plan occurred because he ignored the use by date on the foil wrapper. The barber had been flogging his old stock. Jack, in his rush and panic at the vital moment, would not have noticed the microscopic tear. Downstairs, she asked Jack if he knew the time, as her watch had stopped.

"Why, everything ok?"

"No. Can we go now?" He scowled at her, not understanding the rush. The pair finished collecting up the bottles and washed up the glasses. They left the house, walking along the road a slight distance apart in abject silence. Outside, the air had changed, a mist had settled and the street lamps offered a muted, flat light, echoing their mood. As Beatrice walked, the pain in her stomach grew tighter and she had to take a seat on the low wall by the school gates. Her head spun, and she thought she might be about to faint with the potency of the cramps.

Jack assumed she must be a little pickled and unused to drink; she'd only had Babychams. How many had she drunk? Maybe three or four? As he pulled her to her feet, she wobbled and grasped his hand. Honestly, he felt relieved to say his goodbyes after finally arriving at her front door. A girl unable to handle herself would end up being more trouble than he could deal with.

"Goodnight, Beatrice, or can I call you Beattie now, for short?" He chuckled.

"You can call me Bea if you like, but not Beattie."

The raised eyebrow and direct stare caused Jack to shrink back. She would not tolerate a nickname of his choice! Surprising herself by delivering a small peck on his cheek just near his dark sideburn.

"Do you fancy going to the cinema on Tuesday? *All About Eve* is showing at the Carlton?" she bravely suggested. Jack thought it sounded like a good idea. Maybe he would be on safer ground inside a cinema.

"Can I think about it and let you know?" He paused with a cheeky grin and a wave of the arm. He had already got another plan in mind. First, he needed to dash home to make sure nothing was out of place before his parents returned. The youngsters had no inkling that the two sets of parents were attending the same bingo session that evening. Possibly sitting on the same table, making polite conversation, or comparing bingo numbers as rivals. With the house tidied, Jack went off to the pub to find Albert and discuss his evening. Of course, they would discuss the small matter of their recent bet. His best friend owed him a few bob and a couple of drinks. Should he tell all, or spare him certain details?

"Good," thought Beatrice, surveying the house in darkness. Nobody was home yet. She quickly retired upstairs, thankful that she had the bedroom to herself. She flung her clothes across her sister's bed and rushed to the bathroom to clean herself up for a second time. Her stained underwear would need to be rinsed. But where could she leave her knickers to dry, away from prying eyes? She slipped on her nightdress, crawled under the covers and shivered. She tried to reconcile the events of the last couple of hours. Had she just lost her virginity? Had the other girls been through the same experience? And would Jack be the one, even though her father had expressed he didn't like the sound of him or his family? They had already laid out their expectations for her life. So no use asking Rosina as she had become all serious and sensible prior to joining her order. Beatrice decided not to tell her what they had done, keeping the details to herself.

Two weeks later, the newly acquainted pair of lovebirds had their second date. They were in the cinema as the lights dimmed to signal the start of the film. They settled into the burgundy velour seats. Jack saw this as his cue to place his arm gingerly around Beatrice's shoulder. The pre-film adverts rolled across the screen. Beatrice thought about it for a split second and reciprocated the move by placing her left hand on his knee, unsure what she should do. She didn't want to over excite him again. After the pain she had suffered following their last date, she had been reluctant to see him a second time if it meant another session on the sofa. The discomfort she felt the other evening still remained. Somehow she felt more secure in the darkened cinema, surrounded by people. The pair continued to talk in low voices, discussing the virtues of Bette Davis and Celeste Holm, annoying the girls in the row behind them, who shushed them loudly as the film got underway.

Jack slipped out of his seat at the interval to collect two vanilla ice cream tubs from the usherette hovering down at the front. Still not convinced their relationship would work out long term, he felt something about her was unfathomable.

The following day Rosina and Beatrice were out in the garden, lying on the grass, engrossed in idle sisterly chit-chat.

"So, how did it go at the cinema?" asked Rosina

"Oh, ok, I suppose," came the dispirited reply.

"Only ok? It sounds more like a flop to me."

"Well, I'm not so keen on being fondled in public."

Rosina threw her head back and guffawed at her sister's comments. Gathering her breath, she responded, "I'll soon be gone, Beatrice, and who will you confide in then?" Laughing, she let slip that she and Albert had again been talking.

"We think it would be much nicer for you to have a regular companion. And we have agreed that Jack might be just the perfect match for you. You need to give it another chance, ok?"

"Oh really? So I'm not allowed to decide these things for myself?" Beatrice's mouth twisted itself into a petulant pout.

"Anyway, Beattie, if you don't find a boyfriend soon, you will end up living at home with just Mother and Father for company. How else are you going to find someone to marry?" Who mentioned anything about marriage? Rosina rambled on and on until Beatrice could hear no more of it, and stood up to go inside. She would make up her own mind. Not when her siblings told her.

Jack and Albert were propping up the bar in their local when he raised the subject of Beatrice. Though Albert seemed more interested in telling Jack about his newly received sign-up papers. Jack attempted to steer him back to the topic at hand.

"So, what did you think?" Albert finally asked.

"I do like her, but not in that way, you know. If we could just be friends with no strings attached, it might work?"

"Did you do it?" he asked with a wide grin.

"Yes, of course we did it and by the way, you owe me," boasted Jack, omitting some of the more personal details.

"What's your problem?"

"To be honest, Albert, I don't fancy her, she's not my type."

"You know what your problem is, Jack Gardiner?"

"What?"

"You're too picky. Don't you go getting her in the family way, do you hear me?"

But Jack wasn't listening. He seemed to be already eyeing up a girl in the corner booth, making soulful eyes at him.

"Do you know who that is?" he casually asked, turning back to Albert.

"Yeah, that's Marguerite! Everyone knows her. She lives in

one of the flats in the big house… opposite here, you know, where Big Joe runs his operation."

"Oh right, cheers for that." Jack beamed.

"Listen, I have to get going. See you around, mate." Albert strolled off towards the high street to catch his bus. It would turn out to be the last time Jack saw his best mate.

The two youngsters were still blissfully unaware of any consequences from their first date. Beatrice had always been regular with her monthly cycles, so four weeks after her date with Jack, when nothing happened, she panicked. Who should she confide in? Not her mother, the priest or her family doctor. The sisters were casually chatting up in their bedroom with the door shut. When fit to burst, she could no longer contain herself as Beatrice lowered her voice and confided in Rosina.

"Yes, of course I'm sure. Shush, keep your voice down and don't go telling anyone yet, especially Mother and Father," hissed Beatrice. Rosina promptly fled downstairs to find their mother and break the terrible news.

"Beatrice Amelia Hamilton, you come down here right now! What in the name of the Lord Jesus have you gone and done?" Crossing herself.

Beatrice paused a second in her bedroom, and still being subservient, did as her mother asked. Down in the kitchen, she took one look at her mother, who had developed the biggest frown line across her forehead.

"You promised!" Beatrice wailed, scowling across the room at her sister, looking smug.

"Beatrice, you are in grave trouble, my girl. Are you sure? How could you have been so stupid?"

"Yes, I think so, Mother," she whispered meekly. Tears started to stream down her cheeks.

"You know you are underage. It's against our faith to have 'you know what' outside marriage." She couldn't utter the word 'sex'.

"It's no use. You'll have to see Dr Thomas up at the surgery."

The surgery hours were nine till five, so closed until the following day, as the living room clock chimed six o'clock.

"I'd better see Father O'Flynn, too. He will know what to do." Flo had made her point, dried her hands and hung up her apron on the back of the kitchen door.

She disappeared into the hallway to find the number for the priest's house and arrange an urgent appointment. Perhaps, she should go straight to confession instead. Yes, she would go and ask for God's inspiration for the words to a letter, and then visit the priest in that order.

On her return, with the words of her priest ringing in her ears, she wrote a letter to Jack's parents expressing her disgust that their son had got their youngest daughter in the family way. And what were they going to do about it as they (Harry and Flo) could not subsidise them? The letter was brief but succinctly written.

Dear Mr & Mrs Gardiner,

We feel you should know that our daughter Beatrice is pregnant, and that your son Jack is the father. We think it best that the baby is offered up for adoption as they will require much financial support when it arrives in the spring. As rumours spread quickly in Consett, please keep this matter confedental a secret. [Flo couldn't spell confidential]

Yours truly,
Mrs F. Hamilton

Flo bravely signed it and rummaged in the drawer for an envelope. Before Harry appeared she put on her hat and coat and scurried out of the house. Determined to deliver the letter herself, she didn't want anyone to see it, especially her husband.

Beatrice, feeling full of remorse, went into town hoping to bump into Jack before Flo delivered the letter. She hung around outside his house, pacing the street until she spotted him coming towards her. Just missing her mother, who had made her letter delivery and was now walking away in the opposite direction.

"Oh, Jack, I'm so glad to see you. Have you got a minute? Can we talk?"

"Of course, come in, nobody's here," quickly glancing around inside.

Before he had time to remove his jacket, it all came tumbling out. She'd spotted the envelope on the mat with her mother's handwriting. Before he picked it up, she blurted,

"Jack, I'm pregnant!" She watched his cheeks change colour as he turned away to light up.

"What? How can you be sure?"

"I know I am because I'm late with my monthly thing." She tried to hold back the tears, but they spouted regardless. Dabbing at her cheeks with the back of her hand, she regained a little of her composure.

"I'm going to see my doctor in the morning. You don't seem bothered, Jack," she observed, feeling a trifle disappointed by his first reaction.

"It's a shock, that's all. What are you going to do?" Jack already knew what his father would do when he found out. As Beatrice went to leave, Jack caught her arm.

"You'll need to get rid of it. You know that, don't you?" he hissed, spitting the words in her face. His persona changed rapidly to one of terror, resembling an animal backed into a corner. Beatrice couldn't understand why his mood had changed so quickly. He seemed to be more terrified of his parent's reaction to the pregnancy.

"You should leave now, Beatrice, before my father returns." That sounded more like a threat. She responded to his request, her words still ringing in his ears. How could she spring something like that on him without due warning? His mood darkened. He didn't know that the letter sitting on his doormat had been from Flo, addressed to his parents, waiting to change everything. He imagined the pain his father would inflict on him when he got to hear about the pregnancy. Jack envisaged a wild animal with its teeth bared, seething with anger as each strike of the belt hit his skin. Although he found it difficult to see his expression, as he had his back facing him during the beatings, Jack wondered what went through his father's mind as he inflicted lash after lash. Did he ever regret what he had done afterwards? Jack wanted to stand up to him now. He'd become an adult but thought things might turn ugly and lead to further upset for his mother.

Five

Father O'Flynn

Father O'Flynn had always been known as a parochial mediator in County Galway, because of his flamboyant personality and affiliation with the Catholic Church. He worked with churchgoing families who were wrestling with sensitive domestic problems. Recently, he'd befriended Harry and Florence Hamilton and considered them to be part of his regular flock. Father O'Flynn learnt they had encountered some deeper family issues. He'd also learnt that the burden had threatened to upset the harmonic balance of the Hamilton household. In the local shop stood Harry Hamilton. He'd spotted Father O'Flynn in the queue and taken him to one side. Out of earshot, he'd explained he needed to see him urgently. He sensed discord within his family, and he needed the priest's help to resolve it. Each member of his family was at odds with one another. Father O'Flynn said he would call round once he had secured a solution.

Flo's answer to their problems always started with a visit to the church, and she stayed behind for confession. Struggling to put her jumble of words together and shaking her head, she confided in the priest that one of her girls had "bejesus" got herself lowering her voice to whisper "in the family way". She crossed herself twice and bobbed. Father O'Flynn's first piece of advice: to recite Psalm 51 for cleansing and pardon. He hadn't been paying too much attention to the words, as he inspected his shoes that were in need of some boot polish. But his ears pricked up at the mention of the unwanted pregnancy and, crossing his own chest, he mumbled a prayer of absolution. One of the three worst sins in their faith, a lustful appetite. Beatrice should know this, being a good Catholic girl and a regular attender of his church. She should also know that as she had attended his Bible classes prior to her confirmation not so long ago. He must try to concentrate harder. His recollection was that those classes had been interminable, full of unruly children. His mind kept drifting onto other matters. First, the Mass he had to lead shortly, and his favourite meal of the week, his weekly roast. Served after Mass on Saturday evening. He would have to curtail his audiences with his parishioners or there would be no roast potatoes waiting for him in the pretty, blue serving dish.

On this day, Father O'Flynn concentrated doubly hard as he attempted to give this latest domestic matter his fullest attention. Waiting patiently to ask the priest for forgiveness sat Flo. Seated in the confessional box and clearing his throat a little, he remembered Flo still waiting and listening through the screen. He blessed her several times and drew the sign of the cross over his chest a second time. Whispering two more Hail Marys before standing up. He took a deep breath before telling Flo that, in the eyes of God, her young daughter had committed a mortal sin, as a practising Catholic herself. So why did he have to remind her again? Her daughter would suffer eternal damnation unless absolved. God considers ending a pregnancy completely unacceptable for a good Catholic girl. Therefore, we need to find a solution that satisfies all parties.

The priest's advice that fateful day to send Beatrice to confession backfired. Flo thought she detected a slight whiff of alcohol on the priest's breath, but instantly dismissed the thought. Father O'Flynn had probably overindulged in an extra sip of communion wine. Priests were permitted to have some privileges. Her pudgy fingers had wrapped themselves tightly around the tortoiseshell rosary beads that lay across her lap, and, looking down, she noticed her little finger turning blue.

Beatrice dutifully followed her mother's instructions. First, they went to see her doctor. At the surgery, her mother sat by her side, answering all the questions Beatrice didn't know the answers to and breaking any awkward silences. She found the whole procedure behind the curtain undignified. The doctor, a locum aged about forty, asked her to lie down on the bench and take off her regulation navy knickers. Blushing and cringing with embarrassment, she did as requested. He felt her stomach and asked her to wee into a tiny pot the size of an eggcup. When the doctor had finished, she felt quite faint and asked her mother if they could go straight home. They scuttled out of the surgery under their matching paisley headscarves, avoiding questions and enquiries from the other patients seated in the waiting room. Beatrice thought she saw an old school friend, Cathy Malone, but didn't make eye contact.

The following Saturday, Beatrice dutifully went along to confession. As she sat in the box waiting for Father O'Flynn to appear, she read aloud the prayer written on a nearby wall hanging aloud in a small voice.

'Count not my transgressions, but my tears of repentance. I long to be true to Your Word, and pray that You will love me and come to make your dwelling place within me. I promise to give you praise and glory in love, and in service all the days of my life'.

At that moment, the words seemed to reach out and speak to her and gave her a small crumb of comfort to cling to. Beatrice sensed the priest was in situ after smelling his breath through the screen. When he talked, she forgot about the smell, and listened intently. When the time came, Beatrice confessed everything. Including the more intimate details, which made the elderly priest blush and shift uncomfortably in his seat. She left the confession box lighter in spirit, having shared her burdens with the priest and, of course, with God.

In the early hours of the morning, the priest had been out reading the last rites to an elderly lady, Mrs Smee of Andover Street. Now he had to deal with an urgent issue in the Hamilton family. He found himself a little short on sleep and concentration. The median time for one of his homilies would be roughly fourteen minutes. Not long enough for his parishioners to fall asleep, but just enough to make his point before swiftly exiting the large wooden church doors. That way, he never got to see the faces of the regular moaners lining up outside his office door. The congregation was made up of a variety of people like a human zoo, in his opinion (the priest's own term for a bit of everything). There were clerics, teachers, nurses and his favourite person, the baker. Father O'Flynn's chosen homily focussed on the theme of morality.

Morality, a timely subject considering the audience seated in the front pew. The Hamiltons were regular congregants and their beloved priest more accustomed to them hanging on his every word. Father O'Flynn had received feedback from the congregation about his tone of voice and delivery being too blunt. He'd previously upset the bishop, who had put aside some time to speak again with the priest as he had received yet further complaints.

One villager had told the bishop they preferred to stick with tradition and didn't take kindly to change. He had agreed with them entirely. He took the opinion of the parishioners seriously. The bishop knew that Father O'Flynn had occasionally overstepped the mark but remained a popular priest full of sincerity. He lacked the snobbery of those priests from further afield. The small petty-minded ones had since bent the ear of the bishop. The two men seated themselves in the bishop's office. Through the window, the sun streamed directly into the eyes of Father O'Flynn. The bishop stood up to pull the curtain a little and continue with their conversation.

"Now, look here, Father, we have received yet another complaint about your recent homily about morality." The father blushed and wriggled uncomfortably in his seat. He knew it had been close to the mark.

"And who might it be this time? Let me guess?" Running short on time, he felt irritated that the bishop had summoned him to his office about what he considered a petty issue. There would always be folk who disliked his words, but his biased opinion stood firm. You could not please them all every week. This time the bishop interrupted him.

"I'll thank you for not trivialising this matter, Father, as the whole thing might blow up in our faces, and I'll have no reason not to suspend you."

"Bishop, I know who it is and want to reassure you they are just picking faults. They don't like me. But I can't help that."

"Well, let's just leave it there and you do your best to heal the rift and remember to tone down the words, Father." Father O'Flynn nodded, but inside he thought he would track down the bloomin' eejit and explain they could always look elsewhere for another priest. Maybe we should assign the role to Father

Patrick, who is renowned for his attention to detail. On this occasion the bishop had rattled his cage.

Now, where exactly had Father O'Flynn got to? pondered the housekeeper, rechecking her watch. It wasn't like him to be late on a roast dinner night. Father O'Flynn wondered if the housekeeper would fret about his whereabouts? He would miss his supper if he didn't hurry himself. His homily reading had just ended, and he followed it with a short intercessory prayer to close the service. Stepping down from the pulpit, he checked his watch, hoping to avoid the gaze of any parishioners wanting to detain him. He didn't feel in the mood for discussing the incoming weather. After a couple more friendly interactions with the O'Hanerahan family, and the bonny Miss Flannery, he escaped his depleted Saturday flock. Swiftly, he made his way across the churchyard. He disliked running, and he reminded himself to get out and about in the village more on his new bike. He wished his legs would move a little faster, but, as he'd aged, his knees were getting stiffer and unable to speed walk like he had done in the past. Nowadays, he spent most of his cycle rides pushing the bike uphill. He had become unfit and struggled with the hills surrounding the village, as his eyes strayed past the church gates to the hills beyond them.

As he pondered pumping up the tyres on his bike, Father O'Flynn noticed another job that needed doing. The grass had overgrown, and the gravestones badly needed some attention. He noticed the one under the laburnum tree had lost its wording beneath a layer of lichen. The surrounding shrubs and trees needed trimming back, but the regular gardener had left his post and his replacement had yet to arrive. It all looked a mess. Tomorrow, he would ask his housekeeper to make a poster for the church notice board, asking for volunteers to assist with cutting back the hedges and mowing the grass. The gravestones were getting buried beneath the brambles. Soon the visitors would moan when they could no longer read the inscriptions on their loved ones' headstones. Father O'Flynn picked a browned leaf from his sleeve. The leaves had become a nuisance when you were in a hurry and the brambles kept getting caught on his cassock. Tucked under his arm, he had a bundle of rolled up papers. He'd been on a personal mission. The purpose of his mad dash back to the house, the same dash he took every Saturday, was to secure his seat at the head of the dining table and ensure he received the first, and most generous, serving of the weekly roast dinner. He did not want it snaffled up by his less worthy counterparts. Sorry, God, but it was true. The elderly priest knew greed to be a mortal sin and promised he would make amends after dinner. They served roast dinner always on a Saturday rather than a Sunday following the early evening Mass. On Sundays, supper would always be the leftovers of cold meat, pickles and cold potatoes fancied up a bit with some salad cream. Would he make it back to the kitchen in time to watch the housekeeper carve and serve up?

"Phew, just in time," he thought, as he came flying through the door with a minute to spare, placing his hat on the coat stand and savouring the smell of roasted beef fat wafting along the corridor. He dashed into the cloakroom to wash away the handshakes and crossed into the kitchen and a sea of expectant faces. Thank goodness I'm not so late. Father O'Flynn's gaze drifted to the mercifully untouched contents of his favourite dish. A pyramid of golden, steaming roasted potatoes.

"Praise be," he whispered under his breath.

"Who would like to lead our prayers?"

They all paused and looked at Father Patrick as he sang grace before the chatter resumed around the table. Father

O'Flynn greedily spooned six or more crisp roasties into a mound on his plate, trying to hide the quantity beneath the vegetables and the oversized Yorkshire puddings. Muriel, the manse housekeeper, made the most perfect roast potatoes. The secret, she revealed, hot beef fat. Unable to cook himself, but always more than happy to talk about food, he thought, as he slathered his meat with a large spoonful of horseradish sauce. There were two jars on the table and in his haste he easily covered the four slices of rare pink roast beef with carrots, cabbage and tinned peas, drowning them in lashings of hot beef gravy.

It was his lucky day twice over and, Lord, he was truly thankful. The weekly roast dinner always followed a pattern with a special dessert, and today proved to be no exception. Great, his favourite apple and blackberry crumble with berries picked from the graveyard hedgerows. Served with dollops of vivid yellow custard, some double cream or ice cream. Or all three if you were feeling greedy! Well, why not? he thought, trying to justify his actions. He'd had such a busy, stressful day. It all went wrong when he shovelled the first of his steaming roasties into his gullet. In full flow, he began by describing the vagaries of that afternoon's confessions to his captive audience, when he felt his breath hitch in his throat and choked. It turned out the horseradish sauce was the culprit. His face reddened and his lips turned a funny shade of blue. He attempted a long intake of breath and he grabbed a napkin as a precaution. The damned potato had chosen to come up or go down in the next few seconds. He put his hand to his mouth in preparation, but the scalding pain in his throat prevented him from coughing. With tears streaming down his florid cheeks, those around the table looked on in alarm, halting their knives and forks, their mouths full and waiting for somebody else to intervene. Down went the potato. To the others around the table, it had become a familiar episode. The priest sitting alongside braced himself to perform the Heimlich manoeuvre. Pausing for a moment to swallow, Father O'Flynn took a large gulp of red wine to soothe the burning sensation and clear his throat. A thumbs up indicated to those watching the spectacle that all was well. The heat from the horseradish burnt all the way down.

He managed to discreetly stifle and swallow his third belch before scraping his chair backwards and excusing himself from the room. Perhaps some of Muriel's fruit crumble and ice cream would calm the scorched lining of his throat. He served himself from the sideboard, before vanishing to the study to allow it to cool down. The others around him continued their meal in silence. They too had heard whispers that something might be afoot, but deliberately chose to steer clear of the elderly priest's study. Gathering momentum in his head came a plan to assist poor Mrs Hamilton. Now, a week after hearing the Hamilton girl's confession and the father's mind had been on other matters. He had taken umbrage at the latest summons to the bishop's office. At nine o'clock, the office door remained closed. The room, not overly large, came with two Georgian chairs and a rectangular desk with a green leather insert. Flecks of spilled ink ingrained in one corner and a worn patch in the other. A circular stain from a cup imprinted in the middle. Father O'Flynn paced the floor as he reread the letter from his compatriot Count Vouvier in France. They became friends when Father O'Flynn was posted there three years ago. He realised that the amiable connection to Count Vouvier could work to his advantage. The nobleman and his wife had sent an urgent request to find a suitably qualified young woman required to work as their governess. The term would be for a minimum of twelve months. His habit of rushing into these matters usually backfired. Father O'Flynn knew full well that Beatrice could not work for the twelve months in her current condition. Last time he checked, most pregnancies lasted for forty weeks not fifty-two. But Father O'Flynn, no expert on these matters, had still been trying to work out the logistics of getting the young Hamilton girl to France. Father O'Flynn was trying to work out how soon they could arrange it and whether the girl's parents would consent. His thoughts strayed to thinking of the surcharge he would apply to the deal. Lured by the suggestion from the count of a substantial sum of money into the parochial coffers. This would look good on his track record, surely. The bishop would reconsider his recent opinion of him if he brought in extra money to the church funds. But he had a swift change of mind and thought he might keep those extra monies for himself, meaning a win–win for all concerned.

The family concerned were living near the capital of the Hauts de France region, in the north of France, close to the Belgian border. The Hamiltons arranged for their daughter to work as a governess for a wealthy champagne family who owned over two hundred hectares of vineyards. Father O'Flynn sat down and wrote a succinct letter to the count in response to his request, detailing his terms.

The following afternoon, he called in on the Hamiltons for a cup of tea to discuss his proposal. Trying to give the appearance of a learned man and showing off his limited French, Father O'Flynn boasted he felt the situation had become "a fait accompli". Harry and Flo were relieved to hear the outline of a plan forming for Beatrice. An hour later, the parents were in raptures and in full acceptance of his proposed assignment. At this stage, there had been no consultation with Beatrice. The priest appeared delighted and left them both thinking what recompense there might be for his kind offer of assistance. At once, he must contact the count and inform him that the deal has been secured. Mr and Mrs Hamilton would be happy to have their daughter out of the way for the duration of her pregnancy, and Father O'Flynn would gain the gratitude of the high-ranking family in France.

Arriving back from her walk, as she approached the house, she saw Father O'Flynn standing on her doorstep, saying farewell to her parents. He eyed her up and down rather cautiously, before nodding and bidding them all goodbye. Curious to know what his visit had been about, Beatrice followed her mother into the kitchen. Flo had prepared the evening meal, and had been peeling potatoes at the sink with her back to her daughter. Beatrice sat down at the table and asked what was for tea. On the menu were thick slices of pink boiled ham, mash potato and fresh garden peas. Beatrice had little appetite that day but happily agreed to help with the preparation. She made a start by shelling the peas.

"So, who is going to tell me why Father O'Flynn was here?"

Harry came into the kitchen to look for a pen. He took over the conversation.

"Sit yourself down, Beatrice. We have something to say."

After an awkward pause, she looked from one to the other and dutifully took her seat.

"Listen carefully, Father O'Flynn has come up with a solution to your predicament. You have been offered a very important job in a place called Lille, in northern France, with a wealthy family – a real count and his wife, no less! You would be away for eight and a half months at least. When you return, you will have the baby in a special unit in Elswick. Remember, you now have no choice. You don't want to end up in one of those awful Magdalene laundries over in Ireland, do you? You know, those where they mistreat the inmates as young as fourteen. Father O'Flynn has told me all about them. Yes, Elswick is the next best solution, we think. Don't we, Flo? Flo knew better than to pass comment. Anyway, we have arranged everything now. But where is Jack? He seems to have disappeared at the first mention of supporting you. And to be honest, Beatrice, who will want to marry you now you have tainted yourself?"

The last sentence stung.

Flo did not maintain eye contact with her daughter. Silence can say as much as words. Her father had never mastered the art of tact and diplomacy, always brutal with the truth, and called things exactly as he saw them. He adopted this approach when dealing with his daughters, but seemed to avoid the tactic when dealing with his son. Beatrice's first reaction to the news was shock that turned into one of horror, looking up at Flo with pleading eyes.

"I don't want to go away. I want to stay home and have the baby with you, Mother. When did you decide all this?" Her mother's face looked similar, almost a reflection of her daughter's, eyes brimming with tears. "I want to have the baby upstairs, just like you did with all of us. I want you to be with me, Mother, not some grumpy nurse or, even worse, a nun who does not speak English."

Wiping her nose on her hankie, she reached out her arms to hug her mother's back for comfort, and she immediately felt the pain emanating from her daughter's heart. Flo still held her back towards them and found herself unable to turn around from her peeling duties. Her own hot tears were on the verge of spilling down her cheeks. Holding them back, she sniffed, not wishing her daughter to witness them. She would have dearly loved to have been there alongside with her youngest daughter when she gave birth. Only she knew what childbirth felt like. Now she felt unable to pass on that knowledge when her youngest would be at her most vulnerable.

But Harry would not accept any changes to the arrangements now, he'd decided. For the sake of their family's reputation within the local community, she had reluctantly accepted Father O'Flynn's crazy potholed plan. Tongues would certainly wag. With no idea that as the pregnancy progressed, they would accuse her daughter of having a "detectable transgression". The community would be about to shun them despite all the discreet preparations and Father O'Flynn's mediation. What would they tell the neighbours when they noticed Beatrice had vanished from the neighbourhood? Nobody would need to know about the pregnancy, and the baby offered straight up for adoption by the mother and baby unit.

Harry and Flo agreed on the idea so far. Besides, Beatrice would have the elevated social status of having taught the children of a French count and countess. That's what mattered most, wasn't it? Harry considered this to be far more important than his daughter's emotional wellbeing or losing the first impending grandchild to a strange family. Everything had always been about their standing within the town, which had its own blinkered view. Flo found she had no choice but to be swept along with the grand plan.

Beatrice woke up beside herself with worry. She knew she would have no choice but to travel the distance to France alone. And when she arrived she would be responsible for the children of two grand people. At fifteen, she knew it sounded overdramatic but she strongly felt all the upset would be enough to kill her and the baby. Nobody around her would listen to her opinion. With no other option available, later that same evening she pleaded with her father not to make her go but knew he'd already made up his mind. In times past, once he had made a decision it became futile to try and argue with him. Rosina felt her sister's pain, but felt helpless to influence any decisions made by the priest and her parents, and anyway, she had her own future to think about. Father O'Flynn's reputation went before him, working with churchgoing families wrestling with sensitive problems.

When Rosina spoke with Albert about the impending

catastrophe, they both agreed they felt a modicum of guilt. They had encouraged Beatrice to go out with Jack in the first instance. Inevitably Albert got caught in the middle, straddled between his father and his closest friend, unable to intervene; besides, he would never defy his father's wishes. Soon he would be leaving for his own journey abroad, when his regiment got called up on deployment to Africa.

Beatrice's own posting to France would be courtesy of Father O'Flynn, who had met the Vouvier family whilst serving in France, three years ago. His role had been part of the town's Catholic cathedral with two other junior priests. When his three-year posting ended, he readied himself for the return to England. But before he left he made a promise to Count Vouvier. In return for his excellent hospitality at the chateau, if he ever needed assistance with any pastoral matters he must get in touch. Count Vouvier had held him to his word and written to him explaining his latest dilemma of his governesses departure. Father O'Flynn wrote back explaining he had just the young girl in mind to assist his compatriot with his recent dilemma. He would set about organising the papers and putting her on the next available boat to Calais if the count could provide a car to meet her off the Calais train.

Six

France – 1965

The smart burgundy car at the station stood waiting her arrival. As she descended the afternoon train from Calais, the station was bustling with people as she looked around for a chauffeur. Claude Dupont stepped forward; instructed to meet Beatrice at the train station. The car, parked up close to the entrance, stood out among the others. It looked highly polished, with chrome handles that reflected the leafy surroundings. He nodded politely to her as she descended the steps from the carriage. Holding out his gloved hand, avoiding eye contact, he took her largest bag. The poplar trees lined the long avenue out of the station. Beatrice seated herself in the back of the Vouvier family car. The odd-looking pair travelled in silence the short distance from town to the chateau. It would be her first experience of travelling in a car with a stranger.

Beatrice's first proper view of her new hometown came from her window and took her by surprise as they approached the chateau. The ornate, wrought-iron gates swung open as Claude mumbled something unintelligible into an intercom high on the wall. Beatrice gazed up at the face of a stone lion as they passed through and drove onto the estate. The landscape disappeared across the horizon, into the distance, with the vineyards beyond across the hills. Each field planted out in strict furrows of vines, bursting with dark purple grapes. Beatrice would soon learn that Vin de Coteaux had been part of Count Vouvier's family for generations.

The chateau reminded Beatrice of the imaginary castles she had drawn as a child. Its structure had four circular, limestone towers, which housed tens of grey, leaded window frames. The chateau itself was divided into four sections, with a turreted circular tower at each corner, built of limestone, supporting small, thin, grey-leaded window frames. The slate roof tiles looked old and were a blend of burgundy and grey. Peeling cream paint over the entrance was noticeable as they approached the door. The nimbuses of grey smoke sporadically puffed from eight tall red brick chimneys. Beatrice was bowled over by the sheer expanse of greenery surrounding the chateau as the land stretched off into the distance without the interruption of a single fence. The stone folly, with a crenellated top, was the only other manmade structure she could see. Although no longer functional, it had been built as a focal point between the grand lake and the main house. Beatrice drank it all in and, although slightly awestruck, remembered to shut her mouth. On the far side of the house, an estate worker attempted to clean the ground-floor windows. Large oak trees, secure in their places for generations, cast their shadows over the car. Claude remained mute, his gloved hands glued to the steering wheel, casting the odd sly look into his rear-view mirror. Beatrice wondered how many times he had made that journey from the station with a governess on the back seat. She felt as though she may be the latest poor lamb to the slaughter and kept her eyes peeled for any evidence of small children at play. But there was none to be seen. No discarded bikes or doll prams. No swings hanging from the trees. No tree houses or climbing frames. Someone obviously kept the children well hidden from view.

It felt like the drive up to the house had taken an age, but in reality it had been merely a few minutes. Beatrice tried to take her bags from the boot of the car but the chauffeur intervened, shaking his head and waving his arms.

"*Non, non,*" he mumbled, twitching his mouth, as she stood awkwardly, blushing, not knowing where to go or what to say to him.

"*Merci beaucoup.*" The first words that popped into her head. Before she left, Rosina had taught her a few simple phrases to get her started on her French adventure. Claude looked at her with renewed admiration. Ah, perhaps she had broken the ice.

"*De rien.*" Claude's eyes lit up. This one seemed different, he thought, and smiled. Beatrice wondered why there had been no handover, and why had the outgoing governess left the chateau so abruptly?

Within the chateau walls, the two youngest family members were filled with great excitement and anticipation.

Today, the children looked smart. The housekeeper, who dressed them in their best outfits in honour of the new governess, had spruced them up. The children eagerly awaited the sound of the car on the gravel as they sat in the large window seat in the drawing room.

"She's here! She's here!" squealed Edgar, waving his arms about excitedly. They heard the slam of the car doors and the crunch of footsteps on the gravel.

The chauffeur carried the case as far as the front door and made polite introductions with the housekeeper as they stood in the grand hallway. Beatrice stood simply in awe of her new surroundings.

She came from the small mining town of Consett and had never set foot in a chateau, or indeed any building as lavish or grand. Long Persian rugs stretched the entire length of the hallway and hung neatly overhead. There were an abundance of grand chandeliers. How did they remain suspended from the ceiling? Beatrice wondered. They looked so heavy, their glass casting reflections across the walls.

Count Vouvier seated himself on the long sofa in the drawing room. Dressed formerly with a cravat and a navy velvet jacket, he reminded Beatrice of someone from a storybook.

Holding out a hand with neat, manicured nails, he asked, "Did you have a nice journey, Miss Hamilton?" He spoke perfect English and couldn't help but notice that Beatrice's cheeks were a ghastly ashen colour.

"I'm not a good traveller," she confessed. "I found the sea quite lumpy, and the train from Calais not much better."

She just wanted to remove her shoes, curl up in her new bed and go to sleep. Her nausea had been bad that day.

"Perhaps you would like a cup of tea?" asked Madame Moreau, sensing the girl's anxiety. The housekeeper spoke perfect English that she had learnt whilst working for a wealthy English family in Kent.

"Yes, please, that would be lovely. If you show me where the kitchen is, I can make it myself."

At that point, she felt not much older than her charges.

"*Non, non*, it is my job. *Sucre*, I mean sugar?" asked the housekeeper, lapsing into a type of franglais.

"*Non, merci*." Beatrice stifled a yawn behind her hand.

"Please, go through to the drawing room. The children are waiting for you." Stepping forward, Beatrice took a deep breath and attempted to straighten her crumpled dress before making her grand entrance. All eyes in the room were trained on her as she stepped through the door. Beatrice took note that the countess was still absent. The sound of small voices broke the silence and the awkward atmosphere dissipated for a fleeting moment. The children stepped forward together. A small girl curtseyed and the boy bowed his head. Beatrice found their greeting odd. She thought it quaint and old-fashioned for children to behave in such a way.

"Hello, you must be Edgar. How do you do?" she asked, addressing the eldest child first, immediately struck by his clothing: burgundy corduroy breeches, long white leggings and patent leather shoes. His outfit may have been more suited to a birthday party attended by small children who'd lived a hundred years ago. Instead, she turned her attention to the smaller child waiting patiently alongside her brother.

"And you must be Flora."

Flora looked as though she might be attending a tea party, dressed in a tartan frock with a large, white bow at the back. It seemed overly large for her slight frame. Perhaps purchased with plenty of room for growth in mind. To complete the outfit, she wore white tights and minuscule black shoes.

"My name is Beatrice. Or, should I say, *je m'appelle Béatrice*."

"We know!" they shouted out simultaneously.

"You speak French?" queried Edgar, looking across the room at their father.

"*Mais oui, et vous parlez Anglais*," replied Beatrice. Touche.

At that moment, the floorboards creaked and a swoosh came through the door as Countess Vouvier swept into the drawing room, looking rather flustered. Her short, black leather boots clicked in a military fashion when she walked. Dressed impeccably in an azure blue skirt cinched in at her tiny waist. The pleated blouse a bright white had a large ruff neck. Her cheeks flushed bright pink from rushing the corridors. After introducing herself to Beatrice, she asked the children to show their new guest to her bedroom, but Count Vouvier intercepted the direction.

"There's no rush, my dear. Let the poor girl sit for a moment and finish her tea. She's had a long, demanding journey." His eyes twinkled at Beatrice, who instantly liked him, feeling compassion hidden behind the blue eyes.

"Yes, of course, forgive me. Please sit yourself down." The countess spoke with such authority. Beatrice took a sip of the milky, lukewarm tea and tried hard not to let her disappointment show. The French pasteurised milk made the pale, watery tea taste peculiar.

"Just let Madame Moreau know if you require anything else." The countess remained seated. Beatrice took that as her cue to leave the room and stood up, placing her half-drunk cup back down on the saucer. The parents stood and watched with keen interest, their eyes following the small group of three as they made their way out of the drawing room, leaving the door ajar.

The children took a hand each without question. As they left the room, Countess Vouvier scrutinised the clothes of her new governess. Aghast at the state of Beatrice's shoes, she raised a concerned eyebrow at her husband about the suitability of this latest governess. At first, she remained silent, but she contained herself for just a split second.

"So, what do you think?" she asked, turning to her husband. The count, who had the easier personality of the two adults, responded.

"I shall reserve judgement until we get to know her a little more. She's only just arrived, poor girl. I wonder if she will be strict enough. You know how disobedient Edgar can be."

"Yes, that's the same problem her predecessors have encountered." Countess Vouvier's personal knowledge of her son was questionable. She had never looked after her children for any considerable length of time. She had, however, seen several governesses pass through the household, who had all cited Edgar as the reason for their resignation letters.

Pausing in the hallway, Beatrice overheard their conversation. What had she walked into? She had never felt so unwanted before and immediately wanted to flee back to the station.

Countess Vouvier had spotted Beatrice's rather shabby travelling case and thought it odd how little luggage the girl had brought with her. Her dresses would need an upgrade if the children were to set foot outside the grounds of the chateau, in public view. Although she seemed less keen to instigate this change just yet. Her own reputation would be considered before that of the children. Perhaps once the girl had settled in, she would suggest a trip into town to be measured for a new uniform. Seated at her desk she reread the letter from Father O'Flynn as she wanted to double check the age of the girl who he had sent.

Vast pillars in the hallway were a terracotta and blue effect and supported the high vaulted ceiling. The door on the left led to the small library and on the other side, the corridor led down to the kitchen. The deep walls hung portraits of previous generations of the Vouvier family.

With polite introductions over, the children led the way, leaving the ostentatious hallway behind them. Beatrice never thought to ask why the count had used English names for the children. A dimly lit passageway took them along to the nursery wing. The small group took their lead from the new governess and made their way up a second imposing mahogany staircase to the children's quarters. The doors all looked identical, with no clue what lay behind them, but the children knew exactly which one to open. They had devoted a wing of the chateau just to them, but with many locked doors and unused rooms.

It smelled musty. They had shut some rooms up since the count himself had been a small child. Beatrice forced open a window in the nursery to allow some fresh air to filter through, years of dust dancing in the air as it settled on the table.

She struggled to find any toy boxes. With nothing to entertain or educate a child in these rooms. What did they play with? There were no yo-yos, no toy soldiers, no dolls or dolls' houses. She had expected a small library of books for them to read.

No surprise that the children were badly behaved. They must have been so bored with such little stimulation. The governess's bedroom led off the same corridor as the children. It offered just a wardrobe, a chair and a small chest of drawers, with a single bed.

The room had a damp smell, so with some difficulty Beatrice wrenched open the small window to let in some fresh air. It smelt strange, a mixture of wood smoke and farmyard. The room, though not unpleasant, had been just basic. A pale yellow basin with a round mirror fixed in the corner, which afforded her a modicum of privacy. In terms of not having to share the bathroom. Beatrice felt at odds with her surroundings. She had never had a room of her own and liked the idea of sleeping alone. But the children had other ideas, as at that moment, demonstrating a lack of social graces, they burst into her bedroom without warning.

"Children, where are your manners?" in a stricter tone than they were used to. "Has nobody taught you to knock before entering?"

Edgar went to respond, but checked himself after he saw the look on her face. This one would not be as kind as the previous governesses, he thought. She examined the lock on the bedroom door, looking for a key, as she had not wanted to be caught out by the children in a state of undress. She unpacked and hung up her few paltry dresses in the small wardrobe. That night, after eating a meagre supper with the housekeeper, consisting of just bread after declining the strong unpleasant-smelling cheese, she wished the housekeeper goodnight.

Once under the bed covers, she cried silently into her pillow, her heart aching with homesickness. Feeling a knot in her stomach. Missing her mother and the comfort of knowing her sister had always been in the opposite bed. She lay her hands on her belly, gaining a little comfort knowing the only family she had at that moment was inside her.

Beatrice would soon outgrow her dresses, and she hoped the tiny matter of her expanding waistline would go unnoticed by her new employers for the next few months. As discussed in the drawing room earlier, the children would only cross paths with their parents once a day. It would be for such a short time she hoped they would not pay her too much attention and notice her dilemma.

But the countess had already noticed that her latest governess might not be all she seemed. She thought the girl had a slight paunch for one so slender, especially when she stood sideways, but dismissed it quickly from her mind. She would have to keep a close eye on this one, so she paid an irregular visit to the kitchen to ask Madame Moreau to let her know if there were any problems. A two-pronged approach seemed the sensible thing in the circumstances. She felt something was not right about the latest recruit, but decided it was too early to speculate what.

Word had spread among the junior staff that yet another new young governess had joined the family. What would this one be like in looks and demeanour, they had speculated. Would she be tall and slender with long auburn locks, or would she be like the previous one, with short raven hair and a severe set of blackened bushy eyebrows? Beatrice had arrived at the chateau with a sole purpose in mind: to teach the children aged five and seven. It would only be the basics in reading and writing, and arithmetic.

Initially, the countess allowed Beatrice to wear her own clothes until they had made the new garments. Beatrice found every excuse not to have her measurements taken by the maid and insisted on doing it herself. What would happen when her bump grew larger? She put the thought to the back of her mind. Throwing herself into her new role of governess, meticulously planning her lessons, all with the approval of the mistress of the house.

In England, the drop-waisted fashions of the previous decades had given way to shorter tunics and patent boots. Clothes for Beatrice's age group came in more vibrant colours, acid pink, orange and lime green. Back home in the summer months, girls now stepped out in pedal pushers and flat coloured pumps. But Beatrice refused to move with the times, remaining curiously old-fashioned and gravitating toward dresses much more suitable for women of a certain age. The contents of her suitcase showed little colour; all her clothes were plain, grey, brown or black.

After a week at the chateau, Beatrice found she worked the long hours required with little respite. At first, the children's good behaviour and attentiveness in their lessons made Beatrice feel secure, but it was a false sense of security. Soon after, Edgar played up. His habit of running out of the schoolroom without warning alarmed her at first. One morning she found him standing on the window ledge looking down on the gardens below. His concentration span reduced to that of a gnat. It seemed the honeymoon period might be over. After some persistence, the breakthrough came when Beatrice asked Edgar to gather the books after the lesson and place them back on the shelf. He responded without question. Beatrice put her feet up on the small sofa in the playroom, at times struggling to fight her increasing nausea as her charges contentedly played their games around her.

At six o'clock each evening, Beatrice brushed their hair neatly, Edgar with side partings, and tied Flora's pigtails in place. Her instruction to present the children to the count and countess in the drawing room for exactly one hour bemused her. The hour regularly dropped to half an hour, as other more important issues called for the attention of the parents. Edgar, waiting until they were upstairs and out of parental earshot, would suddenly change his behaviour. It turned out he could be rude, undisciplined and brattish. The children had few toys or possessions to keep them occupied, despite the lavish material wealth that surrounded them. They were bored, tucked away in their schoolroom with nothing to occupy them other than their studies and the odd small personal toy.

On one occasion, without the consent of their parents, Beatrice took them on a secret outing. Claude had a day off and the car had been parked out of sight at the back of the chateau. It had just been highly polished: perfect for an adventure. Beatrice sensed freedom. Now sixteen, she knew how to drive. Her brother had taught her on an old airfield before she'd left England. Driving on the other side of the road, with a gearbox and a seat on the other side of the car, she didn't think it would be a problem. She soon discovered the French car had an unusually shaped steering wheel with a temperamental gearbox on the dashboard. Despite sitting on two cushions, she struggled to reach the pedals as the car lurched from side to side as she tried to control it. Raucous laughing came from the back seat and the children screamed with delight as the car flew round the tight bends.

"Now, you two, don't go mentioning a word of what we have done to your parents, understand?"

"We promise we won't tell them, will we, Flora?" He winked furiously at his little sister. The world outside the chateau and its grounds had been an alien one to Beatrice. They visited toy shops, museums, and sweet shops that sold confectionery in pink striped paper bags.

As she struggled to steer the car home, an officer with a droopy moustache, dressed in a blue uniform sporting a peaked cap and white gloves, stepped out on the road and flagged down the car. The local police had suddenly taken a keen interest in the car with an unusually erratic style of driving. Beatrice obediently brought the car to a halt. They were so close to home the gates were in sight, but the officer's white-gloved hand continued to signal firmly, insisting that she bring the car to a stop. As he looked over the car he recognised the youngsters, who were still giggling in the back seat. He asked her to identify herself and supply her papers. In her pidgin French, she pleaded with him not to tell Count Vouvier. Beatrice held her breath for a moment. The papers were duly returned through the window with a smile, as he nodded and waved her on to drive the last few hundred yards to the chateau gates. Surely he would report her to the count.

Beatrice hung up the keys in the cabinet without being seen. The children were sworn to secrecy, and bribed not to mention the gendarmerie incident to their parents.

Over the weeks that followed, they visited museums and castles, and took picnics by the riverside, though Beatrice would not be behind the wheel for these trips. Claude the chauffeur reverted to being back in charge of the car. He had remained silent on the matter. No one had taken Beatrice to one side and mentioned the police incident. But the potential for a tough conversation with her employers weighed heavily on her.

She introduced the children to exciting shops full of wooden toys and small metal cars known as Dinky toys. She introduced her charges to the delights of the local patisseries, which sold mouthwatering cakes they had never experienced before. If her charges behaved well and completed their lessons without fuss, Beatrice always promised them another adventure. Above all, they must not tell their parents about the expeditions, no matter how exciting they had been. She feared severe chastisement if they got found out.

Beatrice believed that if she had continued to wear loose fitting dresses and underskirts she might have gotten away with her secret until the end of her assignment. It had now become hopeless; her protuberance was too obvious. How long did a pregnancy last she asked herself? Her daily diary recorded the weeks, and she'd reached thirty before she knew it. She struggled to bend down and tie up her own shoes without difficulty, and to get out of a chair in one swift movement. Now felt like the right time to leave France. But no instructions from her father had arrived. The previous night she had lain awake fretting, working through her options. It led her mind back to one thing. The dread of returning home to what her parents might have organised. Her mother had put everything in place for her homecoming, as mentioned in the letter. What did that mean, "in place"? Where would she be giving birth if it wasn't at home? Previously, they had mentioned a baby unit at Elswick but did not know what went on in those places. She wanted to see Jack. What had happened to him? There had been no further contact, despite him knowing the address from Rosina.

Beatrice's relationship with Madame Moreau had grown closer since she arrived. Once the children were asleep, they spent their evenings in the kitchen swapping stories and playing cards. Beatrice had nobody else to confide in. Their conversations left the housekeeper suspicious that all was not well with the young governess. Madame Moreau had already noted that the young woman struggled to eat at mealtimes and would often pick at her food, pushing it slowly round the plate. Occasionally, she would see her nibble at some bread. She offered different foods, thinking at first that it was the French cuisine that did not suit her. But, when she baulked at the plate of cheeses on offer and politely pushed the plate away, Madame Moreau guessed her predicament. As she busied herself making the dessert for supper that evening, she asked a maid to search Beatrice's bedroom for evidence. The next morning Beatrice felt obliged to take her into her confidence. She explained it was time to confess her long-held secret to Countess Vouvier. Madame Moreau invited her to take a seat in the kitchen. The baby kicked and wriggled on the day when she plucked up the courage to speak out, but someone else had beaten her to it. It became clear she had guessed Beatrice's predicament, so little point denying it. A woman of Madame Moreau's calibre would not allow her to avoid discussing something so important with a few well-worn white lies. Beatrice begged her not to divulge her suspicions to their employers. She had wanted to tell them herself, but when she was ready. Now it had all gone awry. Two weeks earlier, when Madame Moreau had voiced concerns about Beatrice looking pale and wan, she'd taken it upon herself to report her suspicions to her employer as requested. Countess Vouvier had already concluded that she had been duped by Father O'Flynn. Her governess appeared to be trying to hide the telltale signs of a near-full-term pregnancy. She too would not want a scandal and a birth to happen at the chateau. What would people think? But she also didn't want to sack her before the end of her assignment. She wanted value for her money. Her frugal nature shone through any emotions swirling in the room. But she felt she had no choice. The girl had become a liability and Countess Vouvier did not want any gossip among her staff that might damage the prestigious Vouvier reputation. She immediately drafted a formal letter expressing her disappointment and plans for the dismissal.

As Beatrice made the final preparations for her departure, she thought the chateau seemed eerily quiet. Everybody had vanished. She peered out of her window to see the estate staff gathered below in a semicircle as if at some sort of meeting outside in the yard to hear Count Vouvier give his annual talk, bursting with pride for his estate and what it had produced to date.

The assembled staff were told the grapes looked likely to produce a bumper crop later in the summer. It meant a small bonus would follow for all those involved. The count expressed his gratitude for their hard work and announced that they would have a party to celebrate the start of the harvest that weekend.

The children were in the schoolroom finishing a maths lesson. Beatrice told them to put on their coats. She wanted to take them for a last walk around the estate. When they returned to the nursery, she asked the children to draw something they had seen out in the grounds.

"I want you to draw something: trees, birds, animals, maybe some flowers." She emptied the colouring pencils and the watercolour paints onto their desks, hoping to inspire their young minds. They could choose whichever medium they preferred.

"Sit down, Edgar. Come away from the window now." Her tone stricter than usual. The tension in the chateau had spread to the upstairs rooms.

"No, I won't," shouted the boy with authority, his face pulled into a deep frown. Beatrice lurched forward, grabbing him firmly by the arm, and marched him back to his seat.

"Ow! You're hurting me, get off!"

"No, I'm not. Look, see? There are no marks on your arm. Don't be silly. Do as you are told."

Oddly for Beatrice, she felt like unleashing her temper on the boy.

"I'll tell my father what you have done."

"Carry on, be my guest."

Beatrice knew he would do no such thing. The boy was terrified of his father. She had heard the horror stories from the mouth of young Edgar and knew he would tell his father none of the events that occurred upstairs in the nursery rooms of the chateau. The previous governess had punished Edgar by locking him in the schoolroom and making him write lines: "I must not be rude" one hundred times. On other occasions, he had missed his meal as a penance for his misdemeanours. Beatrice took a different approach.

"You will do as I ask." She looked directly over at the child. Edgar crossed his arms and sat down, his bottom lip quivering. He continued to sulk for the next half an hour as he painted a picture of a pretty line of trees with a dog running around. Beatrice considered this to be progress, as three months earlier he would not have sat down or made any effort to draw with coloured pencils. Flora had quietly coloured a picture of a small bird in yellow. The masterpieces were stuck to the wall in a gallery-type exhibition. Beatrice had yearned for the parents to have come up to the schoolroom to inspect the children's work. But had resigned herself to the fact they showed little excitement in their children's achievements. Since her arrival, they had never asked to see their children's artwork or taken an interest in their schoolwork. The adage "children should be seen and not heard" was their belief. This meant the children becoming a little detached from their parents, and wanting to please their governesses.

Beatrice had not forgotten her summons from the countess. As she awaited her fate, she sat passively outside the drawing room. It felt as though she were about to be executed. No, she thought, she was overdramatising her feelings. Instead, she focussed on the swirling pattern of the expensive Persian rug in front of her chair. Overnight, the atmosphere within the chateau had changed to one of tension and frostiness like a sky that had clouded over. Why should she take the blame? It seemed unfair when given no other choice. The poor housekeeper had tried to intervene and offer an opinion before Beatrice received her summons, but Countess Vouvier had already decided, and discharged Madame Moreau back to her kitchen duties. Her infamous bad temper was about to be unleashed. Beatrice cleared her throat and knocked timidly on the door.

"Enter," the voice on the other side shouted out.

The Countess barely looked up and got straight to the point. She tapped the letter on her desk as if playing a tune and passed it over to Beatrice without making eye contact. The scent of her perfume clung to the paper.

"Well, I'm truly disappointed in you, Beatrice. You never thought to tell me sooner? I thought you were looking a little plump around the middle when I last saw you." A cruel jibe, given the circumstances, thought Beatrice. Whichever way she sat in the uncomfortable chairs, her mortal sin was no longer hidden. The small paunch no longer shrank back under her clothes. She had tried so hard to disguise it, but the infant inside her belly had been almost full term.

In the last few days, she wondered if she might be bonding with her baby for the first time. At night, as she lay in bed, she'd talked to it, and in soothing tones she reminded it of her promise to always light a candle every year on its birthday.

The countess, still in full flow, had allowed Beatrice to zone out of the diatribe aimed at her, but a familiar name made her tune back in.

"Father O'Flynn will be hearing from us. Did you know we paid him a substantial sum to find and employ you? You should have been with us for a full twelve months, nothing less. And to think, Beatrice, you came with such high recommendations too. Father O'Flynn did nothing but sing your praises." Shaking her head at her seemed ungrateful. "How can I write you a good reference now?"

The lecture ended abruptly. She dismissed Beatrice with a gesture of her arm to go upstairs and pack her bags. Left with no opportunity to defend herself, Beatrice remained silent, passing no comment in response to the accusations. There seemed little point in antagonising the woman further. She wished the damn Persian carpet in the hall would swallow her up and take her back to the comforting arms of her mother in Consett.

The dysfunctional little family had become attached to Beatrice in their own strange way, particularly the children. She knew she'd made good progress with Edgar and Flora; she'd seen a noticeable improvement in their social and academic skills. The children now sat down to their lessons. They were both reading above their age. It was all due to Beatrice's influence.

She'd captured their imagination with her stories and creative classes. You should never tell your parents all your secrets, Beatrice had told the youngsters, as one day you may find your liberties curtailed. An adage far too adult in its meaning and one that went over their young heads. She'd been referring to her own predicament. To Beatrice it felt something tainted the chateau goodbyes with prejudice. The children tried their best not to cry as they stepped forward, hands outstretched. Edgar, the most distressed of the two, seemed to forget all protocols at the last minute, as they clung to Beatrice's skirts and whimpered.

Arrangements for Beatrice's departure had been swift. She would leave the chateau the following day, and take the rickety train back to Calais and a ferry across the Channel to Dover. Nobody had told her who would meet her from the boat. Would it be Father O'Flynn? She did not want to make conversation with him for the five-hour drive back to Consett. Would her father have been a better option? Neither of the men would be pleasant travelling companions in the circumstances. Beatrice had dearly hoped that Jack would be standing at the barrier to welcome her back. But, as he hadn't written to her, how would he know she was about to return? She hoped Rosina had let him know.

She was the best governess ever. Why did she have to leave them? they'd questioned. What had they done so wrong?

"Don't you like us anymore?" whispered Flora.

"No, our mother has dismissed her," Edgar shouted.

"But why? What have we done?" asked Flora in her persistence.

"Let's stop guessing, shall we?" "I'm having a baby. That's why I can't stay."

"A baby!" they shrieked together, jumping up and down flapping their arms.

Beatrice remained stony-faced, unemotional. Explaining any further would be futile. They had already filled their young minds with adult falsehoods.

The car engine revved as Claude tooted the horn impatiently. After a silent drive, he dumped her belongings on the damp station platform, nodded and left without a word, shaking his head as he strode away. He'd liked this one and felt she had been the best to date. Beatrice gulped back the tears, not wishing to break down in a public place. The whistle blew as she wiped her damp eyes on her glove and boarded the train.

As she embarked on the next leg of her journey with dozens of other weekend travellers, Beatrice tried not to think of her future. Young couples, families, and even a soldier returning from leave were aboard. Everyone knew exactly where they were headed, which made Beatrice contemplate her future. They were unlike herself; there seemed nothing worse than not knowing what lay ahead. Rosina's last letter had been a little vague, but, after rereading it, she'd grasped the gist of it. Whether she agreed with the plans, well, that became a different matter.

Seven

Beatrice Returns

In Consett, Father O'Flynn stood on the Hamiltons' doorstep, with a deep look of consternation on his face, asking to urgently speak with Harry. This time, Flo eyed him with a degree of suspicion and asked him to take a seat in the living room. Harry had been gardening outside, she explained, as she shouted to him to come and see their visitor. His hearing had deteriorated recently, so it took several shouts before he meandered back into the house. She hovered by the kitchen door, trying to listen to the conversation. They spoke in hushed voices.

"Hello, Father. What brings you here again?"

"This is awkward, Mr Hamilton. Actually, may I call you Harry? I've received a letter from Count Vouvier."

"Good news, I hope," interrupted Harry.

"They are dismissing Beatrice. They know about her predicament and found out she is 'with child'. The Countess will not have her at the chateau a day longer. Count Vouvier has demanded a replacement straight away."

"What do we do?" asked Harry.

"You will have to leave at dawn to meet the late afternoon ferry at Dover and bring her back here to Consett."

"I have arranged a place for her to give birth and the subsequent adoption of the baby over at Elswick."

"Do you remember our financial arrangement some months back?" Harry blushed; yes, he had remembered the awkward conversation, and a sum of money exchanging hands.

"That now falls short of what we originally agreed, Mr Hamilton. Let's see if we can come up with a solution to cover any losses. Um, losses, shall we say?" He wrung his hands and looked down at his feet. With that, Father O'Flynn swept out of the door, returning a moment later to snatch his hat from the coat stand.

Flo darted back into the kitchen, out of sight, horrified by the suggestion that they might have to cover the shortfall of funds expected by the priest. She waited for an explosion from Harry, but the house went eerily quiet as he retreated to the garden.

When Harry checked the car, he found his front offside tyre flat. He knew there wasn't enough time to get a replacement from the garage and meet Beatrice's boat. Well, the priest would have to go. This mess was all his fault. Harry left the garden and marched down the hill to Father O'Flynn's house. The priest had barely hung up his coat when he heard the knock on the door.

"Hello Harry, what has brought you back to my door so soon?"

"My car is out of action. It's got a flat, so you'll have to accompany me and read the map."

"Well, I suppose that might work. Ok, if you collect me at just after five tomorrow morning, I'll make sure I'm ready."

"Oh yes! And Harry? Don't forget about that money!"

Harry fumed at the preposterous idea that he should hand over any more money to the priest. For a moment, he considered writing to the bishop and telling him that Consett's priest had been running a corrupt sideline, besides his parochial duties. But he knew he could not do so without implicating himself in the whole unseemly business. Harry, not a vindictive man by nature, felt sorely tempted. Perhaps if he offered to pay for the petrol, the priest would let him off.

The return journey to Calais passed without incident for Beatrice, but when she finally walked down the gangplank at the ferry port her worst fears had realised. In front of her stood the two familiar figures of Father O'Flynn and Harry. A right double act, chatting and smiling together at the barrier like old school chums. If Beatrice had seen another exit route, she would have taken it. Waving at her were two old men she had no desire to see. She wanted Jack to be there to meet her. The idea of spending a long car journey in their company made her feel nauseous, before the car had even left the ferry port.

"Hello there, Beatrice!" shouted Father O'Flynn, waving furiously in her direction.

Her father behaved a little more restrained and gave her a stiff hug, avoiding eye contact, though. With the brief formalities over, they loaded up the priest's car with their precious cargo. The two men sat up front, leaving Beatrice and her bump confined to the back seat. The two older men laughed and chatted, but Beatrice failed to hear the content of their conversation over the noise of the car engine. She tried closing her eyes to take away the rising nausea in her throat; it was no use. They would have to stop the car.

She yelled out at Father O'Flynn to pull over and the car came to an abrupt halt on the grass verge. The bump hindered the speed of her exit from the back seat and as she vomited she caught a little liquid on the hem of her skirt.

The radiator required topping up as it had sprung a slow leak on the outward journey. The engine kept overheating and clouds of hissing steam had come from beneath the bonnet. A lot of non-biblical cursing of the vehicle came from Father O'Flynn. God refused to listen, though. The garage attendant commented that the car needed a new radiator, and they thanked the man. Some old rags stemmed the leak and the sorry party continued on their way. Beatrice just wanted to lie down in her old bed and sip some fresh water from a tap that didn't leak brown residue like the taps at the chateau had.

Back at home, the Hamilton family was in a state of flux. They'd had a little over twenty-four hours to prepare for their daughter's homecoming. Flo spent her time rushing around upstairs changing beds and putting a baby layette together for her grandchild. Her nerves were on edge as she waited for their return, pacing the floor. The morning had passed with some baking, and sorting and clearing the bedroom. On the kitchen worktop sat a lemon drizzle cake, one of Beatrice's favourites. Desperate to see her youngest daughter, wondering what shape she would be in when she arrived. The guilt she'd felt after banishing her daughter abroad had been difficult to express, so she'd kept her thoughts close by.

Flo had found it difficult to adjust to a home without the hustle and bustle of her youngsters coming and going. She missed the incessant chatter at mealtimes. She wished she'd been stronger and stood up to Harry when he suggested his plan, but it was too late to change course now. Soon she would lose Beatrice yet again.

Outside, they could hear a distressed car engine sputtering

as it struggled to get up the hill. She recognised the car as Father O'Flynn's. Now it sounded fit for the local scrapyard. The car drew to a halt outside their door. Her eyes flicked to the figure heaving itself out of the back seat of the car. Surely that wasn't her Beatrice. With a hand firmly clamped to her mouth, Beatrice rushed past her mother, straight to the bathroom.

The two men stood on the pavement and shook hands as if they had struck a deal. Harry retreated to his garden for a smoke of his pipe to recover. Father O'Flynn left (whilst mumbling under his breath about ungratefulness and monies owed) and fleeing back to his rectory.

Beatrice reappeared, the pallor of her skin the colour of putty. Flo reached out for her daughter and put her hands on her swollen belly. There were no words to describe that golden moment when both women found each other again. Only a mother and daughter could comprehend the unspoken understanding that lingered between them. If Harry had not intervened, Flo knew she would have mellowed and let Beatrice have the baby at home. She would have been happy to risk all the rumours and gossip attached to such a notion and life for mother, daughter and grandchild would have looked so different.

Whilst his daughter had been away in France, Harry had paid a visit to the matron at the mother and baby unit. The papers, had been signed without consultation with Beatrice about the future for her baby. In Harry's view, her opinion was of little consequence at this late stage, it only complicated matters. A sorrowful resentment slowly built up inside her. She had always had a warm relationship with both her parents. But felt hurt that her mother had not risen to her defence, bitterly disappointed that she had sided with Harry. Each member of the family felt the ripple effect of one crucial decision surrounding the birth of the baby.

In the days that followed, Beatrice became a virtual recluse, locked down within the confines of her home. She spent the last days of her pregnancy drifting from the sofa in the living room, curling up to read, or lapsing on her bed into a fitful sleep. She found out there were only so many times you could pack and repack a hospital bag.

Crawling under the bed, Flo retrieved a specially lined box covered in layers of dust. She gently pulled it out. Inside were the precious garments belonging to all her babies. All washed, dried, and neatly folded. Beatrice inhaled the scent of the Lux soap flake residue, and vowed the baby clothes would remain with her after her discharge. She'd laid out the tiny clothes on the bedspread, some still wrapped in lilac tissue paper. The matinee jackets, nighties and tiny bootees remained a bright white. A pale yellow bonnet, knitted by herself. One had a monogram embroidered AH hand-sewn into the label. Flo kept the cardigans and baby nighties that her four babies had worn, wrapped in tissue paper, and stored in drawers under the spare bed. In a separate box, there were two items that had belonged to Arthur, her baby that had died at birth.

The other items had been purchased discreetly from church bazaars in neighbouring villages, eager not to raise any eyebrows in town, as she was well past childbearing age herself. Folk were quick to judge, and tongues easily wagged, with no foundation on the street corners of Consett. Cruel assumptions were always the work of the devil, she'd repeatedly told her children when they'd been younger.

The downward spiral of her relationship with her father had overshadowed Beatrice's instinct to nest in readiness for the impending birth. He'd been in denial about the impending birth and did his best to avoid sight of his heavily pregnant daughter. Whenever she entered the kitchen, he would mumble some excuse about the garden needing his attention. Harry would not take the risk of her being seen full term outside the house.

With the audacious plan almost complete, he did not want Beatrice to be found out. He reminded her more than once that the family reputation took precedence over any feelings of her own, especially after what she had done.

Bowing to parental pressure, they would force Beatrice and Jack into a doom-laden marriage... Flo and Harry refused to allow their daughter to live in sin. Such powerful opinions were forthcoming, whether or not Beatrice agreed with them. She had given up battling against her father's will long ago. The recent period of isolation had given her time to think about her parent's latest idea for the baby, that they should give it up for adoption. There had been plenty of time to think of outcomes whilst she'd been away. Back at the chateau, Madame Moreau, the housekeeper had floated the option of having the baby in a French convent to avoid further embarrassment. At first Beatrice felt quite taken with the whole idea. But on reflection she told Madame Moreau she felt obliged to return to England, so declined her kind offer. At that point, she'd become so desperate to return home to see Jack.

Jack felt differently, and relented under pressure exerted on him by Harry. His father had made his feelings known too, after beating his son into a confession. The doorstep diatribe between the two fathers, in full public view, had come tumbling out in what the neighbours later described as a 'shocking manner'. He'd described Beatrice as a "little slut" before Harry raised his fist and threatened to punch Jack's father if he did not retract the comment at once. The two men got into a tussle, Harry's hand got smashed against a pane of glass that cracked under the pressure. Harry suggested a comeback line that involved castrating Jack down at the local farm, but he had retracted his words immediately. It took all Flo's courage to disperse the arguing men in separate directions and slam the front door shut. Harry found his knuckle seeping blood from the gash as she went to find the first aid box.

"Don't fuss, woman, it's nothing but a graze."

"But there's blood on the hall carpet, Harry. Two grown men fighting on the doorstep: what will the neighbours think?"

"I don't care. I'll tell them the truth if they dare ask, the nosy bunch."

"That man had it coming to him". It felt quite satisfying throwing the first punch, thought Harry.

Eight

Jack

With Beatrice safely out of the way in France, Jack busied himself working day and night for Big Joe. These days he was courting a new girl in Consett and had not missed Beatrice so much. He had not even bothered to write, despite Rosina giving him the address of the chateau in France. She'd known by Jack's reaction before she left Consett that he'd little interest in the idea of becoming a father. He'd already told himself he was far too young and immature. The news of impending fatherhood had come as a shock. The idea was wholly incompatible with his lifestyle. A small bairn would not fit in. Jack's idea of contraception too had become a little haphazard, and had already landed him in hot water previously, so he was keen not to be caught out again. Jack's father had also made his opinion clear by striking his belt across his son's back until he admitted what he had done. How dare he bring such shame and disgrace to their family? For Jack, the beating was the worst to date. Afterwards, he struggled to stand upright and climb the stairs to lie on his stomach across the bed until the pain subsided.

As he made his way to his room, he caught a glance in the bedroom mirror. A claret-coloured stain had seeped through his best blue shirt. At that moment, he decided. It would be the last time he would suffer at the hands of his father. Lying on his bed recovering, he traced the beatings back to their start, just after his grandfather's death. As a small child, Jack had always felt protected by his authority at home. His father had never laid a single finger on him until that moment. If he left home, his one regret would be that he must leave his mother behind. Oddly, he thought, he had never seen his father strike her. Jack's father had resorted to only bouts of verbal cruelty toward his mother. But the situation at home had deteriorated. Jack felt on the verge of doing something foolish if he remained. Tomorrow, he'd planned to leave. The decision made him feel lighter, as if a weight had lifted from his bruised shoulder. His inner confidence was returning after a period of deep erosion. The wounds on his back would scab over and become a dark crust, slowly becoming scars in a now-familiar pattern of healing. Leaving now would be the safest option.

Pembroke Street lay in a scruffier part of town. Most houses were multi-storied and tenanted; none of the residents cared that much about their properties. Their worries were mainly about where their next wage might come from, and how much money would be left over each week to feed their hungry families. They divided the houses into flats, each one with their own entrance. Here, Jack would feel safe from further paternal beatings. Big Joe, as he was known to the locals, had plenty of work to dish out to the likes of Jack. The flat would come as part of the job, with a peppercorn rent deducted. When his mother found his goodbye note, she struggled to shed a tear. Many years of repressed emotions had taken their toll on her mental health. She secretly felt delighted that her son had taken a bold step and escaped the deeply fractious relationship with his father.

On the first floor stood a young girl with dark tresses, waiting to help him move in. The pair were already firm friends. She had been a regular visitor whilst Beatrice had been away. Jack knew which flat she lived in with her two small babies. The chatter between them was familiar and relaxed. Marguerite, the girl from upstairs, appeared overjoyed when she heard Jack would be moving into the flats. What luck to have him on tap, just a few stairs away. At that point, the consequences of having to manage the affections of two young women had not even entered Jack's young head. Blissfully unaware of events happening over in Elswick, Marguerite helped him unpack his suitcases and offered to help him make the place look more homely. She loaned him some cushions and took him an extra bowl and plate. Although the place needed refurbishment, for now Jack just felt relieved to have escaped the vicious beatings. At last, he relaxed, hoping his life was about to calm down.

Nine

Elswick – 1966

On Manor Road, everybody knew the imposing brick building was a mother and baby unit. Set back from the main road, shielding it from public view and hidden behind a line of tall grey railings, the locals knew it existed. Although some pretended they didn't know, somehow everyone knew what went on behind the large front door. The staff had their families, and tongues wagged in the small community. Even though they spoke of it in hushed tones, rumours escaped from the mouths of those who should have remained silent. Most of the stories focussed on the ill treatment the young women experienced once admitted through the doors.

Out of one hundred and seventy homes run mostly by religious orders, Harry Hamilton had deliberately chosen one a little too far away for visitors to reach without a car, his devious ploy that, if Jack could not visit, he wouldn't be able to turn Beatrice's head and keep her from doing the sensible thing. Father O'Flynn had done well over the years from the Elswick Unit fee, which was akin to a modern-day finder's fee, and someone had prepaid it.

Beatrice's spirits had reached rock bottom since her return. She'd been unprepared for the sheer exhaustion of carrying a baby to term. They took any say in her future out of her hands, leaving her with barely enough time to readjust to life. She'd readily admitted to Rosina that fear had set in. As the countdown began, she felt petrified. Who would hold her hand or mop her brow? The home had a strict "no visitors" policy. How would she let Jack know that she had given birth? She'd promised him one visit, so he could meet his child before they removed it. According to Harry, Matron told him they would inform him in the usual way, via a standard letter sent by post. But she'd already promised Jack he could see the baby once born. Now she would break a promise she didn't want to make to him. She felt sorry for Jack and knew he would be upset. Therefore, she tried to call his family's phone number, but the voice on the other end informed her that the number had been disconnected. She wanted to explain that he could not visit the baby, and the rules were far stricter than she first reported.

Harry blankly refused to accept any financial help from the state. In his view, Beatrice wasn't destitute and had her family to help her, unaware that there were state finances readily available to help single mothers bring up their babies. But, of course, nobody relayed any of this information to Beatrice. She would find this out from an additional source shortly after leaving the unit.

Poor Beatrice had been about to find out that birthing houses had a terrible reputation for brutality and hardship. She had requested a visit to see Jack before she left home, but her father had forbidden it. Beatrice disagreed. She would have liked the opportunity to speak to him in person before leaving. Should she disobey him? The thought certainly entered her cotton wool baby head.

On the day of her admission, she'd stood in her bedroom and sniffled a tearful farewell to her mother. Her father appeared keen to get on the road, and stood in the hallway jangling his car keys, a sure sign of his impatience. Father and daughter spent a tense windswept journey to the unit driving at speed. The trees were arching their branches towards the road in the violent wind. The driving rain came at such an angle against the windscreen, the wipers struggled to offload the sudden torrent of water.

At one point, Beatrice considered waiting for the next red traffic light and throwing herself from the car and running away. She considered the appalling weather outside and promptly changed her mind. It was no use. She didn't have a coat and had not been wearing proper walking shoes. The small matter of a swollen belly prevented her from jumping or running anywhere at a pace. She'd recently found out to her cost on the return drive from Dover. So she sat passively, thinking about what she had suffered in the eyes of God. She thought back to her life before the pregnancy, and how naively she assumed it would all go smoothly.

It had been foolish of her to allow Albert to set up that ridiculous date with Jack. Right on cue, the baby wriggled and gave her a kick in the ribs, as if in agreement. She closed her eyes, sighed and laid her hands on her bump, convinced it was a sign. A sign that told her she should keep the baby she'd carried for nine months, and not give it away to strangers. Perhaps she and Jack could smuggle it out of the unit.

When the car reached Elswick, the imposing gates swung open. Beatrice gripped her stomach, knowing this would be the last time she and the baby would travel over the threshold together. A lump rose in her throat and her eyes filled. Harry seemed keen to offload his passenger as quickly as possible, perhaps out of embarrassment. Beatrice thought he looked most uncomfortable, and a little flushed about the face as he handed her over to Matron in a rather awkward, stand-offish fashion.

"There you are, Matron, she's all yours now." He beamed across the hall at the formidable figure.

"Thank you, Mr Hamilton. Oh, and thank you too for your more than generous contribution to our funds."

Harry shifted on his feet, clearly feeling awkward, eyes cast downwards, avoiding Beatrice's stare. His feet started shuffling on the spot.

"Well, I'll be on my way. Don't forget to call to let us know the news." Beatrice stood bemused by the dialogue between the two adults. They seemed overly familiar with one another. As she turned her face to say something, she saw Harry had vanished through the large double doors before she had time to utter a last goodbye. She tried hard to hold her emotions inward, but her eyes flooded with hot, wet tears. She slumped down on the uncomfortable metal chair to search for a hankie in her gingham pinafore pocket.

Matron summoned a nurse to get on with the tour of the building, and show Beatrice to her room. It would take her mind off her sorrows. It felt worse than being sent to prison, she thought. Of course, she did not know what a prison was like, but imagined it to be full of rules and petty regulations within the small six-by-six cells and solid bed frames.

On their tour of the home, they found several girls gathered on sofas in the lounge, chatting quietly. The lack of warmth in the decor added to the misery of the assembled group. One sat knitting the arm of a small white cardigan, another reading an out-of-date fashion magazine.

Melody sat dressed in multiple thin layers. Her face looked older than her years. They partially hid a small scar at the temple beneath an unkempt fringe. She looked up briefly and mumbled a quiet "hello". The rest of the group took little notice of the new arrival and continued with their conversation. How wretched they looked, thought Beatrice. As she stood in the doorway, she cried again.

"Come along now, lass. Stop your weeping, it won't help. Let's go and find your room and I'll explain the rules of the house". Gushed the bossy nurse. Rules? thought Beatrice. She took an instant dislike to the woman, but couldn't pinpoint why, other than that her sharp, unsympathetic tone made her feel irritated. The nurse's footsteps faded away as the bedroom door slammed shut. In front of her were bare walls painted in a faded magnolia, and the floor was covered in a cold, dark linoleum. The small window overlooked a path that led down to a row of beech trees.

Beatrice looked forlornly around the room as she sat alone on the metal bed, wondering what she should do next. As they would not serve supper until six o'clock, she went off to locate the kitchen. Perhaps a snack would be available. Earlier that day, breakfast had somehow passed her by, and now the rumblings from her stomach were increasing. To find the kitchen in the dingy corridor took you further away than she realised. The chair outside the laundry room gave her brief respite. The weight she'd gained at the start of her pregnancy had tapered off recently.

As Harry drove towards home, keen to escape the dreadful place as quickly as possible, he thought about the damage to the family's reputation. Perhaps the sterile smell had something to do with it, or the thought of what happened behind the units' closed doors upset him more. Deep down he felt a tinge of sorrow for his youngest daughter, but had to do what was right by the words of the priest, and his loyalty would always remain firmly with the Church.

They had admitted his own father to an institution after the First World War, suffering from shell shock when he returned from fighting in the trenches. Harry never had the chance to say goodbye to him, but he remembered his mother's description of the hospital smells, the cold, stark walls and the vacant atmosphere. Harry always found goodbyes difficult to handle after that. It accounted for his demeanour after losing one of his twins at birth.

Her parents had bullied and cajoled Beatrice into the unit, where she was placed in what they called a "coercive confinement". Various unit staff warned her she had committed a mortal sin in the eyes of God and that she would not be going to Heaven. Beatrice understood all the reasons why they'd placed her at Elswick, but she couldn't reconcile herself to her lack of choices. The staff repeatedly told the girls that the only input required from them was to produce fine healthy babies and give them a Christian name for the birth certificate.

On a list of things to expect given to the girls, it stated they were not to form a bond with their newborn babies. It banned all forms of breastfeeding. Immediately after the birth, they administered tablets to dry up their milk, which left a bitter, acrid taste on the tongue and made it impossible to nurse the babies. Without the chance to nurse their babies, they thought the young women at the unit would be less likely to grow attached to their offspring. Subsequently, a nurse told Beatrice that she would find bottles of milk made up in the kitchen fridge. The bottles would be labelled with her name followed by a baby number. The nurse also cautioned her against pinching anybody else's milk, or the girls might set upon you, she warned the wide-eyed Beatrice.

The local county council paid the home a paltry £1 per week, per mother. So it was in the home's interest to pass the girls through the system and out the door as quickly as possible. The fee made a lucrative way of securing a place for the girls. Later, after supper, the other girls were in the sitting room, discussing the subject of adoptions.

"Do you know they adopt some babies from as far away as America?" Melody chirped.

"Yes," chimed Rose. "Apparently the clergy families exchange colossal sums of money for newborn babies."

"I'd heard that our family priest might be involved in a network for baby adoptions," piped up Beatrice, suddenly feeling confident enough to pass comment and join in the conversation. The other girls frowned at her as if she had spoken out of turn. It was news to them that a priest might be involved in the distribution of their babies. They asked where she had got that information from. Beatrice blushed and went quiet, choosing not to answer them.

Five days passed, and the baby had not put in an appearance. Beatrice tried to settle in, struck by the genuine camaraderie amongst the young girls. A few had never been away from home before and became plagued by extreme homesickness. She knew what that felt like from her time away in France. Although the home used the girls as skivvies and made them feel ashamed for being there, they also felt grateful to have a roof over their heads.

One or two of the other girls were homeless, living outdoors in barns and outbuildings or in filthy hostels. Their own families, often staunch Catholics, had kicked them out when they found out about their pregnancies. The unit felt luxurious to those who had been turfed out of their homes and left with nothing because of their misdemeanours. Rose told her she came from a large family of eight girls, a village over Liverpool way. Her sisters had been through the same process and so Rose knew a little of what to expect. She didn't want to scare Beatrice with horror stories and held back some of the more gruesome stories.

"I'm from Consett. Where are you from? My parents didn't want me to keep the baby." Beatrice spoke with a sigh.

"Why not?" asked Rose.

"My father insisted it would bring shame on the family, you know, to have a bairn outside of wedlock."

"Oh well, my dad threw me out on the streets and locked the front door," followed Rose. "Gave me a right beating first, mind. Now I'm thinking I don't want to go back home." Beatrice felt sorry for Rose. "You need to understand the daily chores and try to pick the easier ones. Mind you, it's difficult being nine months pregnant and trying to mop the dirty floors. You'll need to hold your nose if you get chosen for the damned toilet duties, mind," lamented Rose. They gave all the newcomers toilet duties during their first week. She described to Beatrice the arduous daily chores, the least favourite being the cleaning of the dilapidated toilets, many with broken wooden seats. The staff cleverly disguised the overarching stench of urine and faeces with a turgid brown liquid known as Jeyes Fluid, made from cold tar and found in the large blue tin canisters in the shed in the yard.

The girls all agreed that, although it caught in the back of your throat, it overrode the gut-wrenching stench lingering in the corners of the toilet cubicles and sluice room, adding, "Oh yes, and mind out for the rats in the shed, giant ones as big as cats."

Staff lectures came as simple brainwashing. The nurses reiterated the girls had committed an evil sin by going with a boy or a man and committing the sexual act. A common lecture offered by the staff to the girls was one about repentance for their sins and asking for God's forgiveness. The unit was bogged down by petty rules and regulations, unchanged for many years. The nurses advised Beatrice that she must not get attached to the baby in the hours following the birth, as it wouldn't be hers for long. How soon would it happen? enquired Beatrice more than once. Honest answers were not forthcoming. It depended on the time of day the baby arrived, she was told. If the birth occurred during the night, the handover would take place the following day. If the baby arrived in the morning, the adoptive parents would come in for a handover and collect their child the same evening. Beatrice hoped she would have the baby in the evening and be able to spend a few precious hours with it during the night, before the enforced separation the following day.

They escorted some babies, especially those bound for America, into special vehicles under the cover of darkness instead of taking them straight away. It all seemed very cloak and dagger, thought Beatrice, and wondered how much a baby would cost an American family. Beatrice realised the enormity of her father's actions to protect his reputation. Panic and realisation set into her thoughts when she thought about her own baby. Perhaps it would be the baby destined for America. How could she find out? Doubting her father's integrity again, had he lied to her about the destination of her baby? But Harry did not know the address or location of the prospective parents of his grandchild. The secret list was always kept locked securely away in the office. Beatrice had a dumb idea to raid the office and locate Samuel's file. Would she have the nerve to carry out such an audacious move? She wanted peace of mind that her baby would remain in England at least.

One morning after breakfast, the girls were in the kitchen tidying up. Rose, with whom she had struck up a closer friendship, announced she had a secret to share. The girls lowered their voices, out of earshot of any passing staff. In the days preceding a birth, the staff would photograph each girl completing a chore, such as doing the laundry or washing up in the kitchen. The photo provided the basis for a glossy annual brochure. Many churches across the area received the unit's prospectus, as a type of recruitment drive. Father O'Flynn had been one priest tasked with finding girls who were with child and destitute. With each birth, they could make money, which the priest supposedly would place in the church coffers.

The girls had come up with their own plan to identify themselves in the photos, a secret way of leaving a clue behind. Once the pictures were up on the wall and sealed in their frames, they would wait until no one was looking, remove them from the wall and write the initials of the girl in the photo on the back. The initials corresponded with the faces on the front. If anybody came to Elswick searching for their mothers in years to come, there would be a clue for them to follow on the reverse. The practice had been occurring for some time. One or two staff knew what the girls were doing but turned a blind eye. So maybe they had hearts after all, thought Beatrice. She added her initials BH to her picture. With her heart pounding, she quickly replaced it in the space left on the wall before being caught out and punished.

A genuine camaraderie between the girls developed quickly. A commonality of their impending births made friendships easier to form. Working together in the kitchen, they swapped their stories, which made the time pass more quickly. Those smitten by homesickness took comfort from the more experienced girls, who took the lead and showed them how things were done. Beatrice preferred kitchen duties, as these were more akin to her home life. She became competent at baking, with the chef; preparing pies and cakes became her favourite task. It reminded her of home in the kitchen at Consett with her mother and sister.

That afternoon Beatrice, Rose and Mary-Ellen had been tasked with making the evening meal. They rolled out the pastry into large rectangles and filled the pies with boiled scrag end of mutton and a layer of onion soaked in a thin brown gravy. They sealed the edges quickly to stop the seepage of the brown liquid. Beatrice had not got a word out of Mary-Ellen since she'd remained silent all the while they were rolling out the pastry. Had either of the girls been in the home more than once? asked Beatrice. Again, Mary-Ellen remained silent. Beatrice felt sorry for her. She had no family awaiting her return and had lived rough, moving from place to place. Playing on her mind were thoughts about her own impending birth. Rose had offered to help her when she went into labour, but the nurse who overheard their conversation told them nobody else could be in the delivery room. A penance had to be paid.

Beatrice and Rose were taking a break from their baking duties by the back door of the kitchen. Rose, desperate for a sneaky smoke, suggested they take a walk across the grass. They took off their aprons and left Mary-Ellen covering in the kitchen. Beyond the row of oak trees at the rear of the garden lay a small, unobtrusive building, hidden from view from the main house. Beatrice looked at Rose.

"What's that used for?" enquired Beatrice.

"Come on, I'll show you around." Rose didn't flinch.

In front of them was a small white chapel, with tiny windows and a glass door left ajar. Rose pushed the door open to get a better view.

"Hello, anybody there?" shouted Rose, though she already knew the answer. She'd been before. She had all the answers. Silence. What? They had no words. Inside, there were rows of tiny inscribed plaques bearing names and a couple of low wooden benches with no cushions. As far as Beatrice remembered, they had not been told to attend any chapel services. Rose softly explained that they used the chapel to lay to rest the dead babies. Beatrice shivered at the thought of losing the baby wriggling in her belly and placed her hand on it for comfort.

"Come on, let's go. This place gives me the creeps."

With shoes covered in wet grass, they tottered back to the kitchen as best they could, before someone reported them missing from their duties. Mary-Ellen remained silent as they quickly donned their aprons and finished the awaiting pies before placing them in the ovens. Would she tell the nurses about their visit to the chapel? Beatrice thought she might snitch on them. She seemed like that sort of girl. A sneak to gain attention and favouritism from the staff.

The tragic scene inside the chapel played on her mind for the rest of the afternoon. She thought about the lost babies and how their young mothers must have felt. She wondered if they were telling the truth. There were no records of the deaths in the chapel, so they must hold the details in the main office. Rose, going one step further, asked Beatrice if she would dare to search the office. The thought had crossed Beatrice's mind earlier, but she felt unsure if she had the nerve. Rose took it upon herself to wait until nightfall and with Beatrice covering for her in the corridor went in search of the paperwork. They found the office in darkness and Rose found it difficult to see the cupboards. The keys were nowhere to be seen. She would have to abort her mission. The two girls met again in the sitting room to discuss further tactics. How could they get their hands on the keys? The grand plan got scuppered as Rose went into labour later that night and by the following morning Matron had sent her home. The baby had been quickly collected and her room cleaned and readied for the next inmate. So now

Beatrice had to decide if she felt brave enough to try again alone. As a nod to Jack's maternal grandfather, the couple had pre-chosen Samuel as a name for the baby. Leonard Samuel, Jack's grandfather, had had a significant influence on Jack as a small boy. He took him everywhere, balanced on the small seat on the crossbar of his push bike. His favourite hobby was fly fishing, on a Saturday morning, alongside the River Derwent. He allowed Jack to put the bait on the lines and became fascinated by the maggots wriggling in the perspex box. He liked to poke them with a stick when his grandfather wasn't looking. An early memory for Jack was watching his grandfather smoke his pipe; he must have been about four years old. He allowed him to tap the tobacco into the pipe holder. The stain of the tobacco always lingered on his grandfather's index finger and the smell seeped into his clothes. When not working in his overalls, Leonard wore the same thick, mustard coloured cardigan with two deep front pockets and four leather buttons. His round tortoiseshell spectacles, worn right on the bridge of his nose, always amused Jack.

He kept mint sweets in his pockets, which he offered to Jack if he had been good. As a steelworker, Leonard had lived a hardened life. Jack's father's temperament changed after the loving protection of grandfather Leonard was removed. He became brooding and sour, and trivial domestic incidents would be enough to set him off. After Leonard's passing, the family unit fell apart, and for Jack the regular beatings began. As a result, he stayed out of the house as much as possible to avoid his father, he grew up quickly and was only driven home by hunger or the cold. He worried about leaving his mother behind to defend herself, but it wasn't enough to override the fear. Once, after a particularly bad beating, Jack had given her the option to leave with him, but she'd declined. She knew that Jack's father's temper would follow her wherever she lived.

Besides, she had no money of her own, only her paltry weekly allowance to support herself.

Jack vowed to his mother that, if he ever had children of his own he would never beat them. He would remain fair but firm. He also vowed that, if his father laid a finger on her, he would return and kill him. But his mother, who knew him so well, knew her Jack was always full of such dramatic words. She'd heard them all before. But, on this occasion, the look on his face told her differently, and she felt she should believe him.

The nurse had explained a little about labour and what to expect, but nothing could have prepared poor Beatrice for what followed next. Labour arrived rather unexpectedly. In the laundry room, she sat pressing piles of bed sheets when her stomach gave a sudden lurch. A rush of clear liquid came gushing from between her legs. At first, she thought she had wet herself. But her waters had broken in a spectacular fashion. Not as a trickle but like an almighty waterfall, flowing past her stockinged feet and her only pair of sensible shoes. It seeped over the dark linoleum floor. She quickly scooped up the bedsheets and attempted to clean up the mess with the dirty towels on the floor. The contractions hit Beatrice's abdomen in rapid succession. Nobody told her it would be a thousand times worse than period pains. If only they'd told her what to expect. It all lies, lies, lies anyway, according to Beatrice.

She bent over in agony. Labour had started. Several times she yelled out.

"Help!" she screamed. After a time a worried-looking nurse arrived at the door looking more shocked to see the floor awash with a mixture of embryonic fluids and faecal matter. After calling for backup, she tasked the other girls with clearing up and took Beatrice firmly by the arm and guided her down to her room. There, she had to lie on a hard, narrow bed, fitted with overly large leather stirrups. They left her alone, with barely a sip of warmish water at the bottom of a plastic cup. Mother of God, she felt she was paying her penance now, as the pains steadily increased in intensity across her lower stomach. She felt like she wanted to open her bowels, but was petrified in case the baby came out of her bottom.

"Help! Oh, God, somebody help me!" she cried again. Nobody came to her aid. It felt as though her body would split itself in half. The nurse poked her head around the door to see how she was doing and told her to "keep the noise down". She would upset the other girls, yet to deliver. The nurse looked under the sheet and saw the dark, rounded shape of the baby's head crowning. The urge to push intensified. Beatrice screamed at full volume, gripping both sides of the bed.

"Oh! The bairn's here, lass, now let's have one more push and it'll be out!"

"Ow, ow, ow," she wailed, losing her composure and squeezing her hands together. One final contraction sent her pain level soaring off the scale of humanity. By the time the nurse had pulled on her purple rubber gloves, the baby had entered the world. She'd only just caught it, as the baby shot forward onto the bed. The newborn was safely delivered.

"Never again," Beatrice whimpered to herself, wiping snot from her nostrils on the sheets.

The baby had been smaller than expected, but, to her delight, he presented as a boy. His lungs were fully operational, and he screamed until warm hands wrapped him in a towel. Beatrice had been praying for the baby to be a boy throughout her pregnancy. She felt it might bring her a little closer to Jack. Weighing in at only six pounds, with a mass of jet-black curly hair, his fingers were long and slender, like starfish, poking out of the top of the towel. He looked like a miniature version of his father. The birth process felt nothing like the other girls had warned her it would be. Gory, agonising, and above all plain embarrassing, she had just suffered a complete loss of dignity, no part of her body left unexposed. Fancy pooing in the bed. The shame of it. In all her teenage years, nobody had seen her genitalia, not Jack, not her mother or her sister. This part of her anatomy had always remained private.

Now, she needed to put all the ghastliness from earlier in the day behind her and try to remain strong. Beatrice turned her attention and focussed on her baby. The nurse passed Samuel back to her, dressed in a white nightie with three yellow ducks embroidered across the bodice. Beatrice wrapped him in the pale yellow shawl knitted by Flo. Beatrice knew the next few hours were going to be precious. It would be just the two of them, as she cradled him to sleep in her arms. The milk suppression tablets had slowed the milk production progress, but not stopped it altogether. As he fussed, she seemed reluctant to put him down. Despite the warnings from the nurses, she attempted to breastfeed him. Knowing that her milk had not fully come in, as he tried to latch on and took up the offer of sustenance. Beatrice wanted the experience of putting the baby on her breast and feeling him suckle. She had an uneasy feeling about putting him down in the rectangular perspex box, just in case they whisked him away earlier than they had agreed.

Unable to move easily from the bed, she inhaled Samuel's scent repeatedly, attempting to hold it as a kind of keepsake. It would be the only memento she could hold dear in the years to follow. She vowed she would never forget him as she finally gave in and placed him in his cot, crying herself into a short but fitful sleep. An hour later, she woke to find herself in a foetal position on the bed. Her left leg had gone numb and her calf had started to cramp up. Her right arm was curled protectively around her head and the other lay stretched out toward the cot. A warm, rushing sensation started down below and she hobbled to the toilet to check for blood. Beatrice found herself entirely alone.

Every bone in her teenage body ached. Perhaps a warm bath would help. She didn't know how best to take care of herself. Someone had entered the room, whilst she slept, as they had placed the regulation-issue sanitary towels and brown paper disposal bags on the chair. She was conscious of the growling in her stomach and a raging hunger as she had not eaten that day. Melody knocked gently on the door. Unable to sleep she came in to admire the newcomer. Beatrice asked her to stay with the baby for a few moments. Gathering her small wash bag and a thin grey towel, she staggered to the bathroom to soak her bruised and swollen body in a shallow, lukewarm bath. The water ran cold after a minute and left barely enough to get herself cleaned up. She watched the pink water form an eddy down the plughole. Feeling clean and dry, she shuffled back down the corridor the short distance towards her room, pausing by the kitchen. Gingerly holding her stomach, she eyed up the stool by the worktop, and decided sitting would be impossible.

Unless you knew where to look, finding food was difficult because of the locked cupboards. The bread and jam were in the large cupboard, unlocked, possibly in error, so Beatrice found a plate and a knife. She smothered the bread with the strawberry jam and stuck it together against the second slice. It tasted so good as she greedily crammed into her mouth.

Back in her room, with the baby sleeping peacefully in his crib, she thanked Melody for her kindness. The girl seemed different that evening, perhaps her acute shyness dwindling a little. She'd grown fond of Beatrice and saw her as someone she might befriend.

"Thank you, Melody. Has he been quiet?"

"Yes, all quiet, not a peep out of him."

"I'm going to miss you, Beatrice. I don't know where I'm going next; my family don't want me no more."

"Will you go into a hostel?" asked Beatrice with a sudden rush of empathy for the girl who had been so silent for the last few days.

"Nah, I don't like them hostels, never have. I'll find a farm with a warm barn. There's plenty around the coast if you know where to look." Beatrice felt unable to offer any help, as she was going through a similar torment. Alone again after Melody had hugged her goodbye, she began burying the guilt and shame of her birth experience. Beatrice decided she would light a candle every year on the eighth day of May to remember Samuel. She hoped it would bring her some comfort to celebrate his birth date. Not wishing to waste any more of their precious time together, she vowed to stay awake and cradle her baby boy until daylight arrived. But, around dawn she must have drifted off, as the next thing she knew was an abrupt knock on the door, the one she'd been dreading, quickly followed by the sound of a now-familiar bossy voice.

"Come along, dear. Don't make a fuss. There's a good girl." The patronising tone came swooping through the door. "You know who" had arrived early. The nurse swept into the room and stood in front of Beatrice, legs astride and hands on her hips.

"I'm not ready. Go away," Beatrice whispered. Just off to her right, through the open door, she glimpsed a large blue pram. The time had come. She braced herself as best she could. At any minute someone would prise Samuel from her arms, and whisk him down the corridor, through the double doors and away to his new life.

"Just one more minute, please; can't you feel my pain?" thought Beatrice.

The nurse told her that the new parents were waiting for their new baby down in the lounge, so she had better hurry and finish getting him ready. Beatrice deliberately took her time, fastening each button of the cardigan. She would not be rushed in those last few moments with Samuel. They could all wait. Samuel's prospective parents had three little girls of their own, all identically dressed. Yellow gingham pinafore dresses, red shoes and matching pigtails. It had approved them as the adoptive parents for the baby known simply as "No 3-733480" on the departures list. It listed all the babies in this way. The unit had simply listed Samuel as a number, with no formal identity. Tears flowed as Beatrice, unable to look round, stood there facing the window, her back to the door. Not wishing to witness those final few seconds, she bent to kiss his forehead and placed her finger first on her mouth and then against his tiny lips, as he opened his eyes, blinking, and stared straight into hers. The nurse stepped forward, clicking her tongue with impatience. Taking control, she swiftly transferred him to her arms. Swinging her body directly away from Beatrice, she left the room, allowing the heavy door to slam shut. Beatrice collapsed back on the bed, her face buried in the only things left behind were a tiny nightie and her mother's shawl. She had hidden them discreetly under the pillow, and changed the baby into clothes she'd stolen from the laundry.

It began with a guttural wolf-like howl, akin to a wolf looking for its lost cubs and heard throughout the entire unit. Other girls stepped into the corridor, knowing full well what had happened. In her emotional delirium, another of her madcap thoughts rushed through Beatrice's mind. *In her mind's eye, she saw herself sprinting down the hallway, shoving the nurse aside, and taking her baby boy from the pram. She'd locate the office and rip apart the paperwork. In her mind, she saw herself escaping through the gates with her one-day-old baby and not halting. She saw Jack waiting for her by the gates and her little family speeding away in his car.* But, of course, none of that was going to happen. The nurse returned to the room to complete her tasks empty-handed, having relinquished Samuel to his new family. They had strategically positioned the car park at the rear, out of sight of the girls' rooms for good reason.

"You'll soon be back to normal," the nurse chimed in that dreadful matter-of-fact voice, whilst stripping the sheets from the bed, the same voice that got Beatrice's hackles up. On the other side of the room, the emotional mood of the young mother rose. Beatrice ignored the first comment and continued with her packing. Maybe it was just the ill-chosen words or perhaps the tone of her voice. Whatever it was, Beatrice suddenly lost control and snapped back. She had never been rebellious by nature. The condescending look on the face of the nurse was the trigger. Many were unused to verbal chastisements from the young girls, as most were biddable young things reliant on the nurses.

"I don't want to go back to normal. That's the whole point. I've changed my mind. I want my baby back." Still not looking round. The nurse remained silent. "Do you hear me? I want you to get my baby. Right now." Her voice rose a couple of octaves towards the end of the sentence, baring her teeth.

"Ha! All the girls say that. Well, it's too late, lass, that baby will be far away from Elswick by now. You should have kept those scrawny little legs together, shouldn't you?" Beatrice may have been mistaken, but thought she may have glimpsed a faint grin appear at the corner of the nurse's mouth. Did the woman have any idea what had happened in that room less than twenty-four hours ago? Beatrice flipped.

"That's it! I've had enough of your snide comments. You're an insensitive bitch, and I want you to leave this room now. Just get out!" Beatrice screeched. In frustration, she grabbed a teacup filled with the remnants of some lukewarm tea and launched it across the room. The cup smashed into pieces and left cold dregs of tea dribbling down the magnolia wall. The nurse neatly ducked her head and flung the sheets into a mobile laundry basket before bolting smartly out of the door.

—⁓◯

During her stay at the unit, Beatrice had changed her mind about her future and made a new decision. She would not return home. The unit allowed the girls to make a single phone call to their families to arrange their transport home after giving birth. Beatrice had spoken with Rosina the previous evening and pleaded with her to seek out Jack. She'd decided she would live with him.

"Rosina, is that you?"

"Hello, Bea, have you had the baby?"

"Yes, a boy, yesterday. Listen, Rosy, I'm not coming home," with a wobble in her throat.

"What do you mean, you are not coming home? Don't be silly, Bea, of course you're coming home. Father is coming to collect you."

"No, I'm not. I've decided I'm going to live with Jack, and I need you to do me a favour and find him, tell him to collect me tomorrow morning at ten."

Rosina stammered.

"But, but, I'm not sure where he lives. Who do you think is going to tell Mother and Father?" Realising before the words had left her lips, she had fallen directly into her sister's trap. Silence met the conversation at the other end of the line. Beatrice had already hung up. Anything would be better than returning home, where her parents would make her feel guilty with a simple look, or an unspoken word, or dragging her off to church to repent. After making the phone call, she felt a sense of relief and returned to her room to finish packing.

The clock in the hallway read five minutes to ten. The next five minutes ticked by slowly until the hands on the clock aligned themselves vertically. Beatrice sat waiting anxiously in the corridor for Jack's arrival. Surely Rosina would have found him. It all seemed perfectly logical. That morning Beatrice had lied to the staff about her transport arrangements. Internally, she'd blamed Jack for the mess surrounding her, so why shouldn't he help now? She needed him to arrive quickly before she did something stupid and embarrassed herself further. With anxiety levels sky high, her poor body was racked with intermittent pain after giving birth. It had been the longest twenty-four hours of her entire life.

Samuel – 1966

Samuel Gardiner's life had begun at Elswick in a small mother and baby unit. Removed from his mother at barely a day old, he was placed with a family whose surname simply read on the form as Mr & Mrs 733480. They recorded baby Samuel as No 3-733480. But the adoptive father died prematurely, leaving a young widow with five small bairns under ten. Unable to cope, she had been forced to give up Samuel, who had by then reached school age. The authorities decided they should place Samuel in a Roman Catholic orphanage. Before the collection went ahead to the orphanage, his adoptive mother had written a few notes in a book. It gave a more adult explanation that he could read when older. Since his arrival, she had told him little about his parents, only enough for him to understand that he differed from all the other school children. At five, his move to the Buckinghamshire orphanage coincided with the start of his change of personality. To cover his intense feelings of insecurity, he quickly learnt to play the role of a chameleon.

It all came with an ability to change his persona according to the audience. The other children referred to him as Biffo, the house clown. He became a master storyteller who hoodwinked and embellished his tales, frequently making himself into a hero. Samuel liked to be the one to be congratulated and patted on the back. The craving for adult love and attention cleverly disguised his secret.

The constant seeking of approval and reassurance from those around him had begun. The adult attention he naively mistook for love. But, as he had never known genuine love, he made the most of what presented itself to him. Samuel learnt how to not only manipulate the adults but survive them.

They pinned the rules to the walls of every room. They threw the impressionable youngsters into a chaotic routine that swept them along at such speed they either clung on tightly, or fell off and perished. The first rule came at mealtimes. They instructed the children to eat everything on their plate or they would receive no pudding. Breakfast would be a slice of bread and a scrape of dripping to eke it out and add a flavour. Out of earshot, the children said that the taste would linger in their mouths afterwards. The last dining room rule was that all plates had to be inspected before being excused from the table. That became their routine.

The two-inch groove across his right shoulder bore testament to Samuel's difficult youth years. It came as the result of a playtime incident at the orphanage. The outdoor apparatus, after overnight showers, had become slippery. Samuel had been swinging on the climbing frame that suddenly became untethered at one end. Taking a giant swing through the air, he lost his grip on the metal bar, landing with a thump on a metal truck discarded earlier, its frame crushed into a lethal shape of jagged metal under his weight. He lay slumped on the ground, winded. The razor-sharp edge pierced his jumper and shirt and split his delicate skin open. Blood seeped quickly through his clothes, to the horror of the other children surrounding him, gawping. One girl went pale, saying she felt dizzy in the head. Another child nobly sprinted off to find help and, within minutes, the staff rushed outside to his aid. Samuel, in shock, barely uttered a squeak as he lay on the ground.

The lad sat in the emergency department at the hospital, proudly holding his arm. It had stung a little, but he happily lapped up all the attention. The white towel against the wound had turned pink. They discarded some of his clothes in the hospital waste bin. The nurse had to use huge scissors to remove them. The stitches didn't hurt, Samuel boasted to the nurse. She gave him a look and seemed to take a kind of sadistic pleasure in jabbing a large needle in his good arm. For once, he spoke the truth and felt no pain as the local anaesthetic kicked in.

Once back at the orphanage, he became the wounded hero.

"There's no more climbing frames for you now. Do you hear me, Samuel Gardiner?" Matron teased, poking her head out of the office door. His peers gathered round. Those brave enough wanted to inspect the damage done to their steely friend. Samuel peeled back his bandage so they could see. They grimaced and the two kids turned their heads away. At suppertime in the dining room, one or two guffawed at him behind their hands, because he had needed help to cut up his food. Samuel didn't give a jot. He lapped up the attention. One of the staff gave him extra sweets while he recovered. Jelly babies became his new favourite.

During his eighth year, he began stealing from the other children, first befriending them. Many of them had little in terms of personal possessions. But the scheming Samuel led astray those who did. The innocent-looking boy, with the piercing blue eyes and dark curls.

As night time arrived, and the dormitory fell silent, he lay in wait until he heard the gentle snores coming from his sleepy roommates. Once confident they were asleep, he began his secret mission. He crept out of bed to raid their personal bedside cupboards. The hiding place was already prepared to hide his spoils. At the far end of the corridor, in the linen cupboard under the shelves, he had loosened a floorboard. And, without a sound, he slid the items out of sight and replaced the wooden panel, before creeping back to bed, bragging to himself that he, Samuel, would forever be the smartest kid in the house.

He remained unmoved by the intense emotions of the other children, when they protested to the staff about their misplaced belongings. If a scrap occurred between the inmates, Samuel stood somewhere on the periphery, as more often than not he had been the instigator, pitting his fellow orphans against each other. He found he gained genuine pleasure in other children's heartache.

As the months passed, nobody came forward to offer him a permanent home, despite many interviews and adverts. The process cast a shadow over the youngster. It meant he spent the ensuing ten years roughing it out in a variety of orphanages across Yorkshire and County Durham. With no formal roots, he felt ungrounded, as if he didn't belong to anybody or anywhere. Not surprising, considering the type of orphanage regimes they had forced him to endure. Most of his childhood he had spent without being shown any love or affection from adults, with far-reaching consequences. Why should he care about the terrible things he inflicted upon others? Nobody had ever cared about him. "Life's tough," he would say in his defence, offering others little empathy.

At fourteen, he walked away from his last orphanage placement, into a darker underworld, where he would learn how to fend for himself among adults. Living in grimy digs in a poor part of Newcastle, he learnt to feed himself, while he worked long, extended hours. Big Joe had been running a racketeer service for many years. Samuel started running errands for the local reprobate, from whom he took his daily orders. Although known to the authorities, Big Joe liked to keep his life under the radar from the local constabulary. At that point, Samuel was unaware that his father, Jack, in his mid-teens, had also worked for the same man. Although advancing in age, Big Joe still raked it in. Contrary to his name, his looks were that of a wiry, weedy guy with horn-rimmed spectacles who now carried a slight limp.

He still liked to enlist the help of the youngsters, who were otherwise drifting about getting themselves into trouble. Young men such as Samuel were grateful for the roof he provided over their heads. There were pretty girls on tap, if you knew who to ask. And money to be earned if you kept your snout clean and your mouth firmly shut. It had become Big Joe's mantra: he liked to keep the young men sweet. Any spare cash left over on a Friday went into a float he held at the pub. This would cover their drinks and anything else they might fancy on the side!

Samuel's accommodation had descended into a squat, but it served its purpose. The main front door stood permanently on the latch and clunked open and shut at frequent intervals during the night, as the young men came and went. Some visitors were dubious characters, and he wisely kept his distance. The flat, sparsely furnished, held a small double bed with a squidgy mattress that made your skin itch. An armchair stood in the corner with a grubby shag pile rug in the middle of the floor. Its original colour was difficult to determine. Not too much to sing about. She found a tiny kitchenette behind a grubby curtain. Any electricity had to be metered, and the single stove worked only on a low setting. Others shared the bathroom. The toilet sat behind a separate door in the corridor with a broken lock and no toilet paper. You only ventured in if you were desperate. Samuel quickly learnt to keep one foot firmly against the door. The toilet was always dirty because no one ever cleaned it, and you could see evidence of the previous visitors. The local pub became a preferred place to the toilet facilities at the house.

Life was about to change and lead him down a fresh path. One evening, he returned from an errand and found a letter on the hallway carpet, franked London. They proudly displayed the names Lucknow and Hardcastle in bold letters across the top edge. Forwarded several times, the letter explained Beatrice had named Samuel as a beneficiary in her will, and he should get in touch as soon as mutually convenient. He kept rereading the letter, wondering who would have named him in their will. The name in the letter, Beatrice Hamilton, meant nothing. His fantasies ran wild, imagining a large country estate, strutting around in a peaked cloth cap carrying a large walking stick trailing two large black dogs. Or maybe someone left him several properties, and he could walk proudly on the street, collecting huge rents every month as a landlord.

Maybe the solicitors had some new information or documentation concerning his birth mother. Samuel had started the long process a few months back to trace her. He hoped the culmination of their efforts would lead to the discovery of an address or phone number. In seeking his birth family details, he discovered that his father, Jack, had died the previous winter from pneumonia. The Lost and Found Agency referred him to his original birthplace in Elswick, where he would find more details surrounding his birth.

When he telephoned the mother and baby unit, they informed him that, yes, they had a small wallet of archived personal information. He would need to bring proof of his identity for the information to be released. What paperwork had he got to prove his identity? Forgeries were scarce. Samuel needed a quick solution. Big Joe had the perfect answer. They copied a pay slip showing an address and full name. With the copied paperwork in his jacket pocket, he borrowed a dilapidated van from the pub and drove over to Elswick.

The van just made it. The engine kept stalling and petrol fumes drifted into the cab, making him nauseous. Pulling up outside the grey railings, he sat for a moment trying to compose himself. He took in the expansive, neatly trimmed lawn and the line of beech trees with the gravel drive. To Samuel, it looked dead posh, like a hotel of sorts. It took him a couple more moments to compose himself, casting his eyes over the imposing building. How did he feel knowing his birth had taken place in that building? He felt sick to his stomach. His legs trembled as he locked the van. He tried to compose himself, wiping his sweaty hands on the back of his trousers. Nearing the front door, he paused and swallowed hard before pressing the small brass bell. His heart thumped just as he cleared his throat and whispered softly into the intercom.

"Hello, I have an appointment with Mrs Harding at two o'clock. My name is Samuel Gardiner." The buzzer made him start as the front door opened. Mrs Harding hovered in the lobby area, waiting for him. Still unsure what to expect, her appearance took him by surprise. The woman before him wore a dark green polyester suit and cream pussy-bow blouse. His eye was drawn to the perfectly matched shape of her dark burgundy lips. The institutional smell he found overpowering. Blimey, he thought, it reminded him of one of his old orphanages. Perhaps that had been more than the smell of boiled mutton coming from the kitchen.

"How do you do? We were expecting you." Mrs Harding extended a warm hand, and Samuel followed her into a room full of archive boxes.

Before they got started, Mrs Harding asked him for his ID. Without looking at the lady, he flashed up the copied pay slip made by Big Joe. The woman's face remained unchanged, and they continued with the interview. On the table in the centre lay a red plastic wallet from a box file, already open. Emblazoned on the front, the numbers had been his baby identity number. Disappointment suddenly cast a shadow, as he realised there were hardly any papers. One thing, though, stood out from the rest. A small brown leather notebook, the pages neatly handwritten. As Samuel leafed through, he asked why there were no photographs of his birth mother or her baby. Tucked inside the brown leather notebook, they found a letter. The unit encouraged the girls to write to the babies. He had frequently dreamt about this moment and tried his hardest not to let it overwhelm him.

Mrs Harding revealed his birth mother, just before the birth, had written the letter, possibly whilst she awaited his delivery. It explained how she had made one error of judgement with his father, Jack. She wanted to explain how she came to be in the birthing unit and how others had decided what would happen on the outside. They sent her away to Lille in France to work as a governess. Why? All the bold decisions her parents had taken that out of her hands and the local priest, Father O'Flynn. As he tried to focus on the words, his eyes filled; instead he tucked it in his inside jacket pocket. He took a seat at the table alongside Mrs Harding, her sweet scent a little sickly and overpowering. He tried not to let it bother him, as he continued with his questioning. Where were the copious number of documents he had always imagined? After so many moves, he must surely have a full box somewhere. Where were the notes from the previous parents? Their name had slipped from his confused mind. Where were the exit notes from the string of orphanages? Three quarters of his life remained unaccounted for. Who could fill in the gaps? Those important gaps that gave him some sense of identity and security. Without those, he would still feel lost.

"Where is the rest of it?" he asked Mrs Harding, who was already checking her watch; noting her action, Samuel assumed she must have had another appointment or a more pressing matter?

"Would you like a drink, Mr Gardiner, a cup of tea, or some water perhaps? I appreciate it's a lot to take in."

"No, thanks."

"Have you come far today?" she continued. He couldn't answer, his emotions scattered like marbles across the room.

"Do you know why my mother chose this place?" he asked, rushing headlong into the loaded questions. "Why did they insert the word 'unknown' instead of my father's name on the birth certificate?"

"Your birth mother gave up her baby and at the time she would have been in what they called 'moral disgrace'. So, avoiding any trace, the mother and baby units chose not to name the fathers on the birth certificates."

His voice choked as he envisaged his mother, alone in her room, giving birth with no kindly support of a partner or her mother. Before he'd arrived, he thought he might like to see one of the delivery rooms, but he changed his mind once he walked through the door, so didn't bother asking. The signage stated that they permitted no males beyond the entrance corridor.

"I just need a moment, please." Holding his head, he squeezed his brow with his forefingers. He was rarely lost for words.

"That's ok, take as long as you need, there's a lot to take in." Mrs Harding paused for a moment before her next bombshell. "That's all the information we have, Mr Gardiner. Apart from one last thing I need to tell you: there are some group photographs in the hall."

He paused a few seconds before answering. "Can we look? I'd like to see if I can spot her. There were no single photographs of my mother taken at the time?" Mrs Harding couldn't help but witness the pained desperation in his voice.

"No, I'm sorry, there were none. Perhaps the family didn't own a camera; few households had one."

The pair went to find the large dining hall and stood awkwardly under several framed landscape photographs. Samuel was unsure what he was looking at. The pictures depicted some girls at work and others babies sitting up in large prams. Perhaps awaiting adoption. Your mother may be in one of them? Or you may be the baby in that line of prams?

The names purposely left blank, so the girls and their babies remained anonymous. Known as transparent placements, so not wishing to draw any attention to the stream of young girls stepping through the door. Mrs Harding had been most helpful in that respect, but she already knew what lay behind each photograph. Though he had nothing to compare her face with, it might ease his mind. She didn't know why, but she felt sorry for the young man. She'd seen many youngsters come through the doors searching for answers. So why should she feel empathy for this one she didn't know? Perhaps it was the sadness in his eyes.

Squinting, Samuel scanned the rows of young girls. Their sombre faces returned his gaze. They reminded him of the old school photographs where everyone sat on wooden benches, smiling falsely at the camera. One picture frame caught his eye. Samuel studied it carefully. It showed several girls in regulation pinafores and headscarves cleaning the kitchen and a second figure alone in the laundry room. A pinafore barely covering her slight frame with a slight bump at the front. The tall, thin girl staring straight into the camera looked just like him, with a similar facial bone structure and thick, dark curly hair. Was that his mother? His stomach fluttered, making his eyes water. Mrs Harding agreed she could see a likeness, but couldn't be absolutely sure. Samuel wondered if every orphan had the same comment when they came seeking answers? He reached forward and took down the frame for a closer inspection, gingerly turning it over. The frame seemed fragile enough to split without due care. Handwritten on the back in faint pencil, the clue he'd been looking for. At the bottom in the corner, written in faint but neat handwriting, were the initials BH alongside a few others. Placing it back on the wall, he turned to leave. Someone had suddenly sucked the air in the room out of the door and the atmosphere seemed to suffocate him. With a lightheaded feeling, he clutched his folder tightly.

"Thank you for your help," he stuttered in a mild panic. He'd turned a little pale. Tiny beads of sweat had broken out across his upper lip. She thought he might keel over.

"Are you ok, Mr Gardiner?" asked Mrs Harding, following him to the door. Having waited so long for that moment, it had been a shock to be confronted with such intimate details about his start in life. Seeing the photograph had pushed an emotional trigger. He just made it back to the driveway before throwing up behind the van. Although the visit had been fruitful in terms of information, and the photograph, he felt it all too much to absorb at once. His mind felt totally unprepared for the pull that had lain buried within him for such a long time. For several minutes he stood staring at the pool of yellow vomit on the grass, rooted to the spot, the image on the wall indelibly imprinted on his thoughts. At last he'd found a picture of his birth mother, and felt content to cling to that memory.

Once home, he sought comfort in the bottom of a tumbler of whisky, the amber nectar burning away his pain as it slid down his throat. He poured himself a second, much larger one before settling down to read the letter from Beatrice. Referring to her as mother still seemed strange.

May – 1966

My Dearest Samuel,

I hope when you read this it will help you understand more about me, your mother, and the decisions that were taken about you following your birth. I was a young, unmarried teenage girl when I fell pregnant by your father Jack, my first boyfriend. When my parents told our local priest of my predicament, they hatched a cruel plan and had me sent away to France. My job would be a governess to a local count and his family. Of course, they promptly dismissed me when they discovered my hidden pregnancy. My parents felt they had no choice and placed me in a mother and baby unit, where I gave birth to you. They wouldn't tell me the name of the family who adopted you. I cried for many long hours and knew that, despite everything, I would always love you, and never forget you. As you grow older, you will face many challenges, but remember, I will always be with you. I'm resolved to find you, despite knowing they will discourage it. Whatever happens, I will always be your mother.

Yours in love, Beatrice x.

In his mind, Samuel thought about when she had written it and whether she was alone at the time. He wished he had left it unopened for fear of knowing the contents and what they would do to his mind. As Mrs Harding mentioned, the letter had been written on the night before his birth. The raw emotion conveyed in Beatrice's feelings at the time came through clearly by her choice of written words on the page. He'd instantly felt a strong connection and wanted to hold her and reassure her. He wanted her to know… but soon after the whisky worked its magic and he fell asleep clutching the letter, the empty tumbler close to his chest.

Reading it again now, as an adult, it changed his viewpoint. He saw it through fresh eyes. Anger seeped in and he challenged the contents. In the following days, he started taking the words out of context to suit his emotional decline. He researched his mother's whereabouts, but where to begin? He did not wish to work for Big Joe indefinitely. Perhaps this was an opportunity to break away and start a new life. His imagination ran away with him.

Moving straight on to his next mission, Samuel felt determined to seek the lady from the photograph. It felt weird to say the word "mother" out loud, as he had never known the use of that word. Did he know the correct definition of a mother, anyway? How would he know? Years ago, back in his classroom days, he'd looked it up in the dictionary just to prove a point. He remembered the words clearly stated. Mother – to show empathy, to be strong, to guide. The following analogies were from the mouth of Beatrice, who likened it to using a butter pat to mould her offspring into decent human beings. Or to allow them to fly the nest out into the harsh surrounding world. Of course, it varied from family to family, but Beatrice had always had her own theories.

Samuel had never experienced the unconditional and selfless love of a mother. Or a mother who loved their offspring with such a deep devotion through any sacrifice and pain. Beatrice agreed that interpreting love may vary, and it can manifest in different ways. A child may look upon it as a devotion to a person or situation, characterised in Samuel's case by a strong feeling that they had denied him parental love from birth. That left him with intense feelings of insecurity. He'd been too young to remember his adoptive family, or the Christian names of his clutch of sisters with the matching dresses, pigtails and freckles.

Beatrice was reading her newspaper in the kitchen at Ocean Cottage when an article caught her attention. It referenced a new Children's Act, recently granted by Parliament, that regulated any official intervention between families of fostered or adoptive children. This gladdened her heart, as this new legislation would protect Samuel. It gave her the last nudge she needed to register her name with the Lost and Found Agency. Maybe in her own mind she had thought about starting the search, but not pursued it hard enough? Sometimes she had simply reached a dead end with her enquiries, and felt her pain too much to bear and easily admitted defeat. If only she could wash away her guilt like water down a drain. She wished, too, that she could forget about the emotional triggers that ebbed and flowed through her mind at four in the morning. Sometimes they caught her by surprise, and she thought it best if he didn't find her. She still believed she'd sacrificed that right when forced to let him go. She had thought about his life with his new family and tried to imagine what it may have been like? Would Samuel be safe in their hands as the only boy?

Would the father use forceful discipline? Beatrice railed against corporal punishment in any form. She still remembered the harsh beatings that Jack had suffered at the hands of his father's belt. No matter how many faults Jack had had in the past, Beatrice saw no reason for his father to beat him with such severity. With that last thought still fresh in her mind, she filled in the forms and went to the postbox, hoping to catch the last post. Then all she could do was sit and wait for news.

Ten

Beatrice and Jack

After receiving a desperate call from her sister. Beatrice had instructed Rosina to find Jack. She told her he must collect her from the unit at ten o'clock the following day. Poor Rosina also had the unpleasant task of informing their parents of her sister's latest plan. Probably best that Beatrice remained blissfully ignorant of the fact that Jack had grown close to another person whilst she had been away in France. And the friendship would be set to continue after she'd given birth. The place Beatrice had chosen to live had taken her sister by surprise. But Rosina was only following instructions and not there to judge or express an opinion. In a matter of days, she too would be gone from the clutches of her parents' grasp and her sisters' demands.

Rosina pulled up outside the pub. She felt a little awkward about asking the stranger having a smoke outside if he knew of Jack Gardiner. She gave him a brief description, but felt too uncomfortable to go inside herself. The man with the ginger mop agreed to help and returned a moment later with an answer she was not expecting. Inside stood Jack, enjoying a drink, but before coming out he wanted to know who was asking for him. Rosina explained an abridged version of her request. A few moments later, Jack casually sauntered out of the pub, his sleeves rolled up and his shoes looking worn. Pulling another cigarette from his top pocket, she noticed his fingernails stained dark yellow.

"Hello, Rosina, what brings you here? Aren't you a bit far from home?" He blew a puff of smoke over his right shoulder. He had no beef with Rosina. Actually, he felt sorry for her, conducting her sister's private business out on the pavement. She seemed so anxious, fit to burst with worry. "Whatever is the matter?" The cue for her words that came tumbling out. She barely took a breath.

"I've come about Beatrice. She's desperate, Jack, and needs your help. Got herself in a terrible state. You see, she had the baby yesterday, a little boy, and they have given it away to a family already. The thing is, Jack, she's refusing to come home, and has declared herself homeless. Can you take her in with you for a while until she sorts herself out?" A deep frown cast over his brow. Poor Rosina, she was not at fault, just the carrier of her sister's bad news. His response took her aback.

"Damn it, I told her I wanted to see the baby before they handed it over. Beatrice knew that!" Now feeling less than generous, he responded, irked.

"Anyway, what does she want from me? I've no money to offer her, you know. And I'll have to clear the flat up a bit. I suppose she can move in with me, but just temporarily, mind. When will she leave the home?" Rosina grimaced.

"They are chucking her out tomorrow. Can you fetch her at ten o'clock? Here's the address."

Jack took the piece of paper and thought about the consequences for a second before giving Rosina a reluctant nod. Briefly, she lost control of herself and hugged him before realising what she had done. His life had just got a lot more complicated. Would he be able to handle it?

The following day, Jack stuck to the hastily agreed arrangement and collected a weary, emotional Beatrice. Matron feared she might cause more disruption to the other girls by staying a day longer. The acerbic comments were not helpful; besides, they urgently needed the room. Another poor lass with a rounded pot belly clutching a small suitcase sat in the corridor looking wide-eyed and petrified. One in and one out. She wondered how much the girl's baby had cost?

For Beatrice, the place was how she'd imagined hell to be. She hid the baby clothes, out of sight of prying eyes. After the fiasco the previous day with that awful nurse. With the paperwork completed and signatures long dried, she seemed rather keen to leave. Rose and Melody came to say goodbye and one wanted to keep in touch as they swapped addresses. Beatrice didn't know Jack's full address, so wrote down her parents' instead.

She seated herself by the window in the reception area so she could spot Jack when he arrived. At five minutes past ten the doors flew open and in rushed Jack, cigarette hanging out of his mouth. The pair leant in towards one another in an awkward, clumsy embrace. Gosh, how he reeked, she thought. Without saying goodbye to the staff, the pair walked out of the main doors unchallenged. Jack helped her into the car and sped out through the gates. Clutching her stomach tightly, she suggested he might drive a little slower. As she glanced back for the last time, she saw Matron watching them at the window. For the next ten minutes, the pair travelled in silence. Jack eventually broke the impasse. His next comment spilled out without thinking.

"You had a boy, and chose the name we agreed on, yes?"

"Yes, Samuel." Beatrice nodded, staring blankly out of the car window, not feeling in the mood for an argument.

"But you knew I wanted to see him before he left. I told you that."

"They forbade me to call anyone, Jack, honestly. I'm so sorry." She choked back her tears. "Now he's gone and I'll never be able to find him again. Harry has made sure of that. Well, at least they gave him his own baby number – No. 3-733480. That's all we've got, Jack. Here, I wrote it down on this piece of paper." Jack stared at the road ahead, his face stony. "A number is no good, Beatrice. We need a name, a proper name."

Harry and Flo

Rosina went to the confessional box early that day. Father Patrick sat behind the screen, which had given her hope that God would answer her prayers. Hoping that the conversation with her parents would be a reasonable one, and already knowing the answer. Her prayers had recently gone unanswered, and she'd asked Father Patrick why that might be? He had reassured her that her faith had been tested for a reason, and advised her to keep on with her daily prayers; asking the Lord for further guidance. Rosina was unsure how to interpret the priest's instructions and left feeling more confused than uplifted. She was dreading returning home.

She felt she had done her duty in terms of finding Jack. But her next task was going to be more unpleasant whichever way she presented it. She'd already told Harry not to go and collect Beatrice and that she would explain after her confessional. When she arrived home, he was standing by the back door. Quickly, she ushered her mother into the kitchen, patted the chair and told her to sit down. Flo did as she was told and listened intently, her face fixed in a scowl as Rosina explained the new situation. The conversation started well, but quickly went downhill. Flo chose that moment to spill out months of pent-up feelings about the loss of Beatrice and the baby. Harry had joined them and sat in silence, his stony face twitching and fiddling with something in his trouser pocket.

Still sniffling, Flo uttered, "Does she not think I haven't wept every day about losing my only grandchild to the hands of a strange family? And I am likely never to set eyes on him again. And now you tell me that my youngest daughter will not be returning to her family home either? Where's she going to live?" she asked.

During the conversation that ensued, Rosina felt sick to her stomach. She had been sworn to secrecy, so Flo asked her again where she was going to live. The sight of her mother in such a distressed state made Rosina let slip the plan. Beatrice would go to live with Jack! There, she had uttered those fateful words, thinking the house would soon be empty of her offspring and realising the possibility of never seeing Beatrice again! She had nothing to lose, so blurted out the words her mother didn't want to hear. She sighed loudly and readied herself for the explosion about to follow. Experience told her what was coming next.

"No, no, no, over my dead body she will," screamed Flo and flung her dishcloth down in the sink full of washing up. The bubbles splattered her new blouse. "I'll not have a daughter of mine living in sin."

She paused while her mother stormed off to find Harry, who had slipped away to the living room out of the maelstrom. Why should she always have to clear up her sister's mess? Flo turned and directed her anger at Harry, waving her arms about.

"Now look at what's happened. Your idea should have made our life easier. Now it's all a terrible mess." Not normally stuck for words. He glanced up at his wife, a look of resignation on his face. Fearing to interject now, he remained mute. Leaning forward, he turned off the radio and placed his folded paper on the coffee table. Once Flo had reached the end of her rant, he spoke calmly and directly, taking her gently by the shoulders.

"What do you want me to do, Flo? If that's what she wants to do, who are we to stop her? Besides, if she continues with that lad, Jack, I want nothing more to do with her. She will have to marry him and be done with it."

"You don't mean that, Harry Hamilton. You and Father O'Flynn have got us into this dreadful mess, so you better find us a way out of it. Do you hear me?"

If he was honest, he couldn't see the current nightmare ever ending either, but would not admit it to his wife. Harry had decided. He would never pursue Beatrice or deign to beg her forgiveness. He believed his decision had been in the best interests of the young mother and her baby. Both father and daughter had a familiar stubborn streak, never liking to admit they were in the wrong. He continued to gaze out of the window as if looking for some divine inspiration, indulging his wife with the opportunity to get it all off her chest. He believed that shouting and gesticulating would not achieve anything. When she'd reached the end, Flo flounced off upstairs to the sanctuary of her bedroom for a lie-down. All her outpourings had given her a bad head.

They served tea late at past six o'clock, with the tense atmosphere failing to improve once they'd eaten. Their appetites somewhat diminished after all the drama. Rosina thought the sooner she left for the Philippines, the better. They were driving her crazy. The family troubles were taking its toll on her own emotional health. Everywhere she turned, she found chaos and unhappiness, with Beatrice at the core.

The following morning, Flo and Rosina set off to church together. Rosina had been hoping to find Father Patrick again, but first needed to catch up with Father O'Flynn. He had her liner ticket with a leaving date for her passage to Manila. Flo entered a confessional box first, seeking solace from Father O'Flynn. Father Patrick in the next box expressed concern that Rosina had returned to confession so soon. She confessed that her family unit had imploded with everything ruined. This time with a bit more added drama. Unusually, she sniffled through the screen, twisting her rosary beads round her fingers as she asked Father Patrick to turn the clock back. The new priest frowned and began another prayer. His own mind strayed to new areas of sin. He shook his head and, crossing himself, advised her to continue with her plans and have faith that God would answer her prayers. Clearing his throat as a hint that her time had run out. There were several other young ladies who had now joined the queue. Some had never set foot in a church. Word had spread across the tight-knit community about the dishy new priest with dark eyes and sideburns. Would Father Patrick absolve them of all their sins? Rosina remained sceptical. The two Hamilton women emerged from the confessional boxes at roughly the same time. They walked home in the familiar Consett drizzle, linking arms. Rosina had not wished to leave her mother on bad terms. She chose that moment to reiterate that she'd only been carrying out Beatrice's instructions. But the situation had turned the family into an argumentative, disparate group of adults, not the family she knew from twelve months ago when Albert and Beatrice were still living at home. She'd had reservations about the new set-up between her sister and Jack, and how long it would last? Was Jack wholly committed to Beatrice going forward? Rosina, knowing her sister so well, felt unsure it would work out long term. Jack seemed ill at ease when she met him outside the pub. He'd only stepped in at the last minute as a favour, after taking pity on Rosina, and had reiterated that the deal would only be a temporary arrangement. The baby was the only thing that the youngsters had in common, and it had been removed.

Eleven

Jack – 1967

As the car drew up outside the flat, Jack tried his best to explain about the set-up as he hadn't been living there long. They carried her suitcase up the steep flight of stairs, arriving at the battered green front door with no letterbox. Big Joe had not delivered on his promise of replacing the threadbare doormat. Jack apologised again after opening the front door and catching her face. Beatrice took a deep breath.

"Oh, yeah, sorry about the manky smell; you'll get used to it after a while. I bet you won't even notice it once we are inside." Beatrice begged to differ, and covered her nose and mouth with her scarf, trying hard not to retch. The set of her pursed lips was enough. She didn't want to appear ungrateful on the first day, but it smelt as though something had died in the kitchenette. Perhaps a mouse had curled up and surrendered its life to the smell under the sink. The greasy sink with a large tea-stain running across it sat full of old washing up. Jack had left it to grow mouldy and, besides, he thought Beatrice would like something to do when she arrived! The pungent scent of fried cooking oil lingered about in the kitchenette. Jack thought he had worked quite hard the previous evening to tidy up the mess about the place, putting away clothes and stuffing his dirty laundry out of sight under the bed. He disliked the launderette in town. They coloured your clothes without apology, so stopped using them. But, without a washing machine, he struggled. Despite his best efforts, the flat still resembled a war zone. Jack had never shared a room with anybody else for longer than a one-night stand. Mostly his type of visitors were gone by early morning. He'd hoped Beatrice wouldn't be overly fussy, as the place needed a woman's touch.

The pair had been on two dates, one involving a fumble on the sofa and a second to the warmth and security of the cinema. The first culminated in a baby nine months later, the second in a vanilla ice cream. This amounted to the time he'd spent with the girl. He didn't really know her at all. In fact, he felt unsure whether he liked her enough to share his bed. Already regretting his response the previous day to Rosina's request. Damn it, he should have stayed in the pub.

In the days that followed, Jack would disappear from the flat without saying where he was going. When he returned home, he had a guilty look on his face, and avoided eye contact with Beatrice. He went straight to sleep, often feigning exhaustion. Beatrice suspected he was hiding something from her, but hadn't concluded what.

From that first night in the flat, Beatrice made it clear to Jack that everything about the place seemed wrong. It started with her criticism of his paltry efforts at tidying up. She tried changing the furniture round to make it more homely, but that meant more areas of dust and mould became exposed. The black pattern had crept upwards behind the sofa and the lino flooring looked damp in the corner. Jack reminded her she needed to find herself some work, to pay her share of the rent.

Maybe she'd deluded herself that she'd been in love with him whilst away. She questioned whether she had actually missed him during her stay in France. Now, when she thought about the idea of them becoming a proper couple, she found they had not so much in common.

On the top floor of the same house lived a single mum, Marguerite, with two babies under a year old. She quickly became Beatrice's only real friend. She told Beatrice a story about her ex-partner who had disappeared, causing another scandal. So women can manage on their own? pondered Beatrice. At first she felt sympathy for Marguerite, a single parent with little financial support. She spent several hours in the flat upstairs, helping with the little ones. Marguerite would call upon her when she needed to run errands for formula milk or a loaf of bread. She would often hear the clattering of her high heels rushing around on the wooden floor upstairs. Marguerite would run from one baby to the other as she tried her best to pacify their fractious, hungry mouths. The girl would frequently appear at Jack's door asking for help with DIY, peering round the doorframe with her wide brown eyes.

So why had Jack not come clean about Marguerite from the beginning? She suspected that both the babies upstairs were actually his. Nobody knew the name of their father. Jack had been supporting them with some of his earnings. It helped ease her financial burden, paying a paltry sum towards nappies and formula milk.

"Oh my word," when it dawned on Beatrice that she may have made a dreadful mistake as the penny dropped. So that may be why Jack did not want to commit to any more children, and why he freaked out when she told him about her own pregnancy. When she visited Marguerite upstairs, she'd spotted the photograph on the sideboard of a small infant in a crib with looks identical to Jack's. Of course, what a perfect arrangement.

He had two women under one roof, with plenty of sex on tap. He even boasted about it down at the pub. A male fantasy, of course, and not reality with Beatrice.

Months later, more problems emerged, partly caused by the lack of income and partly by Jack's wayward behaviour. Beatrice had been into town looking for work, but returned yet again, defeated. The sole job available was cleaning toilets for a group of men in an office block. Just the wolf-whistling put her off as she looked around. The manager had offered her the post to start straight away, but she'd declined and left quickly by the rear entrance. She concentrated on cleaning and cooking and trying to keep a watchful eye on Jack. His lifestyle had turned into a heady mixture of smoking, drinking and staying out till all hours. Lately, if she were being honest, it had grated on her. She foolishly relayed her woes to Marguerite, who, though sympathetic, had advised her to persevere. Besides, she added, Jack had been the only constant in her life. He provided her with stability and a roof over her head, so why would she contemplate giving him up? She should be more grateful.

Beatrice wondered if her new friend might be right and tried to rationalise her thoughts. She felt guilty talking about Jack to Marguerite, but had nobody else to confide in. Did she not realise that Beatrice knew about the affair? Secretly, she'd hoped Marguerite might confess, as this would give Beatrice a valid reason for leaving Jack. In time, she gave up trying, as it only added to her confusion. Jack spoke so highly of Marguerite, and how spotlessly she kept her flat. Beatrice felt guilty and thought she should try harder and be more like her new friend. Though, when she had last visited the flat, she saw the effect of the damp and it did not appear as tidy or clean as the one downstairs.

Maybe she should attempt to dress like her too, if Jack liked that style. She asked Marguerite if she could borrow something to wear for a night out. What she gave her varied from her usual style, but she felt determined to squeeze herself into it. Beatrice's first reaction was she thought it looked tarty. The magazines she borrowed from upstairs were showing women of her age dressed in vibrant colours, not frumpy brown linen. It was the late Sixties. The latest fashionable hairstyles were shorter and piled high, some resembling the latest beehive look. Beatrice had squashed her hair flat and stuck it down at the side with her grannie's hair grips. The plan to dress up for Jack backfired. The couple had agreed to go for the night out and Beatrice thought she would try to squeeze into the dress and do her make-up, desperate to make a point to Jack that she could be sexy and voluptuous if she only put her mind to it. At Beatrice's insistence, Marguerite had lent her the dress with the plunging neckline.

The embroidered shawl woven in a coarse black thread belonged to Rosina. Jack looked her up and down and asked where the dress had come from. He thought it looked familiar. As he moved forward to inspect it, he picked at the fabric on her hip. It looked out of shape on Beatrice's slender body and needed the voluptuous figure of Marguerite to fill it in just the right places. Beatrice had tried stuffing the top half with a pair of Jack's socks to make her appear more well-endowed. But the socks just made the dress look lumpy. Frustrated, she'd flung them down and drawn the surrounding shawl to cover her flat chest. Her borrowed shoes were slingback heels in burgundy velvet, not her usual style of shoe. She still felt frumpy, and even more dejected. They went to join Jack's friends at the pub. The group in the corner lowered their voices when the pair walked in. Jack saw their faces. He tried not to let it spoil their evening, though he knew what his friends had been thinking! After several rounds, they moved on to another pub, as Jack couldn't stand the atmosphere. The night out ended with Beatrice suffering blisters on her heels from the ill-fitting shoes and Jack drinking heavily to drown his sorrows and embarrassment.

After the dress incident, the more intimate conversations between the two women cooled. They lacked any spontaneity as before. Beatrice returned the dress to its owner, saddened and deflated. Jack had been distant too, his loyalties divided. His life had become too complicated, managing two starkly different women who lived in the same building. He needed to decide what to do, as things could not continue.

One evening, his affair nearly became public knowledge. Jack and Marguerite were in town standing round the back of the bus station, just before heading home. Locked in a passionate kissing embrace, out of the corner of his eye Jack spotted Harry Hamilton cycling towards them. Surely he would have seen them with their faces and lips locked together? Pulling up the collar of his coat, he buried his head in Marguerite's long auburn tresses. After a minute, they pulled apart and split up to make their way back to the flats. Jack came in whistling a merry tune, his coat smelling vaguely of hairspray. Beatrice, curled up in a chair, briefly looked up and continued reading her book. Jack went straight to the bathroom, this time she followed him. The reflection in the mirror showed his mouth tainted red across his top lip.

"Have you cut yourself? Your lip looks red; here, let me wipe it for you." He pushed her arm away and grabbed some toilet paper to wipe the remnants of Marguerite's lipstick off his lips.

"Where have you been all evening?"

"Nowhere."

"Gosh, you reek of hairspray, Jack. "Do I? Must have been the girls in the pub. They are always spraying it about."

"You must think I'm stupid?" Glowering at him.

Beatrice got herself ready for bed, but that night Jack didn't come to bed. He slept in the armchair under a blanket.

For Jack, the constant complaining niggles were grating. Commenting on the aftereffects of his smoky breath on her skin. It impregnated the bedclothes, she told him. She had already stated that she did not enjoy going out with her hair and clothes smelling of smoke. But all her pleas for him to smoke outside went ignored. Sometimes he deliberately lit up in the bed or in the bathroom whilst using the toilet.

One evening they were lying under the bed covers trying to keep warm. They had no money until the end of the week to pay for the electric meter. The atmosphere between them had turned as frosty as the inside of the bedroom window.

"What's the matter, Bea? Don't you fancy me no more?" he asked. After she'd pushed him away for the second time in a week, when he tried to get lucky with a quickie under the blankets, on the premise they were trying to keep warm. Beatrice exploded.

"Are you bloody crazy? The nurse told me I'm not meant to 'do it' for at least six weeks or more after having the baby. Besides, I have not had my checkup at the clinic yet. Those rubber things from your barber's shop are dodgy, Jack. You need to throw them out. We don't want another one and end up like her upstairs." And she raised her eyebrows to the ceiling. Right on cue, a baby's wailing began, which did not help with her own baby separation issues. "Anyway, I've already lost one, and I'm not giving up another." Jack thought about the last comment for a minute. Was this the right moment to tell her?

"S'pose not," he grumbled selfishly, wrapping himself in the blanket. He looked across the room with a painful look of guilt.

"Anyway, just so you know, I don't feel so close as we were

before," she continued. This time, she turned away to face the bare wall.

"Well, that's a turnaround," swaggered Jack. "You needed my help a few weeks back. You should remember who gave you a place to stay when you had no other options. Remember who fed you? Remember who came to your rescue?" He threw back the covers and dressed before launching his cruellest parting shot. "Oh, yeah, did you get rid of that dress hanging on the wardrobe door? It doesn't suit you. You don't have the figure for it now."

If he had been an inch closer, she would have slapped him hard. She didn't want to see his face; it only added to her distress. Those last few words stung. But she forced herself to turn around to watch him, as he pulled on his trousers, and tied his shoelaces slowly in a double bow. The scars on his back looked deeper than she remembered, as she hadn't seen him fully naked for some time.

"Now, where are you going?"

"Out," shot back the reply.

"Why? What for? It's late, Jack, past nine o'clock." He chose not to answer. Sorely tempted to follow him, she changed her mind. Outside the weather had turned, and, besides, she had just got her feet warm, despite wearing bed socks. The door to the flat slammed, but the footsteps on the stairs seemed to go upwards instead of down, in the wrong direction. She stood by the front door and strained to listen to the muffled sounds coming from upstairs. Marguerite was talking on the landing, but to whom at such a late hour?

The recent conversation with Harry, Jack had kept a secret from Beatrice. He chose not to reveal that her father had been round and threatened him, and coerced him with false promises of finding them a proper home if they tied the knot. Jack would never routinely accept guidance from others. The following day, he suggested they take the bus into town. On the bus he let slip to Beatrice about his wild idea as if it were his own. They should marry and use the same ring as before to save on money. He'd hidden it deep in his pocket, but he needed to persuade her to accept the crazy idea as his own.

They might just about afford it, as he had borrowed another couple of quid. When they reached the jeweller's shop, Beatrice stood outside, saying, "No, you don't understand. I don't want to marry you, Jack Gardiner, no, I really don't." Had he not listened? She had been telling him since her arrival at the flat that marriage was not an option. First, she did not feel ready for that sort of commitment. Second, she did not trust him. At Jack's persistence, dragging her by the wrist, they went inside. He flashed the wad of borrowed money under her nose. She panicked, still unsure. But Jack, tenacious in his quest, wanted the initials J & B inscribed, effectuated by the jewellery engraver, who asked no questions, and just took his money. The ring, though not expensive, was pretty. A memento of what they had created together, soon to be a symbol of their wedding day. Beatrice frowned, deep in concentration, staring at the floor, evading the jeweller's penetrating stare. Too late, the jeweller had spotted his own engraving: a simple birth date on the inside of the gold band. Jack asked for a second inscription, a wedding date. Would anyone notice the significance of having two inscriptions on the gold band? What the heck? He'd not thought about the consequences. Was he ready to get married and settle down? His relationship with Marguerite was about to be forced out into the open. He might end up losing both women through his own pride and stupidity.

The jeweller disappeared behind a door. The pair stood awkwardly, trying not to look at each other in the mirrors. Beatrice nearly died of embarrassment, convincing herself that the jeweller had worked out her guilty secret. When he reappeared he had the velvet-lined box in his large, pudgy hands and a wry smile. He handed over the small silver bag bearing the name of the shop. Hoping there would be no further questions, they thanked the jeweller for his speedy efforts, and scurried out onto the street.

"Did you see his smirk?" whispered Jack.

"Yeah, he gave me the creeps. Do you think he remembered us from last time?" Beatrice pulled her woollen scarf tightly around her neck, claiming the moisture on her cheeks had been from the windchill, as she brushed his hand away. They turned to walk along in step.

The jeweller, a shrewd man, had been curious whether his keen observations would make a decent story for the local *Evening Echo*. Some people commanded a high price for that sort of material, but… he would have to live with his conscience. He'd assumed that a domestic misfortune had caught the Hamiltons, a staunch Catholic family from Consett, out. With the potential to become a town scandal, had the jeweller from Granville's got the nerve to sell his story? Believing he might make some money, he took it to the local paper. Sitting before the chief editor, he repeated the finer details and juicier story to write about in tomorrow's edition. The editor failed to grasp the excitement of the story in the same way. He left without the large cheque he had been expecting. To his disgust, they didn't print it. The editor contacted the local priest, Father O'Flynn, and asked him if he would verify the alleged story. Father O'Flynn slammed down the phone, the editor's hastily scribbled notes discarded in the rubbish bin. He would mention nothing more to either party. The jeweller thought the editor had made a serious mistake and missed a grand chance to increase the paper's readership.

Months later, the rift between Beatrice and her father had still not healed. She had not seen him since he dropped her off at the Elswick Unit. Communications had reached an impasse. Flo, always keen to hear her news, felt trapped, unable to reach out. Beatrice hoped she would never have the misfortune to bump into Father O'Flynn again or she might slap him hard across his florid cheek. The priest had made many errors of judgement, exacerbated further by the discovery of transferring monies for the babies at Elswick.

Jack had kidded himself that he enjoyed having a woman around the place, but he remained unsure he'd picked the right one, despite the ring fiasco. Overlooking the fact that his flat looked tidy, she had cooked all his meals properly. This suited his tardiness. Even the smell in the kitchenette had dissipated after Beatrice swept out the decayed mouse and a rotten green potato from beneath the sink. Yes, he thought she was handy in the domestic department, and he had high hopes she would improve in the bedroom. He wondered how she would respond to some pictures in one of his dirty magazines from the barber's shop. They were in a stash under the bed.

So, despite the mounting debts, the marriage would go ahead. In desperation, Beatrice turned to her only friend, Marguerite, to borrow a dress for her nuptials. But this time she found her friend not so helpful, with a sudden change of heart. That day, she'd pleaded for her *not* to marry Jack. Why the unforeseen change in her feelings? Beatrice left her flat more confused. Marguerite explained she had known him far longer than Beatrice and, in hindsight, she thought they were not so compatible. As a result, Beatrice found herself in a state of flux.

Just when she thought their troubles were over, Harry had come up with the second part of his plan: marriage. Beatrice's parents were about to force it upon them, whether Jack was the most suitable man for their daughter or not, after Harry's visit, which had scared him to a point where he felt he had to agree. The Hamiltons were keen to avoid any local scandal that might bring further shame upon the family. Beatrice questioned whether they were the same parents that had brought her up. They had changed beyond all doubt. Were they the ones who had banished her to France? To her dismay, she found she no longer understood them. In fact, she questioned her love for her father at all. Her dreams for the future did not lie in Consett. Her only option was to flee, and staying with Jack was just a temporary solution. He must not influence her, she told herself. She must remain strong and make her own decisions without being influenced by anyone, including Jack. From this point, she was determined she would remain in control of her life.

They posted the wedding banns outside the registry office. As Beatrice was under twenty-one, it allowed time for any objections to be aired. Jack had been along and paid the fee, despite all the anxieties and negativity that surrounded them. The wedding would go ahead with Big Joe and Rosina as witnesses. With no particular theme for the wedding, the sisters plumped for blue for the cake decorations. Rosina protested at first but relented once Beatrice asked her to be the maid of honour. She'd volunteered to make the bride's bouquet using blooms from Harry's garden despite them remaining uninvited to the wedding. The couple had one ring between them already inscribed for the bride. The small wedding group was to gather at five minutes to two at the doors to the registry. Beatrice never got to hear that her father had threatened Jack, a snippet he had still withheld from her.

The sisters had been at the flat all morning, getting ready. Beatrice had dug out her best frumpy frock and plain brown shoes. She'd smoothed her unruly hair down and painted her lips bright red. The cake, a home-made Victoria sponge, was decorated with blue iced roses, and a blue ribbon tied in a bow attached around the edge. They made their way to the registry office, hoping that Jack would be there waiting to greet them at the door. But Jack had gone AWOL first thing that morning and left without his wedding suit. They could only second guess where he'd gone. By the time he'd arrived at the registry office, he was half cut, dressed still in a casual pair of trousers and an old tatty jacket, the shirt untucked, open at the neck and missing a tie. Beatrice stuck a flower from her posy in his top pocket. That would have to do. The service began and by the time the registrar uttered the infamous words, signalling that Jack may kiss the bride, in his haste, he missed Beatrice's mouth, smudging her lipstick across her cheek. She grabbed at his elbow to avoid him falling over. His drunken eyes looked her up and down and almost laughed in her face. Rosina stepped forward to help hold him upright as he tried to kiss her on the lips too. The sisters escorted him to the pub and gave him a black coffee and a large glass of water.

"You're a bloomin' idiot, Jack; you need to sober up and quickly," Rosina told him.

"Why should I?" he burbled. "I've just got married. Don't spoil my fun. I wish I'd married you instead, Rosy, I think I love you." He lunged at her chest.

"The only thing you love, Jack Gardiner, is yourself. You are a useless bag of shite." Then she blushed as she was unused to using vulgar language. She was more furious with him for spoiling Beatrice's special day. If the reservations were true, he'd certainly confirmed them by his foolhardy actions.

The pub had agreed to put on the smallest reception party for six to include Marguerite, at Jack's insistence. Beatrice tried hard to remember if Jack had smiled at her during the day. Big Joe stood up and raised his glass as he proposed a toast. Jack held up a glass of water, thinking it was whisky. He took a long gulp and spat it out over the table and down his trousers. Beatrice looked at him aghast and instantly regretted all of it, the whole sorry spectacle.

Despite his alcoholic haze, Jack seemed preoccupied and gave most of his attention to others around him and not to Beatrice. By nine o'clock, he could no longer stand up. Someone at the bar had been buying him yet more whisky. Marguerite exited quickly, after spotting Beatrice heading her way with her infamous scowly face. They had not invited Harry and Flo to join in the celebration at Jack's request. He had nothing more to say to his new father-in-law and feared his quick temper would flare when combined with too much drink.

To finish the sorry miserable event, when they returned to the flat, the wedding nuptials failed to happen. Jack had ended the day far too drunk and dribbling down his best shirt. Somehow, Beatrice managed to half carry him up the stairs to the flat, landing him with a thump on the sofa before he passed out cold. She removed his jacket with the limp solitary flower still attached, tossing it aside in the kitchen bin, then propped him up before she curled up alone in their bed. The slices of wedding cake still wrapped in serviettes stood on the side, she felt saddened about the whole sorrowful day, still unable to cry.

Jack awoke in the early hours feeling disorientated, and nursing a thumping head, his eyeballs felt as though they were pirouetting in their sockets. It took him a moment to recognise his surroundings. The chill overnight had penetrated his bones before he realised the blanket had fallen on the floor and his trousers were soaked in urine. The air around him smelt rank. A heady mixture followed him in a vapour trail towards the bathroom. He attempted to run a bath, but when the water ran cold he changed his mind. He wanted to clean himself up and change his clothes before nausea set in, then he crawled back into his bed, puzzled as to where his new wife had got to. They'd been married for less than twenty-four hours. He wanted to congratulate her in person, but the flat remained quiet. Beatrice had taken herself off for a walk. She'd met Rosina to clear her head, which felt fit to bursting with ideas. She thought maybe talking to her sister would help calm her down. The sisters walked around the leafy park arm in arm. The conversation easily led back to Jack and what he had or hadn't done. Beatrice, in full flow, remonstrating with her arms in frustration, hadn't noticed the frown growing on her sister's face.

"What have I done, Rosy? Jack doesn't love me; he loves someone else." Rosina tried to speak but couldn't get a word in. "I didn't want to marry him in the first place, but he forced me, do you hear me? He forced me," she wailed. Rosina cocked her head to one side as if she were thinking of a plan. Still, Beatrice rambled until her sister lost interest and stared vacantly at the path ahead.

"Are you even listening to me, Rosy?"

"Yes, of course I am. Look, I think I may have the answer." The sisters continued their conversation for a further few yards before arriving back at the gates. Beatrice was in no hurry to return home to the flat. Rosina planned to go to Mass and find Father Patrick to offload her own troubles.

$\sim\sim$

Jack

What the heck had he done? Had he really tied the knot the previous day? It all remained a blur to Jack. Why had he given in to Harry's demands? His brain would not function correctly. The alcoholic haze muddled his thoughts. Marriage to Beatrice would mean an end to his bachelor's lifestyle. It would mean an end to his affair with Marguerite, who he'd also promised to marry the previous year. She had always been there in the background. He had fathered at least one of her babies, hadn't he? Jack had always denied it, but this time Marguerite insisted. The gulf between the two women had widened. Marguerite had kept her baby close to her on the understanding that Jack supported it, whereas Beatrice had to give hers up. His thoughts had all come too late.

When his stomach finished its lurching, and hunger took over, Jack went out. Knowing his dad would be at work, he wanted to tell his mother what they'd done, knowing she would be upset if she found out from anyone else. No surprise to find his mother already knew! He'd taken a slice of wedding cake round as a peace offering.

"Got any bread, Mother? I'm starving." Rummaging in her larder, he found a cob loaf and sliced off the crust. Spreading it with beef lard, he crammed it into his mouth whilst listening. He found her flat in spirit, showing little or no emotion at his news. She placed the cake in the larder, tucking it out of sight. They exchanged a look, with no spoken words. Jack broke the silence. He felt obliged to ask the obvious question. Wiping a splurge of fat from his chin.

"Dad isn't hitting you, is he?"

"No, no, it's nothing like that," brushing his question aside but avoiding his eyes.

"What's the matter? What are you hiding from me? I know something is amiss."

"Your father went to pay Harry Hamilton a visit last night and has not returned home. He found out about his threats."

"What time did he go out?"

"At seven o'clock. I've been awake all night worried sick, listening for the front door."

His dad had heard about the wedding and gone to make his point to Harry Hamilton. In his current frame of mind, he would be unlikely to be able to control himself and back down from any physical argument.

"Don't worry, I'll find him. He probably lost track of time and ended up in the pub or, worst case, drove himself into a ditch in a drunken state."

"Perhaps he slept in the car." He was making light of it as by his mother's face she looked clearly worried.

"He's been gone all night, though, Jack." Her voice wobbled with distress.

Jack left his mother to her dour thoughts, setting off on his father's ancient push bike to locate him. It didn't take him long. Parked further up the street outside the Hamilton's house looked like the answer to his mother's worries. The windows were steamed up from the cool air trapped inside the car. Jack banged his fist on the window. He could just about make out the figure inside. His father lay curled up asleep on the back seat under his overcoat, his bruised knuckles hidden from view.

"Oi. Wakey, wakey." He hammered on the window and waited a few seconds until the body moved. A mop of grey, ruffled hair sat up, blurry-eyed, disorientated. Once Jack knew the old goat was alive and moving about, he nicked his bike and set off for work. He felt a tad guilty that he didn't return home to let his mother know the good news.

∿

Marguerite

Six months later, with the tensions between Jack and Beatrice unresolved, Beatrice had decided and reached her own conclusion. Marguerite's opinion proved to be right; she and Jack should not have tied the knot. It all came to a head after Beatrice had seen two tickets for a theatre show, which mysteriously disappeared from the kitchen drawer. She knew what she had seen and in a frenzied state tipped the contents all over the kitchen floor to prove to herself the tickets were real and not just a figment of her imagination. But they'd vanished. Had he returned to seeing Marguerite so soon after marrying her and promising the affair had ended? Had he bought the tickets to share with her and she had ruined the surprise, or were they to share with somebody different?

For now, she had more important things to consider. Wisely, she had noted the date and time of the show and prepared herself to be proved wrong. As the day approached, she checked and rechecked the kitchen drawer in case they reappeared. Had her hunch been correct? Beatrice doubted Jack. Her self-esteem and inner doubt sank her mood to a new low. Had Marguerite, the one person she'd trusted and confided in since moving to the flat, been seeing Jack on the sly? She would have to confront him.

The day before the theatre show, Marguerite asked Beatrice to babysit, and for the first time she lied, saying she felt unwell and was coming down with a heavy cold. She took to her bed to keep to the fabricated story, already noting that Jack seemed to have spent more time in the bathroom preening himself that night. The overpowering smell of aftershave sealed his fate. He seldom wore it on the few occasions he took Beatrice out. Her heart told her she had found "the other woman". Early that evening, Beatrice casually asked him, "So, did Marguerite find herself a babysitter for tonight?"

"Yes, that woman from the Coop agreed to help her out. The poor girl deserves a night out."

"What makes you say that?" asked Beatrice.

"Why did you say no when she asked for your help?" He had taken no notice of Beatrice's excuse for not babysitting or enquired how she was feeling.

"What did you say?"

"Oh nothing. Gotta go. Don't wait up; I won't be late." Jack fled the flat as fast as he could, with no enquiry about the state of Beatrice's health, and the last comment ringing in her ears.

Beatrice lay in bed, silently weeping. She didn't want to get up and feed herself. She felt so stupid. Why, oh why, had she agreed to marry him? Marguerite had never been the right person to turn to for advice on relationships. She felt trapped. It seemed the sensible solution when she had no roof over her head, emotionally withdrawn after having the baby and unable to give Jack what he needed. They were unsuited. In the beginning, she'd tried to find some positive comments about what she found attractive about him. His looks were quite dishy. The cheeky grin exposed a set of perfectly aligned teeth despite his nightly tooth-grinding habit, although she noticed the teeth were more tarnished because of his heavy smoking habit.

Marguerite had agreed with everything she shared, and of course, now she understood why. Her friend's opinion had swung like a pendulum, from encouraging Beatrice to leave him to in the next breath coaxing her to marry him. She knew his trips upstairs were for another reason. She had been such a naïve fool while her guard was down and spirits low.

Jack failed to understand her mood swings. When he

arrived home after work, he felt tentative about how she would behave. Would she be happy or miserable? If she were miserable, he knew there would be no cheering her up by offers of going to the pub or out for fish and chips at the cafe. They would end up having a row and Jack would storm out. If she was happy, a rarity, he would suggest the cinema. Beatrice rarely questioned him as to his whereabouts in the evenings when he "popped out" to do a last-minute but urgent errand. Frequently, she found herself alone in the flat, looking at the same four damp walls that seemed to close in on her, suffocating her mind. Perhaps she should make more of an effort. She realised how little she really knew about her husband, knowing nothing more than he ran errands for a man called Big Joe. She bore a deep reluctance to interact with his friends, who hung around in the public bar of the local pub. In her head she'd made the case to leave, practising her goodbye speech many times over. Beatrice continued planning her exit plan. In her mind, she had planned it by having the conversation with Jack in one of three ways. The first one would boldly start with:

"Jack, we're just not compatible."

The second she would get straight to the point:

"I'm leaving you, Jack. I know you've met someone else."

The third was much stronger and far more direct:

"Jack, I'm leaving you and I want a divorce. I have the grounds for it, you know."

Divorce was such a dirty word in the Fifties. People spoke about it in hushed tones. She told herself to be brave. Repeating it out loud in advance might have helped for a smoother transition and speedier exit. But she didn't feel like sharing much with "you know who" upstairs, so never got to practise her exit speech. Marguerite had not been as lonely as she made out. Frequently, she still popped down to their flat with an excuse about something she needed or wanted to borrow. Beatrice resorted to saying Jack was out, even if he was at home. Distrust had raised its ugly head and Beatrice had had enough. After days of agonising with her decision made, she plumped for option three.

Restless since the early hours, exit day had arrived and first she set about cleaning the flat. It helped take her mind off what she had to do. Her fingers were red raw and her lower back ached. You'd never have guessed that she had given birth a few weeks before. Her body had rapidly returned to its previous shape. The stomach looked flatter, but perhaps that was because of the lack of nourishment. Her possessions lay discreetly hidden out of sight. She paced up and down, wondering if she had the nerve to carry it through. What would happen if he didn't return? Would she just leave without saying goodbye?

Her last task: to hide the wedding ring in its box, but the sound of the key in the lock interrupted her packing. Heck, Jack had returned early, so she quickly wrapped the ring box in a small hand towel and stuffed it into the back sleeve of her suitcase. There would be no further discussion about the ring. She would keep it and one day pass it on to Samuel. She planned to deceive Jack by telling him that the ring was lost if he asked about it.

Jack had arrived home in a jolly frame of mind, expecting his food to be ready. He'd already been downing a few pints at the pub and as he entered the flat the post-beer whistling ceased. The atmosphere chilled. Jack realised something was afoot. Looking around, he couldn't see his tea on the table. Checking the kitchenette, he saw it out on the side, unprepared. The flat looked too tidy; it smelt of cleaning products. Beatrice, hovering behind the door in the bedroom, was about to leave. "*Be strong, now; there's no going back,*" she told herself, but her body trembled. Taking a deep breath, she stepped through the door and the pair came face to face. Before he had time to ask the first question, she blurted, "Jack I'm leaving you. I know about your affair with her upstairs, and the baby, and I want a divorce on the grounds of adultery." The woman's name stuck fast in her throat. She couldn't bear to say it out loud. She finished her brief speech and witnessed the colour drain from his cheeks. His eyes narrowed, staring at her in disbelief. She expected a different reaction, but he just stood there looking at her with a look of horror. The words had come as a shock. He'd no idea that she felt that way. Overwhelmed by a sudden rush of guilt, Beatrice gathered up her bags. Jack, with nothing to say, watched slowly as his new bride disappeared through the door, shutting it behind her. Breathe, Beatrice, breathe, don't look back. She'd done it! As she fled down the stairs she became conscious of the outline of a figure above her head, straining forward over the bannisters. The shadow darted back and she knew immediately who it was, but didn't bother to look up.

"He's all yours now, you vixen, and there's me thinking you were a friend. You're nothing but a devious cow," she shouted up the stairwell. Silence came from the upper landing as she heard the flat door shut quietly. In her haste to leave, she'd forgotten to tell Jack about her letter. He had gone straight to the bedroom and howled into his eiderdown, such was his emotional immaturity. In Beatrice's eyes, the couple were free and would no longer have to lock themselves together as a symbol of their unhappy union. "It came like a punch in the guts" is how Jack described the feeling to Big Joe later that night, whilst drowning his sorrows in the bottom of a pint glass. He'd been unprepared for her bombshell.

Dear Jack,

I realise in the last few months how little we know each other and how little we have in common apart from our baby Samuel. I no longer feel the romantic love for you I did before. Our connection has faded somewhat over recent months. Allowing it to continue is unfair to us both. I will always cherish the brief time we were together, enough to create our baby. You also know that our friendship has reached a natural conclusion since I discovered the affair between you and Marguerite had begun before we met. This has made my decision to leave you somewhat easier. I also heard that you had fathered another baby! How you can love two women simultaneously is hard for me to comprehend. I think I was in love with the fantasy of loving you and that means that I cannot love you as I know I should. Perhaps I never really loved you, and maybe it was little Samuel that bound us together and not true love. You will be much happier without me, Jack. I intend to make a fresh start and move to the south coast, where I intend to find work in a local school or maybe another children's home. I wish you luck, Jack, in whatever you choose to do next. Please say goodbye to her upstairs and her babies. I had no issue with her two little ones.

Best wishes,
Beatrice.

Jack

Jack didn't find the crumpled letter until a couple of days later, stuffed under his pillow. Scratching around for his cigarettes, he found it by accident. At first, he studied it with the palm of his hand. Turning it over and over with his fingers, he laid it back on the table. An hour later, he returned to it and this time ripped it open. The words were neatly written on pale blue notepaper. He knew that type had been her favourite. He tried to recall its name. Yes, he remembered now: Basildon Bond, with the faint lines to aid neatness. That's how Beatrice had explained it to him every time he asked why she bothered to write letters that nobody would read. Jack had developed a poor scrawly style of handwriting, and never had the patience to write letters himself. Words had given him trouble early on, after an impoverished exposure to books in his childhood. He sniffed it, inhaling faint traces of floral cologne. He'd read it over again until he knew the words by heart. The faded ink smudged by the time he'd finished and tears fell amongst the words. The letter lay crumpled on the bedroom floor among the detritus.

Twelve

The Rescue – 1968

The skies were leaden, stygian. The rain was of pebbles, the weather for May had been atrocious. It had not stopped for three consecutive days. The grounds in the local parks were sodden. Running rivulets of rainwater poured down the car windows and left windscreen wipers struggling to clear the deluge.

Beatrice, devoid of any visible emotion, assumed a deadpan face as she stepped through the main door away from the flats and crossed the road to take shelter from the rain. Rosina had pulled up opposite. She spotted Beatrice under the trees. How long had she'd been standing there? Her coat looked saturated, the trees offering her little protection. Shocked at the state of her sister's appearance, with hollow cheeks that made her skin look paler than normal. Her hair, normally neatly coiffured, was plastered to the side of her head. Rosina thought she looked fragile, as she took the bags and placed them in the boot. She spread out the old family tartan blanket across Beatrice's scrawny legs. Her sister shivered violently because of the dampness and cold. Rosina had accepted the abrupt change of plan without question, as she whisked her away towards Dorset.

There were no words between them for the first part of their journey, just a mutual familial silence. With the deed completed, her nightmare marriage exit was over. An hour into the journey, she found her heartbeat had ceased its galloping and settled back into a normal rhythm. During the last few months, she had suffered a deep corrosion of her spirit, and lost the real Beatrice. Could she ever find herself again?

They stopped overnight at a modest bed and breakfast. It would be the last night the sisters would spend together. They had no inkling a torrent of sharp words between them would mar it. Their personal grievances had been simmering beneath the surface for some time. The argument should never have happened in such an explosive way. True, sibling tension often bubbles beneath the surface, erupting without warning but, here, this marked a change in temperament for the normally docile, biddable Rosina.

The sign for the bed and breakfast stood at the end of a long, tree-lined driveway. As they pulled up, the last of the rain had given way. The two women were soon drinking tea and eating warm buttered scones outside in the weakened sunshine. Rosina sat calmly, discussing how much she was looking forward to her new life in Manila. Her floral plate laid out with clotted cream and strawberry jam. The excitement about what lay ahead for her had been building for weeks.

Beatrice mumbled something rather sharp and out of turn, and before she knew it her sister erupted like a volcano. She started remonstrating with her arms. Beatrice told her to keep her voice down, so as not to upset the guests sitting at the other tables. Months of pent-up anguish and apprehension about what lay ahead, came tumbling out of Rosina's mouth. The tensions back at home had played its part.

"Do you know how much effort it has taken to get you here?"

"Yes, I know that, and I have already told you how much I appreciate it."

"You have not stopped and thanked me once, Beatrice."

"Well, I'm thanking you now. Is that not enough?"

"You have created a division in the family and brought shame on all of us, especially for Mother and Father." There, she'd finally spat it out. Beatrice looked at her sister, her mouth wide open.

"Why would you say such a thing? I repeat, do you realise your selfish act with Jack Gardiner has affected how many people?" The pair lowered their voices, but continued their disagreement. The scones on her plate were left untouched, with cream and jam piled high.

They retreated to their twin bedroom on the first floor. Beatrice slumped on the bed, the view looked out of the small window across the fields. She wept quietly. Because of her siblings' encouragement, she had gone out on that stupid date with Jack. But it felt much too late for that retort. How was she to know that a baby would be the outcome? The atmosphere in the bedroom suddenly felt stifling. She snatched her towel and wash bag and went to find the bathroom. Locking the door, she turned on the large bath taps. It filled quickly with hot water for a change. Beatrice lowered herself into the bubbles and allowed the water to fill to just below the brim. She submerged her body as low as she could physically bear the heat of the water, leaving just her nipples floating above the surface. It had an immediate calming effect on her mood. She took some more deep breaths. Now seemed the wrong time to do something stupid, like submerging yourself under the water and holding your breath. Her feelings suddenly overwhelmed her. No, she needed to put some space between them, and allow Rosina time to calm down.

Her sister had buried her feelings for many months. This made Beatrice feel doubly guilty. Had she taken her for granted all this time? She had been a little preoccupied during the last few months, but sometimes she found it impossible to view these things from the inside out. The sisters had always been close and done everything together. Now she had ruined it all, and just as Rosina was about to leave the country too. She stayed in the bath as long as she could before the water cooled and the skin on her fingers resembled pink wrinkled prunes.

By the time she returned to the bedroom, she had a rosy glow about her, and her crying had ceased. Rosina had already got into bed and turned out her light, lying with her back to the door, pretending to be asleep. It had been a long day, so Beatrice whispered goodnight and switched out her bedside light. She lay in the dark, feeling hot and wretched. How could she do that to Rosina? She was all she had left in terms of family, and now that was hanging by a tenuous thread. Her thoughts persisted in her dreams, and she woke up several times, conscious that she had been muttering gibberish in her sleep and her mouth bone dry.

A cockerel strutting about under their window abruptly awoke the sisters the next morning. They stayed in their room, warm under the bed covers, reading their books in silence until half past seven. Breakfast had already started in the dining room by the time they descended, so the two women joined the other diners. After twin poached eggs with the deepest yolks served on slivers of thin white toast and steaming cups of tea, the sisters' spirits felt buoyed once again. With their stomachs replete, both felt in a better frame of mind. They avoided any questions from their hosts, and Rosina settled the bill before they left.

The rugged Jurassic coast offered the perfect setting for Beatrice to recover from her recent personal traumas. The

Hamiltons had taken their annual summer holiday at the clifftop cottage near Swanage. Over the last few years, several family members had taken advantage of its healing atmosphere and therapeutic sea air. The cottage left to the family by Harry's brother, Wilfred, had been in the Hamilton family for the last three generations. Rosina held the title deeds and her intention had been to sign them over to Beatrice. She held one stipulation that they should not sell the cottage to anyone outside the family.

After unpacking the car, the pair were sitting on the terrace in the autumn sunshine. Neither wanted to make the first move. Beatrice tried her hardest to make simple conversation.

"I've had a brilliant idea. What if I follow you to Manila in, say, a couple of months?" She suggested she might work alongside the nuns, perhaps as a housekeeper. She knew, having had a pregnancy, that she would not be eligible to join a nunhood.

"What? No, absolutely not, Beatrice, that's a crazy idea." Rosina looked aghast, and rushed to explain. "For a start, you would not enjoy life in Manila. You would hate the heat, and the rich spicy food."

Rosina thought the last thing she needed would be an extra person to look after. No, this time she would stand firm with her sister. She'd wanted to find her own way in Manila without the encumbrances of a younger sibling. Before she left, she told Beatrice she would visit the solicitors and sign over the cottage to her, before she caught the boat out to Manila. The family curse seemed at large. Beatrice knew saying farewell to her sister would be doubly hard after their explosive argument the previous evening. Following the outburst, she'd tried her best to express her appreciation for all Rosina had done for her in recent months. But perhaps she had left the deeper sentiments a little late. When the sisters hugged goodbye, they found it difficult to let each other go. Had they restored the unspoken bond between them? Beatrice found the eyes of an optimist on her sister's face. Would she see her sister again? Rosina had already mentioned she thought it a high possibility she would not return to Consett.

"Promise me you won't forget to write, and send me your new address." Rosina nodded as she handed over the keys. As she turned and placed her coat and hat on the passenger seat, the sun was warm on her skin. Slowly she exhaled, relieved; finally free from her shackles, her duty was done.

"Goodbye, Bea," and she waved furiously until the car was out of sight. The cottage readied itself for a new chapter.

The new tenant at Ocean Cottage stood for a moment, slightly bewildered, examining her surroundings. First, she wiped her eyes before going inside to explore. She had plenty to do, but she had never lived alone, with only the experience of looking after the flat she'd shared with Jack until the previous day. For Beatrice, at last she felt a sense of freedom. It was the Sixties, after all, and the era of free love was flowing. But Beatrice was way behind the curve in terms of courtship mores. Other women felt liberated and started experimenting with the newly released contraceptive pill. She'd read all about it in the magazines at the clinic. Some had even burnt their bras in defiance of the establishment and what they believed to be discrimination against women. She'd been ill-equipped, too immature to handle the birth repercussions from her time with Jack.

Now she would concentrate on unpacking the cottage after months of closure. It had a musty smell that lifted a little after throwing open the windows. Despite the carefully placed sheets, a thin layer of dust had settled on all the furniture. She went to rummage around in the dilapidated lean-to shed and found an old push bike. Apart from the cobwebs, it looked in good nick. The pump still worked, and the air inflated the tyres. Tomorrow she would cycle into town for some essential groceries.

But first she needed to finish opening the windows and unpacking her cases. The only thing in the fridge was half a pint of milk in a bottle purchased from the B&B hosts earlier that day. The half loaf of bread, already going stale. To get to the nearest bus stop, you had to head down the zigzag lanes for a mile towards the village hall. The cycle would do her good and cost nothing. That first night she was homesick, but for what she was unsure. She had broken ties with her parents. She missed her friends back at Elswick. Rosina was the only person she had left in the world. Her mother didn't count. Beatrice felt so lonely she cried herself asleep. She kept stirring, afraid of the noises and gurgles of the strange house.

Builders had constructed Ocean Cottage in the Thirties, setting it back above the cliff tops with dry stone walls as borders surrounding the property. Someone had evenly placed layer upon layer of grey stone slabs. Rickety steel steps at the bottom of the garden led down to a private beach cove. The grass was covered in a blend of pink and white clover and daisies, resembling a carpet. They had laid the mature garden out with shrubs in abundance. Alliums, azaleas, rhododendrons would all be manageable after Beatrice visited the library to learn how to prune them. The cottage came with a small apple orchard, which apparently bore autumn fruit. A sprawling laburnum creeper, rich in colour, covered the back of the house.

The cottage interior had a square hallway with a bench to sit on and remove muddy or sandy beach shoes. The cosy living room had a centrepiece brick fireplace that housed a stout log-burning stove that left faint traces of wood smoke lingering in the air. At the front of the cottage, the bay windows curved gently, shielded by corduroy curtains in a deep turquoise colour. Rosina had found them years ago in a church bazaar. Opposite the window stood a black onyx rectangular coffee table. A large three-seater chesterfield sofa had little support left in its voluminous cushions, all showing signs of wear with shredded piping around the edges. In the living room, there was only one armchair in the corner, which used to belong to their grandfather. The girls had recalled him sitting there and smoking his roll-ups. The daily changes to the panoramic view out on the water were magnificent.

They had simply decorated the walls with artwork from a local artist. Not to Beatrice's taste, but she could ill afford to replace them. The far wall remained covered in bookshelves, stuffed floor to ceiling, the contents covering all genres and authors. From Shakespeare and Dickens to modern-day authors like Fleming or Woodhouse and Daphne du Maurier. Over the years, visitors had left behind their own books to add to the now eclectic collection. The other doorway led through to a long kitchen diner with a table angled at the end that captured the sea view from the window.

In the kitchen, they had arranged the larder cupboards in a purely functional manner. Beatrice named the large kitchen drawer as "the really useful drawer" and found it stuffed full of kitchen paraphernalia. It overflowed with Sellotape, a Stanley knife, a half-used book of stamps, a lightbulb or sometimes long white candles for the winter blackouts. You had to be prepared to rummage around at the bottom to find what you needed.

The layout of the upper landing looked more traditional, with four stripped pine doors, with white ceramic handles, one for each of the bedrooms and one for the family bathroom, not designed for anyone over six feet tall, with low-slung ceilings running the length of each room. The master bedroom had wallpaper, showing a little threadbare behind the door, but only if you knew where to look, originally a popular print from a new up and coming stylist, Laura Ashley. Primroses scattered on a pale lilac background. The layout of the room was based around the optimum position of the sun rising through the large window. The oversized bed with an ornate brass headboard faced out towards the sea. Next door, the twin bedroom had changed little since the family had stayed there when Rosina, Albert and Beatrice were small; still laid out with a clutch of small teddies on matching blue candlewick bedspreads. With Enid Blyton books and *Beano* comics stacked on the painted bookshelves. The guest bedroom looked a little more adult, with a lilac floral quilted bedspread and matching curtains, all home-made.

The bathroom seemed overly large for the size of the cottage. Its plain walls had white tiles down one side and a roll top bath in the corner. Not much colour other than that offered by the accessories, in a now-faded turquoise blue to match a faded blind. Although the bath seemed indulgent, it allowed its bathers to submerge themselves entirely beneath their bubbles. With plenty of room for two people, if one was forgiving about the plughole and the large gilt taps at one end. Beatrice had never experienced the shared intimacy of bathing with another person.

It took several weeks before she began to feel settled. Although an isolated existence at first, the solitude allowed Beatrice to find herself again. Her modest savings came in handy. She joined the local library and found a weekly evening class that taught reupholstery and curtain making. This gave her an opportunity to meet other people.

Beatrice reminded herself of her promise after giving birth to Samuel. The promise that she would not give up hope of finding him. The letter to Jack had taken her several days to write. She felt confident that Ocean Cottage would be her home for the rest of her life. It added to her overall feeling of security.

The family boat *SailDreamer* still had its mooring on a fluorescent pink buoy in the small private cove. It needed some maintenance to make it seaworthy again. The deck needed some varnish, and the sails had perished through a lack of use. Beatrice knew nothing about boats, especially sailing boats. The ferry to Calais had been the only boat she had set foot on. She would need to find some lessons from someone who knew how to sail. Perhaps the man next door might help if only she could remember his name. Before she left, Rosina suggested she call round and introduce herself. But, before she had a chance, Freddie had taken the bold move first. She thought it a strange way to introduce yourself, leaving vegetables in a garden trug on the doorstep with a note that the trug needed returning to its owner next door.

September, always her favourite month, saw Beatrice settling down into her new routine. When the new term started, she began work at the local school. For the first month, she acted as a volunteer and progressed up a level to become a teaching assistant. During her cycle rides to and from school, her mind would drift back to Elswick and Samuel. After a while, it developed into an obsessive thought that preoccupied her head when she wasn't busy with the children in the classroom.

She'd promised herself to try and find Samuel, and have him back in her life. How would that be possible, as she had no means of tracking his adoptive family? Where to start, though, with no paperwork available to pursue such a search? She began by getting the number from directory enquiries and tried ringing the baby unit in Elswick. The splashes from her launched teacup were probably still marking the drab wall in room number five. A few minutes into the conversation with the old matron, the line went dead. Perhaps it had been too soon after her departure. Paranoia set in and she thought perhaps the dead phone line might have been a deliberate act. The only firm fact that she had to work with to find Samuel, was that she knew the family was not American. Perhaps the first key to unlocking her dilemma rested with Father O'Flynn. But no, she couldn't face that, and, besides, wouldn't that require a trip back to Consett?

The letter from Beatrice to Father O'Flynn requesting information remained unopened when it was returned to the cottage. Either someone deliberately misplaced the records or the priest, who ran the scandalous adoption system, had died and left no trace of it. She took small comfort in the belief that Samuel had to be somewhere in England, but where? It was no use. It would mean a lengthy train trip to London to the Lost and Found Agency to register an interest.

One evening, she plucked up courage and rang her mother's home number.

"Consett 4223," came the familiar matriarchal voice.

"Hello, Mother, it's Bea here."

All her recent anxieties melted. Without thinking, she plunged right in, and asked if there were any records or papers at home connected to Samuel's birth. She was confident that her father must have signed the baby over and would have known the family's address. Although Flo felt sorry, she reaffirmed the news Beatrice had been dreading.

"No, there were no records kept at home. And what would she be wanting with them?" She deliberated during the conversation whether to confess her intentions to her mother. Feeling braver, she continued, "You see, I'm going to find him, Mother, despite what you say, and have him come and live with me." A pause, as her mother took a sharp intake of breath, before giving her an answer guaranteed to upset her plans.

"*No*, you can't do that, Bea. You see, your father and I signed an agreement. We can't go back on it now. That would be illegal. You don't understand. The baby is not yours to have."

On hearing her mother's response, Beatrice's patience snapped and she slammed the phone down, sending a book flying across the floor. She paced the kitchen, agitated. Furious that any decision she made about Samuel could still be thwarted by her mother. She took herself off to bed with a thumping headache, still without a satisfactory conclusion. When she awoke the next day, she felt no better. With consternation written across her brow, the morning tea and toast routine had failed to shift it. She sat staring at the business card on the coffee table. The Lost and Found Agency would know what to do. They would help her find Samuel, so she planned her train journey to central London for the following Saturday.

Beatrice booked a seat on the early train to London, unsure about the exact location of the Lost and Found Agency. She needn't have worried. The address was easy to find. Within easy walking distance from the station. The plaque outside on the wall was newly polished. She took her ticket at the enquiry desk and sat down to await her number to be called out.

"I'm sorry, we have nobody of that name on the list," responded the woman with the large hairy mole on her cheek. Beatrice's heart sank, and she asked her to look again, this time giving a birth number instead. The woman scowled at the screen and stopped typing. "Well, we have one name that has appeared on another list. Does the name 'Elswick' mean anything to you?"

"Yes, that's the one," said Beatrice, trying hard not to screech with delight.

"Is there a name or an address?" The woman scribbled a few details on a piece of paper and handed it over to the counter. Beatrice, ecstatic, could have hugged her. She had gone against her mother's advice and proved her wrong. Her intention was to keep her search a secret from now on.

Thirteen

Rosina Departs

Father O'Flynn had quoted from his pamphlet that the passage to the Philippines should take only thirty days depending on the weather. Rosina had taken him at his word. Harry and Flo paused at the barrier to hug their elder daughter.

"Is this what you really want, Rosy?" asked Harry for the umpteenth time.

"Yes, of course, Father, it's what I have wanted all my life, from being a small girl."

Not a man of prominent emotion, he took out his handkerchief and dabbed his eyes. Pity he hadn't shown the same emotion when saying farewell to Beatrice. But those circumstances had been different, he convinced himself. Flo withdrew from her daughter's warm embrace, their eyes fixed upon one another. That mother and daughter bond still existed, despite her lack of forgiveness for moving Beatrice so far away.

But today was different, and those feelings were all forgotten now as the ship's klaxon signalled their time was up. The welcome crew bellowed through a megaphone, asking the passengers to line up in an orderly queue by the gangplank. Rosina shuffled along and waved at her parents one last time. She joined the crew and passengers on deck for another roll call for the first leg of her journey, Tilbury to Naples.

When she set sail, she did not know how her younger sister's life would pan out in Swanage. And had little idea that Beatrice would end up finding love too, and sink herself deep into a comfortable domestic arrangement and live in sin, fueling her imagination. But Rosina was no longer responsible for her sister's actions, and had revelled in the fact she had now had her own freedom. Beatrice needed to find her own way now, a theme they had argued about on their recent trip to Dorset.

It took a little time to locate cabin 1625, deep in the bowels of the ship. She felt she'd walked quite a distance before the ship began to roll. Rosina flopped on her bunk once she had stowed away her passenger cases, suddenly feeling exhausted and a little queasy. She drifted off to sleep. The ticket had bought her a third-class cabin with twin bunks. So far, nobody had claimed the bottom bunk. Taking out her daily journal she attempted to describe her thoughts in a little more detail. She noted the smart decks, painted in strong Italian colours of red, white and green. The cabins created a peaceful ambience and drummed out any noises from the engine rooms. The funnel spluttered black soot, landing across the deck on unused white plastic sun loungers. As the wind speed picked up, the crew neatly folded and tied down the jaunty, coloured parasols. She tried to think if Tilbury might be the furthest she had strayed from Consett. Life had been frenetic for the preceding weeks, managing the organisation on behalf of Beatrice, with little time to think about what lay ahead for herself in Manila.

Self-doubt regularly plagued her thoughts. Had joining the nunhood been what she'd desired or what her parents had desired? She thought she had wanted it from being a small child. When she awoke a few hours later, slightly disoriented, she could hear the ship's engines throbbing. Feeling refreshed and braver, she escaped the confines of the cabin to find some fresh air and seek out the other guests. But the decks were empty, and her stomach told her otherwise. Wishing she had stayed put in her bunk, Rosina made her way back down below. The ship had made its way out into the open sea as darkness had fallen and the beginnings of the approaching storm hit. As feared, during the first forty-eight hours the ship hit gale force winds. Most passengers took to their cabins for modesty and dignity's sake. After three days, the swell diminished. Those who'd found their sea legs slowly emerged into the daylight from below decks, like animals emerging from hibernation. Rosina tied up her dark tresses into a tight bun, applied some Vaseline to her lips and a dab of Pond's Cold Cream to keep her cheeks supple. The crew had posted the route up on a large notice board. It would take them through the straits of Gibraltar to Naples, and east through the Suez Canal and past Ceylon, then through the Straits of Malacca, before arriving in Manila.

Surprising herself at how quickly she recovered her equilibrium, she set off to explore the ship and find something to eat. It reminded her of a hotel in the high street back home. In the lounge area, the rounded tub chairs are covered in either vivid pink or luminous green velour fabric. The height of fashionable colours. There were nine decks, with four restaurants to choose from, where one could sit and eat your meals.

After breakfast Rosina was on a mission, searching for something in particular. The sign for the chapel was on C deck, and to her delight it was empty on her first visit. A gold altar stood at one end, with six white candles placed at regular intervals inside wooden candelabras. Statuettes lined themselves up, ready for worship. The baby Jesus on his mother's lap painted a deep gold and red. Behind it sat an angel with golden wings. She found if she sat still in the pew and kept still the spinning in her head subsided after a few moments. She likened the experience to being drunk and losing control of your legs. Not that she had ever been in a state of drunkenness. Rosina had only once tried her father's pale sherry as a teenager at Christmas. It had burnt her throat so badly she spat it out in the kitchen sink. Her mother's voice still rang in her ears days later, exclaiming how silly she had been wasting her good sherry.

In the peaceful ambience of the chapel, she sat quietly, crossing her chest and saying her prayers with her rosary beads set loosely in her lap. Her thoughts were distracted only by a sound behind her as the chapel door creaked. She noticed the young man wearing a white dog collar, but she thought it would be impolite to stare right away. After concluding her prayer, she sat back in the pew and studied her new compatriot out of the corner of her eye. Boldly, he'd moved into her pew.

Why had he not chosen one of the many other empty pews available? The outfit of her new acquaintance suggested he might be a priest. The proximity of their seating filled her nostrils with a potent scent. Or perhaps that was just incense burning at the altar. Rosina had always been a poor judge of these matters. The man, in a neatly pressed black shirt and white dog collar, filled a medium frame, in complete contrast to the tall and slender Rosina. His dark hair appeared wild, possibly because of walking outside on the deck. What did she expect, as the chapel opened its doors twenty-four hours a day to all passengers and crew, no matter their denomination? When the priest had finished his prayers, he extended his warm hand and introduced himself. His name sounded so unusual. Rosina asked him to repeat it, twice. She had difficulty in pronouncing it and instantly flushed with embarrassment.

"Thabo Nkosi."

"Sorry, can you repeat it?"

"Thaaabooo." He chuckled, his white teeth gleaming. "It means in Zulu, 'to be thankful to God'. Few people have heard of it, but you can call me Baabo for short. Most people do. In Zulu, it also means king."

Rosina felt a sudden warm rush creeping up her neck. Suddenly, she came over all hot and placed her hand discreetly over her neck. Had he noticed? She must be committing a sin to have such feelings, she told herself, promising God she would pay a second visit to the chapel later that day, to repent. Would she recognise what love at first sight felt like?

With prayer time over, the pair took a walk along one of the upper decks to check on the horizon and the state of the weather. They noted the eight lifeboats hanging on ropes on either side. Laughing, they both agreed they were a comforting sight. The lurching in Rosina's stomach had subsided, but her full appetite had not returned as yet. Despite her doubts that she would feel like eating, the pair met for dinner at six. Choosing to go their separate ways for the rest of the afternoon. Rosina returned to her cabin to record her personal thoughts in her daily journal.

Over dinner that night, Thabo explained how he came to be on the ship, and that he was returning to the Philippines for his second posting. Although his origins were back in Zimbabwe, he had been in London for six months, completing a ministerial training course. The texture of his smooth, blackened skin fascinated Rosina the most. She had never seen a black person in real life, only in picture books at the library. His long, brown, slender fingers and neatly trimmed nails, clasped together in prayer, drew her eyes. Thabo's eyes were enormous, with irises the colour of dark chocolate. On his feet, he wore tan leather sandals with brass buckles, which displayed perfectly aligned toes. Before that moment, Rosina had only witnessed her brother's bare feet as he sprinted to the bathroom at home.

Thabo continued to impart his superior knowledge about ocean liners and their distances. He explained that, at the start of the voyage, with the ship fully loaded with cargo and food for the passengers and crew, the ship sailed slowly. As more passengers disembarked and more food was eaten, the ship went faster. Rosina hung on his every word. Whether the tale of the ship's speed was true or not, she didn't care.

The couple met every morning in the chapel before breakfast. They prayed for their families back home and for a continued safe passage. In Thabo's company, she found her self-confidence growing. Alone in her cabin, she found she thought of not much else. When not with him, she missed his laugh, his warmth, and the rolling whites of his eyes when she spoke something heartfelt. By explaining that her domestic shackles were cut loose, he helped her lighten up and relax. Now she was at liberty to be true to herself. The real Rosina with the broadest sense of humour. Did she know the real Rosina, no longer anybody's daughter or sister on the ship? Rosina found she had an attraction to the dark-skinned man she had known for only ten days. Could this be actual love? She felt unsure, but knew something inside her had changed.

Thabo talked knowledgeably about what to expect in Manila, and the hotspots she should avoid as a young white woman. He offered to show her the sights and introduce her to some of his pastoral friends. Rosina didn't want to arrive at their destination; their journey was already going much too fast. She wanted to stay at sea for longer, listen to more thrilling conversations, stories of Thabo's travelling adventures.

Poor naïve Rosina had not realised what was happening.

By the time the ship reached Manila, she found herself head over heels in love with Thabo Nkosi. Now she had to decide if she wanted to fully commit to the Order of the Sisters of Mercy. To do this, she would need to dismiss him from her thoughts. Or take the less complicated emotional route and become a missionary. The latter would allow her to continue her relationship with Thabo.

She started a letter to Father O'Flynn twice, explaining briefly that she had reconsidered and she would not be joining the nunhood after all. She'd made up her mind. Before sealing it, she asked Thabo to read it and confirm whether he felt the same about her. His answer: an overwhelming yes, he did. So we need mention nothing more. He declared he loved her to the moon and back. That was enough for Rosina. When they disembarked in Manila, she posted the letter straightaway. Would Thabo be required to assess his own future as a priest? Would he honestly give that up and become a missionary too? Would he do all that just for Rosina? Everything he told her over the course of their passage held true, and he kept his word.

The ship docked, and the passengers disembarked to various locations across the main island. It turned out Thabo had been right: Rosina found the first few weeks difficult, acclimatising to her new surroundings. The heat and the food were the first challenge, as she had been used to the murky British climate with four seasons. They both had to be interviewed by the head of the mission. Thabo Nkosi had been abroad before and felt comfortable in the humidity and intense heat. The second challenge for Rosina: the local food. Her first foreign dish, *adobo*, a stew made of braised pork, went down well, apart from the heat of the spices that numbed her tongue; she likened it to one of Flo's casseroles back home, only stronger. They slept in separate basic accommodation under rattan roofs, and shared outside toilet facilities. Thabo, a popular, generous man, made time for everyone he met, true to his word, and stayed at Rosina's side.

~~~

A few months after Rosina's departure, Father O'Flynn received a letter franked in Manila. Pulling a frown, he scanned the letter and his face quickly changed colour, he sat down to steady himself.

"Well, I'll be d...," he exclaimed. It explained that Rosina and Thabo were now married and settled in Manila. Her new name; Mrs Thabo Nkosi; Father O'Flynn flew into an instant rage and scrunched up the letter tossing it into the bin. His head thrown into yet another spin. He'd been convinced that Rosina would have never been the one to renege on her decision to join the holy order. He felt bitterly disappointed. She had let him down. What would the bishop think? Did her parents know? He would not be the one to tell them. Now he'd failed at both missions concerning the Hamilton girls. A sign he should take early retirement somewhere in southern Ireland, perhaps Cork, or Galway, to a town called Burren, his childhood town. True, Father O'Flynn had made grave errors of judgement during his ministry. This time, he'd crossed the line, as he took a call from the bishop, demanding to see him. Could they sack a priest? In his heart, he knew his time playing the saintly parish priest might be drawing to a close. Before he met with the bishop, he wrote his letter of resignation and sealed the envelope. He set off for the church for an extended confessional followed by his meeting with the bishop that ended with a handshake and a mutual agreement. Father O'Flynn would leave his post at the end of the month.

Back in Consett, winter had come early and a shale grey sky had descended; the icy breath of a freezing winter had come calling. Icicles were hanging from the shop signs and water dripped from the roofs, making pools of water on the pavements. The street corners in Consett were empty of folk. It matched the mood of the town as people disappeared indoors to sit by their fires in an attempt to keep warm. Marguerite, now six months pregnant with her third baby, defiantly announced to everyone who would listen that this one had been Jack's too. So, as Beatrice suspected, he had fathered two out of three of her babies. Left with little choice and partly to save money, Jack had given in to mounting pressure and nagging, and agreed to move upstairs with Marguerite. The flat, a substandard building, had large cracks in the outside plasterwork that had led to water ingresses. Upstairs, Marguerite's flat reeked badly of damp, the curtains covered in black mildew. The mould had spread under the threadbare carpets. The town council had recorded higher than usual cases of flu amongst the population of Consett. Within such a close-knit community, everyone knew someone suffering with it, or, worse, dying from it. The authorities had called it an epidemic rather than a pandemic; they compared it to the Spanish flu, which had been far worse after the First World War, killing millions globally. The funeral directors worked round the clock to keep up with the local increase in demand.

Marguerite had returned to the flat with a baby on her hip, a second growing in her belly, and a toddler lagging a few steps behind. She unleashed herself for a moment and stepped into the bedroom. She wanted to check in on Jack. To her horror, he was lying on his back, his eyes wide open, the face waxen with no rising and falling of his chest, completely still. A bit of yellow spittle had settled at the side of his open, unshaven

215

mouth. His arms lay flat by his side, and his purple toes poked out at the bottom of the blankets.

The poor woman sat on the end of the bed and shivered just with the shock of it. Marguerite had never seen a dead person before. She pulled her shawl around her shoulders. Poor Jack. She had left him alone for barely half an hour whilst she collected his medicines. What should she do? Whom should she tell? As far as she knew, he had no family to tell. For the next few moments, she panicked, leaving the babies alone for a moment in their cots, and dashed over to the pub. Someone would know what to do. The ambulance arrived quickly, followed by a local doctor, who certified the death. With the body removed, Marguerite felt numb. The death certificate confirmed Jack had died of bronchial pneumonia.

For Marguerite and her babies, the situation had suddenly become desperate. Heavily reliant on Jack for financial support, there would be an extra mouth to feed soon with baby number three, due in ten weeks. It took until January the following year for the town council to condemn the flats as unsafe and unsanitary. Marguerite and her family moved out into a hostel for unmarried mothers. She wondered how to let Beatrice know about Jack's passing, but had no forwarding address. Perhaps Big Joe knew where her parents lived, and could pass on a message. Marguerite had never learnt to write properly, so a letter would be out of the question. It would have to be verbal.

Jack had not been the only family member to succumb. Harry Hamilton had also caught the flu and passed away. To date, it had not yet spread to the southern counties, keeping to the densely populated towns across the north east. Beatrice remained blissfully ignorant of the fact that her father and Jack had passed until Flo's letter arrived. The news about Jack upset her more than the loss of her father, if she were being honest.

Beatrice felt puzzled why her mother had not rung to tell her the news. The letter came with a firm request to return home immediately to assist with the funeral arrangements. Beatrice couldn't face the idea of attending Jack's funeral, either. She had no desire to be confronted again by Marguerite. So Flo had none of her children alongside her for Harry's funeral, led by Father Patrick.

Beatrice had weighed up her choices and opted to stay home at Ocean Cottage. She wrote back to say she could not make the long trip north. Gone were the days when she jumped at her mother's demands. She cited the flu epidemic, and that she'd been keen to avoid it, thinking by staying at the cottage she could remain fit and well. But that winter the flu spread quickly across the country and finally it hit Dorset, where Beatrice succumbed.

She arrived home from work feeling chilled and her body shivery. Her throat felt like barbed wire. Since leaving home, she had not fallen ill. It turned out to be the first time she'd had to look after herself. Her head felt hot with a fever and her hands and feet were icy cold. She boiled the kettle to make a warm drink of honey and lemon, dug out an old hot water bottle, and took to her bed. The demon flu virus had finally struck. Every limb throughout her body ached, and she'd lost her sense of smell. On the bed, she had two eiderdowns and several blankets. Her feet were still freezing despite her woollen bed socks. Two days passed before she emerged from a deep sleep to hear knocking at the front door. Too weak to get out of bed, she ignored it. When Freddie saw the curtains were drawn, he was worried. On day three – or maybe it was four; she couldn't remember – she ventured downstairs to replenish her drink and saw the note on the doormat. Holding onto the wall, she bent down to retrieve it.

Hello, Beatrice. Hope you are ok. Ring me if you need anything. Freddie.

Short and succinct, her eyes filled when she read his kind words. After another lengthy bout of coughing, she retreated to the comfort of her bed. It took a further week before her legs would stand without wobbling and the dizziness dissipated. Each day Freddie left her a small package of food neatly wrapped in baking paper on her doorstep. It took a few weeks before she had recovered enough to return to work. On her first week back at school, she returned home to find a letter from Rosina. It immediately lifted her spirits. Tucked inside the envelope: a square black-and-white photo of her sister in a posh frock, holding a small posy; standing arm in arm with a dark-skinned gentleman. Mmm, thought Beatrice, he looked quite handsome. On the reverse of the photograph were two names in bold print.

The Marriage of Rosina Hamilton and Thabo Nkosi

With a loop to show a knot and a flower.

"Oh my goodness," exclaimed Beatrice out loud. The news of the wedding from abroad came as a shock. The couple opted to spend the next three years in the Philippines. Oh yes, Rosina was expecting a baby in the autumn. Beatrice wrote back at once, saying how delighted she felt that her sister had found love with a like-minded individual, and to send photographs of the baby when born.

Beatrice would need to buy some more writing paper and write a letter to her mother in Consett immediately. It would perk her up. Did her mother already know the news or had that been left to Beatrice to share it now the sisterly roles had been reversed? She wondered what Flo would have to say on the subject when she saw the picture of Rosina's new husband. Beatrice had looked after children with many skin colours and had no issue with Rosina's choice of husband. But in Consett, in the Sixties, people were still prejudiced against folk who originated from a different country. Perhaps Flo had softened over recent years. Beatrice hoped so, unable to contain her delight that Rosina had chosen not to become a nun, reneging on her promise to Father O'Flynn. The most obvious question in her letter would be when they were going to make the journey home. Beatrice already knew the answer to that question before she had written it. Whilst rereading the letter, she had another of her madcap ideas. The following day, she would find the travel agents on the high street and book a trip abroad. It would be a surprise for her sister and coincide with the birth of Rosina's baby. Within the week, she would have it all settled.

Fourteen

Ralph – 1969

To understand Ralph Barclay, it would be more helpful to return to his roots. Born to a rather conventional couple, Colin and June, who in modern times would be known as "beige". The couple never liked to venture outside their regular comfort zones. Growing up, Ralph had to share everything with Max, the older boy, by two years. Their upbringing was simple, and they considered their family financially stable. Colin owned a car considered a luxury back in the day. A mustard-coloured Austin Maxi – his pride and joy. Meanwhile, his wife became a traditional stay-at-home mum.

But the role of motherhood had simply not suited June. As small kids, they had had to suffer the indignity of their mother's meticulously hand-knitted V-neck sweaters in various bland colours, the only version that she knew how to knit without referring to a pattern. Their school chums teased the brothers mercilessly about their home-styled jumpers. Perhaps this stymied childhood gave Ralph the impetus and motivation to flee the confines of the small, closeted Dorset village so early in adulthood. He yearned to broaden his horizons with some travel escapism. Colin had a more hands-on approach. For example, he taught the boys how to assume responsibility for sharp tools. First, he showed them how to use a penknife, and taught them how to use it to whittle shapes out of chunks of wood. Ralph had his own whittle too, with a loop to hang around his neck. He felt most grown-up.

Ralph traced the start of his abhorrence of religion back to his mother's cruel trick, whilst still dressed in shorts. Without advance notice, she'd signed him up for the local church choir. A prime example was Sunday Evensong. He dutifully went along to the service, innocently believing he was going to tidy the hymn books and assist his mother in sweeping up the petals from the altar flowers before the next service began. But, once there, the vicar's hand landed on his shoulder. He gave him a robe with a cassock and guided him firmly to the vestibule. Not wishing to make a scene, or upset his mother in public, he obliged the vicar and got changed like the others without question. He felt unable to find his voice and say there had been a dreadful mistake and he couldn't hold a note. Whilst attempting to sing the closing hymn whilst holding in his emotions, he realised his own mother had duped him.

They spent family holidays within their safe county of Dorset. Colin Barclay booked the same hotel in Bournemouth, with the same bedroom numbers, where they ate the same type of flavourless food each summer. Everything had to be just the same. A psychologist, perhaps, would view this as a sign of their deep insecurities. Colin and June would counter argue: why bother to change things just for the sake of it?

Ralph found it a struggle to express himself coherently. They had always taught him to keep his emotions in check. His parents had not been the best role models, with few displays of affection. If he thought hard about it, he found he held few memories of them holding hands whilst taking a walk, for instance. For certain, he had never witnessed them kissing goodbye on the doorstep when his father left for work. None of those scenarios came to mind. His mother was a bit of a cold fish, lacking any warmth towards her offspring. June would never have harmed them physically, but frequently confessed she had few maternal instincts. The children arrived only to please her husband, as she felt a duty to provide him with an heir. Her personality came across in stark contrast to their father, who was a warm and affectionate man. The boys would climb on his knee for a bedtime story and he would readily get down on the floor to play games with their model trains. Colin, being the antithesis of his wife, always had something kind to say about everyone.

Being kids, and particularly boys with voracious appetites, they turned their attention to the person responsible for feeding them. June fed the boys on time and adhered to a strict nursery schedule. On offer were three square meals a day, with nothing to be left on the plates. The food provided was simple home-cooked meals: shepherd's pie on a Monday, liver and bacon on a Tuesday, and so on, with the treat of a roast chicken on a Friday. For Sunday tea, after the chicken paste sandwiches, the boys had a choice of their favourite desserts: rice pudding, or tinned peaches served with evaporated milk. In the Barclay household, there were no animals to slurp up the plates under the table. "Animals spread diseases, and should eat and sleep outside," June would tell the boys. This conversation took place after the boys asked if they might have a puppy for Christmas. It had been met by June with a firm "no". Their father raised his eyebrows and thought better of it than to pass comment.

The boys had no hidden agenda and no real complaints about their mother. On the advice of their father, if they were wise, they should play quietly to avoid further chastisement.

She made it clear to them she disliked small children. So they kept out of her way, following their father's instruction. Either playing upstairs in their bedroom, making Airfix kits or Meccano or playing out in the sizeable garden making dens and elephant traps. Perhaps it would all change as they got older and became more independent. June preferred knitting and making strawberry jam for the Women's Institute to looking after her offspring.

The only time holidays varied from the same Bournemouth hotel had been when the boys went to the Kennet and Avon canal. Some school friends had invited them on a barge holiday. By now, the boys were both teenagers and the canal trip seemed a perfect opportunity to test out their muscle strength and prowess in handling the lock gates. The brothers agreed they'd had the best adventure yet, and much more fun than on their family trips to Bournemouth, perhaps because they were free from their parental shackles.

Unbeknown to Beatrice and Ralph, they had gone about their daily lives within a short distance of each other. They regularly passed through the same country lanes that led to their respective homes, unaware of what lay ahead.

Max had escaped the clutches of their mother and moved away to work in fashionable Kentish Town, in London. But for Ralph, though there had been a brief dabble in the art world, he had never settled comfortably against the backdrop of the talented Dorset artists.

Over time, he gathered many books on lock-keeping and boats, preferring to be on or near the water. In his early twenties, he became inspired by a long-held pipe dream to become a lock-keeper and landed his first job away from home, in response to an advert in a *Waterways* magazine. Ralph had applied for a job working on the Kennet and Avon canal as a lock-keeper. His knowledge of waterborne jobs limited to fishing with his father in his younger days and the brief teenage holiday on the canal. To his surprise, after his interview he received a letter to say he had got the job. And would he be available to start at the beginning of March, just at the start of summer? He packed up his stuff and sold or gave away the remaining pieces. His father had asked him directly: why a lock-keeper? Such a strange and lonely profession. Ralph's response disappointed him. The job market in Swanage would never give him what he was seeking.

~~~~~~

The canal job came with accommodation, a cosy, roughened stone cottage. One double bedroom and a box room he might use for his junk. A central doorway had a cambered arch with the main stove in the living room, which provided much-needed heat to the rest of the upper floor. The floorboards remained bare, painted with a black gloss, creating a darkness to the aura in the rooms. The previous tenant had brought it up to date, by bringing the toilet inside and adding bathroom facilities with a modest lower-ground-floor extension and a flat roof.

For Ralph, the modest salary had not been the attraction, nor the extended hours, as he started at six and finished when the last boat had gone through the lock. The peppercorn rent might have given a clue, but he secretly enjoyed the responsibility combined with the isolation. He had always had an interest in the environment and its long-term effects on the planet.

The outgoing lock-keeper had left copious notes in a large blue plastic folder that covered everything from boiler issues to stopcocks and bin collection days. But, like everything in a new place, until you experience it for yourself first hand, you don't have a clue where to find anything.

After settling into his new role, he enjoyed the daily ebb and flow of the canal traffic. Sometimes the barge owners would be in such a rush with their entry into the canal locks, if only to gain the best mooring pitch for the night. Ralph gathered a collection of phrases he nicknamed in his logbook as "The Weekly Splash". Over time, he collated the comments he'd overheard on the locks. He thought they might come in useful, if he ever wrote a book. His latest idea had been to record the "shout outs". One barge owner who continually barked orders at his crew:

"I steer the boat, I don't do the menu." "This is a lock boat rather than a yacht." "No room for slapdash techniques."

In Ralph's experience, the twenty-five-to-thirty-year-old group were the worst offenders. They always thought they knew everything. His hackles were raised before the young "eejits" arrived in his lock; he could hear the voices in the distance echoing off the walls, frequently jibing at the other boat owners whilst battering their own boats. Ralph thought they showed a deep lack of skill and judgement. Had none of them listened to the instruction handover at the boathouse? They were always mouthy until they got stuck and unable to operate the bar. He would mumble under his breath that he was "not their mate", and reluctantly assisted with a false smile. The look of abject terror appeared on the face of the newbies, causing unnecessary panic to a rise in tension as the engine cogs ground together followed by shouts of *'look out'*, followed by the crunch of metal on metal or wood on wood.

"Sorry! I'm a first-time captain." "No damage done, I think."

I'll be the judge of that, thought Ralph with a wincing smile, yanking the rope out of the inexperienced hands, leaving yet more canal walls destroyed. Ralph enjoyed the human interaction and won over many folks with his winning smile.

In the winter months, perhaps that's when the true isolation got to him, so he would share a couple of pints in the Five Ducks pub, along the canal embankment. Within an hour, he would put the world to rights alongside Nigel and Sonja, the hospitable publicans. Ralph became well known behind the bar and had recently prided himself on the challenge of trying every item on the hot food menu. His favourite dish, the steak and ale pie with the deepest crust on the top and not a vegetable in sight, trying not to think of his childhood nemesis, green vegetables. He bravely recalled their mother's repeated attempts to convince him they were good for him after boiling on the stove for half an hour. A grey washed-out mush.

It took him a few months before he started to relax and found the job restorative. In time, he forgot how he came to be beside the canal. The long hours had not allowed him much time for dating. The last girlfriend from Swanage hankered after lots of children: at least four, she'd declared to Ralph in a fit of passion. Ralph remained unsure that he would be fatherhood material. He still felt far too young to commit to a long-term relationship. The closeness with his mother evaporated long ago, after she'd clarified that his choice in women did not suit her. This happened after he took an ex-girlfriend, Wendy, home. Despite the girl's amazing looks, June gained a sadistic pleasure in making her feel uncomfortable. Ralph questioned his mother why she behaved as she did and reminded her that at his age he should be old enough to make up his own mind.

June's mental health had been in decline for some time and Colin found himself unable to manage. The formal diagnosis of dementia left a devoted husband struggling to cope alone. It would mean selling up the family home. The decision to put her into a nursing home offering round-the-clock care hadn't been easy. When he'd rung to enquire about his mother's progress in her new home, it dismayed him to hear she had passed away in her sleep. Ralph had taken a call from his father requesting that he and his brother return home. So he felt they had given him little choice but to hand in his notice with the canal job. The water continued to flow through the canal.

It shocked the brothers to find the family home had been sold at a property auction. Things had moved fast in a matter of weeks. Max, the prodigal son, had not yet showed up. With another box held high, his father muttered under his breath as he squeezed past that his errant brother would arrive any minute. And, with that, the unmistakable sound of a battered silver Renault pulled into the yard alongside the campervan. The mutual slapping of backs ensued and quickly the grown men reverted to familiar brotherly banter. It ended in pleas of desperation for help from their dad to just "get on with it". They needed to clear out the house before the new occupiers arrived the following day, jangling keys in their hand. The removal lorry stood in the yard, filling with a lifetime of memories. Furniture, books, clothes are all replaceable items. A mixture of inherited items from a previous generation when you made do with cast-offs and hand-me-downs. They felt no shame in it after the war years. The modern view was that everything had to be brand new.

Each room of the 1940s semi looked in a chaotic state of undress. They had stacked removal boxes of different shapes and sizes very high, some labelled and some unlabelled. Large patches of dust surrounded floor lamps or sideboards. Sorely tempted, Ralph felt an urge to write rude words on the packing boxes to confuse his brother, but thought better of it when he glimpsed the ragged state of his father sitting on the stairs, head in his hands. It must have been something about being back at home and alongside his brother that caused the regression to childhood antics. The boxes contained a complete Dinky car collection and family memorabilia. The discovery of the family photograph albums passed another nostalgic hour. All twenty cars, wrapped in tissue paper in a large cardboard box. The model railway set had provided the three men with hours of pleasure. Colin had set it out as a model village and the trains were at a perfect height for the young boys to interact with the small carriages. The smash ups on the 00 gauge tracks were all part of the train set fun. Something nostalgically captured the smell of the engines in the boxes, with a heady mixture of oil and metal.

~~~

Ralph had always prided himself on his physique, a testament to his hours spent exercising on or in the water. Bearing the looks of someone much younger, with smooth skin and sparse lines. He put it down to his bachelor lifestyle, without the stresses and strains of having a permanent partner or any young dependents. Whilst clearing out the house, the lure of the open sea so close to the house became a temptation, enticing him away from a lifetime of memories. Without explanation, he ducked out for a quick swim and made his way the short distance down an unmarked track lined with pine trees on either side. His front crawl sliced cleanly through the clear, cool, turquoise water, instantly calming his mind. His safe swimming markers on the near horizon were two fluorescent mooring buoys. One of them had a yacht attached, looking a little battered and unloved.

Unaware of the distance he had covered, and well before the invention of the Fitbit watches and iPhones, he did not know how far he had swum, the only clue that he felt his legs tiring. As he swam back and forth, he grew more determined to check out the name on the side of the boat. It had been bobbing about on its tatty mooring rope. As he approached the far side, he saw the name *SailDreamer* proudly displayed in faded royal blue paint. What an enchanting name, he thought, and vowed to find its owner. Despite the onset of cramp in his right foot, he continued with his swim for a few more minutes.

On his way back, his other foot cramped up so badly he had to swim using one leg and limp up the beach. Rubbing his foot, his attention was drawn to a figure lying on a striped beach towel reading a book, sporting a broad raffia sun hat with tanned shoulders and long legs that crossed neatly at two petite ankles. Transfixed, he swallowed a mouthful of seawater from a gentle wave whilst attempting to weigh up the situation lying on the sand. He wanted to know who owned the boat as it needed some serious maintenance before it could safely set sail. Outstretched on a beach towel lay the answer to his query. He vowed he would return the following day to pursue his enquiries in person, next time taking his mask and snorkel for a closer look at the bottom of the boat in more detail.

Beatrice – 1969

It was the summer holidays; school was out for six weeks. Beatrice lay horizontal on a striped beach towel in a more relaxed posture, occasionally moving across, leaning on one elbow and posing on the other. As the sun moved round, it cast a shadow across the pages of her book. She had bought herself a new pair of sunglasses with white frames, the height of fashion chique. Unable to concentrate on the pages in front of her, despite the fresh glasses, she'd reread the last few lines several times. The new plot had not captivated her. The protagonist she found irritating, a weak individual, and, in her opinion, there were major flaws in the storyline. Bored with reading, she sat up to take in the view. The floral swimsuit drying at her side implied she may have had a dip in the sea. Earlier, she'd discreetly removed it, rinsed it out and placed it on the rocks to dry. She'd changed into a loose white linen top and a pair of faded shorts, leaving her underwear in the beach bag.

Recording her thoughts in her diary that evening, she wrote about the male swimmer, whom she noticed, when she looked back at the previous day's entry, had featured in her scribbles. She wrote about the changeability of the weather and her abject loneliness that enveloped her in the evenings and weekends when she was not working. Her reflections revolved mainly around her family. How she felt about her mother and the distance that had grown between them. She missed their womanly conversations in the kitchen. Reconciling her fate on the pages seemed to assist in her emotional recovery. Back to her obsession, she referred to him simply as Mr X. But he had already taken up two pages of her scribbles that morning, and she realised he might become more intrinsic to her daily routine. Well, more than she'd cared to admit. Her stomach grumbled with discomfort and she remembered she had not yet eaten that day. So gathered up her things and took the steep steps back up to the cottage. Looking back over her shoulder, she noted that Mr X had also left the scene. Why did that irritate her so much? Perhaps she was making something out of nothing.

The fridge looked bare, with nothing of inspiration to satisfy her appetite. She struggled to find something to put between two pieces of bread, on the verge of mouldiness. The tomato and soggy lettuce nestled in between a slim covering of cheddar shavings. After a couple of bites, she threw the rest out of the window onto the grass for the birds.

⌒⌒〜

Over at Colin's house, all sorting out and clearing had ceased for the day. The first removal van had departed as the sun dipped. The next lorry was not due until the following morning. So it would be the last night in the family home. The brothers went down to the town quay to pick up supper and have a couple of cheeky sundowners. On the menu: fish and chips. They plonked themselves on a bench, cool beers in hand, while they waited. Filling in the missing pieces for the few months they had been apart. They relaxed and chatted about the sad demise of their mother and the plans for Colin.

On a clear day, looking east and west, you could pick out the landmarks of the two headlands, Ballard Point and Durlston Head, popular places on the local maps. Swanage had its origins as a small fishing port to the west side of Chesil Beach with its famous long shingle bank.

Ralph couldn't help himself. He was itching to tell Max about the lady on the beach, and how captivating he found her. But he had to wait, as like all siblings when reunited the conversation quickly led back to memories of their childhood. Sipping their beers, they listened to the gentle clinking of the lanyards against the masts. Max recalled the smell of their father's two-stroke engine and the small family motor cruiser. Cormorants were taking a rest from their foreign travels perching themselves atop of the mooring posts. Ralph pointed out the familiar Old Harry Rocks as he recalled the story of their motor cruiser stalling its engine alongside the rocks and being rescued by a lifeboat. Their father was red-faced and apologetic when the RNLI turned up and towed them back into the harbour.

The chief attraction of the marina, too, with an intense smell of ozone as the tide went out. On the same quayside stood the Spinnaker Cafe, a familiar meeting point for people with young families. The Barclay family had spent many joyful hours in the cafe eating cheese and ham toasties, and slices of Victoria sponge or warm scones served with jam. During the school holidays, they would line youngsters up along the harbour wall with their fishing rods loaded with bits of string and pink lumps of streaky bacon dangling from their hooks. Clutching their brightly coloured fishing nets, scooping out the contents from the bottom of the harbour at low tide. Ralph explained again about the lady he'd seen down on the beach. But their conversation got interrupted a third time by a dramatic scene developing right ahead of them.

A visiting Chinese family were eating their pasties when an out-of-control seagull swooped down to steal it from a pair of small hands in a pushchair. With black tips to its wings and a beady pair of dark eyes, it was easily identifiable as a herring gull with a pale grey mantle. Unable to defend himself, the child let out a scream as the starving gull landed in his lap. It had the golden prize in its beak, flapping its wings and looking for an escape. Cawing right at the boy's face, his tiny hand let go of the pasty to shield his eyes. Max leapt forward and grabbed the bird, flinging it high towards the sea, with dregs of pasty shell hanging out of its beak. Its neck swung round to peck at Max's hand. The skirmish was over in a matter of seconds. The chopped beef skirt, diced carrot and potato flew through the air, landing on the stones, immediately surrounded by a dozen or more other hungry gulls. They pecked and scavenged for scraps amongst the melee of feathers and screeching. The piercing childlike screams had shattered the peace. Spectators stood transfixed by what they had witnessed.

The family thanked Max, placing their hands together in an oriental gesture, and scurried away to the sanctuary of their car. The brothers peeled away to find their own supper packed into boxes along at the chip shop. Ralph took his chance to tell Max he had seen someone of interest on the beach. By the time they reached the house, Ralph had unburdened himself.

"Hi, Dad, we're back. We've brought fish and chips with us to save you the bother of trying to find the plates and cutlery in the packing boxes."

"Here, take this box out to the garden and we can sit outside on the garden chairs if it's warm enough for you. Do you want to borrow my fleece?"

"Are you ok with cod?" queried Max, opening the boxes to display the bulging contents. Their dad had not much of an appetite, but did his best to show his appreciation. He enjoyed having his sons around him after the last few weeks of heartache. It brought back warm memories of their relationship years back.

~~~

Ralph set out for his daily swim. An hour later than usual, he'd taken his father into town before nine. Hot and sweaty after rushing around town, he was eager to get down to the beach, the coolness of the seawater bracing as he plunged in head first, instantly cooling his body down. His front crawl sliced easily through the water, uninterrupted. That day he had a plan to introduce himself to the lady on the striped beach towel. He'd noticed her body had turned around this time, and she faced the water. Her hand was raised to her forehead; her eyes needed shielding from the glare of the sun. Ralph lifted his right arm in a semi-wave to acknowledge her presence. She hesitated before offering him a short wave and returned to the pretence of reading her new book.

Since Beatrice arrived at the cottage, she had led a solitary, almost monastic life. She worked, she swam, and she went shopping when supplies ran low. More out of necessity than a desire to mix with others. She kidded herself; she enjoyed the low-key existence and solitude, and didn't need anyone else, and that living alone had its advantages, with nothing to consider but her own mood and wellbeing. She could eat what she liked, when she liked. If she wanted to eat toast in bed, who could stop her or complain? Not being beholden to anyone else suited her. Or did it?

Freddie, the neighbour next door, was also on his own, but for a different reason. They passed pleasantries on the doorstep, but it stopped at that. She barely knew the man when he confessed over a cup of tea that his solitary life had been because of the result of an abandoned relationship. Whilst he delved into the details, her mind drifted away to the man in the swimming trunks, or Mr X. Beatrice told herself she should not be interested in Mr X. If that were true, why had she turned over to get a better look the previous day? And why did Mr X have so many mentions in her diary? She had not paid him too much attention, had she?

That summer saw Beatrice on holiday from her job at the local school. A heatwave had started in late April and went on for several months. A national ban on the use of hosepipes started. Pavements steamed and road tarmac melted. They had set a water ration station up on each street. Disgruntled villagers queued with their plastic flagons of various shapes and sizes. They stood and spoke in low voices, asking when it would end. Wiping perspiration from their brows as they took their turn at the water station taps.

Freddie's home-made contraption for wheeling the heavy water canisters along the lane came in useful. Beatrice paused momentarily to speak to him about the issues of the day and the lack of sleep at night with the heat and humidity. Once they had completed the daily water run, Beatrice returned the Heath Robinson trolley to his front garden.

She was too tired to water the wilting shrubs with the dirty water from the watering can because of the intense heat. That afternoon Beatrice could not concentrate on anything for any length of time. Her body had reached boiling point, and was simply too hot to deal with the usual routine stuff. Her appetite had disappeared. She felt it was too hot to eat. She nibbled on a tiny cucumber sandwich on white bread with no crusts, but after a couple of feeble bites laid it down on her plate. After lunch, she'd planned to go for a swim, to cool her melting body. Packing up her large beach bag with a book and a towel, she hunted down a bottle of sun cream. She disliked the latest craze of using olive oil bought from a chemist's shop. Beatrice decided she didn't fancy looking like a greased-up goose. She prepared a thermos flask of tea and took the rickety steps down to the cove, reminding herself on the way down to get the loose handrail repaired after nearly losing her footing again.

On reaching the last step without further incident, she looked out at the sea, which that day resembled a mirror. The water gently lapped at the bank of small shingle, and the sky was cloudless. She made herself comfortable in her usual spot, where the sand moulded itself around her form. She spread out the towel and pinned it down at the corners with four large stones. Off to her left, she spotted a pair of blue flippers on the rocks. The cove was clearly marked "Private Property" so there should have been nobody else using it. He had tucked the small blue backpack out of sight behind. Unsure whether to be angry, bemused or curious, she tried to ignore the articles on the rocks and get stuck into her new book. This time, the pages gripped her attention. But, after a couple of minutes, human curiosity got the better of her and she glanced around to see if anyone else was visible. Taking a few steps forward, she stooped down and picked up the rucksack and undid the zip, hoping the contents would identify its owner.

A voice behind her spoke first. "Sorry, I know it says private, but I needed to leave my rucksack in a safe spot. It's much busier round the corner and I…" the man paused his excuses, when he caught the look on her face. Startled by the sudden voice, Beatrice's arms flew up in the air at the sound of his voice and threw the bag down on the sand. The contents scattered in front of her. She clutched her chest, startled.

"Yes, and the sign says, 'Private Property' for good reason, you know. Officially you are trespassing on my land!" She felt embarrassed by her rather spiky retort.

"I'm Ralph. You'll find nothing of value in it," he responded with a salacious wink. Mr X stood there sporting a pink and black wetsuit rolled halfway down a tanned, muscular body. Beatrice couldn't help but stare and, in doing so, almost forgot to close her mouth. The elusive Mr X stood before her, explaining and offering his hand. Beatrice had heard little, her mind running away to another of her fantasies. This one was more sexual than she'd expected.

Apologising again, the man asked her to zip up the back of his wetsuit. What a cheek! Had he not understood anything in her last sentence? The effect of her cool, damp hands on his warm skin made him smile. He deftly pulled on his flippers and reversed backwards into the sea, pulling his snorkel over his face, submerging himself under the water and waving an arm as he went under. A sense of humour came as part of the package. She cracked a small smile at his antics and waved back; the pair had reached an amicable impasse. And the rucksack stayed in position on the sand.

Beatrice felt unsure whether to be livid or excited. Probably the latter, by the look of her flushed cheeks. He had a bloody nerve, for sure, but she rather liked his manner. Nothing to do with the ripple of his toned body she'd felt under her fingers. It had been a while since she had such stirring feelings for the opposite sex, if ever? Perhaps it was time to rediscover them and no longer keep them suppressed.

The chance meetings between the pair soon became a daily habit, and Beatrice found, when she had not seen him during the morning, she became eager for his welfare, concerned to discover whether his sunburn had healed. Ralph varied the timings of his swims to ensure they passed a conversation at least once or sometimes twice during each day. After quitting his job as a lock-keeper and returning to the village, he resorted to living in his camper van and wanted to confess it. He'd resigned from his role as lock-keeper and returned to the village. His father had sold the house; besides, life in Swanage was far more interesting. Not to mention he'd fallen for the lady on the beach.

Over that summer, the pair became more than beach friends, both admitting it had been a while since they'd had partners, so they wanted to take things slowly. The camper van was no longer in its previous location and parked up outside Ocean Cottage. They reaffirmed to one another that they were not looking for any long-term commitment, such as marriage. Neither wanted that. Ralph found he enjoyed the company of a woman again. Soon, the overnight visits led to Beatrice's large double bed, far more comfortable than the lumpy camper van mattress. He offered to help with the repairs to the shed roof and the handrail down the rickety beach steps. In return, Beatrice cooked them romantic meals that, when the weather permitted, they ate out on the terrace.

Ralph introduced himself to Freddie, and the two men struck up an immediate friendship, their commonality being a love of water and boats. Together they repaired the *SailDreamer* and both took great delight in escorting Beatrice nervously out on the water to inspect their troubles. Sea swimming had been her thing and not sailing boats.

One evening, they were sitting in the garden, and after several glasses of red wine Beatrice popped the question. It came out of the blue, not the type of question akin to a marriage proposal. Neither party wanted that. But she asked Ralph to move in and become her live-in partner. Beatrice didn't care a jot that they would live in sin. How she wished she had dealt with her feelings about the Catholic Church a long time ago. She always blamed it for sending things so awry. She knew she must allow him into her life or spend the rest of her life alone, adrift and miserable. She did not wish to end up like her mother, cold, lonely and frigid. Ralph, observing her consternation, agreed and hugged her again. The timing was perfect. They unloaded the camper van the next day and placed all the remaining items on Beatrice's porch. The couple settled down to a perfect domestic arrangement.

Their first trip abroad together was to Brittany, spending two weeks travelling the coastline. They stayed in rural *gites* and laid out on the beaches at night, under the stars. When they returned, Beatrice made an appointment with the health clinic. She'd realised all the symptoms were there. The tender breasts, the queasiness, the overwhelming tiredness. All early signs. She bravely tried to bury all her doubts connected to her previous pregnancy. She'd blanked them out for good reason. As she took a seat in the waiting room, the nurse appeared, clutching her notes and beaming at Beatrice, who studied her face to determine the result.

"Good news, you are 100% pregnant." The nurse beamed.
"Oh!"
"You'll be celebrating tonight, I expect."
"Yes, for sure it's a much-wanted baby." Beatrice found her

voice, pushing any niggling doubts firmly to the back of her mind.

Driving home, she considered how Ralph would react to the news of impending parenthood. She wanted to tell Rosina immediately and promised herself she would write and share her good news. As she pulled up outside, Ralph looked up from the flowerbed. Judging by her face, he downed tools and rushed over to greet her. Before he could speak a word, Beatrice smacked him with a kiss full on the lips, beaming from ear to ear.

"Wow, I'm guessing we have some positive news?" Searching her eyes, his own already twinkling with delight. Ralph tidied away his gardening tools and followed Beatrice into the kitchen. Boiling the kettle, he asked, "What shall we call it? A French name, don't you think?" As he reminded her of their night in Brittany on the beach with a wiggle of his eyebrows. "It's Guillaume or Fabienne, if you remember?" "Please promise me one thing, won't you, love? Not Harry," she begged, adamant that the name Harry would feature nowhere on the birth certificate of her next baby.

Ralph closed his eyes for a moment, allowing his mind to take him back, a happy flashback to how his firstborn had been conceived. His mind led him back to the last night of a beach holiday. They were staying in a holiday home in Brittany, a couple of hundred yards from the sable beach. A broad house painted grey, with a living room on the upper floor, built especially for the panoramic views. On the last night, they had made their way down onto the sand, through the grass dunes along a well-trodden path, and spread out beach blankets. The fish and chip van out on the point supplied a meagre supper. The picnic bag held two cold beers and a bottle opener. The food tasted so much better eaten out of a cardboard box. A wedge of lemon and a fiddly sachet of salad cream. Stuffing their faces, the pair munched on thin fries. The perfect supper treat, Beatrice thought.

Both were keen to do some stargazing, as the light pollution in Brittany stood at zero. With the pink sun hovering below the skyline, partially illuminating the sky. With stomachs replete, they lay down on their backs to watch the emerging galactic display overhead. Once the sun disappeared over the horizon. The usual constellations were all there. The Plough, Perseus, the North Star, all twinkling their magic. An enchanting sky and, as night descended, it wrapped a smoky blanket around them. Beatrice instantly reminded him of her favourite Henry Wadsworth Longfellow verse, "Evangeline". She knew it off by heart.

"Silently one by one, in the infinite meadows of heaven, blossomed the lovely stars, the forget-me-nots of the angels." Ralph enthused about the notion of three twilights; a civil twilight, a nautical twilight and an astronomical twilight, desperate to impart his knowledge. He explained the derivation from days when sailors used the stars for navigational purposes. Beatrice had heard the facts before but indulged him with his ramble. It seemed the perfect moment to share a secret. She wanted to reveal the full story of Samuel. But Ralph had other ideas with a full belly. He thought they should take full advantage of an uninterrupted moment and an empty beach, as he took Beatrice in his arms, sliding his hand under her fleece and T-shirt to a certain spot.

"What did you want to say?"

"Oh, nothing, it can wait."

"Tell me what?"

"Just something I feel you should know about me."

"Ok. Later," he whispered, slightly breathless as passion overtook him.

Beatrice felt she needed to give him her full attention. She knew what needed releasing, and it wasn't just her bra, as his cool hand slid down the inside of her jeans, now loosened around her middle. It took all her concentration to focus when he yelled out into the dark. With her mission complete, her partner returned the compliment. His finger knew the familiar spot to work his magic, achieving the desired result. She arched her back, clutching the sand between her slender fingers. If Ralph had bothered to look down, he would have seen the beatific look on her face.

Leaving his French memories behind, he tried to get his head round the news that in nine months' time he would become a father. Beatrice had to reconcile that it was time to reveal to Ralph that she'd already had a child at seventeen. So this would be her second pregnancy. She hoped it wouldn't complicate their relationship. The conversation would be a little difficult to start. Where to begin?

Fifteen

Beatrice – 1970

The following year, Beatrice gave birth to Fabienne. How did she feel about the birth experience the second time around? Giving birth at home, with just a midwife present, an altogether unique experience from Samuel's birth. She needn't have fretted. With Ralph by her side, it all went smoothly. Both parents were instantly besotted. Beatrice kept the baby close to her. She strapped it to her back in a papoose-type contraption, deliberately refraining from placing it in its own bedroom until the little mite turned one. Breastfeeding went on a little longer than strictly necessary, but, as mother and baby enjoyed the experience, why should they stop? There would be no rules this time round.

Beatrice held an irrational fear of the baby being forcibly removed. Terrible nightmares haunted her at night, all set back at Elswick or on an empty beach riding a horse in pursuit of her baby. A recurring dream, lying on a wrought-iron bed and giving birth in the laundry room with Matron bellowing at her to stand up. The dream was so intense her body awoke trembling. Another dream in a hospital, and the babies lined up in perspex cots except the one at the end, which looked empty. Beatrice heard herself screaming, "Where is my baby? What have you done with it?"

In her panic, she believed Fabienne to be stolen, as the pain in her abdomen intensified. But, when she woke up, Ralph was sitting with the baby in his arms. It only needed feeding.

The birth of Fabienne triggered some old post-birth trauma feelings she experienced after Samuel. Guilt, anger, betrayal, loss, all jumbled together. Trying to separate them for a deeper analysis became impossible. They accounted for her fractured relationship that ensued with her parents, which she never repaired. As Beatrice matured, she reminded herself not to lose touch with her own youngsters. She was determined to break the cycle.

A year later, in 1971, when the next baby arrived, to Ralph's delight, she delivered a boy. They both agreed on the name Douglas. By the time she had her fourth pregnancy, in 1972, she felt far more relaxed. She put the baby to sleep in the Moses basket straightaway. This time, her behaviour swung to the other extreme. Not that she failed to bond with her latest daughter, but they all rushed her off her feet. Baby Eloise had to fit in. Following the trend, she put her to sleep outside in the pram, in all weathers. She picked her up to change and feed her before placing her back in the pram.

For most of her adult life, particularly after having four children, Beatrice struggled with her weight. A chance conversation with a friend after she'd remarked how slim she looked. She had discovered the latest phenomenon. The Cambridge diet worked its magic and the low-carb regime shrunk her body back to its original shape. The slender figure returned. Ralph was more than delighted to have his wife back. What had he meant by that comment? Beatrice felt the same inside, but her new body gave her a renewed confidence. A new wardrobe of clothes complimented her new looks; she went mad and splashed out on bold linens, tunics, cropped cardigans and even a popsicle dress, all in bright colours. To complement her new style, she bought herself some white pumps. Choosing bright cheerful colours felt a far cry from the frumpy brown linen dress and thick brown stockings she'd worn on her first date out with Jack.

~~~~

Now in their thirties, the couple had grown a good social life. They were part of a friendship group that had all produced children at around the same time, so they could easily arrange babysitters and play dates. Dinner parties were loud, lengthy and boozy. They languished in the early heady days of Liebfraumilch and Blue Nun, the food on offer an interesting mix of old and new recipes. Prawn cocktails were always popular for starters or spaghetti Bolognese, advertised as the height of haute cuisine. None of the men in their friendship group could cook. The kitchen remained a woman's domain. Ralph had been in the minority. The other dads looked at him with cookery envy when he put the final touches to his prawn cocktail.

The loyalty of those early friendships stood the test of time, as the parents continued to socialise once their offspring had left home. Before she had the children, Beatrice worked as a teaching assistant in the local school. This became trickier once she had three under-fives at home. Together they made a collective decision that, if finances allowed, she would become a stay-at-home mum, at least until Eloise went to school. She blended into the community with the other young Mums volunteering at play school and gym club.

They spent annual family holidays camping, sleeping outside in a faded green canvas bell tent. Pitched in damp fields, often surrounded by livestock. Meals cooked on simple camping gas stoves and the children fed from tins and packets. After boiling the plastic bags, he emptied the steaming contents out onto chipped white enamel plates edged in blue.

Typically, the children suggested it looked like something already digested and regurgitated. One raised eyebrow from Beatrice and they bowed their heads and greedily tucked in and scoffed at the lot. If they were still hungry, they filled up on angel slices, jaffa cakes or jumbo-sized bars of Cadburys fruit and nut.

The following year, things progressed from roughing it out in a wet canvas bell tent to luxury tent accommodation abroad. Following his success in artwork sales, they were temporarily in the black at the bank. Ralph's success in artwork sales led him to choose a EuroCamp holiday, which he organised through a travel agent. The family went abroad for their first inter-continental holiday. A first experience of an all-inclusive break: Calais, close and easy to get to and only an hour on the car ferry. So not too long for the children to be cooped up. Before the days of deep tyres on mountain bikes, most boys could only dream of owning a chopper bike with the high chrome handlebars. The mixture of bikes went with them to the campsite tied to the roof rack. The tents on site were pre-erected and considered a real luxury with proper beds, and came equipped with standard features such as fridges, plates and cutlery. It had overjoyed Ralph to see there were no camp beds to build or mattresses to blow up, and no tent pegs to bash in.

The freedom the children enjoyed on the campsite to cycle, swim, and make new friends all contributed to a happy family holiday. At last, they could relax. They drank copious amounts of local red wine and ate French cheeses with baguettes and croissants.

They happily occupied the children, either with the entertainment provided or playing with their fresh groups of friends. The site was a quiet wooded location where you heard nothing but birdsong and the odd scream of delight. During the holiday, the youngsters learnt to swim. Douglas, the stronger swimmer, liked to swim underwater. He held his breath for the longest.

On the third day, when everyone had relaxed and perhaps let their guard down a little, a shout went up from the pool area, followed by the long whistle of the lifeguard sitting high in his chair. A dash along the pool edge saw the young lifeguard stripping off his T-shirt. Parents were standing and pointing to something happening in the pool. A little girl struggled against the wash of the activity; one boy had tried to drag her to the side but gone under himself. Within seconds, two children were in serious trouble, arms thrashing in desperation. Two pink armbands lay abandoned by the steps. Beatrice dived in, fully clothed, instantly recognising the flailing arms were those of her youngest. The sloping pool meant she'd quickly got out of her depth. The lifeguard threw the ring, and the boy grabbed at it in relief. Beatrice hoisted Eloise out of the pool by her swimming costume, trying not to panic. After a lot of spluttering Eloise took a breath, vomited a lot of water and burst into tears. Beatrice thanked the boy, who had made a valiant rescue attempt. Before she began chastising her youngest daughter she deliberated her choice of words.

Fabienne

Fabienne had been blessed with the looks of a model. Her colouring more akin to Beatrice's, with dark, flowing chestnut locks surrounded by an oval-shaped face and blessed with small ears. The soft brown almond eyes bearing long extended lashes were her own, she reminded those who asked. Her peaches-and-cream complexion covered a smooth, unlined forehead, carrying a smattering of pale freckles across her nose. For such a tall person, her small hands were delicate, with neatly trimmed, manicured nails. In the bedroom was a set of full-length wardrobes bursting with clothes from all the top haute couture ranges. She liked to dress at the height of fashion.

Whenever the family gathered together at the kitchen table, inevitably the conversation reverted to their childhood. What did Fabienne remember most about it? Stories frequently degenerated in tone and weight. The siblings brought up their worst moments. For instance, whose behaviour had been the worst? Douglas won that one. Or who had committed the most heinous crime at school? Again, Douglas won the prize. At school, Fabienne had always been a smart child, placed in all the top groups. One subject she loathed was PE, in any form. She excelled at art and English. In English literature she allowed her imagination to be fuelled by the wide range of storybooks at home.

Her university days at Exeter proved invaluable. After attaining a first-class degree in English, she landed her first job back in London in Canada Square as a junior editor for a newspaper, writing a weekly column for the entertainment team. The perks of which meant plenty of nights out at film premieres in Leicester Square, trawling book shops such as Foyles or Dillons, checking out the top ten bestsellers before writing up her reviews.

Fabienne never appeared to be short of male friends. By the time she turned thirty, her parents were becoming less hopeful of her settling down. An agreed moratorium on the subject reached between them long ago. Working long twelve-hour days with an equally hectic social life meant that men came and went in her life, but rarely stayed long. Fiercely independent, and bullish in a manner, her softer side remained hidden beneath a cool exterior that rarely revealed itself publicly.

The well-paid job had funded the plush riverbank apartment in the city. The flat boasted a wide balcony that stood proudly overlooking Tower Bridge. She lived her current life as a city girl, known then as an "it girl". To escape the smoke and grime of the city, Fabienne took her holidays in the solitude of the hills and mountains of Scotland or Switzerland.

Unlike her younger sister, she abhorred all water sports. Perhaps it had been the overzealous enthusiasm of her parents when small. But she still remembered the thrill it gave everyone else. After being coerced into the water, just to please them, she would make a feeble excuse to get out and shiver purple-faced, scowling under her towel. The joy of her family splashing about, squealing with delight, bothered her. She had had no desire to get wet or have her skin wrinkle up like a prune.

The newly built offices at Canary Wharf were minimalistic in their furnishings. Fabienne's office had a few executive offices and one large board room that overlooked the Wharf. Employed for her fierce reputation, she managed a team comprising mainly young hopefuls. The office ethos was: work hard and play hard or you would fail. One by one, the junior staff came and went, working under the illusion that they were at the office for a bit of a skive or gossip. If she caught them hanging about in the staff kitchen, they would instantly receive a verbal warning. Firing staff had become a large part of what she did, and other senior staff looked to her to do the deed that many found so awkward. Although there was no violation of the rules, the methods appeared outdated by modern European employment standards.

On that Monday morning, the call came out of the blue. Fabienne and the senior team were sitting in the boardroom in the middle of the weekly team meeting. After a knock on the door and a whisper in her ear from her assistant, she excused herself and exited the room. There was an urgent phone call, said her assistant. After dashing down the corridor by the time she reached her office, the call had gone straight to answer the machine. With her finger trembling, she pressed the flashing red button. Beatrice's voice sounded frail, a little choked in fact. Fabienne, puzzled by the urgency of the request, returned to her meeting. Would she be able to visit at the weekend, as her mother had something important to reveal? At last, the big reveal of the long-held family secret, if her hunch turned out to be correct! So she left a message for her siblings, apologising for the short notice, but they all must try to be at Ocean Cottage on Friday. The logistics involved for Eloise, living in western France, and Douglas, who was living who knows where, made the plan tricky to coordinate. Fabienne did not know where to find her brother. It would prove impossible for the others to find their way to Swanage by Friday at such short notice!

By one o'clock, Fabienne needed a break. She left the confines of the stuffy office for a quick takeaway lunch. Back in the queue at the Chinese noodle shop. The number of choices confused people on the takeaway menu. For Fabienne, it proved easy: Singapore noodles with lots of hot chilli sauce. Chinese food was no longer a novelty on the streets in London. Rushing back to the office, clutching her warm box in a bundle of serviettes, she quickly ate whilst she prepared for her next meeting. Slurping the last of the noodles from their cardboard nest, she scrunched up the box and tossed it in the bin. That day she was hoping to finish on time, but thought her meeting might get tricky as the boss had disliked her latest review, rejecting it prior to the publication deadline.

$\sim$

Fabienne felt she had the closest relationship with her mother, their bond sealed from the very beginning. Beatice had likened her daughter's personality to her own, citing familial traits. From an early age, her mother's jewellery had caught her interest. In particular, she had a fascination for her rings and necklaces, in fact anything that sparkled. They took the jewellery box down from the shelf, laying it carefully on the bedspread. One particular ring always held her attention far more than the others, partly because it had hidden in a special tortoiseshell box lined with rich blue silk. She had only glimpsed it once before. The sheen on the stone caused by the light reflections always fascinated her. Beatrice allowed her to put it on but, of course, it instantly fell off when she wiggled her fingers. Her mother explained about the colour of the stone and why it had inclusions. Fabienne, far too young for conversations about inclusions, looked at her mother quizzically, but Beatrice, oblivious, ploughed on.

"What are intrusions, Mummy?"

"Not intrusions, darling, inclusions. It means the stones look like gardens or green plants. Look at these." She held out her hand and young Fabienne nodded as though she understood the significance. The thorough explanation soared over the head of young Fabienne. But she never forgot the word inclusion. And the ring with sparkles that always held such a fascination. Fabienne was too young to have known it held such key information. The type that would come back to haunt her and her family. Beatrice closed the lid and promised to tell her more of the secret story when she was old enough to understand. For reasons only known to her mother, that had never happened. She felt convinced that Ralph knew far more than he revealed.

Fabienne, an avid reader, regularly used her local library. She liked to pop in every month to check out the latest popular novels for her book reviews, never one to spend money where it wasn't necessary. Whilst her head buried itself amongst the pages of the books, she picked up a dictionary, curious to understand the meaning of the word "inscription" and to understand why people reacted so differently to the word. She was trying to understand the true meaning of the words that her mother had left inscribed on her ring. Her eyes scanned down the pages.

They inscribed rings for many personal reasons. She read the last few words out loud. What did they mean? Every word has its own connotation depending on the letters or sentiment involved. An engraving, lettering, epitaph, etching, carving, a dedication, or a coded message?

What lay behind the inscription of Beatrice's ring and what did it mean to the family? Two dates, with a link.

Beatrice had had the ring inscribed as a memento to her baby and a brief marriage to Jack. Fabienne wondered why it had been so short? Nobody had asked that question yet. Feeling thwarted, she closed the books on the table, gathered up her belongings and headed home. Later that evening, she would attempt to call her brother and sister again to discuss her findings prior to their meeting and the implications for them.

Beatrice

Standing in the kitchen Beatrice had made two cups of coffee, but didn't recall how whilst deep in thought. That morning, she and Ralph had entered a tense discussion.

"It makes perfect sense to me," he murmured in a clipped tone. His retorts had been turning sarky. Recently, he'd found the complications of Beatrice's early life hard to fathom. He found himself irritated. Why had she not told Eloise about her health issues whilst they holidayed in France? It felt like one of the stormy squalls they endured whilst sailing, about to erupt around them.

"What does? What makes perfect sense?" snapped back Beatrice, who found the sudden tension between them hard to deal with. As usual, she'd been overthinking it. "I'll tell them when I'm ready, Ralph. Stop telling me what to do, ok?" She trailed off.

"You just need to be honest with them, that's all I'm saying." He was walking away towards his garden in retreat, coffee in hand, newspaper tucked under his other arm.

"I have always been honest with my children, and with…" Her voice trailed off through the open door. The last word of that sentence she couldn't utter as it was not quite true. Ralph had already seated himself on the bench with his newspaper open at the sports pages. The reason for her irritability, she knew she had not been totally honest with Ralph in recent weeks. She flung the remaining washing up in the sink and went upstairs to take a shower. Still in a huff, she loathed it when they had words. She also hated to admit that perhaps Ralph had been right. The scalding water cascaded down over her head. She tried to ignore it. In the middle of washing her hair, with her head completely covered in shampoo, the phone in the bedroom rang out.

"Am I the only person who answers the damn phone?" she roared out to nobody. Wrapping her soapy hair in a towel, she got out of the shower, muttering. Refilling his cup, Ralph paused by the back door to listen in. He couldn't hear properly so climbed the stairs to check on the ID of the caller. The bedroom door stood open, so he listened to the conversation.

"Hello, can I speak with Beatrice Gardiner, please?" spoke the deep voice with an air of familiarity.

"Who is this?" Her voice immediately changed to one of minor irritability, the soap in her eyes beginning to sting.

"It's me, Samuel. We met the other day at the hospital. Sorry, is this a terrible moment? I'm wondering if we could meet up properly, perhaps in a cafe?" Beatrice melted as she sat down on the edge of the bed, quivering. She had not expected his call to come so soon.

"How about the Spinnaker Cafe, on the seafront at Swanage?" The voice was a cross between Jack and Douglas, persuasive, almost a tad coercive, she thought. How did he know the whereabouts of her local cafe?

"Tuesday? Yes, that should be fine," Beatrice suggested, randomly picking a day without checking the diary. Ralph gave a serious nod and a shrug.

"Yes, fine, see you there, say ten thirty?"

Taken aback, her bottom lip quivered a little. The grimace on Ralph's face spoke enough. The time had come.

"Don't say a word, I can guess by the look on your face, love."

"Brace yourself, Ralph." Beatrice held back and chose not to tell him the full story about the hospital bench.

"Didn't you register some time ago on the Lost and Found Agency list?"

True, she had registered, but she hadn't told Ralph yet about the hospital meeting. It had raised so many questions.

Her life was slowly unravelling. Blowing her nose, she returned to the shower to rinse her hair. When she'd dressed and wandered down to the kitchen, she still felt in a bit of a weepy daze. Ralph had his own suspicions and thought it best to keep quiet for the minute and see what materialised. So why Samuel's sudden interest in finding his mother, after so many years? Ralph's chief concern was that Beatrice might not handle the emotional side of a reunion in her current state.

Beatrice had a totally different take on it. The reunification between the pair would be a relief. For years, she had carried the emotional baggage associated with her teenage troubles. No longer angry, just sad that she'd been so young and under such influence from her parents. On reflection, Harry and Flo had been under the influence of their priest. Reuniting with Samuel when things were so uncertain about her health felt like a positive outcome. Despite differing expectations from those around her, now was the right time to engage with the other siblings. She told Ralph she had already left them messages to come down for the weekend. She wished to tell them about Samuel and the changes to her will.

For Samuel, his mission would be to simply to screw her for every penny: a means to an end, cold and calculated. Even a hardened individual like Samuel Gardiner would have a softer side. Nobody had ever got close enough to find out, though. He had never had a steady relationship. He used women to satisfy his sexual urges without the respect they deserved. In the past, they had challenged him about his sexuality, and vehemently denied that he felt leanings towards same-sex relationships. Someone would raise the question again about his sexuality when he arrived on Mull to introduce himself to Douglas. They had challenged him about it in the past and he had vehemently denied any same-sex leanings.

Tuesday came round quickly for Beatrice. They'd referred to it on the calendar as "Meet Up" day. The meeting at the Spinnaker Cafe with Samuel would go ahead. Beatrice showered and dressed before Ralph stirred. Unable to face anything for breakfast, she made herself a strong cup of tea instead. The previous evening, she'd asked Ralph to drive her over to the cafe and hover around outside, just in case.

"Just in case of what?" he'd asked gently.

It would be an ideal opportunity to take his watercolours to make a start on a new landscape painting. Beatrice wanted him on hand in case she had cold feet at the last minute. In reality, she might have had a funny turn meeting Samuel face to face. Or she wanted Ralph to be somewhere in the vicinity in case Samuel started a scene; she wasn't able to define what kind of scene she might expect. The scene where she'd run out of the cafe sobbing into Ralph's arms? Or a scene where Samuel got tetchy and made unrealistic demands? Or a scene where he'd stand and shout at her for abandoning him, and storm out? Last but not least, would she find it too emotional to handle and wave Samuel away, too distressed? Having waited so long for the golden ticket moment, would she be strong enough to handle it emotionally? Though perhaps Ralph was right when he'd hinted that it would be too much. Beatrice felt comforted by having him nearby anyway, whatever the outcome!

They took the back roads to the cafe. Parking up at the far end of the promenade. Stooping to kiss her head, Ralph wished her good luck and watched her walk away. He thought she had visibly aged since hearing about her diagnosis. She no longer walked with such a spring in her step. The crinkly laughter lines around her eyes seemed to have diminished a little with her recent weight loss. The real Beatrice had become a little more introverted.

Ralph unloaded his frayed painting bag and folding stool from the boot of the car, taking the familiar walk towards the beach. Great, he thought, an hour of uninterrupted painting. Looking upwards, he squinted: the weather perfect with cerulean skies. What could be nicer? The satchel contained a pad of painting paper and a small box of watercolours and water in the glass jar with a screw top. The new brushes made of horsehair were a recent birthday present from Beatrice. He found the spot where the vista gave him nigh on perfect colours as the light bounced off the water, scattering reflections across the bay.

Samuel had arrived at the cafe early. Showing no obvious sign of nerves, he'd tucked into a hearty breakfast. His seat in the far corner had a bird's-eye view of the harbour and the entrance door. During his visit to the mother and baby unit, they had shown him an old photograph, taken many years ago. Now Beatrice's figure and hair looked so different. He would just have to rely on instinct. Using the paper serviette to wipe his bearded chin, sweeping his teeth with his tongue, he sipped the dregs in the bottom of his empty coffee cup and waited.

First, he fidgeted with his hair, tucking it behind his ear, twiddling it around his forefinger. The exposed ear showed off his gold stud earring, the one thing he'd kept from his teenage years. He briefly remembered when he'd walked into the jeweller's shop, aged about thirteen, to have an ear piercing. When the shop staff asked why his mum wasn't with him to sign a consent form, he boasted loudly that he didn't have one to ask. Just for effect. He persuaded the woman to carry on and pierce his earlobe. It probably had something to do with the substantial wad of cash he waved in her face. With the deed completed, he returned to the orphanage, where nobody seemed overly impressed or interested in what he had done.

The matron told him to take it out straightaway when the bleeding stopped. Feeling miffed at her request, he'd refused. He'd expected a greater reaction. The mantra repeating in his head: "big boys don't cry", though the ear piercing session had pushed him to tears. The following day, he nearly ripped the thing from his earlobe in frustration at the throbbing, persistent pain.

Tuesday came round quickly. Samuel had prepared his questions with care, over and over in his head, until he knew them off pat. Mostly they began with the word why? Why did you? He was hopeful that she could give him some of the missing answers. He'd also hoped that she would provide him with some honesty in return for his questions. Ones that were true to the dilemma she faced.

In his mind, he had meticulously planned what he intended to say and felt confident all was going to go his way. He ordered a second coffee and a slice of raspberry flapjack for old times' sake. He had a sudden memory from his orphanage when they ate poor man's flapjack. Served as a dessert, and swamped with thin pale liquid that the staff called custard. Interrupting his memory, the bell jangled above the door and the next customer came in. The woman looked around as if she might be meeting someone but unsure where to find them. Her eyes cast around the crowded cafe and settled on the curly-haired, bearded man alone in the corner.

For the occasion Beatrice had chosen her favourite dress, a pale pink linen number, with flat white summer sandals. A blue patterned scarf hung loosely around her neck. The choice of outfit complimented her hair, recently cut into a bob. Samuel watched as she passed the till. She asked the waitress for a pot of tea for one. Her eyes were quickly drawn to the man in the corner, who had already had a drink. Once inside, she removed her cardigan, placing it on the back of the chair. Samuel stood up, uncertain if he should shake her hand formally, kiss her cheek or hug her. When they'd met briefly at the hospital, they had remained cold and clinical when Beatrice had been in complete shock. In his head, he'd planned to offer a hug, but didn't want to overwhelm her so soon on arrival.

"Hi, Mum." He grinned awkwardly, relaxing some of the tension on his shoulders. He instantly liked her eyes, warm and friendly, with faint wrinkles around the edges.

"Hello again, Samuel." Beatrice, with no qualms, instinctively leant in to kiss him, grazing her face against a bristly cheek. Even though she detected a trace of smoke on his beard, this did not affect the instant rush of maternal feelings. Within half an hour, she felt the void between them shrinking, so she took his hand across the table. Things were moving too fast. Samuel, unsure, thought it a little forward. She wanted to study his face for every minor detail. Noting the non-existence of a wedding band, she'd already spotted the earring and a chipped front tooth. The colour of his eyes, flecked with hazel, set deep within blue irises. The chickenpox scar on his temple looked fresh. They were the smallest of things that only a mother would trouble to notice, as she tried hard not to stare at his face.

Beatrice inhaled. Where should she begin her story? Like Samuel, she had rehearsed this moment so often in her head. She suddenly felt at a loss for words, her chest taut with unspoken emotion.

Samuel had his own motives for this meeting, which were cold and calculated, so he concentrated all his efforts on ingratiating himself. No! He reminded himself: not just any woman... his "mother".

"I guess my first question should be why you didn't keep me after my birth. And why did you have to hand me over?" Ouch. She felt that question aimed straight at the heart.

Beatrice felt her chest muscles tighten again. Slightly winded, she took a deep breath and quickly regained her composure enough to continue.

"Well, I'd prefer to start at the beginning, so you understand what reasons lay behind the decisions. You have a right to know the sequence of events as they occurred. I had no choice whether I wanted to keep my baby or choose a partner and get married."

Samuel interrupted her again with, "Did you love my father? I don't even know his name. It wasn't on the birth certificate."

"Jack. Jack Gardiner. Oh, yes, at the start, I think I did. Being so young, I naively thought he loved me, too. He cheated on me before we married and again soon afterwards. We were totally incompatible after that. Your father messed about, and I ended up mistrusting him. It took a lot of courage to walk out on him. Divorce was frowned upon within the family, but I knew that I could have a life beyond Consett."

Over an hour later, they finished the second round of drinks just as the cafe filled up for the lunchtime peak. The pair took some fresh air and, leaving the security and warmth of the cafe, walked towards the harbour. Samuel had far more questions than Beatrice. As they walked, she attempted to fill in some gaps.

As Samuel had always mistrusted adults, he found it hard to show and receive any form of affection without an ulterior motive, looking for that missing something in his life that he had never quite fathomed. He always spoke with such convincing authority nobody doubted him, and those who did were soon met with his foul temper. For the next hour, Beatrice became his new captive audience. Desperate to impress, he worked hard in a brief space of time to convince her that her firstborn had matured into an honest, hard-working guy. That he had a secure job, had money in the bank, and lived in an affluent part of London. Most of the aforementioned facts were of course lies and fantasies. He had to make a quick decision about whether to disclose his place of residence or the type of car he owned. They had become a compensation for the disastrous paths and life choices he'd taken since leaving the security of the orphanage. The plush house in London was simply a pure fantasy. He lived in the roughest part of Barking, his car a knock-off from the dodgy garage on Dagenham High Road. A converted Ford Escort with twin exhausts and an engine far too big for the chassis. Bought on tick, and years before he had the finances to pay it off. With not a penny in the bank, far from it, and a hefty overdraft, the bank letters had stacked up in the bin. The bank refused him further credit recently. His job history bore testament more to a man who'd struggled with the basics of day-to-day life. He'd recently had a crazy new idea of becoming a loan shark. That he wisely left out of their conversations.

The weather had been kind to the pair. Being outside in the fresh air took a little of the tension out of their meeting, as they linked arms for a walk. This allowed Beatrice to unfold a potted history of her life. Starting with Jack, followed by her banishment to France, and by serendipity finding Ralph. She felt she ought to broach the subject of her three other children, and spoke of wanting to introduce them. She told Samuel about the inscriptions on her wedding ring and the meanings behind it. Samuel frowned and nodded in all the right places. One question he wanted answered: why had his mother never remarried? Beatrice thought this to be an intrusive question that she would prefer not to answer. So she didn't.

As the pair walked the length of the prom, neither had any inkling that her life would draw to an early close. This would be the only time they would get to spend together alone. Beatrice kept the reason for her hospital visit to herself, overlooking the fact that the details were in the envelope that she'd given Samuel when she'd scribbled her phone number down. She kept glancing sideways at this man on her arm and imagined herself back in the day doing the same with Jack. The small pencil moustache with a beard and the way he dressed, a few of his mannerisms, were identical. Perhaps she was trying a little too hard to make her story fit together. How could Samuel consider betrayal and coercive plots whilst smiling sweetly at his newly discovered matriarchal figure? Skilfully, he portrayed his character without issue, striking revenge for the way his life had panned out to date. A sick act for his motive and form of payback. Would he betray and double-cross the folk he fought so desperately to know? For now, he had nothing to lose as he perceived he had already lost everything at birth.

Beatrice shivered, and Samuel kindly drew her cardigan around her shoulders. The meeting had reached a natural conclusion, as they found themselves back at the car park. Before she left, she gave him a family memento. A silver horse pin that had belonged to her brother Albert.

"I'd like you to have this. It's only a small memento."

"Thank you," faltered Samuel, examining it in his palm and putting it straight in his pocket. He wasn't keen on sentimentality or mementos. Beatrice waved him goodbye, and walked back to the car, her thoughts spinning. She found Ralph packed up, waiting patiently, engrossed in a crossword. Beatrice got in and let out a sigh before she slumped down in the seat. She hated goodbyes, in whatever form. They always gave her a lump in her throat. They had a bad association with giving away her baby.

"Did the meeting go well?" he gently enquired. On second glance, he thought she looked drained, wrung out. She'd been in such a state beforehand, but actually nothing had gone wrong. In fact, they'd planned to meet up again, next time with the rest of the family beside her.

Ralph listened, raising an eyebrow in consternation, and started the engine. Before they reached the top of the hill, Beatrice burst into floods of tears. How had she expected to reach this stage in her life without all those dormant feelings bubbling up to the surface? Ralph took the drive at a slower pace and refrained from asking any more questions until they got home. She promised him she would share what had passed between them later when she'd had time to fully digest it. Ralph couldn't help himself and, in his haste to find out more, he forgot his earlier vow to tread carefully with too many enquiries.

Once home, he set about organising a glass of dry cider and some crisps before attempting the conversation again, this time with a blinder guaranteed to rile: perhaps a male attribute he never learnt.

"So, you are seeing him again?" Followed quickly by, "You didn't give him our address, did you?" Beatrice thought it best not to confess to the envelope incident at the hospital.

"Jesus, love, give me a chance to get my cardigan off and sit down."

"Sorry, I can see you are upset. Let's start again. I only saw him from a distance. He looked like a decent bloke; thought he resembled Douglas a little."

Now seriously regretting her decision to allow him to drive her to the meeting, Beatrice took a large slug of her drink and let it slowly do its magic, pausing only to reflect before answering him. Did he fully understand the significance of the wedding ring inscriptions? Were there any secrets left between them?

Later that evening, with delicious smells coming from the kitchen that met with Beatrice's approval, Ralph set about cooking supper. The table was duly set with her favourite French tablecloth with flowers and chocolates at one end. They eagerly consumed another glass of chilled cider. He busied himself in the kitchen cooking her favourite comfort food: macaroni cheese. A box of Black Magic chocolates superseded the dessert. Ralph's plan had worked, and they'd restored some calm and order to their lives. The day ended in peace and harmony. How long for, he couldn't say; he was content things would work out.

Beatrice

After their meeting, Samuel had been playing on her mind and she had spent much of the night thinking about what to do first. She felt in a slight quandary; she had to make a tough decision. Should she change her will to reflect the wishes for all her rings, or leave it all to Ralph's judgement, to sort out after the event, which seemed unwise, as she now had the added complication of Samuel to acknowledge. The consideration led her to the thorny subject of the cottage and whether to leave it to Samuel too, therefore bypassing Ralph. The itemised bequest list was easier to solve. She would leave a copy in the jewellery box. Carefully, she lifted the oriental wooden box down from the top of the wardrobe. Inside, the lining still captured the aromatic scent of camphor. Inhaling deeply, the memories came flooding back. It had been a birthday present from Rosina. When Fabienne was born, Rosina sent a box carved in Manila as a present.

Her family had passed the set of rings down, each ring with a personal story behind it. As an important part of her legacy, she felt her youngsters should know the backstories. By the time she'd finished writing her wishes on the list, she hoped she had made the right decisions.

Eloise would inherit the large Edwardian emerald ring in a claw setting, which Ralph had bought for Beatrice following her birth. The emerald ring sat in a chrome box lined with royal blue satin. Emeralds represent luck, love and peace, a mantra adopted by Beatrice early in her adult life. A good choice for marriage proposals, but Ralph had never proposed and, even if he had, Beatrice would not have accepted. She slipped it over her thin ring finger, thinking how strange it looked now on an older person's hand. The green-blue veins were nowadays more prominent with raised gnarled knuckles.

The second ring, a male signet, had belonged to her grandfather. It was wrapped in black tissue paper and tucked inside a small wooden box with a brass hinge, no bigger than a matchbox. Unlucky onyx: she remembered his words. They would leave it to Douglas? Still undecided, she left a question mark alongside it. That left the golden topaz ring with smooth tones of yellow saturation in a bezel setting. Ralph had given it to her to mark their twenty-five-year partnership. The topaz ring came in an unusual oriental silk pouch secured by a brass popper. Each ring in her collection had a unique box, and the jewellers provided information on where it was originally purchased. It made sense to leave that one to Fabienne.

Lastly, the gold wedding band with the two inscriptions in a round tortoiseshell box. This one, she decided long ago, must be for Samuel. Yes, they were her wishes. She had decided each person would have a ring. With the list complete, she placed it back in the envelope, sealed it, and returned the box to the shelf.

Would anybody work out the inscription and the birth was three months before the wedding? That inscription hid a dark Hamilton family secret.

Lucknow and Hardcastle had been family solicitors for generations of the Hamilton family. Considering her health news, Ralph and Beatrice had changed their current wills. His affairs were far more simple and his will, in the event of something happening to him, left everything to Beatrice. The main issue to be acknowledged was that Beatrice and Ralph remained unmarried. Would this affect the legality of the will? They both asked the same question. Mr Lucknow tutted, shaking his head. He didn't interfere in her plans or attempt to sway their minds. But reminded them of his role, acting purely as an advisor, aware of the complexities of this family set-up. He felt he should start by advising Beatrice to itemise the smaller bequests. The pair explained the recent added complication of Samuel, with little idea it would be contested at a later date.

But, as Ralph stepped into the corridor to find a toilet, Beatrice made another change that she chose only to share with Mr Lucknow. When he returned, he found Beatrice ready to go, her coat slung over her arm, sitting out in the corridor. The meeting had ended rather abruptly, and she chose not to reveal any of the last conversation that he had just missed. Why did she feel she needed to keep her thoughts and plans from Ralph and share them only with her solicitor? Would Beatrice now put Samuel before Ralph?

Sixteen

La Baule

It had been six months since Beatrice's diagnosis and there had been no cancellation appointment. Ralph had told Beatrice they needed a holiday. He'd become concerned that they should not delay their arrangements to visit Eloise and Romuel. The plan was to take the boat across the Channel to La Baule.

Built in the 1950s, *SailDreamer*, was a neat thirty-four-foot yacht with smart teak decks. It boasted distinctive navy-blue sails and a main and foresail with a proud blue and white spinnaker. Two single berths filled the forward cabin, and a double in the main cabin. The galley, although narrow, came equipped with a three-ring burner hob and a small grill, the lockers beautifully hand crafted with ornate brass handles. The boat had taken them on many jollies across the English Channel, taking in the beaches and towns of the west coast of France, La Rochelle and La Baule, and exploring the west Cornwall coast, down as far as the Scilly Isles. They thought nothing of spending two or three weeks sailing their favourite stretch of coastal waters. They challenged themselves to live frugally, buying fresh food from the local quayside markets. Their passports held an array of destination stamps issued by the local harbourmasters. Like many older boats, *SailDreamer* held its secrets close to the decks.

Their romantic trip across the Channel had been planned with meticulous precision. Ralph took charge of the boat, and Beatrice became the crew, hoisting sails, and duty deckhand. The latest trip to La Baule would turn out to be their last one together.

"Ready to cast off?" barked Ralph. Bea raised her hand in acknowledgement. Ocean Cottage up on the clifftop soon became a tiny speck in the far distance. They took the light force-three breeze with them for the first two hours, on course to reach the French coast by evening if they continued on that tack at a steady speed without the need to make too many sail changes. Their crossing took them across one of the busiest shipping lanes. Ralph continued to bark out his orders. Beatrice did not object, familiar with her role as deckhand. She knew Ralph's instructions had to be followed on command, to avoid veering off course into the path of larger ships. They had spent many weekends at sea choosing random places along the south coast to moor for the night, sometimes with no harbour wall to moor against, or dropping anchor and taking the small rib up on to the beaches.

This trip would be different. They had planned to visit Eloise and her family. When the harbour came into sight she strained her eyes to see if any of the figures waiting on the jetty resembled their daughter. With the light fading, the trip across the Channel had taken longer than expected. Eloise stood on the quayside waving furiously. She strode along the jetty to grab the mooring rope. *SailDreamer* glided into the mooring, fenders at the ready. Ralph cut the engine and let the ropes ease the boat to a halt.

The plan was to moor the boat at Douarnenez for the first night and sail on to La Baule for a weekend reunion with Romuel and Amélie the following day. After lingering hugs, they realised they hadn't set eyes on their youngest daughter for some months. That night they dined on board just the three of them. Eloise had come prepared with a magnificent supper. Moules bought from the quayside, with a crusty baguette for mopping up, followed by a selection of French cheeses to compliment the new bottle of Beaujolais. She updated her parents about the recent events in France and plans for the future.

At dawn the following morning all three set sail for La Baule. On Saturday evening a table for five had been booked at La Pastiche, a local restaurant, for eight o'clock. The atmosphere around the table felt upbeat and relaxed. Ralph and Romuel plumped for entrecôte steak and Eloise and Beatrice went for fish, all with piles of frites. Young Amélie surprised them all by ordering a seafood pasta dish, spaghetti allo scoglio. So grown up, thought Beatrice.

Why did she feel nervous? She felt it would be such poor timing to start the conversation she'd been dreading. Looking around her at the tanned happy faces of her family, full of bonhomie, Beatrice changed her mind. She thought it selfish to create an unhappy memory at a place they all loved on such a joyful occasion; and more important to talk with her granddaughter about her life at school, and her own hopes and dreams. At thirteen those subjects seemed far more relevant than her own worries. So Beatrice kept the news about her health to herself. Ralph nudged her a couple of times to start the conversation; she frowned at him and chose to keep quiet.

~

On their return to Swanage things started to unravel. Between them they couldn't agree on the best approach. Beatrice felt she owed Samuel the chance to meet the others, unsure how they would react to a stranger coming into their close-knit unit. Discussions became heated and divisive, one morning erupting over breakfast. Ralph kicked off the conversation.

"You need to come clean, Bea; they should know what's happening. They have every right, don't they?" Trying not to think that the worst might happen before they got to know.

"Ralph, please let me take care of it, I'll sort it out in my own time."

"You know that I just want the best outcome for you, don't you? You owe it to me and the three children rather than leave me with the murky job should anything happen to you, love." It felt strange to be thinking purely of himself for a change. He did not want to be the one to clear up the mess left behind by his beloved partner. He disliked any form of confrontation.

Seventeen

Samuel – 2000

Samuel had taken the same seat as his mother two weeks earlier. He was at the solicitor's office to discuss his late mother's wishes. The office decor was typical of a solicitor's office, all wood panelling and vintage plaster roses with lavish ornate fittings. The old-fashioned muted desk lamps had been in situ for many years. His body twitched, a sure sign of nerves despite all his external bluff and bravado. He'd stifled a laugh when he'd read the latest version of Beatrice's will. Mr Lucknow's bushy right eyebrow raised itself to its limit, on hearing the request from the young man opposite him. He had only seen Beatrice a couple of weeks ago. And now Samuel Gardiner had the audacity to convince Mr Lucknow that he'd become reliant on a promise made by Beatrice. He claimed it had forced him to quit his position at work, to his own detriment, doing his best to convince the solicitor that he lacked any funds. The second claim from the young man was outrageous, in the solicitor's eyes. He believed they had updated the will through the undue influence of her family.

The solicitor calmly reminded him he would still not have a valid claim on that basis. Samuel responded he did not need reminding about an interpretation of the law. The solicitors had discreetly completed comprehensive security checks. And had found nothing but debt attributed to his name. Of course, he had a legal right to contest the will, for a valid reason. The solicitor explained items like money or property bequeathed in return for care and support would indeed give one a legitimate reason to make a claim. They stood fast, despite Mr Gardiner's protestations. The solicitor saw straight through his counterarguments. Samuel had gone as far as contesting the legitimacy of the nominated executors, Fabienne and Ralph. In Samuel's opinion, he believed Fabienne had not been serving the best interest of his mother, and failed in her duty to remain impartial. For example, if Fabienne had her way, he would receive only the inscribed ring. The others would surely dispute the amendment. That caused outrage when he posed a further question over whether Beatrice "might not have been of sound mind" when she amended her will, citing Ralph as having an undue influence on her recent changes.

Mr Lucknow cleared his throat again. He felt he had to intervene. The man was ill-informed. His assumptions were all made in haste and facts were unsubstantiated. Again, he explained the vagaries of common law. Despite meeting with his newly acquainted mother, he knew she had added a second valuable asset to his name, a property, Ocean Cottage. Nobody had mentioned it yet.

Mr Lucknow checked his watch and sighed as Mr Gardiner vacated his office for the second time that week. The pair of solicitors had decided not to indulge him any more of their precious time. The secretary had already noted his endless chase up calls. His ultimate question was, "Why hadn't they granted probate yet? Why was it taking so long?"

The grant of probate would allow the executors to get on and administer the estate. Samuel felt he had a strong legitimate claim and held this over the other stepsiblings like a leaden weight and lost patience. The arguments had set them all against each other and within a few short weeks of Beatrice's death the infighting had begun. Ralph kept his opinion to himself. He empathised with his youngsters and felt in some ways they were right.

Why should they accept Samuel into their close family group as they looked to him to resolve the matter? He felt out of his depth for the contents of Beatrice's will and how to divide her estate equally, all within the confines of the law. Samuel's arrival on the scene had complicated matters, each sibling with a differing point of view on the subject.

Fabienne's take on Samuel: they should fight his claim to inherit any part of her mother's estate, in particular the inheritance of the property. She firmly believed he had no right to any of it. They should not pass even the inscribed wedding ring over. She thought it outrageous that he should show up and lay claim to any family jewellery. Fabienne did not wish to meet him and made this clear to Ralph. She'd wrongly assumed that her mother would leave the cottage to herself and Eloise once their father had passed.

Eloise, the adult who was softer, more forgiving than the others, had no issue with meeting Samuel or sharing any part of her mother's wishes. Nothing but an intense curiosity had taken over her thoughts and she asked Ralph when and where they were going to meet. She wondered what he looked like and whether he had a family of his own.

She asked Romuel if he would mind Samuel coming to stay with them in France, so she could get to know him. Romuel agreed in principle with her idea, although he'd heard from her sister some strange stories about Eloise's stepbrother.

He wanted to make up his own mind and meet him in person. They had all overlooked some basic facts like where he lived, or how he found Beatrice in the first place. Or was his claim to be Beatrice's son legitimate?

Douglas, the dark horse of the three siblings for reasons he'd omitted to tell the others, had met with Samuel in Scotland. The affinity between them was quickly established. Douglas remained forever the gullible fool.

Eighteen

Douglas

As a small boy, Douglas had always been indulged by his mother, because of an irrational fear that Beatrice had about losing him, a fear akin to how she felt when she'd lost Samuel. Beatrice always denied it when Ralph had questioned it. At school, Douglas found his popularity heightened when he discovered he had a talent for creating chaos and distractions by becoming the class clown. He became adept at covering up his true feelings. Like most strong-willed, needy children he never enjoyed being told what to do by those in authority. Content to exploit the good nature of others, though. Perhaps this similar trait could be found in another member of the family. He recalled the teachers making idle threats to have him removed from the classroom or to sit out in the corridor for his misbehaviour. Soon, he got the measure of the idle threats that were never carried out. His sole aim was to be removed from the class so he would not have to listen to those unlucky enough to educate him. School life sucked, in his opinion, and he simply gave up learning.

About the same time, aged sixteen, his relationship with his parents nosedived. He started staying out late, and lying in bed all day, and became a slob.

The close circle of friends had changed, and he no longer spent time with his school peers, preferring to seek the company of men a few years older. They drove their tatty souped-up cars at speed in the car parks in town, performing flashy donuts on the tarmac. The locals complained about the foul language and smell from the burnt-out tyres. The police paid frequent visits to the cottage. They returned him late at night or the following morning after a spell in the cells if no one picked up the phone at home. The cannabis smoking had become a regular habit. He'd become difficult to manage, and learnt to lie with ease, his primary aim to deceive and avoid authority.

The final straw came when Ralph caught Douglas armed with a large bag of stolen bottles. Wine, spirits, whatever he could find in Ralph's cupboard. The hullabaloo between father and son brought the rest of the family out to the kitchen, curious to see what the commotion was about. Father and son were in a tussle over a bag weighted down with bottles.

"No, you are not, you're still underage." Ralph was yelling.

"We all drink," responded Douglas.

"Well, bloody well buy your own." He quickly regretted the last comment.

"I don't have any money. You stopped my allowance, remember?" This was through clenched teeth, glaring at his father with flinty eyes.

"Well, you know the bloody answer to that!" shouted Ralph, eyes ablaze with fury. "Douglas, the bag, *now*, or else."

Douglas looked his father straight in the eye, defying his command. He swung it round, clipping his father's ear, and shot out the door. Lurking in a clapped-out car in the driveway was a group of friends. The loud rev of the engine could be heard aiming for a quick getaway. Ralph stood helpless, red-faced, shaking with rage, clutching his ear. Yelling after him, "And don't come back," as the car vanished, honking its horn, with a one-fingered salute from his son, chortling on the back seat.

Ralph felt a warm trickle of liquid running down the side of his neck. Slamming the front door, he dabbed it with his hankie, as a pink stain appeared on his T-shirt. He slunk off to calm himself down, knowing he could have handled it better. That was the final act. He'd reached the end of his tether with Douglas. Instinctively, he wanted to protect his girls, who had witnessed everything.

Beatrice felt mortified that things had come to a head after such a stupid argument. In the early hours of the morning, after another restless night, one thing had been decided. They would send Douglas to live in London for the sanity of the rest of the household. The girls needed protection, with Fabienne preparing for finals and Eloise still too young to fully comprehend what had happened. The belongings in the hallway were enough for them to know it was serious. Douglas, led astray by the others, failed to reappear the following day.

After three days, he returned dishevelled and unapologetic to find his belongings still in the hallway. Officially kicked out, with no questions? That's how he saw it. He told them he wasn't bothered; they could get stuffed. Ralph delivered him to the train station in silence and handed over a single ticket to Paddington. Banished to his uncle's house in Kentish Town. Max Barclay worked with children who didn't have a privileged life like Douglas. His experience of working with disadvantaged youngsters would stand him in good stead for dealing with his young, errant, cannabis-smoking nephew. Friends had reassured Beatrice and Ralph, "It's just a teenage phase. Don't worry, he'll soon grow out of it."

Ralph had gone out to do some shopping. Standing in the queue at the grocer's, he felt in his pocket for his wallet. The bank card was missing. A red-faced Ralph returned home with an empty shopping bag and his blood pressure about to explode. Later, he contacted the bank and discovered that someone had made a £200 withdrawal from his account. A familiar calling card of Douglas. It had happened before. Would Max have any more success with their son?

Three years later, Max made him a doctor's appointment. He felt a burden of responsibility for his young nephew and believed Douglas might be harbouring a serious medical complaint. Recently, his late-night vomiting had been getting worse, not helped by the copious amount of alcohol consumed. The GP appointment had not ended well, despite the vain promises made to the doctor on his previous visit.

"How old are you?" questioned the doc.

"Nineteen," he replied. "Are you sure those are my test results?" he asked, studying the doctor's face. Douglas focussed on a long black hair that protruded from the GP's cheek.

"Yes. How many pints do you consume in a week? These liver results look like someone who drinks heavily." He shone a small torch directly into Douglas's eyes, making him squint, clearing his throat.

"A fair few. I've lost count. Why?" He never kept count.

"Your results show a liver belonging to an adult, advanced in years. I have to tell you that you have the early signs of liver disease." Teenagers never bothered with the minutiae of such information. Looking down at his feet seemed far easier than making eye contact with the doc, knowing the units were possibly higher. The doctor tore off two prescriptions, one for painkillers and one for stomach buffers to crush the persistent nausea in his gut. When the doc told him there might be the start of an ulcer too, he thought those things were only for older people.

"I'd like to refer you," he continued. Douglas had ceased listening, his gaze elsewhere focussing on the birds pecking worms in the flower beds. Something snapped, and he decided to take a swift change of direction with his life. Entirely normal behaviour for Douglas, who, when finding himself in an impossible situation to extricate himself from, would instinctively bolt. Straight away all his plans shifted. The doc stood up and opened the door, calling after him as he strode down the corridor.

"Before you leave, Mr Hamilton, make another appointment for a month's time. I'm going to..." Douglas never heard the end of the sentence. He waved his arm in the air, dismissing the doctor's words. *Bugger that*, he thought, and strode out past the receptionist with the smart blonde ponytail and open mouth. He classed the conversation as a "near miss" situation.

Back at the house, his head thumped and his stomach ached. With his mouth stuffed with buffers, he started to gag, but swallowed them down, helping himself to the bank card from the kitchen worktop. Douglas already knew the PIN number. He'd seen it written on a scrap of paper pinned on the fridge. For the briefest moment, he felt tinged with guilt. On his way past the hall table, he helped himself to the stylish brass lighter.

With all his thoughts twirling around, he'd suddenly had enough of living in Kentish Town. Too many pressures to deal with. Stuffing a bag with a few bits of food, he went upstairs and packed. Out in the garage, he had to check something. The Renault turbo stood neatly parked in the garage, the temptation just too great. He darted back into the house and grabbed the car keys from the hook by the front door. With no insurance and a full tank of fuel, he'd already planned his getaway plan. Well, how else was he going to get to the Isle of Mull?

~⁓~

Douglas

As he drove through the streets of north London heading for the A1, he thought about how misplaced he'd been feeling recently. The doctor's diagnosis had shocked him into action. He'd thought about his relationship with his parents. He missed them and had had no contact since the day his father had driven him to the station. Did his mother have much love for him? These thoughts always followed a disagreement. But it had been three years, and he'd chosen not to communicate with his parents since they delivered him to the station. In his mind, he justified his actions by blaming his parents. Beatrice would have argued that she loved all her children equally. Beatrice always believed that people misunderstood Douglas, and that's why he pushed them away. The traffic stopped moving, which brought his mind sharply back to the road. After a brief pause, the car in front moved forward again, and the blue signpost for the north beckoned.

He stared into the rear-view mirror, he studied his face. His looks had always puzzled him, and he wondered why the girls had not flocked his way. Wasn't he appealing to the opposite sex? His fashionable style of beard held tiny flecks of ginger, visible in the sunlight. He stood tall, lean in the body, with broad shoulders. He considered himself lucky, blessed with neat ears. Behind the piercing blue eyes, he had no requirement for glasses, despite squinting at the road signs. The recent eye test recorded his vision at 20/20. So, with all the good looks, why was he still single?

Criticism had been his major downfall, and as a result he found it hard to settle down anywhere. Everyone expected him to fail at everything he did. To date, he had achieved little in his life, nothing to be proud of. Since moving to London, he'd drifted from job to job, falling out with bosses whenever things became too tough. He would quit and move on. Quick-tempered flare-ups happened without warning, catching co-workers and managers by surprise. Douglas had received more P45s than anyone else he'd known in his brief working life. He almost felt proud of that last fact.

Earlier that day, he'd experienced one of those quick flash moments. The travel poster on the wall at the surgery had caught his attention advertising the Scottish Isles. The plan was to move to an island on the most northerly coast of the British Isles, where nobody would find him. To reinvent himself and stop running away. In doing so, would he be laying past ghosts to rest? He had not been the epitome of a perfect son. He knew that deep down. But he knew life would be different in a new environment without further pressure. He knew starting afresh would be his only hope, and now seemed the perfect opportunity to try it. Nobody in Scotland would know anything about his past. He decided he would move to the Isle of Mull. The car behind in the queue gently tooted, and they all inched forward again – for Douglas, another step closer to his new life.

Having driven over five hundred miles, Douglas pulled onto the quayside at Oban. The queue for the car ferry to Craignure was short. At the kiosk, he purchased a single ticket with Max's cash. After a short crossing, his arrival would signal the commencement of his new life. Once on the ferry he deliberated whether to keep his real name or make up a phoney one. For now, Douglas sounded Scottish enough, which he liked to think might go in his favour. Looking at his reflection in the window, he pondered: should he shave the head and beard to create a new persona too? But that seemed a little drastic. First, he needed to seek an income and somewhere to live. He knew that much. Why go as far north as possible? What was he running away from? Debts to family, unlucky relationships; he'd been described as "unstable and unreliable". But no one here knew any of his past.

By early evening he'd arrived in Fionnphort (Gaelic for fishing port). It offered easy access for tourists to ferry hop over to other islands such as Iona and Staffa. After a lumpy crossing over the Firth of Lorn, the Caledonian MacBrayne ferry, known among locals as CalMac, docked. On the ferry, he'd picked up a free booklet stuffed full of local facts. He would need to absorb everything about the island in the coming days, if only to distract himself from the reality of what he had done. Quietly, he read the information about the island.

"Welcome to Mull" it stated on the front cover. Mull, an island that measured 875 square kilometres. Inside it asked a few weird questions that he didn't understand, such as: Why are the oceans so blue around the island? The leaflet explained that the water absorbs the colours in the red part of the spectrum and leaves behind colours in the blue part of the light spectrum. He struggled to comprehend the words. The oceans take on green, red or other hues as light bounces off floating sediments and particles of water. It all sounded fantastical, though, over his head. The Scottish Islands, renowned for their inclement weather cycles, even had special words to describe such things as snowflakes, known as flaggies, or frets, which were the cold, wet mists. Douglas read on about the sterrms, which were clearly seen at night because of the shortened daylight hours.

None of these elements fazed him. The weather would be one of his first new challenges.

Holding up the local map, he traced the road across the island west to the furthest point, through the Ross of Mull. Not more than an hour's journey and some thirty-five miles later along the banks of Loch Scridain, Douglas landed.

A small row of pretty shops lined up along the pavement. Outside the first one stood an advertisement: "a shop that sold everything". From stamps to fishing bait. Behind the narrow counter sat Janet Campbell, a buxom lady, known locally as the shrewdest lady on Mull. Over the rim of her thickset reading glasses, she eyed the newcomer straight from the ferry. Things had taken a downward turn in her shop during the winter months. Takings were disastrous. Her winter finances were totally reliant on tourists' wallets, which hailed mainly from the cruise ships. Casting on her size-four knitting needles, she had just begun knitting a cream Aran jumper.

This shiny new face standing in the shop was no tourist, though, and remained a mystery to Janet for the next few moments. Janet liked mysteries. Her reputation as the "Miss Marple of Mull" went before her. Quickly calculating the young man at her counter with no visible bag across his chest, no baseball hat, no designer sunglasses or expensive trainers. Not off some cruise ship, by any chance? This guy looked normal. Besides, the next ship was not due to dock for another week.

The whispery grey hairs that grew in a cluster on Janet's lower chin drew intense speculation from the visitors to Mull. Some questioned in hushed tones that she might have been a man. But her voice sounded softer than a tenor when she spoke, and her features, although a little masculine, were not those of a male. Nosy by nature, she cleared her throat and struck up the first conversation with the new, bearded man standing in front of her, looking anxious.

Douglas looked around and stepped to one side to allow the other person to get to the till. The shop suddenly felt busy with two customers. His mind was in a mild panic over what to buy. Something? Anything? Grabbing a wire basket, he hastily added yesterday's reduced cheese and pickle sandwiches, a pint of blue-top milk and a packet of custard creams. At the last minute, he grabbed a free local paper. He knew what she must have been thinking – a strange collection of goods – but avoided her beady eye. That would have to suffice until he'd found somewhere to live. Something he hoped to resolve by the end of the day. Paying by cash, he seemed ill at ease, almost fretful, his eyes darting about when he handed over the money. Janet thought it odd. Why look over your shoulder in such a small shop? Perhaps he was being followed. Her mind was already concocting a wild tale. Douglas promised he would return to stock up as soon as he had secured some accommodation. Janet thought, why would anyone arrive on Mull without booking a bed first? She knew the answer to his problem before he spoke. On the notice board, the advert told enquirers to ask at the local pub for Campbell. He read it.

"Aye, that's my wee brother's advert, they're looking for deckhands," she continued, clicking away with her needles. The raglan sleeve of her latest creation almost completed for her next customer.

"Are ya on ya holidays?" came the thick Scottish accent, reaching across for her mug of tea whilst still eying up the stranger. She stood up to put the items through the scanner and took the crisp new money, enjoying its smooth feel on her fingers.

"Don't suppose you'd have a bag?" Janet clicked her tongue and handed over a brown paper bag. "I'm Douglas, by the way. I'll pop back later." He stuffed the items into the bag and headed out of the door before Janet had time to pick up her needles or place her glasses back on her head. The telephone set to auto-dial the pub across the way. On the first ring, her brother picked up.

"Halloo, it's only me, aye, a young man called Douglas is coming your way, seems a wee bit shy, says he's looking for work aye, and somewhere to live."

"He's already here, hen." Campbell hung up. Damn it, she always liked to be the first to know; this time her brother had beaten her to it. Campbell seemed accustomed to his younger sister's nosiness, which came in useful in the tight-knit community. She knew everything about everyone, or so she liked to think. Nothing got past her: her speciality was listening in to other people's conversations. Campbell knew incorrect assumptions were also her speciality, which had led her down a shady path on previous occasions.

Douglas thought it would be easy to blend in with the active fishing community on the island. The small island held a miasma of hidden scandals, but nothing got past the McCampbell siblings. The pretty quayside covered itself in lobster and crabbing pots. At the far end, the ancient stone slipway led down to the palest of sandy beaches, when the tide was out. He had withdrawn the contents of his bank account plus helped himself to Max's money before leaving, hoping that it would be enough to see him through the first month with enough for a deposit on a flat, and pausing a moment to eat the sandwiches on the quayside before tossing the stale crusts to the hovering gulls.

He decided the best place to ingratiate himself with the locals would be in the pub. Outside on the pavement, a warm welcome sign with the lure of fresh fish and chips all cooked to order. The landlord introduced himself as Campbell McCampbell. Like his sister, he knew everyone and their business, and everyone knew and respected him in return.

Campbell weighed in at eighteen stone plus. He towered over most men at six foot six with a low-slung girth, supported by a wide leather belt. Even though he had gained two stone, he was the guy you would always want on your side.

Following up the advert and with no proper plan in mind, his mood lifted when he read "cash in hand". He liked the idea of a hand to mouth type of living. It suited him. Though many of the questions from Campbell were out of a natural curiosity. Douglas asked him where the *North Western Star* might be moored up as he'd seen the advert in the shop wanting trawlermen.

"Do you have much sea time experience?" asked Campbell, looking him over and getting straight to the point. To Campbell, the man in front of him did not look like the outdoorsy fishing type. With his smooth skin and manicured hands, he looked more like someone who'd nick your last fiver with a wink. True, the *North Western Star* was hiring to replace the skipper's son, who'd been injured in a rigging incident. John Maclean liked nothing better than to sit in his own booth by the bay window in the pub. His daily catch of lobster and crabs had been delivered to the kitchen earlier. The menu was true to its word as fresh meant fresh off his boats. Campbell pointed out John with a booming voice, giving a nod to the corner, pulling another pint. Douglas opened the conversation by elaborating on his meagre experience of sailing with his father's mackerel fishing. John required deckhands, and Douglas seemed to fit the bill in terms of his strength and availability.

"Another pint, John, and one for yourself, Campbell?" proffered Douglas, splashing the cash. He would need to find a secure place to hoard the stolen money, as bank facilities were few and far between.

"Aye, I'll take a pint from you. So, where are ya staying?" came the next question.

"I'm new to the island today, and I've not got my bearings yet. Can you recommend a room anywhere?"

"Tell me, where does that accent come from?" Douglas ignored the question and didn't answer. "I can offer you a few weeks' temporary accommodation, of course, as I have a wee cottage that's used as a holiday let during the summer months. At the moment it's just out of season, so lying empty. Do you want it for a week or two just to see you settled? It's a bit run-down, mind, and needs updating. But it has all mod cons, running water and electric etcetera. As part of your wages you could take it on?"

"Drink up your pint and I'll take you across the road and show you around." John, keen to get going, took an instant liking to the bearded younger man. He definitely had the brawn required for the job, but did he have the stomach for the sea? That would be the test. Taking his second sip, he licked the creamy froth from his lips and turned to Douglas, his mind made up.

"The job's yours if you want it, starting on Monday, five a.m. sharp, mind; meet the skipper at the boat."

Douglas smiled and considered how his luck had changed after only two hours on the island. Yes, his life might finally come together. He'd liked the people he'd met so far. They seemed genuine enough. But that woman in the shop, Jan, or whatever her name might be, he might have a spot of trouble with her later. They picked up his stuff from the car and wandered over to the grey stone cottage. The name "Stoneymollan" had been set into the grey brick wall. From the outside it looked unloved; the windows were covered in smears of salt spray. The front door, although made of solid oak, didn't shut completely, leaving the cottage draughty. John handed Douglas the keys and added, "Welcome to Mull," as he held out his hand. John pointed out the cottage needed some running repairs as they examined the small number of rooms. He had never had the responsibility of looking after a property before. If Douglas was happy, he would leave him to it. The windows were difficult to prise open and needed easing. The front door had no letterbox, just a brass knocker. Any mail went into a small American-style aluminium box attached to the wooden gate post at the end of the path. Douglas began by spraying the door hinges to get the front door to shut. He thought he remembered John saying it had been used as a holiday home. The only form of heating came from the small log-burning stove that served the boiler with hot water. Douglas, keen to try out his latest acquisition, lit up a cigarette with the new brass lighter. The hearth looked neatly laid up with logs and kindling, ready for a roaring fire. It didn't take long before it burst into life, the flames flickering in the grate, and the sweet smell of woodsmoke wafted through the downstairs rooms.

The kitchen had a small sink and a wooden draining board, with one cupboard for storage. The kitchen table had a large fruit bowl on it, and a dated light swung on a long flex above it. Better still, it would come in handy for his keys, wallet and cigarettes, though he had not got enough to last him the week, and he did not know where to source more, so would have to ask Campbell. Upstairs, Douglas noted the small loft hatch on the landing with no obvious ladder. It might be a suitable place to stash the stolen money currently hidden in one of his duffel bags. He would remember to check it out later to see if it was dry enough for storage. He started unpacking and rearranging the furniture.

By Sunday morning a howler had blown in, and the bobbing fishing boats nestled tightly side by side in the harbour were all grounded. The barometer had dropped to below nine hundred millibars and foul weather was predicted. The swell and winds were vicious, whipping sea-foam and spume over the harbour wall across the road. Douglas stood at the edge of the steps inspecting the green swollen water, the flotsam gathering in the corner. His stomach felt nauseous just looking at it. If the strong winds had subsided by Monday morning, he wanted to check for himself which trawler to report to. The *North Western Star*, easy to spot with a distinctive logo, was moored securely to the harbour wall.

By Monday morning, the winds were still blowing but only a force six, gusting seven. Had they subsided enough for the fishing fleet to set sail? The swell would still be high, making it not impossible to trawl the fish. Douglas felt a little apprehensive about the new job but, to his credit, stuck with the idea. He wanted to prove to himself he was no longer one of life's quitters. Dressed like a banana, in yellow oilskins on loan from the skipper, John, he descended the steel ladder on his first outing as a trawlerman. The fella in the wheelhouse, wearing a mauve beanie hat, swung his head round.

"Douglas, isn't it? I'm Jed, the skipper, standing in for John, just for this trip. She'll sail for two or three days based on the haul and the chase." In terms of float ability, the boat seemed watertight to Douglas. But what did he know when it came to boat safety management? The other men quickly eased into their roles and a strong Scottish banter commenced. They cast off the ropes forward and aft. The crew tried their best to include him in the conversation. But the thick dialect proved a problem, with the winds whistling around the ears covered by woollen beanie hats and yellow waterproof coat hoods.

The men adopted sign language, which came in useful once you could interpret it. Within an hour, Douglas wished he'd opted for a land-based job in the pub, or in an office on the quay. As the deep swell took a toll on his stomach, his pallor changed to a pale shade of green. He kept his vomiting at bay, a difficult feat leaning at an angle into the wind. He had to adjust his body quickly to the motion of the boat and he avoided embarrassing himself in front of the crew, even though he felt warm vomit rising in his throat. The gulls encircled the boat overhead, cawing loudly and picking out the remnants of the faded, battered fish boxes loaded in the stern. The discards of the fish offered an easier meal for the gulls than diving under the swell of the white horses that day. To save their energy, some brave enough hitched a ride on the stern guard rail.

The rota in the galley listed the crew, who all took it in turns to cook. For newbies like Douglas, they did not expect them to take part until they'd found their sea legs. The first shift took their seats at the table. Simple, hearty, easy-to-prepare food for all those with stronger stomachs. They filled deep bowls with a greenish-looking pea and ham broth, served with thickly sliced, white buttered bread. Douglas glanced at the bowl and raised his hand, declined and bolted back up on deck. He badly needed some fresh air. He opened his mouth wide and, this time remembering to face downwind, he let out the contents of the enforced porridge breakfast from earlier in the shift. In the wheelhouse, Jed smiled to himself as he watched Douglas wipe his beard. The poor man would soon get used to it.

Nineteen

Mull – 2001

For the first time in his life, Douglas had found his niche. He had a proper job among the crew that took him at face value, his sea legs improving each shift. He earned a proper wage each week with cash left over. It was the first time he'd taken orders from management without responding negatively, and the first time he'd belonged to a local community. Locals acknowledged him in the street. His renewed confidence had led him to pluck up the courage to ask out the young barmaid over at the pub. Or maybe it had been the other way round? Molly had come on to him. Ten years his junior, a fact that didn't seem to bother either of them at first; the feelings were mutual. He found it comforting to have someone to share his bed with after such a long period of abstinence. Molly had been through most of the younger men her own age on Mull, Iona and Staffa and not settled down with a regular boyfriend. Soon after they started going out, she asked him if she could move in. Two weeks later she'd moved in three black bin liners and a cardboard box. With Douglas's shifts on the trawler and her own bar shifts they would pass literally like ships in the night. The bed would be still warm and most welcoming when Douglas arrived back from sea just after dawn.

Molly's family, originally from Harris, had all left to find work in the larger towns. She'd found few friends on Mull, and in the beginning clung to Douglas like a limpet. At the start she had free board and lodging and thought she might be onto a winner with no outgoings. Douglas had put off the conversation about sharing the rent and food bills.

Having just returned from three days trawling the waters off the Irish Sea, he found himself not in such a good frame of mind, with only two hours of sleep. He felt he was starting a head cold, his nose felt bunged up. The stench of the fish guts had made it difficult to breathe. The smell lingered in his nostrils long after leaving the boat.

While he had been lying in his bunk taking a brief break, being tossed about by the waves, he'd been thinking about his recent family estrangement. He knew the feelings for his two sisters had diminished. Beatrice and Ralph had had no contact with Douglas either, only a rambling letter from Uncle Max saying he had done a runner with his car and, by the way, his bank card was missing. Oh, and another thing, just so they knew, he'd cleaned out his (Max's) bank account, to the tune of nine hundred pounds. The brass engraved cigarette lighter that Ralph had bought his brother for his twenty-first birthday had gone missing too! They promised to repay him.

But, typical of Douglas, he never felt guilty for long before he moved on to his next ruinous project. But all that was in the past. Life on Mull had looked pretty peachy. He'd tried to kid himself that he had honestly changed for the better. For the first time in his adult life, he felt settled, and wanted to stay and put down some roots. Nothing would throw him off course this time, not even young Molly. Hearing the captain's voice booming from the wheelhouse, Douglas swung his legs into action.

"All hands on deck, you lot. We've got a large catch coming in," bellowed John through the portside window. With the haul safely boxed in ice, the trawler headed for port and the men for a decent rest. Glad to be finally ashore, Douglas had been looking forward to his pie and a pint with Campbell later that day, but first he needed some well earned sleep.

~~~

Samuel

After Samuel's appointment with the solicitors, he drove straight up to Mull, with the sole intention of finding and introducing himself to his stepbrother. Douglas and Molly were cosying up beneath the quilt, enjoying themselves, when a loud rap on the door disturbed their early morning lovemaking. Leaning out of the bedroom window, a bare-chested Douglas hollered, "Who is it? Hang on just a minute." He rushed naked down the stairs two at a time, dragging on some shorts. Whoever had been standing on the doorstep would have heard the shout from Molly a minute earlier, in the throes of her second orgasm of the morning. Douglas had tried to cover her mouth to stem the screaming, but in the heat of the moment she'd bitten him.

"Jesus, Molls, that hurt." He sucked his finger, dabbing at a few specks of blood that had bubbled up. The impatient, embarrassed visitor, who'd heard everything, walked away towards the gate. The guy with the faded blue backpack and a short attention span, bored with waiting and listening, turned on his heel. Why would he know that the front door always remained unlocked? Reaching the end of the path, he'd turned to glance past his shoulder when a man appeared, hastily buttoning up the flies of his shorts.

"Sorry, I may have got the wrong house. I'm looking for Douglas Hamilton."

"Who is asking, mate? You have the right bloke; that's me."

"My name is Samuel Gardiner, and I believe we are related." Taken aback by the familial looks of the random stranger standing in his doorway, he felt he should welcome him inside.

"Like I told you, I'm Samuel Gardiner." He held out his hand.

Douglas ignored it and kept his hands in the pockets of his shorts. "Excuse the mess, come on through." They made their way into the kitchen. Douglas, still frowning, pulled out a chair for the unannounced visitor and sat down stuffing newspapers under a cushion.

"It took a while to find you!" he said as he rummaged through his backpack for a plastic wallet.

"I'll get straight to the point, Douglas, if I may call you that. I think we share the same mother, Beatrice Hamilton, my father—" he didn't get to finish his sentence before Douglas interrupted him.

"You've got a bloody cheek coming up here. How did you find my address? Now you have truly mucked up my Sunday morning. I should throw you out. Why have you chosen to seek me out? Nothing to do with my mother's will, is it?" Ignoring the last comment, Samuel ploughed on with his prepared explanation. Something had suddenly flashed up inside Douglas, taking him by surprise.

"Yes, it's about the will. Were you aware that she changed it recently?" Samuel's eyes focussed intently on a dusty green pea in the corner of the floor. Alarm bells rang out in Douglas's head.

"Yes, though I've not seen her for a while," Douglas lied. "Give me one good reason why I should believe you."

Not wishing to reveal too much too soon. Samuel switched tack. "Listen" – scratching his head – "perhaps I'll call back later when you've had time to adjust to my news and get over the shock of what I've just told you."

Douglas, aware that Molly might have been listening at the top of the stairs, needed to get shot of him quickly. The meaning of tact and diplomacy was not something she'd fully grasped. And he did not want her spreading false rumours around the small insular town just when he was settling in and finding his way. Scraping back the chairs across the flagstone floor, the two men stood up as Samuel signalled his departure. He'd noted they were of a similar height and build, and their voices threw a similar intonation when they spoke. Casting his eyes around the place, Samuel assured himself that he'd made the right decision in coming up to Mull.

He left feeling upbeat, and that he would win him over, whatever the cost to him personally, financially or morally. They agreed to meet next in neutral territory, away from the cottage. Lucknow and Hardcastle delayed the letter, but Samuel already knew the contents. No point in scaring him away. He would soften him first with a wee dram. But, hey, now he was getting ahead of himself.

Douglas considered how he could check out Samuel's validity. It all sounded so plausible. So why the suspicions? The letter had still not arrived. The post-boat weather was dependent as always on the islands. Douglas's impatience led him to telephone the solicitors and speak with Mr Hardcastle to check out the facts. Yes, it was all bona fide. Samuel was related to Beatrice – everything he'd been told was true? Douglas queried. With no reason not to believe him, given the stranger's storyline, and reassured by the solicitor's stance, this temporarily put his mind at ease.

The following day, the dialogue between Douglas and Samuel took on a more serious tone. They met in Campbell's bar. With their voices purposely lowered over on the corner table, Samuel explained the reason for his visit. Listening intently, Douglas decided Samuel had a real likeability about him; they even had a few threads of commonality.

"Just so you know, Douglas, I will not be the only person without a chair when the music stops, if you get my drift." Douglas shrugged at him and tried to imagine a game of musical chairs with his immediate family and Samuel standing in the middle without a chair.

Putting childhood games to the back of his mind, he'd heard enough to be taken in by talk of scams and quick-fix money-making schemes. He fell into the trap as Samuel conveniently forgot to mention his own heavy debts, low credit scores and bank loan refusals. His debt to the tune of fifty thousand pounds didn't get a mention. Samuel had already worked out his stepbrother's weaker points and worked hard to win him over.

Douglas left a message for Fabienne with his new number, but chose not to reveal his current address or the identity of his current visitor. The answer machine message was brief and to the point. "Hi, it's Douglas, please get in touch. I have news." Unusually, he left the cottage phone number, the only clue as to his whereabouts. That evening again the message to Fabienne went unplayed on her answer machine. It took a while for her to work out the area code for Mull. Douglas began overthinking the lack of response from his sister.

After a second restless night mulling things over, Douglas rose early to cook up a typical Scottish breakfast for his guest. Square Lorne sausages, fried eggs, streaky bacon, black pudding and tattie scones with mushrooms and tomatoes. He'd loaded up his basket in Janet's shop enough to raise her suspicions that he might have been entertaining.

Later that day, they were heading out to Ben Fore, the highest point on Mull and the island's towering peak. Douglas wanted to show off some of his local knowledge and escape further scrutiny from any of the locals. They always expressed such curiosity with fresh faces, especially in the shop.

With breakfast over, they stacked the dirty breakfast dishes in the sink and got in the car. As they drove through the windy roads towards the peak, Douglas remained unusually quiet, recalling his experiences of judgemental people. Places where, if you did not fit in, they considered you an oddball. Quite a philosophical thought so early in the day. Perhaps he was still in denial. What had he been searching for all these years, a relationship with another man? He had no inkling that he might have been bisexual under that harsh swashbuckling exterior. He believed he'd always been straight and enjoyed the company of women, hadn't he? A female partner was living with him, but he was having second thoughts. His wearisome mind kept playing tricks with his emotions. Would he know the difference between a romantic attraction to Samuel or an animal attraction? Perhaps he was just in a transient period of his life.

Samuel, on the other hand, had been bisexual for many years, with no particular loyalty to either gender. The car stopped as they reached the car park, shaking them both out of their personal reveries. Samuel had been thinking about what he should say to Douglas. He did not want to offend him. Far from it, he needed to bring him on the side, to secure a financial deal, whatever the cost.

The two men examined an old OS map found in the car's boot. They laid it out on the bonnet to discuss the trail, before setting off up the hill. The aim was to reach the summit. They argued about the finer details and the relevance of the key or legend at the side of the page. Douglas boasted he knew his dotted lines from his railway tracks. Samuel thought all he knew were the blue bits were lochs and the yellow roads were B roads. He knew only that. Any geography from his school days had passed him by. Although they disagreed about who knew what when telling the age of the trees, they agreed that the track signage on Mull needed updating, as it petered out towards the summit.

Once at the top, they sat on the patchy grass recovering their breath from the climb, looking across at the breathtaking panorama below in silence. Not a single living thing in sight, apart from a brief glimpse of a red deer expressing an interest from afar. They sat and discussed what had brought them together, and how their individual futures might map out. Samuel thought it too soon to mention money or bank accounts. Besides, he was enjoying himself. He hadn't felt this way for months. They spread out the blanket and Douglas sat down whilst Samuel lay on his back instead. He placed his arm out to the side and it brushed against Douglas's hip. The electricity between them was felt by both parties. Samuel's face broke into a wry smile, unseen by Douglas, who was busy concentrating on the view and trying to keep his heartbeat steady. Samuel was getting frustrated by the lack of action and initiative on Douglas's part. So he stood up and suggested they leave the picnic spot to descend back to the car park. He thought it had been a wasted opportunity by Douglas.

After his trip out to Ben Fore, Douglas remained single. He told himself it would be much easier to manage his life if he were unattached. He knew the relationship with Molly would have to cease. In such a tight-knit community, it had felt claustrophobic. He needed to finish with her. Had this anything to do with Samuel's appearance on the scene? Was he in denial about his true feelings? All his personal affairs were being relayed over the shop counter by Janet. When Douglas heard, it transpired that Molly had been the source. Buoyed by his recent trip to Ben Fore, he re-examined his feelings for Samuel. Could he be behind his pathetic reasoning to nudge out Molly?

October had brought with it a maritime climate, with a light breeze blowing offshore. On Saturday, the two men took another trip, this time across the Firth of Lorn to Oban. A little further afield, but no less scenic. They'd taken the late-morning ferry, hoping not to be recognised. Douglas, keen to show off, pointed out the landmark in the distance, McCaig's Tower. Built in the late 1800s by John McCaig, it had provided work for the local stonemasons. The two men stood and watched as the ferry swung neatly into its allocated berth.

Buried beneath the layers, the bearded neanderthal Douglas had not been keen to attract any further salacious gossip. So he had pre-booked a table for two at the Ferry Boat Inn, on the front, at one o'clock. They could explore the more detailed financial discussions here, with the modicum of privacy the pub offered. It had turned out to be a strange few days, and Douglas felt like he had known Samuel all his life.

As neither of the men was a local, they would not have known the local annual parade was taking place that day. The pretty streets were full of families out enjoying themselves. Trucks were adorned with multicoloured bunting and colourful exhibits. An air of excitement filtered through the streets, with squeals of delight from the small children. The two men, absorbed in their planning conversations, failed to spot Janet McCampbell amongst the crowds, walking arm in arm with her best friend, Morag Maclean. The two men may not have seen Janet, but she'd spotted them. Her jaw dropped and her head swung around the instant she recognised the two bearded gentlemen from Mull. Were they arm in arm, or perhaps her imagination was playing tricks? She couldn't wait to tell Campbell. He would never believe what she had just seen. But what had she actually seen? Two men were deep in conversation, walking in step along the Oban pavement. What was there to tell? Janet, a master of tall stories, would think of something before she returned later to Mull. Excitedly, she looked around for a phone box. She even had some loose change in her pocket! Unable to wait any longer, she excitedly telephoned Campbell with her news.

The barman at the Ferry Boat Inn looked up, giving them a querulous look, as the two strangers entered the bar. Engaging them in the usual banter, his ears remained alert as he prepared two pints of bitter.

After a couple more rounds, they found the drinks slipping down too easily and foolishly let down their guard. Samuel, with the stronger, louder Geordie accent, decided not to whisper. They tucked themselves neatly into a corner booth out of sight of the main window whilst they waited for the barman, who also acted as waiter, to take their food order. They were the only ones eating that afternoon. After an hour, the barman had fabricated an excellent story of his own to relay to his friends at a later date.

The Ferry Boat Inn had an excellent reputation for its fresh seafood, though Douglas always chose meat when dining out and never fish. The menu felt unsuitable for the two foreign diners. Their choices were normally more pie and chips than posh seafood nosh. Dessert became an easier choice of lemon meringue pie. Another weird coincidence is that both men cited this dish as their all-time favourite.

Conversation quickly turned back to the scheme. As Samuel leant in closer to Douglas, his knee deliberately brushed against his leg, making the hairs on his arm stand up. An electrical pulse shot through his body. Douglas wondered if the plot would involve anything on a more personal level. Exactly who was flirting with who here? Unsure whether the drinks were having the dizzying effect, or something else. He tried hard to concentrate, though his mind kept drifting. Samuel might be coming on to him. The wide eyes penetrated his own during the conversation, which soon felt a little one-sided. As Samuel's proposal unfolded, Douglas remained sceptical but deeply curious. He knew nothing about the loan shark business but liked the idea. Samuel asked him to invest in his scheme. Douglas recalled the poster by the Acton Tube station back in London. The bold text in large letters: *"Don't get bitten by a loan shark"*. Samuel prayed on Douglas just as a shark would prey on its catch. The popular Americanism began during the late nineteenth century, citing a slang metaphor of predatory behaviour, such as that of the shark. Securing debtors' furniture or belongings, of course, all this interested Samuel. Douglas thought he had little to offer Samuel except the stash of stolen money in his attic. When asked about his investment amount, he avoided giving a specific answer and the conversation stalled.

As the waiter delivered their order, they barely glanced up, still deep in discussions. They were just finishing up their coffees when a cacophony of noise came from outside. It seemed the entire town had turned out on the streets, cheering and clapping the parade. Samuel insisted on settling the bill. Douglas felt another pulse of electricity when their arms touched at the till. He wandered about, asking the bartender to book them a couple of rooms, but changed his mind when he saw the crowds outside. The men gathered up their coats and joined the throng of people moving slowly along the pavement. Had Samuel secured the money? He thought so. It had all gone to plan. The two men walked at speed against the throng to catch the next ferry back, Samuel assuring himself the money was all but his. He would need to have a snoop around the cottage just to ensure there were no more pockets of cash hidden away.

⌒∽⌒

Up in the attic, Douglas was counting the rest of his money stash when an old newspaper article covering the floorboards grabbed his attention. It referred to an article about an old wreck, a Spanish galleon, *San Juan de Sicilia*, anchored in Tobermory Harbour in 1588. It sat firmly on the seabed off the coast of the Isle of Mull for hundreds of years. The famous ship was well known among the captains and local sailors. In 1586, the *San Juan de Sicilia* anchored for repairs and supplies when the crew had a gunpowder accident that blew the ship apart and sank to the bottom of the bay. On board, the money, jewels and munitions were estimated at nine million pounds. For the locals, they always had the promise of sunken treasure if you knew where to look. The Duke of Argyle at the time laid claim to the haul. Douglas, intrigued by the end of the article, wanted to find the wreck and check it out for himself. And, as he fell into a deep sleep that night, his mind took him on a unique journey:

> *It started off as just another regular fishing trip, but the trawler net became entangled in the wreckage of the sunken galleon. Douglas offered to dive and release it. The men feared it may heave the trawler over on its side. Douglas quickly got into difficulty and struggled to surface, his foot entangled in part of the net. Under the water, he held his breath for as long as possible before disaster struck. He inhaled a lungful of seawater. The situation rapidly turned into one of rescue and damage limitation. Jed, the captain of the day, made an instant*

decision to save the trawler. He dived to cut Douglas free. It took him a few attempts to release the netting, and Douglas resurfaced. After what seemed an age but was in fact only minutes, they resurfaced and hauled out by the crew. Coughing and vomiting water, gasping for air. Not out of trouble yet. The trawler had taken on water and seemed to sit at a strange angle to the waves. With the bilge pumps struggling to syphon out the oily floodwaters, the rest of the crew panicked. Sixteen-year-old Tom jumped over the side into the sea, believing the trawler was about to go under. In his panic, he forgot to put on a life jacket and sank like a stone, before emerging on the rebounding wave, flailing his arms and screaming. The tide pulled him further away from the boat. The men threw a line and hauled him back on board. Ted, the oldest crew member, took him down below. Gradually, the colour returned to his face. Once the chaos had subsided, the men heard the maroon being fired, and the coastguard summoned the local lifeboat stationed at Tobermory to assist.

The listing trawler was slowly towed back into the harbour, its pump struggling to empty the overflowing bilges. Three near misses on one outing. The boat seemed cursed by the famous galleon. And, far more important than the galleon, who had triumphed as the hero of the day? Douglas secured his place on the boat and Jed offered him a permanent job.

By the time they moored up, the TV media had gathered waiting for a scoop. The Scottish reporter was keen to know what happened out in the bay. The notoriety could not go to the heads of the fishermen. Douglas appeared on the front of the paper under the headline "Hero Saves the Day", hailed by his fellow crew members.

His place in the community was firmly sealed on land as opposed to the bottom of the sea, his dream firmly left behind in its rightful place, at the bottom of the bay.

He awoke in a sweat.

Twenty

Molly

Janet had not enough to do, and loudly cast her first suspicions of Douglas's character to anyone who would listen. She had placed the idea in Molly's empty head that her new boyfriend might not be as honest as she first thought. Perhaps a little jealous of Molly's svelte figure and younger, more modernistic approach to life? Janet remained stuck in the past, hidden under heavy knitted jumpers and plaid skirts with thick tights that wrinkled at the ankles. She had never worn a bra and her pendulous breasts had suffered as a result, adding less shape to her already shapeless frame.

They were working a shift together in the shop, when Molly asked a direct question as to why she had never married. Janet's answer surprised her. She mentioned she disliked the idea of committing to one man for her entire life. As the cruise liners came through the Scottish waters one by one like clockwork, she believed she would find herself a rich "sugar daddy" among the American tourists. The men were often loaded and looking for love. Janet had fantasised about becoming an American "sugar momma". The sorry image of a "sugar momma" had never crossed Molly's mind and she had no idea what one would look like anyway. In Janet's head things seemed different. Instead she'd conjured up a largish frame to suit her own looks with manicured nails and lots of gold jewellery. She saw someone who wore their hair piled on top of their head and slathered layer upon layer of make-up with long false eyelashes. If she got hitched they would have loads of money to spend in the casinos on board the ships. Her "sugar daddy" would buy her lots of expensive clothes and jewellery. And they'd dine at the captain's table every night dressed in suits and ball gowns. She'd read articles about the types of women advertised in the cruising magazines from her shop. Janet acknowledged she did not easily fit the image the men were looking for. Why spoil the woman's fantasy? So Molly kindly let her have her dreams; she had her own immediate worries on her mind.

The cottage she shared with Douglas became useful in a secondary way but the new income sideline would be her eventual downfall. Bored with listening to Janet's theories, Molly had been secretly monitoring Douglas's phone. After seeing messages flash up, she'd wrongly assumed they were from a male admirer. She was expecting Douglas to make a confession. With nothing forthcoming to satisfy her deepening curiosity, and having made several incorrect conclusions, she was left bewildered. She knew she had to tie up some loose ends in terms of her own local business venture. But her loose tongue had become a real problem over in the shop; she became unfussy as to where she spouted her untruths. Douglas had recently become aloof, and not giving her so much attention since his new friend had been on the scene. Samuel was about to wheedle his way into her relationship with Douglas, cleverly setting them at odds with one another.

Samuel

Samuel met with Molly and started boasting out of turn about Douglas, leaking the fact that he was due to inherit a large sum of money, speculating that soon he would be wealthier than Campbell. He only wanted to date Molly, to pick at another layer of Douglas's persona after feeling rejected. When finally he got a taste of Douglas's life he vowed to destroy it through jealousy and avarice. Samuel thrived on planting doubts in other people's minds at every turn. And Molly, not being the brightest tool, had shown more interest in what she thought Douglas was going to inherit. It became part of Samuel's quest for retribution. He'd started to enjoy his life on Mull and wanted to be a part of it, even though he did not fit in. Locals had not taken to the stranger with his brusque manner and an unhealthy interest in young Molly. They found him conceited and became guarded in their conversations with him.

His latest plan was to poach her from Douglas, but once he found out Douglas had planned to finish with her the attraction diminished. Having lived the majority of his life with no firm roots, if he couldn't have Douglas his next ploy would be to have Molly instead. Douglas realised early on in their relationship that he was not going to give Samuel the satisfaction of seducing him. At this stage he had no idea that he was about to be double-crossed, twice, once by Molly and a second time by his prodigal stepbrother. "Douglas the gullible fool" had been mumbled on more than one occasion.

Twenty-One

Douglas

The skies were just welcoming a grey dawn as Douglas finished his three-day shift on the North Western Star. That same morning Molly had seemed unbothered by the state of the place. She urgently needed to shift some stock and return home before Douglas arrived through the door. The secret hiding place in the wood bunker would not go unnoticed. She'd considered using the loft but, being short, she couldn't stretch the distance between the hatch and the top of the ladder to lever herself up to the beams. Her primary focus that morning was to drop off her stock at locations dotted around the island. The earnings were far greater than the wages paid by the miserly McCampbell siblings. Cycling around the lanes at top speed she'd spotted the group of fishing trawlers returning to the harbour. "Oh my God, pedal faster, Molls, pedal faster; the boats are coming in. Faster." Determined to finish her rounds, she arrived back hot and sweaty so went straight upstairs for a shower.

Douglas had been looking forward to some downtime as he took his regular route back to the cottage. Approaching, he saw the front door ajar and a familiar smoky haze greeted him, filling the entire kitchen. It looked like the cottage had been turned on its roof. A mess lay on every surface in the kitchen. The stench of something foul in the bin liner discarded on the floor caught in his nostrils. The door of the fridge stood ajar, devoid of any contents. Empty bottles lay strewn across the hallway floor. The cottage resembled a war zone. The kitchen had fared worse. Dirty cups and plates lay scattered across the draining board. The pan on the hob had the remnants of some cheese sauce, or something akin to it. Crusty slivers of dried cheddar were heaped in a pile on the side, offering a small clue. The macaroni jar sat empty on the side as did the kettle. Someone had lost the plot in the kitchen and this time Douglas knew he was not the culprit. He found his cottage in a sorry state. Each room full of detritus, little things guaranteed to rile him when he came back from sea for some shore time, tired out and hungry.

Douglas found the culprit sitting in the lounge staring into an empty cup, wet hair dripping around her shoulders. Fire-lighting had never been her forte. She'd made a hurried feeble attempt and in her haste chosen the wrong type of wood out of the bunker. The last delivery had been damp and needed drying out before attempting to burn, he'd told her. Had she not remembered his firm instructions before he left?

Three days ago, he'd spotted a delivery hanging on the gate. Poking his nose inside the bag, the label scrawled on the lid read "Shepherds Pie × 1". Leaving it in situ on the post he'd gone off to work and thought no more about it until his return. Douglas casually asked, "Did you find the white carrier bag on the gatepost the other night?"

"Ay, a friend dropped it off; it would nay fit in the mail box. There's hot water now in the kettle." Changing the subject, staring deep into her empty mug. Should she tell him or keep it to herself? She knew he would be like a dog with a bone, unable to leave it alone. The bag had contained a foil dinner tray made to look like a takeaway, and labelled "Shepherds Pie". The contents were a long way from a cosy Monday-night supper. A clever disguise for a few small pouches of the white stuff. Molly had come up with the idea to deter snoopers in the sleepy laid-back community. She had her own network of users neatly set up, scattered in small pockets across the island.

"Since when have you qualified for meals on wheels?" Douglas asked before he went to make himself a cup of tea before retiring to his bed. "No milk left, then?" He shook an empty bottle on the side. Still curious, he poked his head round the doorframe.

"We're outta milk," came a miffed reply.

"What was it?"

Not wishing to let it go, Molly kept quiet, looking down at the floor, avoiding eye contact.

"So answer the question. What was hanging on my gate? I demand to know."

"A mate over at Croggan has started a make-up business." She managed to lie her way through another interrogation. Douglas had his suspicions; how many other locals had white carrier bags hanging on their gates with make-up inside? Had he noticed her left eye, which always winked slowly whenever she fibbed? Molly's sodden hair draped itself over her face and neck so Douglas had missed the blush that crept downwards across her chest, as he pressed her for more details.

"Where's the brochure? A weird place to leave it, don't you think?" Douglas felt he was now onto something and wouldn't let go.

"That's my concern not yours," she snapped. He speculated that maybe she was just being hormonal. His body needed some kip; he would have to deal with it later.

As his head touched the pillow, within seconds he'd drifted off into a deep sleep, dreaming of giant black lobsters approaching the cottage. In the dream he tried to fend them off by throwing damp logs at them. The reality of his thoughts mingled with the fantasies of the deep sea.

When he came to, he heard muffled voices downstairs. His immediate thought turned to Samuel. Molly should have been at the shop to start the afternoon shift, so why had she not left? Something in the cottage felt out of kilter. To wake himself up he took a shower. It ran cold; she'd used all the damn hot water again. Pulling on a thick sweater and a pair of tatty jeans, he followed the trail of voices down to the kitchen. By the time he reached the table, the voice and the visitor had vanished. He scoured outside the window for evidence. Molly, still seated alone, looked flustered.

"What's going on, Molls?"

"Och, nothing, Dougie, just leave it, can ya?"

"Did I hear voices, hen?"

"Och, no one you would know, just a mate."

"Well, try me?"

Standing up, she went to the front door to find her coat. "Can't stop now, I'm already late for work. Catch ya later, yeah?" She shot out of the door, leaving their conversation shrouded in mystery. With the bag on the gate issue still rumbling in his head, he cooked up a makeshift meal. Pork sausages in a tin of beans. The only fresh element, the half loaf of bread from Janet's shop, was just starting to turn crispy at the edges, though ok for toasting.

Douglas, still procrastinating about splitting up, had reached his conclusion. The bottom line had been breached, he told himself, all trust now gone. The timing of ditching her bothered him. He'd started to plan the conversation in his head and as usual was overthinking it. He'd vowed to keep Samuel away from Molly for her own protection. The suspected drug issue, well, that had become just another bloody stupid diversion.

After Molly left for work he firmly closed the cottage door, using his shoulder this time, turning the key in the lock and retreating back upstairs to his warm bed. Before nodding off he reached over for his meds on the bedside cabinet. He felt they were not doing him much good recently; the symptoms were still there. His legs felt restless as he tossed about trying to get comfortable; his last thought before falling into another deep sleep had been about dumping Molly. She had become too loose with her tongue. On the plus side, she was pretty good in bed, and this attribute had been hard to source on Mull. Nah, tomorrow, it would always be tomorrow with the procrastinating Douglas.

Twenty-Two

Samuel

Samuel felt his stay on Mull had reached a natural conclusion. So he decided to swing by the cottage one last time, to find Douglas, on the premise of collecting the promised money. When he arrived, the front door was shut and locked, which was unusual. Upstairs the window looked ajar so he yelled up,

"Hello, Douglas, are you there? It's only me, mate." Silence. At the rear of the cottage the back door remained unlocked. He didn't like to miss a golden opportunity to have a snoop around in more detail. Preying on his mind had been the cash in the loft story that Douglas had bragged about in the pub the other night. It would be an added bonus as Douglas had finally signed up to the shark lending scheme. He just needed to hand over the cash, although so far he hadn't revealed how much money he had stashed away. Samuel greedily imagined a few thousand pounds minimum. The fire embers were still alight in the grate, and an empty mug stood on the draining board but no sign of Douglas. He must have popped out to the shop or the pub. Samuel considered for a moment the idea of living in the cottage himself. A creak from the upstairs floorboards reminded him why he had stepped inside the cottage without invitation. Ah, good, that will be Douglas, he thought. He must have woken; perhaps the sound of his voice calling out had disturbed him. With only two bedrooms on the upper floor, Samuel crept upstairs, peering round the first open door. The room looked typically messy, with clothes strewn about, unoccupied. Curious, as to where Douglas had got to, he was met by an unusual smell.

Momentarily distracted, his mission had been to find the hidden cash. Feeling behind the second bedroom door, he discovered the loft ladders. He raised the hatch door and groped around in the dark for the bag. Got it! After checking the contents, he tossed it down on the landing, half expecting Douglas to appear as the bag landed with a loud thud. By the weight of it, several thousand pounds. Focussed on his mission, he continued. He knew the cottage needed some maintenance but today the smell upstairs took him aback. He couldn't place it: was it rotten window frames or damp towels, or a dead bird or a rodent? Before heading down the stairs he took one last look in the bedroom and on the floor poking out the end of the bed were a neat set of toes, but a strange colour. He leant around the side of the bed and saw the body, the eyes wide open, staring blankly at him, the blood already starting to sink from the veins. His fingers and toes had darkened to a deeper shade of purple. A sudden chill swept through Samuel, as if a cold wind had sliced through his veins. The hairs on the back of his neck began to prickle. Samuel knew immediately what had happened and grabbed the bag before rushing out into the garden to find some fresh air. Phew, he exhaled, catching his breath again. His own body wouldn't stop trembling. Still clutching the holdall bag, he strode away. Had anyone spotted him? He checked up and down the empty street. As he looked back over his shoulder, his eyes focussed on the upper-left-hand window of the cottage. Did he see the outline of a pale face staring at him through the glass? Perhaps his mind had started playing crazy hallucinatory tricks again.

When he'd checked the bedroom earlier Douglas must have been already on the floor but out of the line of sight, along the side of the bed. Deceased. Dumping the bag in the boot of his car, Samuel made an anonymous emergency call from the phone box before heading straight to the pub. A double whisky would calm his trembling. Just as he took his first swig, a couple of locals rushed over to the window. An ambulance, with blue lights flashing, sped past, making rare headline news in the small community. Downing the rest of his drink, he reached the cottage gate just as the ambulance gurney navigated the bumpy path out of Stonymollan cottage. A white sheet covered a motionless body form.

"Anyone we know?" he enquired. The crew in green uniform shook their heads, and told him they had to inform next of kin first, before they could release any formal identity.

"We can't say yet, but we know it's not the owner of the cottage," answered the man in green with his blue rubber gloves. So that ruled out Campbell.

The coroner had been called to the hospital morgue to determine a cause of death. Samuel's immediate thought had been for Molly. He started to panic, as he'd been the last person in the cottage. What had he touched? Jesus, had he returned the ladders to the spare room? Yes, thinking back, the rank smell had been a major clue.

His next stop would be the shop. At least six large American tourists stood idly queuing for the till, chatting in loud, bumptious voices. Baskets stuffed with mementos and sweet treats. The jollity in the air irked him; he didn't have time for this. The police would surely ask who was the last person to see

Douglas alive? This time if asked he would not lie. But what of Molly? The next thing she would have to contend with was far more serious than finding somewhere to live. Would she still want to have a drink with him? Who would be the one to tell her the awful news? The previous day the pair had arranged to have a drink after her shift. He already knew the friendship was going nowhere; stringing her along seemed more fun yesterday. Now fun was not on his mind. With his game plan upended, Molly had now become surplus to requirements.

From where he was sitting in his car, he watched her leave the shop to go home. Ten minutes he'd give her before calling round, hoping someone else would have broken the grim news. Not expecting any more visitors, Molly swung open the door, clutching a tumbler of amber liquid in her hand, the bottle from the kitchen table discarded on the floor. Drowning her sorrows quickly had seemed the easiest solution. Her eyes were puffy and still swollen with tears. Janet had been nominated as the one to tell her about Douglas.

In the shop, Janet commented to anyone who would listen, the initial reason given for Douglas's death had been natural causes. With no foul play suspected, they would need to wait until the official results of the postmortem were established to be sure. Or was Janet hypothesising again? Samuel and Molly were interviewed briefly by the local police then discharged with no further questions. Following the stipulation that both were to remain on the island.

"Coming in?" she burbled, swinging the glass in the direction of the kitchen.

"I've come to offer my condolences. I know we'd arranged to meet up later." Samuel gave the girl a hard, penetrating stare that she mistakenly translated into something entirely melodramatic and different. The whisky had started to talk. Seconds later they were having rough, urgent sex in the small, cramped kitchen, pausing only to place a throw on the chair. Their bodies entangled, desperate to release the pent-up emotion of the last few hours. Could this be part of Samuel's revenge? Poor Douglas, lying on a mortuary slab, and there he was having sex with his ex-girlfriend. Samuel felt unmoved, his own tears unshed. Bitterness and anger took over, finishing quickly.

Afterwards, Molly tried to get her spinning head together. Samuel had pressured her into another drink; it would be his last, just to soften the blow. He exited saying he'd meet over at Campbell's place when she was ready.

She didn't want to go into the bedroom to change, despite all her stuff being strewn about. It still smelt odd. Douglas's clothes lay on the chair, untouched. She stared at them in disbelief. Her stomach told her she should eat something, but she felt sick drinking on an empty stomach.

Molly had taken longer than usual to get ready. Her trembling hand applied thick black eyeliner, with darker lips and a smudge of blusher to the boozy flushed cheeks. All extras to disguise her swollen, teary face. Looking in her mirror, she thought about what Samuel had promised, in his attempt to lure her away from Mull into his world. She knew she craved the male attention but her real motive? Was it the money or the lure of Paris that had sounded idyllic?

Molly sat alone on a bar stool, all glammed up wearing her shortest white miniskirt, questioning herself as to why she always attracted wrong uns. An hour later, she was still sitting on the bar stool, checking her watch for the umpteenth time. Campbell looked up from reading his evening paper, feeling a tad sorry for his young barmaid. She looked a wreck, so he sauntered over to keep her company with a pint of water. Puzzled by her stoic attitude, she didn't appear too distressed about losing her friend Douglas. He found it hard to read her thoughts with all the slap pasted on her face.

"Hey, Molls, where's your hot date tonight? Bit soon to be seeing that man from the south, eh? Your fella is barely cold, hen."

"Ach, he's a loser, a no-show anyway."

"Plenty more fish, eh?" Campbell retorted.

"Pity as I'm not interested. All men are the same; a bunch of shits the lot of them." She swigged more of her drink.

"Here, drink some water. Not all men are shits as you call them ya know, hen, there are a few of us good ones left." He chuckled, and winked at John the skipper, sitting in the corner. Campbell took her glass, unhooked her coat and pointed her in the direction of the spare bedroom upstairs.

Word had spread quickly round the small cluster of houses; someone had already laid flowers wrapped in cellophane on the verge outside the cottage gate.

Samuel had driven past the pub with a bunch of the cheap flowers from the verge on the passenger seat. He'd seen Molly sitting alongside Campbell through the window, and felt a twinge of guilt about his no-show with the young lassie, especially after such a massive shock. His mind switched back to his own plans and a new place – Paris. Yes, the cash would come in useful once he'd exchanged it for francs. That could be done at Dover as he tossed the wilting flowers out of the car window. Before leaving the cottage Samuel had helped himself to Douglas's bank account details just in case. Mull had suddenly lost all its appeal, despite the initial lure of Douglas and young Molly. He drove off at speed to catch the last ferry. No time to waste on emotional pulls.

Twenty-Three

Douglas's Funeral

Fabienne had taken the call from a distressed Molly earlier that evening. Between the sobs she explained that Douglas had been found dead. Something to do with his liver, she'd heard, but unsure exactly about the medical terminology. She'd pleaded for Fabienne to go to Mull, saying she had no idea what to do and needed help to organise the burial. Fabienne had been left with the unenviable task of telling Eloise and Ralph.

Half a dozen people stood at the remote graveside, to pay their respects. Eloise had declined the request from her sister and sent her apologies. Uncle Max had sent some yellow chrysanthemums despite the request for no flowers. Ralph clutched his stick with one trembling hand and Fabienne's elbow with his other, unashamed to admit that news of Douglas had knocked him for six. To outlive your son, to have to bury him first? Why had life been so cruel to his family? It must have been a jinx.

Janet, Campbell, John and Jed made up the small group, solemnly peering deep into the grave. Molly kept her distance, preferring to stand alone. Samuel had fled to Paris.

Over at the pub they raised a glass and Campbell uttered a few simple words. The fellow fishermen from the *North Western Star* had started a collection for their temporary crew member. The money would go to the local fishermen's mission.

The Renault turbo was found and returned to Max with a burnt out engine. Ralph thought he recognised Molly's lighter when she lit up in the churchyard. She'd half-inched it, unaware of its connection to Max. Ralph didn't feel strong enough to ask for it back.

Molly had already been to see Campbell and asked to move back into the cottage. He agreed to think about it, and to ask him again in two weeks' time, when all the fuss had died down. Meanwhile, she was welcome to stay at the pub free of charge. The shrewd landlord had already made up his mind, apologising, next time she asked, that she would need to look elsewhere.

"So why canna stay in your cottage? I could look after it for ya." Molly tried her best to persuade Campbell to let her stay. "I can look after myself."

"Nay, Molly, it's not right for a young lassie to stay over there alone. Besides, you canna afford it on your wages."

"Please, Campbell, I canna return to Harris; my parents won't have me back. I'm begging you, I have nowhere to go."

"Molly, the answer is still no. Ask Janet if she has a spare room, yeah?"

With his mind already made up, he'd already let it to a young fisherman, Eddie, from the *North Western Star* who had fallen on bad times. Molly had to consider the reality that her next move might be back to Harris. Her only hope was Janet. The thought filled her with dread. But she realised it was the only option left. Everyone she knew had walked away from her or died.

Twenty-Four

Ocean Cottage 2006

Five years later someone mysteriously put Ocean Cottage on the market, without Ralph's consent. A new estate agent board hung outside. Who had given the instruction to put it up for sale? On reflection, Ralph believed he might have handled his affairs a little better, particularly in respect of Samuel. Dismayed to hear he'd vanished from Mull without a trace, he felt betrayed by the young man. New allegiances within the family had been forged but between whom?

Ralph contacted the solicitors about the cottage; he needed some reassurance. After replacing the receiver, and with the words of Mr Hardcastle still ringing in his ears, Ralph was flabbergasted to hear that Beatrice had made a change to her will that stated the cottage would be transferred directly to Samuel. He vividly remembered her promising him she had changed the name on the deeds. But he thought that she'd meant to himself. Would the sisters forgive their mother for the tangled web she'd woven for them? The sisters still assumed the cottage would become theirs when Ralph died. Now they would be bypassed in favour of Samuel as only one name remained on the deeds.

Eloise still worked part time and Romuel had taken early retirement. She felt her life in France to be perfect in La Baule so why spoil it? She had been content to accept her father's previous explanation that the cottage would eventually be left to the two sisters when he died. What reason would she have to doubt him?

Amélie, now grown up, with two small babies of her own, had married Guy Lavigne, the ex-bass guitar musician from Dax. They were busy making their own plans and looking forward to spending more time in Swanage and being nearer to Grand Papy Ralph. But what plans had they got in mind?

Twenty-Five

Ocean Cottage

Fabienne closed the front door of her apartment. She'd recently accepted a good offer, and now needed to act fast and find somewhere to live.

Mr Lucknow had been in touch with Ralph to discuss the legalities associated with Ocean Cottage. Beatrice had made changes to her will on the day they went to London to the solicitors' office. Sadly the changes were made without his knowledge. All Beatrice had told him at the time was that he need not worry, she would not leave him homeless. But, after her meeting with Samuel, she'd changed her mind. The final outcome had only become apparent whilst he was away on holiday.

Ralph returned to the cottage from his break in Devon with Freddie. As they pulled into the driveway, a French car stood in the driveway, giving him grave concern. The mystery began when he entered the garden with his bags. Baby clothes hung on the washing line. A small football lay dormant in the flowerbed with a couple of squashed flower heads. Ralph marched over to the fence and angrily tore down the SOLD sign and tossed it high into the hedge.

Fresh baking smells wafted through the open kitchen window. Stranger still, the back door remained unlocked. On the draining board lay another clue: two mugs with a baby dish and spoon. Who else had a set of keys? Racking his brains, he couldn't remember how many sets they had had cut the previous summer. In the fridge he discovered some full-fat milk bearing a French label, and some brie. The end of a baguette lay half eaten on the chopping board, the crumbs spread out across the worktop. Nappies on the kitchen chair? For a few more moments the mystery deepened. He struggled to figure it out. Looking out of the kitchen window, it all made sense. Beyond the trees he saw the outline of a figure. A much younger woman, recognisable by the colour of her hair and the back of her head.

Amélie looked up just as Guy appeared carrying a small boy on his shoulders. Ralph watched the scene play out. Guy swung little Arthur over his head, lowering him gently to the ground as he ran off towards the swing. She remained seated, looking down at baby Jacques in her arms, taking her milk. The attentive young father followed little Arthur, who needed help with the swing. Ralph could hold back no longer. The sight of that male figure could have been him years ago playing with his own children. He rushed outside, arms outstretched. Little Arthur trundled over to his Grand Papy.

"Amélie, my darling, what are you doing here?" His face beamed with delight.

"*Bonjour, Papy, ce chalet m'appartient maintenant.*"

"*Que? Non*, Amélie, somehow you are mistaken. Your grandmother left it to me. It's not for sale." That was untrue.

"*Qu'est-ce qui se passe?*" said Amélie.

"What did you say? No, it belongs to me, and is no longer for sale!" he said, looking crestfallen. He would not allow his careful planning to be ambushed, not even by his granddaughter. "We are awaiting the documents from the agents," he told them, thinking to himself he would have to recheck the information with the solicitors to ensure the legal situation complied with Beatrice's wishes. In the last few days he had been receiving calls late at night from an unknown number. The confirmation came through and a new deal had been struck: the cottage had a new owner.

~~~

Since losing Beatrice, Ralph hsad become a virtual recluse, refusing to wash himself or launder his clothes. Refusing to socialise with anyone except his darling Fabienne. This the same man who sunk into a deep depression, became unable to function and closed his door on the outside world. At first, he'd felt overwhelmed, but slowly over time learnt to absorb his grief into a new life. Now he had a real sense of purpose and a safe routine that brought back some of the comfort he'd experienced when living alongside Beatrice.

Whilst away on holiday, he'd hatched his own secret plan. Unbeknown to the rest of the family, Freddie had made him an offer and Ralph had accepted, to move in next door. Eloise and Romuel declared they would be staying in La Baule. And Fabienne, having sold her apartment, was leaving London and moving to Scotland. She confessed to her father she'd always fancied a small remote island, but had yet to decide which one, probably not Mull.

A few days later Ralph heard the sealed bid from Amélie and Guy had *not* been accepted by the estate agent. Amélie immediately rang Ralph and asked him to intervene. She sounded distraught; mentally she had moved her own family into the cottage. Again, Ralph kept tight-lipped, unwilling to share any plans or what he knew. There had been much confusion, something had got lost in the translation between the French and English legal estate systems. Beatrice had no idea when she wrote her will that a simple *inscription* on her wedding ring and a reunification with her son would cause such confusion and heartache for her loved ones.

Later that same day, when things had quietened down, it was Samuel who stepped out of the shadows with a wry smile, keys in hand, before firmly closing the gate. Looking around, he wondered how long he might stay at Ocean Cottage.

Cast of Characters

Harry and Florence Hamilton – Beatrice's parents

Beatrice Hamilton – Youngest daughter

Albert Hamilton – Beatrice's brother

Arthur Hamilton – Beatrice's brother, deceased at birth

Rosina Hamilton – Elder daughter and sister to Beatrice

Thabo Nkosi – Rosina's husband

Jack Gardiner – First husband to Beatrice

Samuel Gardiner – Only son to Beatrice and Jack

Ralph Barclay – Beatrice's long-term partner

Fabienne Hamilton – Eldest daughter of Ralph and Beatrice

Eloise Lavigne – Youngest daughter of Ralph and Beatrice

Douglas Hamilton – Son of Ralph and Beatrice

Colin and June Barclay – Parents to Ralph and Max

Max Barclay – Ralph's brother

Romuel Bacri – Husband to Eloise

Molly Robertson – Girlfriend of Douglas

Janet McCampbell – Shopkeeper on Mull and sister of

Campbell McCampbell – Pub landlord

Amélie Lavigne – Granddaughter to Ralph and Beatrice

Guy Lavigne – Amélie's husband

Claude Dupont – French chauffeur

Count and Countess Vouvier – Beatrice's employers in France

Acknowledgements

Thank you to Mike and Angela for keeping the faith.

Friends: thank you all for your input and support in my ongoing creative writing journey.

Publishers – All thanks to Troubador for their patience in making *Inscription* the best it could be. Special thanks to the copy editing team, and to Holly Porter for her patience.

Thank you to the Portsmouth Authors Collective for all their support during the last year.